BLOOD INNOCENCE

Joy M. Jamison
and
Carole Kennedy

PublishAmerica
Baltimore

At the specific preference of the author, PublishAmerica allowed this work to remain exactly as the author intended, verbatim, without editorial input.

ISBN: 1-4241-5365-4
PUBLISHED BY PUBLISHAMERICA, LLLP
www.publishamerica.com
Baltimore

Printed in the United States of America

To Kathy:
May God
Continue to Bless your
Life Journey with Love:
Peace, Harmony & Carry you
down New Roads for excitement
& fond memories.
3/7/07
Fondly
Carole
Kennedy

Dedication

Joy's dedication:
George, Tavia, Jerry, Bryan and Mama

Carole's dedication:
Jim, Ken, Wesley, Dwayne, Kerry, Kim and Lori

Acknowledgments

Our love and undying gratitude go to Mary B. Arrington and Mary Sue Dye for plodding incessantly through this tome while correcting the numerous punctuation boo boo's. Also love and thanks to Shirlee G. Wilkins and Deborah Sue Lancaster for their unwavering faith in us. And Steve Webb: the behind the scenes man.

PROLOGUE

She knew in her sixteen-year-old heart that she was going to die. She was sure no one could endure such pain for long and not die. Her arms were spread, and tied between two saplings; her legs were splayed, and they too were bound to the trees. A ragged strip of cloth ripped from her blouse covered her eyes, and her sock had been stuffed into her mouth to muffle her cries. She still wore one sock and one shoe, but nothing else.

The frigid, autumn night air had invaded her bones, and she shook violently while her chattering teeth kept time. She could feel the syrupy viscosity of her own blood mingled with semen as it cooled and coagulated between her open thighs. She had been forcefully and brutally raped.

She had lost her virginity only weeks before, in what had been a clumsy, rushed and disappointing episode. But she had sincerely cared for Terry Richards; perhaps she even loved him. She had never been in love before, so she couldn't be for absolutely sure. Though each succeeding intimacy had grown a little easier and more pleasurable, she had doubted that she would ever come away sweating and gasping for breath the way Terry always did. The only comparison she could draw between those times and what had happened to her tonight were the incoherent, guttural sounds; the sounds she suspected all males made when in the throes of sexual ecstasy.

Terry was sweet, and had always been respectful of her body and her feelings. He had told her that he loved her, and she knew he did. This animal, however, whoever he was, had ripped her body and her soul, and now she could sense him calculating her fate somewhere out there in the night. Unmindful, the pale, reflected glow of the newly risen moon peeked tentatively through the bleak, skeletal trees. In other places, other people were basking lovingly in that same glow.

It was 2:05 AM, November 24, the last time she heard him coming toward her. He was crunching through layers of musky leaves that carpeted the forest floor. Twigs snapped sharply beneath his sneakered feet as he approached her. Coming upon her from the rear, he whispered his fetid breath against her cheek, "Bitch!" That single muttered word bore into her brain and coiled around her heart like a putrid snake. It was the last word she would ever hear on this earth.

Her skull collapsed under the crushing blow of the heavy rock wielded in the white-knuckled fist of her captor. With the other fist he brought himself to the most gut-wrenching orgasm of his young life. He was exhilarated beyond belief. He felt like a god!

1

Eight o'clcock in the AM is by no means my finest hour, but some mornings are worse than others. I looked in my rearview mirror when I heard the siren. *Damn!* Blue lights were flashing to beat the band. With a sigh of resignation, I begin to slow down (which can be deadly on the busy interstate). The motorcycle cop had chased me, for God only knows how long, before it finally registered that it was me that he had in his sights. I pulled over to the berm, rolled to a stop and cracked my window open. I looked at him with that "Wha'd I do" expression. He informed me that both of my rear tires were rapidly going flat, and soon I'd be rolling on the rims. He reared back in that familiar superiority stance, with arms crossed emphatically over his broad chest and continued, "You better slow down or it may not be just flat tires next time."

I nodded, and hoped I appeared properly chastised. "Officer," I said, "I'm on the air in less than ten minutes; KRF is just off the next exit. I've only got one spare, and it's probably flat too." I promised him I'd call AAA, if he'd just let me go.

The moment I opened my mouth, he recognized my voice as the "resident psychic" on WKRF where bright-eyed and bushy-tailed, I greet Nashville radio listeners every Tuesday through Friday. Of course, that is, when I'm not in the field working on a case. Being a quasi-celebrity does have its advantages. Sgt. Donald Winslow escorted me to the radio station, and left me tucked safely in the parking lot—but not before extracting a promise from me not to drive so much as an inch without the benefit of fully inflated tires.

* *

My name is Dare Murphy. I'm the widowed mother of three sons, all of whom are grown. My late husband Tim, who I married when I was the tender age of sixteen, died after a brief illness, a little over six years ago. We had

9

nineteen very good years together, and I'll never forget a single one of them. But life, as they say, does go on.

Nearly four years ago I met a man, through my business, with whom I had a very special relationship. That is, until I foolishly decided it was time to move on. Several months later our professional paths crossed again. However, this time it was fate herself who intervened. Two murders at the Opryland Hotel complex had been the occasion for our professional reunion. And as night follows day, we again slipped seamlessly into a personal relationship. He was Jerry Collins, a detective lieutenant with the Metropolitan Nashville Police Department. That had not been the first time I had lent my professional services to the Metro police. In addition to them, I have worked with law-enforcement agencies all over Tennessee and surrounding states, as well as with the Tennessee Bureau of Investigation and Federal Bureau of Investigation. I am a professional psychic.

* *

My hour of airtime was drawing to a close, and I had already removed my headphones when Eddie Stockton, the engineer, alerted me of a phone call he felt I would want to take. We were in a commercial break, so I nodded to Eddie, who was partitioned from my co-host, Marilyn Curry, and me by a heavy plate-glass window.

An Asian accent met my ear; it was colored by a decidedly British undertone. My brain deduced Hong Kong almost immediately. "Ms. Murphy," the cultured male voice said to me. "My name is Dr. Jaing Zhou, and I am visiting my brother in Clarksville, Tennessee. My daughter is living with my brother, while she is attending your American high school, where she will graduate next spring. Her mother and I have come to visit with her and my brother's family for the holidays."

"How nice to talk to you, Dr. Zhou; what I can do for you?" I must admit the other side of my brain was preoccupied with the inconvenience of flat tires and calling AAA. Also I knew that soon clients would be arriving at my office, and Katie, my secretary, hates it when I get behind. *Hell*, I say facetiously to myself, (and only to myself) *they can't start without me.* Unfortunately, my personal predicament was taking precedence, at the moment.

"Ms. Murphy, perhaps you have read about our daughter Marie in your newspaper. She disappeared right before Thanksgiving—it was November

23, to be exact. She had spent the evening with her boyfriend and his family. She had left their home and was driving back to my brother's home—but never got here. You see, my brother is a military policeman on the base here in Clarksville, so after Terry, Marie's boyfriend, called to see if she had gotten home safely, my brother went out looking for her. He found her car parked at the high school. But Marie was nowhere to be found. So far the Clarksville Police have had no luck finding my daughter. My entire family is worried to death that something may have happened to Marie. Her mother is just sick with anxiety."

I knew, perfectly well, the case he was telling me about. The authorities had previously called my office to enlist my aid—(I'd had the flu and...) I had selfishly begged off.

"Ms. Murphy, my brother's wife listens to your radio program every morning, and she suggested that I call you. Will you help us?"

Eddie was counting down to the end of commercial. *Five fingers...four fingers...*

"Dr. Zhou, if you will leave your name and telephone number with the engineer—his name is Eddie Stockton—I'll call you later this afternoon. Right now, the commercial is just about over."

"Thank you...."

We were back on air, and I watched as Eddie spoke into the mouthpiece on his headset. I watched as he scratched what I knew was a name and phone number on a note pad.

* *

"Well, Dare, that's all the time we have for today. As always, it's been a blast, and we'll all look forward to hearing your sage advice next Tuesday morning—same time/same place—WKRF, on your FM dial." Marilyn was being her normally exuberant self, but after what I had been through this morning, I just simply wasn't in the mood for it. I liked her, and I enjoyed sharing an hour of most mornings in her company. But really, effervescence has its place—like sometime after noon.

Taking care that my headphones were secure on the desk, I scooted my stool back. I dumped the contents of my ashtray into a Ziplock bag and sealed it tightly before cramming it into the side pocket of my purse. They (the management) indulge my habit but not my leftovers. I've been giving a lot of thought to giving up smoking. I think, at least, that's a step in the right direction.

"Dare, do you know who that guy was?" Eddie had left the control booth, with all its switches and digital readouts, and was standing in the doorway between the studio and his engineering lair.

"Yeah, Eddie, I do. It took me a moment, but then I put the names and locations together, and *voilà*! He's the father of that missing teenager from Clarksville."

Marilyn looked up from where she was systematically packing her briefcase, as efficiently as I would pack for a weekend in the Smoky Mountains. "Are you going to help them find her?"

I once thought she had the greenest eyes I had ever seen in a human head, until one morning she came in with two sapphire orbs twinkling at me. I remember thinking that I had to pay a visit to Dr. Debbie Ruark and get fitted for contacts, but the good Doctor had died before I even got around to making an appointment. To say I'm a procrastinator would be an understatement.

"Well, I guess I'm going to try. The Clarksville cops already called me not long after she went missing, but I was sick, remember? Then I hadn't thought about it since. Actually, I didn't decide to go until just a few minutes ago, when I talked to her dad."

"Why not?" Eddie wanted to know.

"I haven't done any field work, to speak of, in several months—and besides, you've been outside. It's been snowing and it's cold as a witch's tit in a brass brassiere.

"So?" Marilyn accused, "That's what you *do,* remember?"

Blasé bitch. I swallowed it. "See you two Tuesday morning; have a good weekend…. Oh, shit, (I remembered my twin flats). "I've got to call AAA before I can go anywhere."

Marilyn, with stuffed briefcase, and Eddie, anticipating commercial's end, left me alone to make my call in peace.

* *

The guy at Universal Tire told me I had run over two huge nails, (one in each of the rear tires) and that they were beyond repair. But I got two replacements relatively cheap, due to my tread life warranty. He pumped up my spare, to boot. So, two hours and two new Bridgestones later, I headed for home and office. Katie's impatient secretarial voice was still tattooing inside my skull. "Clients are here," she had informed me in her inimitable fashion, "and they're getting restless."

"Katie," I had told her, "just tell them I'm sorry, but I've been unavoidably detained and I'll be there just as soon as possible." At that point I turned my cellular phone off and shoved it into the bowels of my purse.

Anticipating a typical Friday, I knew I faced an exceptionally busy day with clients working their gallimaufries of unique experiences across my desk. I would do my best to focus my undivided attention and energies on the situations at hand. However, Marie Zhou, *missing* high school senior—her father Chinese and her mother American—was crawling incessantly through the corridors of my consciousness. I could do nothing to stay her.

* *

Until this case, I had not been sought, nor had I offered my assistance in any major law enforcement activities since the infamous Opryland Hotel Complex fiasco that had come to light nearly three summers ago, and had dragged doggedly into the following fall. That was when a small, but exceedingly venomous faction had been ferreted out and exposed to the daylight. It had been a veritable nest of ignominious, self-serving vipers who cared little that their actions could have actually toppled a financial empire. Confessions and plea bargains had dispatched the principals up the proverbial (and also quite literal) river to the new Tennessee State Penitentiary. Even now, they await the outcome of the appellate process.

The bastards had murdered two people. A third death had occurred when one of the killers had committed suicide. The latter, by some unholy quirk of the draw, had met and fallen in love with someone very close to me—Katie, my secretary. I would like to think that at the end, he had finally had the innate good taste to kill himself to avoid ruining her life as he had his own. Yeah, right. That was when his partner had attempted to eradicate me.

The ringleader of the nefarious group was a good-for-nothing animal, who at one time had been a "high-up" in the Metropolitan Nashville Police Department.

The most tragic of all, to me, was the senseless death of my lover. Directly attributable to our relationship, he had been blown to kingdom come, while driving my car. The explosion had been intended for me, but unbeknownst to the bastard who had armed the plastic bomb in my Mercedes 550SL. That day, still so fresh in my memory, Jerry would drive from the parking garage, instead of me.

I was devastated. We had recently rediscovered each other, and we were seriously thinking about a future together. Our intimate circle of friends, especially Lee Graham, who is my long time best friend and working partner, has stood steadfastly by me since his death. I've managed slowly but surely to pull myself out of the realm of bottom-feeders and back to the surface, where the sun will shine on any fool who has the sense to get out in it.

After all had been said and done, one of my most immediate problems had been the purchase of a new car, a chore I didn't particularly relish. But I had coerced Joe Graham, Lee's husband and my good friend in his own right, into accompanying me on my quest.

My only qualification for the impending purchase was that I knew what I didn't want. No practical, economical, sub-compact with no CD player for me. One that when you turn on the A/C everything else—including the clock—slows down.

We had "window-shopped" for a couple of days when I fell in love with a silver Lexus RX400 SUV. The leather smelled and felt like leather, not naughahyde as so many do. It drove like a dream, was extremely comfortable and fit me to a "T". And the Bose multi-speaker stereo system was awesome.

"This is it!" I had announced, driving it back onto the dealer's lot.

"You sure?" Joe was prepared to play devil's advocate.

"It speaks to me," I winked at him.

"Oh," he understood my meaning, "then let's go deal."

I have driven my beloved Lexus ever since. Life goes on.

* *

I had been planning for some time to get out of the public rat race. I wanted nothing more than to get back to the exclusivity of a one-on-one rapport with my clients.

I had grown increasingly disenchanted with several of my former activities: ones that I had previously thought were so important. At the top of my trash list was an organization for businesswomen, where discord and backbiting seemed to reign supreme. I had been, until recently, an extremely active member and past president, but I was tired of it and its seemingly never-ending, sycophantic satellite activities.

Screw 'em, I decided right then and there, while looking at the world from high up inside my new Lexus, *screw 'em all.* So, except for the occasional interesting police case, and continuing to work with my private clientele, I would do nothing more daring, for the foreseeable future, than shave my legs with a very sharp razor. *Ah, but if that could have been.*

2

After my tire-shopping episode, I was in a hurry. So I by-passed the garage, with its decrepit power door, and pulled around back, almost to my kitchen door. Driving through virgin snow, my tires crunched the thin, brittle crust that had formed overnight. As I stepped out of the car, icy fingers of winter snatched at the hem of my coat, and I gasped as the rush of frigid air hit my unsuspecting lungs. The atmosphere veritably crackled in the biting chill of the week before Christmas.

I stepped into the kitchen, planning to tarry only long enough to shuck out of layers of protective outer wear, and pour myself a freshly brewed cup of coffee. Katie nearly always anticipates my every need, so I knew there would be an unopened pack of Raleigh cigarettes in the top drawer of my desk downstairs in my office.

As I stirred my usual four spoons of sugar and dash of Coffee Mate into my cup, I heard Katie's footsteps on the carpeted stair treads. Without turning around, I sensed her watching me from the doorway.

"Don't ask, I'll explain later. Today's been a bear, and it's not even noon." I quipped in a light-hearted manner that I did not feel. "How's your day, so far?"

"You're late." God, she has such a way with words. Not only had I spoken with her earlier by phone, but she had heard every syllable I had just uttered. She still had to get her licks in.

"Yeah, I know, but I'm ready to go to work now. Who's my first client?"

"It's Dr. Henry, you know, the shrink from Madison—the guy whose wife left him, his house burned down and his dog died. Remember?"

I smiled. I did remember. As clichéd as it may sound, those events actually happened to the poor man. On his first visit to my office, he told me he really did miss his dog. I'd liked him from the outset.

"Okay, I'm always glad to see the good doctor." I said, preparing to head downstairs to my little *sanctum sanctorum.*

She put out her hand to stop me in my tracks. "It's the one after him that's going to grab you."

"Why, who is it?" She had tweeked my interest.

"You're not going to believe this. It's a Mrs. Richards and her son from Clarksville. I was talking to them while we were waiting for you—the son is the boyfriend of that girl who went missing from up there."

"Do you mean Marie Zhou?"

"Yeah," she was all smiles now, "that's the one."

"How absolutely bizarre. I just spoke with her father this morning while I was at the station. Which reminds me, I've got to return his call when I finish for the day. Oh, yeah, and I'm going to Clarksville Monday morning."

"I'm glad you picked your day off; I despise shuffling clients around."

"Yes, sweetie, I know you do," I said as I gave her an affectionate tap on her firm, little butt. "Now, let's get downstairs before all those people down there decide they don't really need to see me after all."

"That's not a likely prospect," she grinned at me.

"Oh, Katie, please call Lee and ask her to come over about…what time is my last client?"

"Four o'clock." She answered.

"See if she can be here by 5:30 at the latest. If she's not home, leave a message on the machine and be sure to emphasize that it's important. Okay?"

"Gotcha." She moved toward the door leading to the basement, where my business offices are located.

I watched her move. She reminded me of the cats that she surrounds herself with at home. Years ago she had announced that she had *nada* interest in ever giving birth; all her primal, maternal instincts would instead be satisfied by caring for Bootsie, P.J., Half-pint and whoever might eventually follow in their tiny paw prints. She also claimed a kinship with my cat Hillary Rodham Kitten.

I had joked with her at the time of that disclosure, "You know, kids are not always what their cracked up to be anyway—just look at mine."

"In essence that's what I based my decision on, yours *and* Lee's." She threw her head back and laughed. She had dated my middle son while they were in high school, and later she and Lee's son had been married for a brief span of time. They had dated and lived together infinitely longer than they were legally married.

She considered my boys to be the siblings she never had, nothing more/ nothing less, or so they all claimed. Once in a while dissention reared its ugly

16

head, just as it does among actual siblings. Even though my birth offspring are grown, and very much on their own, at least once a week they either call or drop by to see me. This generally occurs when dinnertime would be, that is, if I cooked with any kind of regularity, which I do not. They usually don't hang around after I offer them a choice of Lean Cuisine, Yogurt, or their particular favorite, sardines and saltines. Hey, after a long day at the desk, I'm into "fast"—what can I say? Anyway, they're all working, self-sufficient individuals, so they could offer to take me to Cracker Barrel once in a while. Even a wannabe-vegetarian needs an occasional cholesterol fix.

3

Mrs. Richards, Terry, I wish we could have met under pleasanter circumstances." I rose from my chair. Reaching across the desk, I shook her outstretched hand, then her son's hand. I knew instinctively that this relatively clean-cut, young man was rapidly becoming the prime suspect in the disappearance of Marie Zhou, for no reason other than he was her boy friend. No disrespect intended, but the police didn't have a clue. In their eyes he was an easy, logical suspect. And as could be expected in these situations, the Richards' were extremely upset at best.

Terry's mother asked if it would be all right with me if she tape-recorded the session, and I told her I had no problem with that—lots of my clients like to keep souvenir records of their readings. At that point I decided I would conduct the session by reading Terry's cards. I could have just as easily given him a purely psychic reading, using no visible aids at all, but I wanted to look at the "confirmation" that would lie on the desk before me when we were finished.

We had talked in generalities for only a few minutes when Terry abruptly begged to be excused.

"Surely, but, hey, don't be gone long. Obviously you've come a considerable distance to see me, and we need to get started. Oh, in case you need it, it's the first door on the left."

His mother apologized and said that he was probably going outside to smoke.

"Terry!" I called with gusto from behind my desk.

"Yes, ma'am?" He peeked around the door facing; he was holding a red, Marlboro flip-top box in his right hand and a disposable lighter in his left—the cigarette between his lips was not lit.

"Come back in here and sit down." I opened my desk drawer. There lay, not only a fresh pack of Raleighs but also a lighter. Beside those lay the regular deck of playing cards (*sans* 16) that I use in my work. I took my time tearing off the cellophane, then the foil, before tapping out a cigarette and lighting it. Blue-gray exhaled smoke tucked me within its coil. Terry brought the lighter to the tip of his cigarette, drawing the smoke deeply, satisfyingly into his lungs and holding it there, while savoring the nicotine *hit* that he had obviously been denied for some time.

I mused to myself. *I'll just bet his mother doesn't allow him to smoke in her car.* I could relate completely. I'm a junky—a freaking, nicotine junky. Some would argue that I'm a caffeine and sugar junky, as well.

"Would you like a cup of coffee? Katie keeps a pot going at all times." I was doing my feeble best to allay their fears and put them at ease.

Terry shook his head, but his mother accepted graciously. "I drink it black, please."

I rang Katie and made the request. She was in my office five minutes later, with not only a cup of coffee for Mrs. Richards, but she also handed Terry a frosty glass of Coca-Cola, ice cubes bobbing to the surface like tiny bergs. Winter certainly was coloring my thoughts.

"Oh, Dare," Katie stepped back inside the office, "I forgot to tell you, Lee will be here by 5:30."

"Thanks, sweetie, I appreciate it."

I shuffled the cards before passing them across the desk. "Terry, shuffle these until they feel comfortable to you, then using your left hand, 'cut' them into three stacks; they don't need to be equal or even."

"Why do I have to cut 'em with my left hand? It'd be easier if used my right one." He looked me quizzically.

"Well, son, only virgins cut right-handed. Now, you can lie to your mother if you must, but do us both a favor, and cut the cards with your left hand."

He did, and he grinned for the first time since we met. I began to lay the cards in their proper positions on the board. Every one I turned up only served to reinforce what I had already *seen* in my mind's eye. All the while, I was reciting my ice-breaking spiel, that is designed to add a bit of levity, and to ease any trepidation a first-tme client might feel. Terry and his mother needed all the help I could give them.

"I don't walk on water or fly through the air...I tend to say hell and damn...however, my preacher...some days are definitely better than others..."

* *

Knowing the answer before I asked the question, I bolted forward, "Terry, have you talked with an attorney?"

They were both surprised by the bluntness of my question.

Mrs. Richards spoke first, "Terry and Marie were in love. He would never have hurt her, would you Terry?"

"No, ma'am, I haven't done anything—why do I need one? " He was seriously close to whining, not that I could blame him.

I rolled right along. "Have you spoken with the police about Marie?"

His mother once again jumped to the fore, "He volunteered to go in and talk to them."

"Terry," I bristled, and I made it abundantly clear that the question was addressed only to him, "did they ask you about your relationship with Marie? I mean did they ask you any really personal questions?" I looked from his face to his mother's, trying to read something, if there was anything to read.

"Just stuff, you know, like how long I'd known her, and if I had any idea who'd taken her off."

"And what did you tell them?"

"Just that I had known her since she moved here about a year ago, same as everyone else around here did. I said I didn't have any idea who'd taken her off. Why?" He was trying valiantly to buck-up, but embryonic tears were beginning to leak from the corners of his pale, aqua eyes.

I took a deep breath and calmly put my hands, palms down on the desk. "Terry, do *not* volunteer anything else. Hire an attorney, if only to protect you to from yourself. I don't know how to say this except just to say it." I took his two, quivering hands into my own, and looking directly into his almost, translucent eyes, I spoke. "Sometimes we all say purely innocent things that may be misconstrued, and we don't want that to happen, do we?"

"No, ma'am."

"Terry, listen to me very carefully. Marie is dead. She has been dead since the night she disappeared. I'm so sorry, but I just don't believe in offering false hope when I know there is none."

I had, in my mind's eye, a conclusive "picture" (not his face, but his personae) of the killer, but I would save that for the police—when the time was right. However, I told Terry and his mother that I was confident that the perpetrator would eventually be tracked down and arrested.

They wept.

After Mrs. Richards wiped her eyes, she sat quietly for a while, staring into that elusive space that can be shared with no one. When she finally spoke, she asked, "Do you mind if we play the tape for the Clarksville Police?"

"Be my guest, but remember what I've said. Talk to an attorney before you do anything."

"Thank you, Mrs. Murphy, you've been very helpful." Mrs. Richards was again on the verge of tears, and panic was stalking like a night-thing.

"Please call me Dare, because I suspect we'll get to know each other pretty well before this is all over."

"Ms…er…Dare, do you feel the police think I did something to Marie?"

Sitting before me was a sad, frightened, seventeen-year-old "man-child", who, in spite of everything, was trying valiantly to put up a brave front. I owed him the truth as I *saw* it.

"They are, in fact, going to try to pin her disappearance on you because right now, you're all they've got. However, Terry, if it's any consolation, I know you're not guilty—and eventually, so will everyone else.

So ended my session with Terry Richards and his mother. No solution and no closure, only heartbreak and countless, unanswerable questions. Questions I would continue to pick at, like the scab on a child's knee.

* *

I lit a cigarette, drawing the smoke deeply into my lungs. I allowed my little *Filipino boys*, which is how I refer to the keepers of my memory banks, to roam at will. I know that reference might cause some to question not only my sanity, but if the world is safe with me walking around unescorted. *C'est la vie.* That's how things go. I can't offer an objective opinion, but I can say that we all have our own individual processes for bringing forth lost or misplaced information. I have given anthropomorphic form to mine, and I have discovered it's a most expedient method, regardless of what others may think. It's even come to the point, when on occasion Lee (my friend and fellow crime-stalker) has asked if she may borrow my little Filipinos. It won't work. I created them, trained them, nurtured them and they work for me. They live inside my skull where they are allowed no time off, even for good behavior.

* *

I have known Lee Graham for over ten years. We met through the school each of our sons attended. By the serendipitous whim of fate, we both volunteered to be homeroom mothers. Through that commonality, camaraderie grew and developed into a friendship that I fear few people are privileged to experience, even once in a lifetime.

Over the years Lee has worked for me and with me. She's answered phones, done research, contributed to, and edited a newsletter for my business—and her efforts went a long way toward keeping both my oars in the water while I wrote my first book. Without her, I'm afraid I might have slipped through the cracks and drowned in a sea of words and ideas before I ever got it between its covers.

We work very well together, and she is ultra-sensitive to my vibes. She has trailed along with me through some excruciatingly difficult terrain. She has not only followed me thorough muck and mire, but she's also my buffer, answering any and all questions that officials might have. She also funnels mundane information back to me. When in the field, I communicate directly with no one but Lee. Cops, being naturally ego-sensitive creatures, don't always like or understand the protocol. But generally they come around—if they choose to work with me.

* *

Lee's husband, Joe, is not only a good sport, but also a staunch supporter of the work I do. He accepts the fact that I need his wife to expedite that work, not to mention that life is so much more fun when Lee's around. Joe has lately taken to using the *sobriquet* tacked onto me long ago by Jerry Collins and his partner, detective Dave Marshall: I am the finder of "lost bodies and diamond rings."

* *

"Yo!"

I looked up, and there stood Lee.

"What's happenin'?" she smiled her inimitable smile, and sat down across the desk from me, crossing her legs and getting comfortable. She drew a Benson & Hedges from a leather case and lit it with a slim, silver monogrammed Zippo lighter. She had told me once that Joe had given her the lighter as a gift early in their relationship. If that be true, so are the phenomenal claims the company makes about the longevity of its products. She leaned forward, her elbows on her knees and her chin in her palms.

I was telling her about my visit with Terry Richards and his mother, earlier in the day, when Katie rang me. "There's a call for you on line 1—sounds urgent."

* *

"Holy shit." I placed the receiver back onto its cradle, amazed at the rapidity at which events were taking place. "That was Emmett Calhoun."

Lee looked up from the sheaf of crossword puzzles that had occupied her attention while I was talking on the phone. She had at her disposal, stuffed into the various nooks and crannies in her satchel, that passed for a purse, brainteasers in varying degrees of difficulty, depending upon her mood and time allotment at any given time. I could see that she had cracked the CRYPTOGRAM in this morning's *Tennessean*, as she wadded it into a ball, tossing it into the wastepaper basket behind my desk.

"Two points off the glass! *Who* was Emmett Calhoun?"

"My God, I wish I could lose myself in something the way you do in those damn puzzles. Emmett Calhoun, for your information, is a lieutenant detective on the Clarksville police force. He's heading up the city's end of the Marie Zhou investigation. And now it looks as though the county may get involved. It seems that Mrs. Richards left here and drove directly back to Clarksville, where she didn't wait to pass go, collect $200, or even take the time to speak with a lawyer, as I had so implicitly suggested. She went straight to the police and played the tape of our session. I don't give a shit, but it doesn't take a rocket scientist to know that one should have an attorney along when presenting what could conceivably be construed as self-incriminating evidence to the cops." I lit a cigarette and flinched as a stray wisp of smoke swiped against my eyeball. I rubbed the smarting eye and felt a teardrop cling to my fingertip. "Holy shit," I reiterated.

"So?" Lee sat poised, blowing smoke across the desk.

"So, he wants to see me first thing Monday morning. Didn't you hear me tell him I wouldn't be able to make it to his office until around ten thirty—or were you too busy with your cryptoshit?"

"Who peed in your Wheaties this morning?" Barely stopping for a breath, she persevered: "Why are only the city police involved, and not the county

Mounties? I read the paper and catch a little news on TV. When the hell are they gonna catch that creep?

There is no need for recriminations for repartee between good friends, but I was surprised by the tone of my voice. "I'm sorry I'm so cranky Lee, but that boy, Terry Richards, really has me worried. Given half a chance, the cops are going to hang him out to dry and then eat him for breakfast—never mind Wheaties." I looked into her hooded eyes while she considered why I had apologized in the first place. I plowed onward. Her car was found in the city limits, and so far as I know, there has been no legal justification for the county to be involved. That won't last though. I'll bet you a dollar to a donut that they're doing their own surreptitious investigation—if for no other reason than she had driven on county roads earlier. They may as well, 'cause this is going way beyond the city or even the county."

"Wow, I had no idea." She set aside her pack of puzzles.

"Oh, I almost forgot, can you go with me Monday morning? As you probably heard, Calhoun wants my presence. Also I spoke with Dr. Zhou just before you came in. I told him I would meet with his family at his brother's house sometime early Monday afternoon."

She held my eyes in check while mulling over the question. "Sure, I guess so. Will we be back in time for me to make dinner, or shall I just tell Joe to fix something for himself? Strike that. You know, I'd forgotten how long it's been since we worked in the field. The last time was with Jerry and Dave. Sometimes I miss Jerry." She smiled, and I was forgiven for my imagined sin.

"I miss him too, but it's easier now. I have my work, which as you well know, keeps me hoppin'."

* *

The piercing scream split the fog. Dogs snapped and growled somewhere beyond the trees. I was so close I could taste it, like cider vinegar along the lateral extremities of my tongue.

Ruts were visibly cut into the earth. Mud had been pushed aside by plodding wheels. Dried leaves had blown and scattered across a small, open area surrounded by a monk's fringe of adolescent cedars. These, in turn, were enveloped within a stand of ancient hardwoods. By no means was clear-cutting evident, but it was as though this rutted, mud-caked trail (it hardly seemed adequate to be called "road") was used for snaking out but a few oak or hickory logs at a time.

The scene arced approximately 180 degrees before the moan of a rushing freshet insinuated itself into the scenario. It was as if a wellspring had materialized out of the palpable fog banks. In a sprinkle of fairy dust, a canvas sneaker appeared, toe pointing, like a beacon, toward a thicket. I visually followed the footwear, as if it were the needle on a magnetic compass. I watched as a soggy, toadstool-infested heap of rotting leaves evolved out of the mist. Therein, lay the partially obscured remnants of a long white cardigan sweater. I could have sworn that none of this had been here only moments ago. It was as if the forest were vomiting forth clues in the form of some Merlinesque paradigm.

The sirens wailed their animalistic mating calls. An internal scream lodged somewhere between my lungs and my throat, never to lend its voice to the night-sounds. Stillborn, it was vaporized before it ever had a chance to make itself heard.

4

I slammed my fist down on the top of the alarm clock to check its incessant wailing. Lying in a cold sweat while my heart beat paradiddles against my ribcage, I hauled myself over the edge of the sleep-pit, lying still but alert. There were nine minutes in which to calm myself before the snooze alarm reactivated itself.

I *knew* what had happened. The nightmare had shown me how, when, and where, (relatively speaking) but not why. What reason could there possibly be, beyond total sociopathic insanity? As it were, I *knew* details that I would have preferred to die, in my bed as an old lady, without knowing. I, it would seem, had not been given that option.

My feet hit the floor. I slipped into last night's gray sweatshirt. And I pulled the matching sweatpants up over my ankles and hips, letting the elastic waistband snap against my stomach, making sure I was actually back where I belonged.

I grabbed a legal pad and pencil from my bedside table and drew a rough map, labeling: logging "road," cedar trees, clearing, stream, and items of clothing. No need to make further notes. The episode was indelibly etched into my memory banks, and my little Filipinos would never let go of it.

I called Lee and asked her to meet me at the radio station. "No problem," she had said. She would be waiting in the lobby when I got off the air. I reminded her to dress warmly and to bring her hiking boots.

I laid out jeans and a bright orange University of Tennessee sweatshirt. I have a small, perpetually packed overnight bag, containing insulated socks and gloves, long silk underwear and a variety of caps and earmuffs. I took my boots from the closet and sat them, along with the bag, at the side of my bed.

I went to the kitchen, where Mr. Coffee had automatically prepared my ritualistic, morning kick-start. I flipped on the Bose Wave. Stan Getz, was playing his incredibly sexy saxophone, and Astrid Gilberto was singing in her incredibly sexy Brazilian accent. What a way to start the day.

I sipped my coffee, *Bossa Nova*-ing my way toward the bathroom. I was actually in a better mood than I had any reason to be—after that dream. I dropped my clothes in the hamper and stepped into roiling steam, where finely honed needles of spray pulsated from the showerhead, massaging my body *and* my soul, while refreshing my mind in preparation for the day ahead.

* *

Sleet-infested snow pelted me as I walked the few steps from my back door to my car. Thank God for remotely controlled engine-starting, heater-activating and seat-warming devices. This Lexus of mine, as my grandfather would have put it, "is neater than snuff, and not half as dusty." Nevertheless, I should have taken the time yesterday for my physically challenged garage door to open and then parked inside. I don't like leaving the car out in the elements.

With the aid of the windshield wipers, the defrosters and a little *pixie-dust*, I made it to the radio station without incident, and did my morning stint on the air. Sure enough, Lee was waiting for me, rearing to go when I returned to the lobby.

"Do we have time to grab a bite to eat?" she queried.

"Yeah," I answered, following her out the door that led to the parking lot, "as long as you remember that *grab* is the operative word."

* *

"Lieutenant Calhoun." I shook his outstretched hand. Emmett Calhoun was a tall, middle-aged man with the pocked residuals of long-ago acne-plagued adolescence. His cheeks and forehead were perpetually flushed, which drew attention away from his soft, sea green eyes. He was a nice man, whom I liked okay, but not at all physically attractive to me, bad complexion not withstanding. "It's good to see you. I'd like you to meet my associate, Lee Graham." They shook hands. The three of us made small talk for the few minutes it took before we were joined by Emmett's partner Harold Riggens, who was, on the other hand, an incredibly good-looking, fair-haired, blue-eyed hunk. I never said I wasn't a sexist. A closet sexist, however.

"Emmett, I've sketched this map that I believe will match the place where Marie Zhou's body will eventually be discovered.

"Whoa, there, Dare. Who's said anything about bodies?"

I locked onto his eyes like a homing device and spoke as emphatically as I knew how. "Look, Emmett, if you want to dance around this, then put on a record, but if you want my help, then let's be candid, please. I didn't drive all the way up here to do the *Funky Chicken*.

He smiled at my mixed (and dated) metaphors. He tapped his pencil on his desk. I held his gaze, waiting for the gears in his head to assimilate what I had just said.

* *

Ricky Dean Harris was lounging against the Sheriff's cruiser. He had forgotten how many times he'd been told not to touch the official vehicles, except when he was washing and waxing them, or running official errands for the sheriff.

Dino, as his fellow inmates called him, was more or less a permanent fixture at the Dickson County lock-up. He was a typical, habitual, so far as anybody knew, a non-violent, petty larcenist. At the moment he was biding his time on a "drunk and disorderly." His *rap-sheet* trailed him as far back as the sixth grade, when Vincenzo Formosa had him pinched for snatching apples from his old, *fly blown* fruit stand out on Highway 70.

"Them shitty apples was full of maggots," Ricky Dean (before he was Dino) had complained to the deputy who had hauled him in. The initial idea for taking him in to the station had been designed to put the fear of God in the young master Harris.

"Young man," Deputy Mark Turner had tried to be patient, but Ricky Dean had had an attitude even back then, "the only maggot on them apples was you." He regretted having said it almost as soon as the words left his mouth, even though he had meant every word.

The deputy had taken the petulant, prepubescent Ricky Dean Harris down to the county jail and given him his famous "Saint Jude" tour, the one where emphasis was on how helping the hopeless often fell upon the shoulders of over-worked, under-paid, but nevertheless, righteous law enforcement officers, such as himself.

Ricky Dean had shaken in his bell-bottoms, but at the same time he had looked upon the petty thieves and puking drunks, that were in residence that day, as anti-heroes of sorts. His mind had dressed them up in black hats and called them the *bad and the ugly*.

Walking the edge would become Ricky Dean's *modus operandi*. He didn't exactly plan it that way—that's just the way it turned out. Not the brightest light bulb in the socket. Nevertheless, he could feign a certain likeability that came just shy of endearing him to folks—who didn't know him.

Today, Ricky Dean, (now Dino) shakes in his boots once more, but this time it's from the cold. He isn't wearing gloves: his bare, balled fists are buried in the armpits of his blue, county-issue jumper. His threadbare knit cap is pulled down around his ears, and stray greasy dishwater-blond strands are wind-raked across his watery eyes. Occasionally, he stamps his boots in the dirty snow, just to see if he can still feel his feet inside them.

He's smoking a Lucky Strike, it dangles between his lips. The ash droops off the tip of the cigarette like the miniature *snotcicle* that has formed beneath his leaking nose. His hands are otherwise occupied, so unless he chooses to push the soggy butt from between his teeth with his tongue, there it is. Smoke stings his half-frozen eyeballs.

"Trustee, get your lazy ass off that cruiser!" Dino leans against the leeward side of the vehicle, attempting to suck a little reflected heat from the metal and window glass. "What the fuck you think this is...your goddam birthday?" Sheriff Ruble Houston strides across the ice-encrusted, parking lot as if heading for the OK Corral, rather than where Dino is standing (caught in the act of copping an illicit nicotine hit in the great out-of-doors).

Sheriff Houston: an *Orwellian* good ol' boy, complete with white Stetson hat and rattlesnake-skin boots. His personal vehicle is a red king-cab Chevy pickup truck outfitted with gun racks and stocked with an arsenal. A locked box full of everything from birdshot to Hydra-shocks sits at the ready behind the passenger's seat. He keeps a spare twist of Granger chewing tobacco hanging from his rearview mirror, and a Campbell's Tomato Soup can is perpetually stationed in his cup holder. He had, after all, been a Boy Scout.

The sheriff is well known in the western end of middle Tennessee as a *shit kicker.* He had made his most pivotal campaign announcement down at the VFW right before he was re-elected to his latest term. "If I had my goddamn way, I'd clean the liberal pussies out of this county and I'd pack ever' damn one of 'em up there for John Ashcroft to deal with (never mind that he was the sheriff wielding almost despotic authority, and John Ashcroft had recently resigned). Now, there's a man with a plan, if ever I seen one." Shit, like I said, if I had my way around here there wouldn't be no crime to speak of. Between ya'll, me, and the gatepost, I wish we had open season on them bleedin' heart, tree huggin' nuts. Me and ol' Johnny could clean up the mess Slick Willie and *Aleen* Gore made of our justice system. God, I miss J. Edgar."

* *

Dino jerked a rigored hand from its hidey-hole and grabbed the butt from his mouth. It stuck between his lips, partially *glued* by the moisture from his mouth and leaky nose. Bits of chapped scab came away on the paper of the unfiltered cigarette butt, as he dropped it onto the filthy, tire-tracked snow and *toed* it out of sight. Tiny flecks of blood sprang to the surface of his lips where they were immediately cauterized by the bitter cold.

The sheriff waited while Dino got his feet operational and moved away from the driver's door. His hands were once again parked in the relative warmth of his underarms. "No, sir, sher'ff, it ain't my birthday," was all that crawled from between his wounded lips.

Sheriff Houston slammed the car door before reaching for his shoulder harness. He watched as Ricky Dean "Dino" Harris turned his back to him, starting his trek back toward the massive gray metal door that led to the lock-up. "Trustee!" he shouted as he rolled down his window. Newly generated warmth was escaping from the interior faster than the heater could pump it out. "Goddam it, trustee, get your lazy ass over here when I call you!"

"Sir?" The ever-vigilant Ricky-Dino turned around and shuffled back toward the sheriff's big, white Caprice with the dark green stripes along the sides, where DICKSON COUNTY SHERIFF had been neatly stenciled. His sneakers were dragging wide tracks in the snow that looked as if someone had been cross-county racing on water skis.

"Trustee, I've requisitioned a squad car so's you can drive my wife up to Nashville in this afternoon. She has a doctor's appointment out in the Rivergate area, but I don't want her out there driving on the interstate in this snow. You can just wait in the car 'til she gets finished at the doctor's, then come right on back, you hear?"

"Yes, sir, sher'ff."

"You go get washed up and pick her up at the house at eleven o'clock. You got all that, trustee?

"Yes, sir, sher'ff."

"Don't forget what I said about waiting in the car."

"No, sir, I won't.

The sheriff had partially rolled up his window, and Dino had begun making his way back to where he was going. The sheriff, without even being aware, had been guilty of *morosity-interruptus*. He had screwed with Dino's own private pity-party.

"Trustee."

Dino stopped, stiffened, then slowly turned to face the sheriff one more time. "Sir?"

"Trustee, wipe that shit off your nose."

He did. He raked his sleeve across his face, knocking the tiny, mucilaginous stalactite to the ground.

Ricky Dean "Dino" Harris was sick to death of being the sheriff's toady, but if he were going to continue to enjoy his modicum of freedom, he knew he simply had to grin and bear it.

Another errand to run for Superfuck, only this time, her majesty Ladyfuck will be goin' along to screw up the trip. No time to pick up another chicky to party with. What a guy can't get, with a little time to spare and a cop car under his butt, ain't even been thought of.

* *

I looked at photographs of the scene where Marie Zhou's car had been recovered. I looked at photographs of the car: an aging white Cavalier, I judged from my limited knowledge in such matters. I expected to see the actual vehicle later at the Zhous, since the police lab had supposedly finished processing, and had returned it to the uncle. Lastly, the Lieutenant laid a studio portrait of the missing young lady in front of me. She was lovely, possessing the best of both the West and the East. Her hair was long and very dark. Her mouth broke the plane in a wide, mischievous grin; however, it was her eyes that bespoke her Asian heritage. They were *almost* almond shaped, but not quite—it was what was beyond the eyes that was so bewitching. Her countenance had a certain Erté-ishness about it. She looked almost transcendental, which was ridiculous—a sixteen year old transcendentalist—preposterous.

* *

I guess Lieutenant Calhoun decided his boots weren't made for dancing because he stopped his pencil in mid-tap and looked at me from across his desk. "You're right, Dare, we don't hold out much hope for finding the young lady alive. She disappeared the night of November 23 and hasn't been seen or heard from since. At first we considered everything from simple runaway to kidnapping. But we have no evidence of either. At this point, I would welcome a ransom note.

His line of thought shocked me. "Why on earth would you welcome a ransom note, Ernest?"

"At least we would have a direction to concentrate on."

"Well," I said, taking my time while lighting a cigarette, looking around for a *no smoking* sign (but not too diligently) "let me see if I can throw you a tiny bone to gnaw on." The Lieutenant pushed a *purloined* McDonald's ashtray across the desk, never taking his eyes off mine.

Lieutenant Calhoun straightened himself in his chair and for the first time, seemed genuinely interested to see me.

"I'm *picking up* some sort of uniform."

He leaned forward in his chair, now chewing on the pencil. My guess was he had recently quit or was trying to quit smoking, judging from the way he was going at it. "What kind of uniform?"

"I don't know…what I mean to say is, I'm not sure. I *see* only the jacket. It's like a flight jacket. I know what they look like because my son has one he got when he was in the Air Force. The jacket I'm *seeing* has some sort of ornamentation on the front. I guess it could be a patch or some sort of…uh…what is it the military calls decoration?"

"Fruit salad," Harold Riggens spoke up. I had almost forgotten he was present. I smiled at him, in agreement.

"Yeah, that's it, but I'm not at all sure that's what I'm seeing. I guess it could be a military or law-enforcement…or maybe even a postal insignia." I drew deeply on my cigarette before grinding it out in the feeble McDonald's tin-foil receptacle.

After some rumination the Lieutenant spoke. "Considering the proximity of Fort Campbell, the first thought almost any one around here would have is military," His expression verged on a sneer. The resentment of an officer of the law, carrying out his duties, shoulder to shoulder with a military installation the size of Campbell, was apparent. "There are several thousand military personnel stationed out there…but actually, they're *everywhere*…I wish to hell they'd keep them on base. There is no way in hell we can keep up with them—reminds me of herdin' cats. I don't know if the army does any better, who knows? Communication with the goddamn base commander is like trying to make contact with aliens."…*and now, Lieutenant Emmett Calhoun…representing the Chamber of Commerce….*

I stemmed my dauntless, mental sarcasm, and jumped back into the conversation. "Speaking of *Fort Campfire,* just what are they doing, if anything?"

He ignored my *bon mot,* or feeble pun. "Well, you know her uncle is stationed out there." The Lieutenant was constructing a scenario for my benefit. "He's a career-man, a Chief Warrant Officer, MP unit with thirty years under his belt. The ink was barely dry on his U. S. citizenship papers when he joined up and went off to Nam. After that he saw action in Grenada, Panama and last, but not least, he took the festive Kuwaiti tour." I was detecting conflict of moral conscience here, but it made me *no-never-mind,* just as long as he and I could concentrate on the problem at hand. My opinion concerning my country's military policies is for the most part a very private matter. I don't think about it often, but sometimes when I do, it gripes my constitution.

The Lieutenant waltzed right in on my self-assessment. "Well," he said, "my initial take on the situation was that they'd probably take the old *wait and see* attitude, but since the Chief Warrant Officer could very well be a force to be reckoned with, publicity wise, they seem to be actively doing their part."

"Like what?" Talking to this man was like going to the GYN; he was beginning to give me cramps.

"Wait just a minute here. Dare, you say you *see* a uniform, well, the girl *did* live in the house with a soldier, and by the way, from what I understand, he is a highly decorated one."

"Forget it Emmett. It's not her uncle or anyone else in the family, and it's damn sure not Terry Richards."

"Well, maybe, but I'm not at all convinced that we're not on the right track in going after that boy friend of hers, that Richards boy."

I silently mused the words of the perspicacious (acutely insightful) poet Bobby Burns...*The best laid plans of Mice and Men gang aft a-gley.*

"Anyway," the Lieutenant began again, "the 101st Airborne has had their helicopters out in force; I have seen them from right here. I've also heard they're running the bloodhounds over there—I don't hold out much hope though. Even if a soldier did snatch her, and even murdered her, he'd be a damn fool to haul her body back to the base. Even though there's a million acres out to hide her in; no, ma'am, I don't buy that. Too many places are off limits to too many of 'em. Of course, the *brass* sees no reason to keep us even remotely informed. Hell, it's like they're in their own little county over there, and we haven't been granted diplomatic relations.

What if he had murdered her on the base? "Emmett, do you suppose there's any way *they* would talk to me? Even maybe let me have a little look-see?"

"Surely you don't mean the military." His demeanor was just a *skosh* condescending.

"Yes, I do."

"Damn, I don't know, Dare. Wait just a minute. I do know the deputy chief investigator with the Montgomery County Rescue Squad. He's just retired from the Army, but he's remained active with the CID (he was referring to the Criminal Investigation Department). I know he's done a lot of liaison work with Campbell and other bases. His job was, and I guess still is, coordinating civilian and military disaster control, often crossing jurisdictions to accomplish his task. That includes everything from domestic violence between service personnel and civilian spouses, or significant others, to a full-blown national emergency and everything in between. I can call him if you want."

"Emmett, I would certainly appreciate anything you could do in that quarter." Already feeling bad about my petty thoughts...well, maybe not *too bad.*

"I'll do it right now." He stabbed the speakerphone button and dialed the seven digits. Between rings, silence skulked like a phantom around the room. Then the phone on the other end sprang to life. A cocky-sounding male voice answered, "Rescue squad, this is Deputy Taylor speaking. Barney ain't here." Well, it wasn't a 911 call, and he probably wasn't expecting a call from police headquarters. I reckoned everyone was entitled to *one.* And actually, I thought it was pretty funny.

Lieutenant Calhoun released the speakerphone and grabbed the receiver to his ear. "Deputy Taylor, *this* is Lieutenant Calhoun at Clarksville City Police. Is Will Bealer in his office?"

I watched carefully as the Lieutenant talked to the errant deputy. He doodled incessantly on his desk blotter. I could tell from where I sat that he was obviously striving to master his art, or control his anger.

"Dare? Earth calling Dare Murphy." I don't know how many times he spoke my name before I reeled myself back from *Zoom Dweeby Land.*

"I'm sorry, Emmett, what were you saying?"

"Will's out of the office, but Deputy Taylor will have him call me, and I'll ask him to call you, okay? He made no mention of the deputy's *faux pas.* It was just as well, all things considered.

"Yes, thanks, Emmett."

I told him how I *pictured* the surroundings where Marie's remains would eventually be found. We discussed various sites and possible locations, or rather he did. I knew very little about his charming city, very little indeed, and even less about the military reservation. I had briefly worked there just once, for which I'm sure the army was grateful.

"Oh, Dare, I almost forgot to tell you something. There's a woman who called me this morning; she claimed she had some pertinent information. She said she's a psychic."

I was surprised. I would never insinuate myself into a police investigation without first being invited by the authorities. "Who is she, and do you know her?"

"No, I never heard of her before this morning, but she said her name was Glinda Güdwich. She asked if she could come in this afternoon. She said she works over at the college." I guess he caught my blank expression, for he explained that she was an assistant librarian, or something, at Austin Peay University.

"Oh, I see." I had forgotten there was a university in Clarksville—if I'd ever known it.

"Shall I have her call you?" he cautiously queried.

"Emmett, I'll let you be the judge of that, after you talk to her."

"Thanks a lot," he feigned (maybe not) exasperation, "okay, Dare, I'll be your screening service just this once. You owe me one. Hey, let's get out of here and drive around to see if anything grabs your eye.

"He goes by a nickname."

"Who goes by a nickname?"

"The guy in the uniform jacket."

* *

The snow had quit the sleet. The mottled, stained, pocked slush in the near empty parking lot had taken on an abstract expressionist quality. It was as if God had given Jackson Pollock a crack at *doing* the day. I know what they say about beauty being in the eye of the beholder. I also know what they say about Rorschach, but hey, this beholder takes her little bit of sunshine wherever she finds it.

* *

As politely as I knew how, I asked Emmett and Harold not to speak directly to me as we drove around Clarksville and its environs unless I raised a question first. I hoped by now they were accustomed to my myriad idiosyncrasies.

I was playing bloodhound, attempting to pick up on some sort of occult scent. Emmett pulled the car to the curb across the street from the high school where Marie's uncle had found her Cavalier on the night of November 23. I stepped out of the car and crossed the street. Walking from slot to slot in the parking lot, I was reminded of the long ago child's game "Hot and Cold," the one my friends never wanted me included in—I *always* won. You see, I discovered my special talent at the age of four.

I could feel my internal radar fine-tuning itself. When I came to the parking space farthest from the front entrance of the school, I was simply dumbstruck. That's the only way I know to describe it. I felt completely disarmed, and I was at a loss for an explanation. Lee stood close by. I knew she had stationed the cops at bay.

"Lee," I whispered. She stepped to my side, and I reached for her hand. She didn't speak for she knew my left-brain was *crankin'* along at the speed of light. "Lee," I whispered again a few moments later, "this is where he picked her up."

"What happened?" We were standing close, with our conspiratorial heads together. God knows what those two cops were thinking, not that it mattered.

I *fast-forwarded* to what had transpired that fateful November evening. That day had been my birthday.

"There was no struggle—she pulled into the lot—rolled down her window and spoke to him. I just don't understand this. I have no inclination that she knew him. Why in God's name would she pull off into this deserted place? We know it was some time after 10:00 PM because that's when she left the Richards' house. The cops said it would have taken at least fifteen to twenty minutes for her to have gotten from out there in the *boonies,* where he lives, to here. But you know what? I *know* she drove like a bat out of hell. Oh, my God, You know what else?" This time I looked into Lee's expectant eyes. *"She was pulled over!"*

"Oh, sweet Jesus." Lee was taken aback, as was I, but I still knew one pertinent fact that she did not. "Do you mean to tell me that a fucking cop did this? That some son of a bitch in uniform flashed his blues at that child, and when she pulled in here he snatched her out of her car...and...just carried her back to his...his goddamn cave?" She was clinching her teeth in belligerent frustration.

"No, not exactly. Just calm down and I'll explain it the way I *see* it."

"Okay, but this just burns my ass."

"I know, but listen. I don't believe he was a cop."

"What? But you said..."

"I know what I said. I believe that somehow this man, and it was a man, had access to the *tools of the trade.*"

"Meaning what?" Lee was looking at me from under that infamous cocked eyebrow. I caught peripheral sight of our official hosts. But ignoring them, I went back to my explanation of events with Lee. "He *appeared* to be a police officer—at least she thought he was. He was driving an official vehicle of sorts, with lights, and maybe he even shot her a siren burst to rattle her."

Lee jumped in. "He could have used one of those rotating red lights that some plain-clothes detectives *slap* on top of their cars when they're chasing after the bad guys. You can buy those things at Spencer Gifts, you know. Scary thought, if you ask me—you just don't know anymore who are the good guys, and who are the bad guys. I'm not even sure there are any good guys anymore: Jerry, Roy Rogers and Gene Autry are all dead. Shit, all I see out there are black hats."

I waited while she vented her spleen, then I continued, "No, Lee, he was driving an official car of some kind—from somewhere."

"What do you mean, somewhere?" You don't think he's from around here? That he's not a cop, and he's not from this neck of the woods?"

"I don't know yet but, no, I don't think so. Well, let's go talk to Emmett. I'll tell him what I've picked up so far and find out when *or* if he wants us to come back. But I've got to tell you, Lee, they're chasing their proverbial tails, big time, on this one. There is more collusion, intrigue and careless behavior surrounding this mess than I've seen in a long time."

"And just who are you assailing with the semantics here?" She was priming me, for every word was being recorded by her ever-present micro-recorder.

"I'm not sure yet, but I don't *feel* it's coming from around here. I *will* find out, sooner or later. Dammit, I wish Jerry were here."

"Well, Dave is, but I reckon that's about as good as we can do."

"You're right, maybe he would help us *ex tabulae.*" She looked quizzically. "Under the table. You know—on the QT." My phone, in Lee's jacket pocket, rang to life, shaking us both out of our contemplative moment. "Answer that, please," then I quipped, "and if it's not Felix Walker, I'm not home." I was referring to a man with whom I had recently re-established an acquaintance. It was said purely in levity. However, Lee didn't appear overly amused. I could see into her head as though it were *plexiglass.* She was filing that one for future reference.

"It's Katie, will she do instead?" she grinned, handing me the cellular phone.

I grabbed the phone and greeted Katie, but before I could be clever, she had announced that Will Bealer, from the Montgomery County Sheriff's office, had called and wanted to know if he could come down to talk to me tonight.

"What time, or did he say?" I quizzed my secretary.

"He wanted to know if nine o'clock was too late. I told him I'd have to check with you."

"I wonder why he didn't want to talk to me while I'm up here already. You did tell him I'm in Clarksville, didn't you?"

"He knows you're out with Lieutenant Calhoun, but apparently he wants his own time. Well, what should I tell him? He said he'd call back in about half an hour."

"Well, tell him okay, I guess. Wait just a second, Katie." I asked Lee if she could come over tonight to meet with this unknown deputy chief from Montgomery County: the one Emmett Calhoun seemed to think might be able to help us in our quest. She nodded. "Yeah, Katie, tell him nine will be fine. We're about to wrap it up here for now, then, Lee and I are going to meet with the Zhous. I should be back in the office by six, but if I'm not, just lock up and go on home."

"Dare, do you want me to come back at nine?"

"Not unless you just want to. I've promised myself I would try not to screw up too many of your evenings."

"I'm not doing anything tonight. Neither the Steelers nor the Titans are playing on Monday Night Football. Besides, who'll make coffee and empty ashtrays, if I don't?"

"Come on then. I'll be glad for your company." I flipped the cell-phone shut and handed it back to Lee. She zipped it back inside a copious pocket in her black Vanderbilt jacket with the university's seal plastered like a gold bull's eye across the back. I remember once when she and I were out for a stroll near my house. We had crawled between the strands of a rusty barbed wire fence and crossed a neighbor's pasture, going nowhere in particular. Suddenly, out of the corner of her eye, Lee caught sight of an angry galloping Black Angus cow—not a bull, but a cow. Not only had I never seen a cow gallop, I had never seen Lee Graham climb a tree. Well, she tried, but the sapling would have none of it. She stood behind that pitiful spindly little tree and turned white as a sheet while we both watched that pissed-off bovine paw at the ground. I told her to take off that damned Vandy jacket and the cow would back off. Guess what? She did—it did. She even has a license-plate guard on her car that boldly states that Vanderbilt *Is* the University of Tennessee. How could two people who are so different be such good friends? After I married at sixteen I got my GED, raised three sons and went to college. And my blood, as they say at UT, which, by the way, is my alma mater, runs *big orange*.

* *

I turned toward the two cops who were sitting on a low barricade. There was a heap of dead cigarette butts on the ground at their feet. They got up: each subconsciously brushing imagined wrinkles from the back of his trousers. They walked over and escorted us back to their *confiscated* red Taurus, complete with spoiler. Somewhere, someone was grieving for the loss of that one. Oh, well, *thou shall not do nor deal while driving, lest thou lose thy beloved ride.*

* *

I explained about my appointment with the Zhou family, and Emmett said he had spoken with Will Bealer. Then he asked if he might call me the next morning. He listened to my explanation of what I felt had happened at this place the night Marie Zhou had disappeared. I could tell the revelation shook him up. He assured me that he would do some serious checking. He asked me if I could come back later in the week. Not before Saturday afternoon, I had told him, and then only if it were imperative.

Pretty well disregarding my need to remain the homebody on the weekend, he asked Lee and me to meet him for breakfast at Sharkey's at nine o'clock Sunday morning. "We'll be able to talk; everyone else will be in church." I guess he just assumed "spooks" don't attend church, but I decided not to go there. "Okay," I said, unless you hear otherwise, we'll see you Sunday at nine." He drew a crude map showing us how to get to Sharkey's from I-24. He drove us back to his office, where I had parked earlier.

Lee and I got back into my car, and turned the key in the ignition. Listening to all those Nipponese ponies roar to life, I smiled. Waiting for the automatic climate control to kick in was the hard part. Our breath escaped like little smoke signals inside the frigid Lexus. "Heat!" Lee slapped her gloved hands on the dashboard. I must admit she did a pretty fair Benny Hinn, and it worked. *And it was good.*

I backed out into the street while Lee rattled off directions to the Zhou residence.

"Well?" she asked.

"A deep hole." I answered, driving on.

5

Some things I never get used to. Parents' grieving over lost children is one of those things. When I watch a mother and a father grapple for comfort from each other, I know, full well, that as time passes, those parents, for the lack of anything more positive, will begin to pick at the edges of each other's reserves. Finally blame leaks across the boundaries and falls about the shoulders of both. Blame, unfortunately, or maybe fortunately, is nature's analgesic. Or in some cases: the doorway to divorce court.

* *

Marie's father rose, waiting for Lee and me. He then led us down a dimly lit hallway to a closed door, stepping back, as if he were afraid of the ghosts that might be lurking within.

"Mr. Zhou, we won't be long, and I promise everything will be left exactly as I found it."

"Take your time, Ms. Murphy."

Lee followed me inside. It was an average-sized room, quite adequate for a teenage girl. The double bed was a veritable parade ground for a collection of stuffed bears in every conceivable size and costume array: soldier bears, dancing bears, gowned and tuxedoed bears. There must have been twenty or more.

Thumb tacked to one wall was a couple of yellowing Harry Potter movie posters (knock-offs, I'm sure). On the opposite wall hung a framed 8x10 glossy photograph of Justin Timberlake. Even this ol' broad recognized him after the infamous Super Bowl wardrobe "malfunction."

There was an Austin Peay University pennant thumb-tacked over the headboard and a University of Tennessee basketball schedule tacked beside it. On the opposite wall, where she would see it first thing every morning, hung an inexpensively framed Claude Monet print. How odd, she must have sought solemnity and tranquility in the impressionistic water scene.

An 8x10 Olan Mills portrait of Terry Richards, was surrounded by partially used-up candles, sat like a Kodachromal shrine on her bedside table. I detected faint, smudged lipstick traces on the glass. I smiled and swallowed the lump in my throat. There were snapshots of Terry all over the room. Some were with Marie, some with other people, and some were of Terry alone. There was one in which he was grinning widely and waving at the camera, with only some unknown's shadow spread across his sneakered feet. She had slid several small photos inside the frame of her dressing table mirror so that when she looked at herself, he was always within her peripheral range.

She, like most sixteen-year-olds, was not the neatest of all people. Her closet was a hodgepodge of skirts, blouses, dresses, slacks, jeans and jackets; no visible sign of rhyme or reason. The items in her chest of drawers were in the same state of disarray—helter-skelter. Only her make-up and toiletry items reflected any signs of organization, and it was totally out of character when compared with the rest of her belongings. I sat down at her dressing table. and I pulled a drawer to its outer-limits. V*oilà*! Behind jars and bottles of various health and beauty aids lay a brown business envelope held closed by an industrial strength rubber band. Its contents, as I soon discovered, were several, neatly folded notes, handwritten on loose-leaf notebook paper.

"Well, well, well." The words escaped as breath from between Lee's lips.

"Shit," I muttered, "now what do I do?" Knowing I should turn the notes over to the police, (or the very least, her family) without first reading them, and knowing at the same time that if I did so, I would be missing a unique insight into the young lady's private world. I slipped the rubber band off the plain unadorned envelope and onto my left wrist. I extracted one folded lined page from its confines. I unfolded the page and read quietly aloud.

...I can't wait 'til Friday night. Marie, every (sic) since we made love the first time I don't think about much else. Coach even asked me what was wrong after basketball practice yesterday. He laughed and asked me if my little head was doing the thinking for my big head. Ha ha. You'd think I was walking around with a hard on or something.

Well, I'm going to go down to the pool hall after supper and shoot a couple of games. I told Jake and Speedy I'd meet them around seven. Like I said before, I can't wait 'til Friday night. Love, Terry

The remaining notes were a variation on a theme. The ones that were written on a Monday, following their being together on Friday, Saturday and Sunday nights, grew increasingly explicit *and* urgent. No doubt about it, the boy was in love—or in lust. It was hard to differentiate.

I refolded the notes and put them back into the envelope, carefully replacing the rubber band, before returning the packet to the back of the drawer where I had found it. Feeling like a peeping tom, I wondered why no one else had found the letters. They weren't that well hidden.

I said to Lee, "Let's go, I've done all the damage that I can do here. I have some questions to ask the Zhous, then let's go get something to eat before we head back home."

"Sounds good to me." She gathered herself together and followed me from the room.

I closed the bedroom door behind us, as we reentered the world of the living. Dr. Zhou and his brother, Army Warrant Officer Huan Zhou rose, as we made our way into the living room.

The two Mrs.' Zhou, both of whom were Caucasian, had sat patiently, and I thought, subserviently, while their respective husbands satisfied themselves that I was, indeed, legitimate before they sat back to ingest what I had to say. After that, the spousal quietude abruptly ceased. The ladies fired questions at me that I could not yet answer.

* *

"Well, what do you think?" Lee was blowing smoke out the barely, rolled-down passenger's window. The car had grown toasty warm with the passing miles.

"What do I think about what?" I asked without taking my eyes from the slushy highway.

"The friggin' Tennessee Titans. What the hell do you think I mean?"

"Oh, that...I think they'll probably win next weekend."

"Jesus Christ, in your dreams. *And you call yourself a psychic?* You know perfectly well what I'm talking about."

I still didn't dare take my eyes off the highway. I thanked God that my car had all wheel drive and ABS, or anti-lock braking system, but I hoped I wouldn't be called upon to test the worth of either this evening. Interstate-24 between Clarksville and Nashville is treacherous in bad weather, particularly in winter. There are signs posted at the top of the plateau warning of dangerous crosswinds. I always find that comforting. "I know what you meant, but, to be perfectly honest, I don't know what I think. I keep going back to the guy in the uniform jacket. Nothing else fits, though. It's like he's the only major player, except for Marie, of course. He like blew into the scenario, just long enough to do the dastardly deed, then blew out again. Almost like a hit man, but of course he's not. He's a psycho, son of a bitch, and he's left the area. Bang!"

"Do you have any idea where he might have gone?"

I could hear her tape recorder's occasional squeak as it did its job. "That's the weirdest part. It's like the guy is on some sort of schedule, and, in my gut, I know he'll be back."

"You mean you think he's going to kill again?"

"No, not necessarily, all I *pick up* is that he frequents this general area occasionally, for what reason I can't say. It's like he's just in and out again."

"Do you think he could be a truck driver, or work for some sort of messenger service? Maybe that could account for what looks like a uniform jacket, you know, with the patch on the front."

"No, he's getting his perverted jollies playing cop somehow; I'd stake my reputation on it."

"Hey, that's good enough for me." She dug the cell phone out of her pocket and dialed Joe at home to tell him about our plans for the night. She asked if he needed anything, had he had his dinner? "Oh, yeah," she added, "I love you." He was fine with the plans, and no, he didn't need anything. He was going to watch the football game. Yes, he had had dinner and he loved her too, then as an afterthought he added, "Ya'll be careful, and tell Dare take her time because the roads will be getting slick".

Getting slick? "I take it Joe's okay?"

"Finer than frog hair split four ways."

I watched the white center lines whiz by until I thought my eyeballs would roll around in their sockets.

"I can't believe I couldn't see her car."

"Well, you heard Lieutenant Calhoun; he said the lab wasn't through with it."

"I surely hope I can get my hands on it next weekend. I know that's where the mystery will begin to unravel. I feel very strongly that I'll be able to get a better handle on, not only Marie, but also on her abductor." Lee tossed her cigarette butt out the window. "Don't do that!" I screeched. "Use the fucking ashtray, that's what it's for, for God's sake."

She looked at me as if I had gone completely around the bend. "Well, ex—cuse me for breathing."

"I'm sorry. I refuse to blame anything else on this case, this weather, or this day in general. And I'm damn sure not going to blame my raw nerves on you. Throw your butts out the window, I don't care…just be careful."

She snapped her fingers and started to sing, doing a *chickenesque* Mick Jagger, "You don't—always get—what you waa—nt…"

I interrupted her halting intonation. "I think we're both ready for a good stiff shot of Irish whiskey when we get back to my house. What do you say?"

"Make it *Jack* and you're got a deal. Oh, by the way, why did you say before…if it wasn't Felix Walker you weren't home?"

"I was only *jivin'* you. He called me the other night. He was just being…neighborly."

"Neighborly, my ass. He lives in Bellevue, that's what…thirty-five miles?"

"At least."

"You didn't tell me he called."

"I know." I put our lives on the line for a mere nanosecond while I stole a glance in her direction. As I knew she would be, she was looking askance as me from under that eyebrow. I grinned, focusing my full attention back where it belonged, straight ahead.

6

I stopped off at the base and picked up my wife after she got off work at the PX—I hope you don't mind." We shook hands all around, and while I helped Katie relieve Will Bealer and his wife Rolanda of their winter coats. Lee showed them where to set their boots.

"Of course I don't mind." Lee was with me on this particular night, but I don't generally welcome strangers into my office *or* my home after dark. Sometimes, however, on occasions such as this, its just more expedient than screwing around with everyone's daytime schedules. Besides, he was recommended by Emmett Calhoun, wasn't he?

I looked around, only to find Katie had left the room and gone upstairs. I showed Will and Rolanda into my private office and seated them across the desk from where I would sit. Lee took up residence in her regular chair.

Rolanda Bealer was a tall lithe brunette, in total contrast to her husband Will. He, over the years, had lost more than a little hair, while what was left had eased from light brown to mostly gray. And he had grown a little thick around the middle. They reminded me of a latter day, Sonny and Cher. They complimented each other, I thought, and I felt comfortable with them, almost immediately. I learned they were acquainted with *all* the Zhous, including Marie. They had met Marie's parents, Dr. and Mrs. Zhou only once. That had been after Marie's disappearance, so they couldn't give me much information in that quarter. Will had worked with her uncle the CWO (Chief Warrant Officer) on base. Rolanda had gotten to know Elizabeth Zhou and her niece Marie at school functions, as well as seeing them around the PX. As a matter of fact, Marie had gone out with the Bealers' son once or twice before she started dating Terry Richards exclusively. So, here I saw not only professional, investigative interest, but also well-defined loss on a certain personal level. I could not have asked for two people who had more special, yet objective, insight into this case, to have walked unsolicited into my office. *Thank you, Jesus.*

Katie came in carrying a huge tray laden with coffee carafe, four mugs, Oreo cookies (she had rescued from her own private stash—she's a chocoholic), cream, sugar and a Mello-Yellow for herself. The next few minutes were filled with small talk and conjectures about UT football and the weather. Coffee poured and stirred, Will broached the subject that had brought him to my office on this nasty night.

* *

"You ain't never felt nothing like it in your life." Ricky-Dino was standing in the yard with fellow trustee Harlan Merriweather. The snow had stopped, but the wind was a mad dog on a leash. Light puddled spottily around the yard, melting into the snow under the few remaining functional security lights. Most of those that hadn't been knocked out by bored inmates had died natural deaths, wheezing and crackling down so slowly that usually nobody even noticed when one fizzled out completely. It was cold, and all of the present inmates were non-violent offenders: drunks, vagrants and the like. They didn't need security lights, or even guards for that matter, to keep them inside (out of winter's icy reach). Hell no, they weren't going anywhere until they had to.

"You're lying, Dino You ain't never offed nobody and you know it." Harlan was known to his fellow incarcerees as Cobra because of the tatooed snake that was coiled around his penis. "Always ready to strike," he'd brag the first time anybody saw it, which was just about anybody who hung around long enough to partake in the weekly communal shower.

"I have too. Why the hell would I say I did, if I didn't?"

"Because you're a piss-in-your-pants little shit, and you want somebody to think you done something besides robbing little old ladies, then jerkin' off in their pocketbooks. Like I said before, you ain't killed nobody, else you'd tell me who it was."

"I can't do that."

"Yeah, right. Listen to yourself. And if it wasn't so fucking cold out here, I'd tell you about some of the murders I've pulled." Harlan "Cobra" Merriweather cupped his hands around the stub of his cigarette and took one last drag. Sparks exploded on the wind as he tossed the butt to the snow, watching as it melted into the slush. "They call me 'Jack the Ripper' you know, cause of all the people I knocked off, cut up and sold for dog food." He cocked his head and sniggered insolently in Ricky-Dino's direction. He

47

turned toward the door leading to the lockup at the minimum-security facility of the Dickson County jail. Here, the trustees came and went inside the compound, pretty much as they pleased. The *lockup* was left unlocked. No smoking was allowed inside at anytime—or outside when the sheriff was around—but he was never at the jail after dark. So in his absence, the staff relaxed the *no smoking* rule for the trustees, as long as they went outside. It just made life easier. An indifferent deputy nodded as Cobra strolled by.

Ricky-Dino hadn't eaten in so long his stomach was sucking air. Supper had been at four o'clock, nearly five hours ago. He knew he would have to go to sleep to escape the gnawing at his insides, for breakfast wouldn't be served until six the next morning. One more drag on the Lucky Strike, and he flicked it into the night.

Ricky-Dino headed for the lockup, passing by the same indifferent deputy. He was glad to leave the *killer cold* behind. His little corner of the world was dark, except for pale dingy light that was crawling around the corner and down the hall from where the deputies were drinking coffee and shooting the shit. Inside, the dormitory style lockup was tomb quiet, except for the occasional cough or ragged snore. Cobra was already huddled under his blanket. It looked to Ricky-Dino as though he *and* his serpent were sleeping. The rest of the skanks lay still in their bunks. TV had been off since eight o'clock, and the lights had been out since nine. He pulled off his clothes and crawled into his bunk with nothing on except a baggy pair of threadbare boxer shorts on which the elastic waistband was alternately puckered and stretched.

He lay on his back, searching for sleep, remembering the conversation he and Cobra had had earlier. The natural progression of his musings led his random thoughts back to *her*....

When he recalled *that* night, and the hateful young thing that filled it so vividly, his balls ached. No matter how many times he jerked off, in the solitude of his bunk, it wasn't the same—not even when he tried to picture that night. Not even when he remembered *taking* her in the back seat of the car. Listening to her scream at the top of her lungs (until he had clamped a hand over her mouth) acting like she didn't like it. He knew she did. The bitch just thought she was too good for him. That showed how much she knew. How could she *not* have liked it? He had taken her to the top of the mountain, and back, and he was sure she'd gone along as a willing passenger. Maybe even liked it a lot. Girls always said no when they really meant yes.

Everybody knew that. Little prick-teases, all of them. He was hurting. Now he had a hard-on that wouldn't quit. The bitch was still tormenting him. He couldn't get rid of her. It was as if she had moved into his head to torture, but to give no release.

"Fuck it!" he said out loud to the pitiful darkness, not even *it* was complete.

Sometimes he considered the *girls* inside: the pansies, the fags or someone who was willing to give a little head for a couple of smokes, some pills, or just to gain the favor of a trustee. But so far, he had not been able to bring himself to that. *"But,"* he decided *"if I don't get out of here for a few hours on a driving job for that prick Houston, where I can take somebody to Nashville or somewhere and come back alone, so's I can pick me up some sweet meat....*

He touched himself. The nerves at the base of his spine stood at attention, before telegraphing their cousins around front. He lay on his back, slowly moving his fingers up and down, establishing a rhythm, of sorts. Finally, making a relaxed but responsive fist, he focused on the serious business at hand. His breath caught somewhere between his lungs and his throat. His back stiffened and his heels dug into the feeble mattress until he could feel the unsubstantial springs underneath. He was flirting with orgasm. It was coming, but he wasn't quite ready. He summoned her to him. Her face materialized inside his head, and in her eyes he could see the mortal, abject terror that he had put there. *"Oh, God, I'm going to kill her...I'm finally going to get rid of her this time."* The tide was rising to meet him head on. The sweating and shaking, due to hatred/fear of this phantom, were adding substantially to his excitement. The incredible spasm rose in his gut and crawled down between his legs, grabbing his balls in its teeth. Every nerve and fiber in his body stretched and sang like a violin string. At the exact moment of orgasmic eruption, he slammed his left fist into the cinder-block wall beside his bed. Involuntarily, convulsive spasms charged through him, spitting his anger, frustration, and a chunk of his all too tenuous sanity onto the mattress, between his pale, hairless thighs.

* *

"Ms. Murphy, Ernest told me that you feel very strongly that Marie is dead."

"Yes, I do. But, please, call me Dare."

"Okay then. Dare. He also said you've drawn a map depicting where her body might be found. Tell me, if you don't mind, how you came to these conclusions."

"I have drawn a map, and yes, it depicts certain landmarks indigenous to that locale. As far as *how* I came to these conclusions, I can only say, and very unscientifically I might add, that I *saw* what happened. It's as if I were present or watching it all take place in the form of a TV dramatization. I just *know*."

"Do you know we've already talked to a psychic?"

"Yes, Lieutenant Calhoun told me. I believe he said her name was Glinda something. He also said that he didn't know her."

"Güdwich"

"Pardon me?"

"Her name is Glinda Güdwich, and no, he doesn't, or didn't until now. I know her slightly, but Rolanda here knows her pretty well. Isn't that right, honey?"

I transferred my gaze and my interest to the attractive face across the desk from me. "How well do you know her, Rolanda?"

"Oh, I've known Glinda for several years. Actually, I knew her parents before I knew her. Her father is a retired Master Sergeant, so I got to know her mother Elizabeth through several of the base auxiliary groups we've both belonged to over the years."

"I see," I said, turning my attention back to her husband. "I told Lieutenant Calhoun that I have no problem working with any particular person or persons. However, to be aware that at the outset I say what I *see*, and then I tend to sit back and wait. If and when the authorities decide they want my help, then I do what I can. If not, then I go on to my next project, what ever that might be, at any given time. What I'm saying is: if you feel, for whatever reason, that you can't use my assistance, don't worry. You won't hurt my feelings." I looked past them both and met Lee's eyes. She nodded. Her micro-recorder was crankin' in 3/4 time.

"No, no, Dare, the CID is very interested in anything you can do to help, and I know Ernest is counting on you. Glinda has never worked on anything like this before, but she has some very strong feelings as well. I'm sure she would be very happy to meet with you, and according to Rolanda, not just a little star-struck. Right, honey?"

Rolanda nodded and added, "She's really looking forward to meeting you."

"Oh, please, both of you, assure her that I'm no different than anyone else." I hate it when people say things like that to me. It makes me feel very self-conscious. Lee was slowly shaking her head and grinning at me from across the office.

I reached inside my desk drawer and withdrew the map that I had previously shown to Lieutenant Calhoun. He had earlier made a copy for his files. I handed the sheet of paper across the desk to Chief Investigator Bealer. He sat for several minutes, studying the map with almost reverent attention.

He finally looked at me, "Dare, did Ernest say that any of this looked familiar to him?"

Well, not exactly familiar," I explained, "but he did say there are several places in the county that are similar. Lee and I are going back to Clarksville, Sunday morning. I presume he's going to drive us around and probably take us to some of those places he spoke about. If so, I will walk the terrain to see if I pick up anything. I don't care who all goes along, you, the other psychic or whoever. I do, however, have one cardinal rule: any communication must be directed to Lee, when I'm working in the field. If we do it any other way, everything gets all balled up. It's like listening to a radio with overlapping stations, all vying for the same airspace at the same time. I have to have my space in order to do my job, and that's why I speak only with Lee. She will relay any questions you might have. I hope that's okay with everyone concerned because that's the way it's done."

My department will comply with your wishes, and I see absolutely no problem. I did, after all, come to you, not the other way round." He asked if he could have a copy of the map.

I buzzed Katie who was catching up on some extraneous work at her desk. She answered immediately. "Katie, will you come in here and get this map I've drawn? Make a copy for Inspector Bealer, please.

She appeared at my office door, almost like a genie, and without a word took the paper from my outstretched hand, departing just as quietly as she had come. I heard the copier hum to life down the hall, and at almost the same time I heard the telephone on Katie's desk ring. Glancing at mine, which does not ring, I saw it was not my private line, but I smiled nonetheless.

Will Bealer spoke up, "Then you're sure you don't mind who comes along while your working?"

"No, like I said, just as long as my privacy is respected, I have no problem whatsoever."

"Well, then, I'll talk to Ernest in the morning and tell him I'd like to come along on Sunday. I know Chief Warrant Officer Zhou will want to be there. He's taken a very active role in this investigation from the get-go. I reckon he feels a certain amount of responsibility for her disappearance, whether it's warranted or not. I'd probably feel the same way if one of my nieces or nephews went missing while they were living under my roof. I'm not sure about Marie's parents, but I'd think they wouldn't want to be there. I know her aunt won't." We heard the copier go silent, and the Bealers waited 'til Katie reentered the office, carrying my original drawing and Will's copy. Lee, Katie and I walked them to their coats and boots. We made small talk while they redressed themselves for their foray into the bitter cold night. I opened the door for them; looking beyond the immediacy of winter's icy grip, I saw clusters of stars, strung like tiny candles, on a colossal cosmic Christmas tree. Winter nights are clearly grand—from the inside looking out.

We shook hands all around, and everybody promised everybody else we would see each other on Sunday, which was the day after Christmas. My God, where had the time gone? Thank God, I had finished my shopping, what little I would do. I had been invited to my middle son's home for Christmas dinner, for which I was grateful. The merest thought of myself preparing a festive meal was totally out of the question.

I shut the door and dropped onto the couch across from Katie's desk. I was exhausted. "Give me a minute to get myself together, that is if I can find all the pieces." Even my attempt at humor was worn out."

Katie looked up, "Do you need me anymore tonight?"

"No, sweetie, I appreciate your coming back this evening, but you go on home now." Looking at my watch, I gasped, "holy shit! It's nearly midnight."

"Oh, Dare, you got a phone call a little while ago. I wrote the particulars on the memo sheet. I guess he forgot to leave his number, but then maybe you've got it in your little black book." She was referring to my electronic organizer. But, no, I didn't.

"Thank you, now go—it's late. Hey, wait. Why don't you spend the night? The weather's rotten, and it's too cold to go out anyway."

"No thanks, I have to get home and check on my babies," she said, referring to her menagerie of cats. She pulled her winter jacket over her sweater and zipped it to her chin before cramming her hands into driving gloves. She never wears boots. So after hugging both Lee and me, she walked out the door into the moon-bathed snowscape, crunching her sneaker-clad feet across its icy surface.

I waved goodbye and watched her take the driveway, like she was steering a Zamboni. I walked around her desk and ran my finger down the memo sheet until I came to the final entry. *Felix Walker called at 11: 05PM. He said he had expected to get your answering machine this late. He apologized for the hour, but said if you're going to be up for a while to give him a ring at home. If not, he'll call back tomorrow night about 7ish.*

I felt Lee behind me. "Well, well," was all she said, but I could sense the resolution in her voice.

* *

Cobra hadn't been asleep after all. He had, in fact, been toying with the idea of a little Narcissistic self-indulgence himself. His fantasy had ground to wilting halt when he had heard the *splat* of flesh and bone against the cinder-block wall, and the groan/moan/gasping for breath that had followed. He jumped out of his bunk and ran over where Ricky-Dino lay whining in the quasi-darkness of the lockup. There he lay, one fist dripping blood, the other, still holding onto a rapidly deflating penis, was covered in what Cobra didn't want to think about.

"Wow," Cobra breathed, he was on his knees trying to get a better look at the situation. "I heard ya shootin' your wad, but this is the damnedest thing I ever saw. What the hell you been doing over here?"

"Fuckin' a ghost, and I think I busted my goddam hand."

Cobra carefully fingered the bloodied fist (he wasn't about to get near the other one) and pronounced it wasn't broken, "just bunged up and scraped pretty bad."

"I gotta go to the can and get this shit cleaned up. When I get done you still want to hear *who* I offed?"

"Shit, yeah, I ain't going nowhere. I'll be right here." He sat on the edge of Ricky-Dino's wildly disarrayed bunk, carefully avoiding the wet spot, wondering if he was about to hear the biggest load of horseshit he'd ever heard, or if he were, in fact, going to be let in on a major secret. He decided he didn't care which it was, 'cause if it had got ol' Dino's rocks off that good, then it would be worth losing a little sleep over.

* *

"You look like a ghost your own self," Cobra said to his fellow trustee when Ricky-Dino finally eased himself back down onto his bunk, where he

53

lay inspecting his puffy left hand. "What do you mean, you was fuckin' a ghost? Goddam, you're a crazy bastard."

Ricky-Dino raised up on his right elbow and got nose to nose with Cobra. "You want to hear this or not? Ricky-Dino's voice was cold, like the ice outside the lockup. "Well?"

"Yeah, sure I do."

"Then shut the fuck up and stay shut up."

Ricky-Dino lay back down, and Cobra slumped forward grabbing his own bare, bony knees for support. "All right, shoot." He giggled a dirty, juvenile giggle, "'scuse the pun."

* *

"Well, are you going to call him?" Lee asked.

"I don't know. Not tonight anyway." I had expected the call, but that's not to say I was prepared for it. I like to keep order in my life, which I guess means no complications. I also knew that when I put voice to those concerns, Lee would remind me that trying to avoid those very same complications had almost cost me my relationship with Jerry Collins. If Jerry had lived, we probably would have gotten married or maybe just lived together. I know I'm not what Gloria Steineim would have at one time called a "today's woman," but I can still think for myself and make rational decisions.

"It's late and I'm tired." I sounded a little testy, even to myself.

"Fine, don't bark at *me*. I'm not the one who called." Lee was making a very good point.

"I'm sorry," I said, meaning it sincerely. "Let's go upstairs and have a cup of coffee." It seemed like I was spending an awful lot of time apologizing lately.

"No, thanks, I'm going home before Joe sends out Sergeant Preston and his faithful Husky, Yukon King. Seriously, it *is* late and I'm tired too. Besides, I've got to navigate your damned bobsled track of a driveway. I should have left my car at the radio station and had you drive me home."

"Hey, I'll take you, no problem. Your car isn't worth a shit in this weather anyway. Wait, I'll get my coat."

"No thanks, darlin', I've got my cell phone. If I have any difficulty, I'll call Joe. Once I get out of *here,* I'll be fine. I'm sure the streets are clear. After all, it's quit snowing, and it's clear as a bell outside."

"Okay, but remember, I offered."

"I know, and I appreciate it, but there's no sense in both of us freezing our tushes off. Call me tomorrow."

We hugged goodnight and I watched as she tried to shake the snow off her boots, before putting her feet inside her precious Pearl: the sporty black Mazda RX7 that Joe had bought new in 1985. I sometimes wonder whom she loves more, the chicken or the egg. That's an idle brain-fart, for I know she loves Joe more than life itself, and it's certainly reciprocal. But, that car is *not* far down the list. She honked when she got to the street so I would know she had gotten out safely.

I turned out the lights downstairs (it's been said that I have as many lamps as the Pentagon) and made my way upstairs. For one moment I almost called 1411 to ask for Felix's phone number. But as quickly as the thought came to mind, I pushed it aside. *Tomorrow is another day.*

I turned off Mr. Coffee, and after preparing a fresh pot (that was electronically timed to greet me in the morning) I poured myself a shot of Jack Daniels Old no. 7 over ice. Walking through the house, I flipped off lights as I passed them, on my way to the bathroom. Then, cranking up the furnace a little, so I wouldn't regret taking a bath at this hour, I turned the hot water on full blast, then tempered it a bit with a little cold, knowing that I would look like a lobster when I emerged—but who cared? No one was here to see me. I was becoming introspective, and that was not a really good idea under the circumstances. Loneliness sucks. I went to the bedroom, pulled the flannel gown from under my pillow, and headed back to the bathroom, muttering into my sour mash. "*It's a damn good thing there's no one to see you tonight, Granny Clampett.*"

* *

Ricky-Dino had returned from the bathroom with his injured fist swathed in industrial strength paper towels. The bleeding had stopped, but the throbbing had not. As he lay supine, he cradled his painful extremity against his groin. It didn't seem cause for concern, under the circumstances. His right hand had been rinsed off too, for that was where his nose pickin' digit lived. He lay quietly for a few minutes. He had already scolded Cobra into being quiet during the telling of his promised tale of murder and mayhem. In his mind, this was his *great* dramatic pause.

"Godammit, Dino, I'll be back on the streets before I hear this yarn if you don't get going."

"I told you to shut—the—fuck—up. Now don't say another word 'til I'm done. You got it?"

"I got it, I promise." Cobra was about to pee his pants, but he wasn't about to move, for fear that ol' Dino might just have a change of heart while he was gone. Anyhow, he knew there was a Pepsi can under the bunk if the situation got really critical.

"Well," he began, "that fuck, Sheriff Houston, got me to drive some big dick up to Nashville one day. I took him to the airport out in Donelson and dumped him and his suitcases at the American gate. After that I had no idea where he went, and I didn't care. All I could think about was gettin' me a little pussy. I went down on lower Broad, and shit, they've got that place all cleaned out. These big cafés and nightclubs are all over the place. There wasn't even a porno bookstore left, much less a whore. So, I headed up to Clarksville to see a buddy of mine, I knew I could find some shit up there. Well, I'll be godammed if he wasn't gone. So, just about the time I'd decided to crawl over in the corner and play with myself, I caught sight of something shiny over in the back seat. I turned around, and I'll be dammed, there laid a nice, new looking police jacket, badge, and even a flashlight. Some ignorant deputy Dawg had just left it in the car when he got off shift. I'll bet his balls were fuckin' icicles by the time he got home."

Cobra was getting antsy and his bladder was beginning to complain, but he kept his word and didn't interrupt Dino, even though he was in a lull right then.

"I was just outside Clarksville when I saw this sweet, young thing driving an old Chevy Cavalier, so I followed her for a while. She drove through the outskirts of town before she headed toward a section where there was a bunch of houses. I popped the old blues in her rearview mirror and hit the siren for just a second. I didn't want to make nobody curious. Well, sir, she pulled right over into this school-ground where it was dark'rn under an old maid's nightgown. The moon hadn't come up yet. I got out of the car and walked up to hers. She had already rolled the window down by the time I got there. I shined that big, old regulation flashlight, right in her face so she couldn't see me, but I could see her real good. Jesus, boy, she was fine. She was real young with all this long, dark brown hair and sort of *slanty* eyes. I heard later that her daddy's Chinese or something like that. Anyhow, like I said, I shined that light in her eyes and told her that her daddy was in the hospital and that they had sent me to find her and take her over there to see her family. Well sir, she got out of that car just as pretty as you please. Then, for some reason, she acted like she was going to crawl right back in. That's when I reached in and grabbed her. I led her to the car, and I guess she was real worried about her daddy cause she didn't act like she thought anything was strange about the way I picked her up. She didn't make a peep. I saw on TV later where they said her car was locked when they found it. But all I did was shut the door, maybe it locked itself. I don't know and I don't care.

By this time Cobra's "snake" was about to explode. He was slapping his legs together, but he wasn't having much luck stemming the tide.

"What in hell's wrong with you?" Ricky-Dino was not in the best of humors.

"I gotta piss something fierce."

"Then go on and do it before you wet my bed."

Cobra, holding himself, ran to the bathroom and aimed his tattooed snake-entwined dick toward the cracked stained urinal, while breathing a sigh of much needed relief.

Ricky-Dino was thinking in Cobra's absence. He was reliving his pre-Thanksgiving dessert, and was loving every minute of it. God, the memory of that hateful bitch made him hot. Cobra broke into his reverie when he sat back down on the edge of the bunk.

"Look at you, you sonabitch, your ready to go again."

"Fuck you, Cobra!"

"I don't think so, massa—I be getting out next week." He grinned at the serious face looking up at him from the pillow.

"Well anyhow," Ricky-Dino sighed, "if you can keep a lid on it, I'll get on with my story."

"I'm all ears, Dino."

"I had her in the back seat of the car before she knew what was happening. I sat down beside her for a minute. You know what she said to me? She said, 'You're not a police officer, are you?'" Ricky-Dino giggled under his breath. "Can you imagine that? I told her no, I wasn't, but that I was working part-time at the Dickson County Sheriff's office, and since I was in the area, they had called me. Shit, she could've read the side of that old squad car and known where I was from. Now, listen, later on I heard on the TV that she was real smart and was getting ready to graduate from high school pretty soon. If that's smart, then I'll stay the way I am, thank you very much."

Cobra, slow as he was, looked eyeball to eyeball at his comrade in chains.

"Jesus H. Christ, Dino, I know who you're talking about. It's that *gook* girlie that went missing a day or so before Thanksgiving, ain't it?'

"Shut your goddam cake-hole, you idiot, if I wanted the whole fuckin' place to know about it, I'd a called a press conference. Now watch it, damn you."

"I'm sorry, Dino, I'm just surprised, that's all. I'll keep it down, I promise." He would have gladly super-glued his mouth shut—if that's what it took.

"Just see that you do. Now, where was I? Oh, yeah, I drove her out to some godforsaken spot out past Cole's Creek Road, down this muddy pig trail that ended in a little clearing. By now she was crying to beat the band, not screaming and yelling, just blubberin' real hard. I got out of the car and crawled in the back seat with her. She started scootin' real hard to get away from me. Hell, I wasn't gonna hurt her. All I wanted was a little piece of ass. I slapped her face and she shut up for a minute. I told her that I just wanted her to suck me off, and then I would let her go. I dropped my drawers, and after a bit of fussing, she went to work. I reck'n she was scared not to. She did a real good job, though. Must have been practicing on that boy friend of hers. I was getting real hot, so I pulled her off me so's I could take her clothes off. It was colder'n a well digger's ass outside, but I wasn't feeling it at all. She started whining again, so I threatened her pretty good. But I didn't hit her again. I just don't know why she had to get so tore up over things. I pulled off her sweater, unhooked her bra, and kissed around on her tits for a little while. I like to never got her britches off, but finally did, along with her underpants. I had everything off her but one shoe and one sock, when all hell broke loose. She started screaming like a banshee or something, so I clamped my hand over her mouth real good. She wiggled, but I reached down on the floorboard and found one of her socks. I stuck that in her mouth real tight. She gagged around there for a little while 'til she finally just seemed to give up. Well, with a mouth full of sock there weren't no room left for me. So I laid her down real nice. I had left the rear door of the squad car open 'cause if you get your ass closed up back there, you're as good as got, but I don't have to tell you that. So I spread her out there on the seat. My, she was nice and so pretty. I took my time with her until I couldn't wait no more. So I then banged her real good. Jesus, Cobra, did anybody ever tell you if you take your time and try to hold off as long as you can, that when it does come, it's so much better than if you just *wham, bam, thank you ma'am*?"

"Goddam, Dino, did you grow up in a fuckin' cave? You're one dumb sonabitch."

"Fuck you, Einstein. Anyhow, when I got through, I carried her over to the edge of the woods while I took a look around. The moon was bright as day, by that time, and I could see as good as daylight. I figured she must be cold out there with no clothes on, so I got her long sweater. It looked like a coat. I buttoned it around her while I looked for a good place to stay for a while. I found this little spot under some trees where the leaves had hit the ground, and made a dandy place to lay down. Well, I told her it was time to *go* again, and I'll be damned if she didn't haul off and kick me in the nuts with the foot that still had the shoe on it. She didn't have no real strength behind her, but it brought me to my knees for a second or two, all right. She started to run away when all of a sudden, she stumbled and fell. I ran over and picked her up. Jesus, I was mad now. Kick me in the nuts, would she? I hauled her ass back to the car where I found some twine in the trunk. I jerked that sweater off of her, then I marched her back to the trees where I tied her hands behind her, threw her down on those leaves and ate her like a big, old juicy orange. Then I fucked her 'til the world looked level. When I got done, I got her up and spread her arms and legs between these two little trees and tied her up real good. She was staked out like dessert for the buzzards. I went back to the car and rummaged around and found somebody's stale old Kools and smoked a couple while I tried to figure out what to do next. I decided right then and there that I couldn't let her go. I'd have to kill her. I hung around the car for about a half-hour or so before I went back to where she was tied up. I'm sure she heard me coming, but she never gave no sign. She couldn't see me 'cause I was coming up from behind. I got me another bodacious hard-on from just looking at her stretched out between those trees, so I stopped to work on that for a while when I got me an idea. I slipped up on her real quiet, still working on my boner. I picked up a big, old rock in my left hand, cause my right hand was busy. I raised that rock up over the back of her head. All the while I was doing the *hand-jive,* which I stopped just long enough to grab her hair and whisper a sweet nothin' in her ear. Then it was back to the business at hand. After a minute I felt it comin', and I slammed that ol' rock down on her head. I heard her skull crack. Jesus Christ, I ain't never come like that before, or since…'til tonight. I saw colored stars and heard the fucking *Star Spangle Banner* all at the same time. I'll never forget it. Look, I get horny just thinking about it."

"That's some story, Dino, damned if it ain't." Cobra was horny too, just from listening to the story, but he didn't think he could do anything about it because the pictures that Dino had painted inside his head were too fresh. He'd have to wait a little while—give the paint a chance to dry a little first.

* *

I lay in my antique ball and claw bathtub, floating in *la la* land, simmering, actually, amidst the aromatic candles and heart wrenching strains of Peter Ilich's *Symphony No.6*, "Pathetique." I thought I knew how a lobster must feel the instant he realizes that he's about to enhance someone else's romantic evening, not his own.

Bathing, by its very virtue, had to have been one of the most civilizing of all activities indulged in by prehistoric man. Think about the first time a hairy, smelly, little knuckle-dragger came home to the cave after having fallen into a stream or river and been cleansed of a layer or two of topsoil. The little woman must have veritably swooned in ecstatic wonderment. The *mystique physique* could have flourished only after Cro-Magnon, or one of his *homo-erectus* cousins, accidentally tumbled into a steaming pool, and called his mate to join him. No doubt that very act was what eventually precipitated the evolution of the thoroughly civilized hot-tub. True romance had surely had its inception (or conception) that day.

I know that where Lee hails from, Hot Springs, Arkansas, was *sanctum sanctorum*, the most holy of holies for all Native American Indians from that part of the country. Warring tribes buried the hatchet and smoked the proverbial peace pipe when gathered around the bubbly steaming pools that emanated from natural thermal springs deep inside the bowels of the earth. The waters had simmered in the cauldron of lava-beds, since before man was the merest twinkle in God's magnanimous eye.

Yes, to me, a steaming immersion in the old ball and claw is a side trip to *Civitas Dei*, or a brief respite in earth's heavenly pleasure dome, not to be redundant or overly dramatic. Candles and other accoutrements, added to the ritual, are merely the icing on the cake of civilized behavior.

* *

Tchaikowsky withdrew sullenly into silence, whereupon the soundtrack from *Sleeping With the Enemy* fell into my lap, to put it bluntly. I supposed that for as long as I lived, I would associate that music with Jerry, and particularly the last night he and I spent together. I felt renewed emotion that I thought had absented itself from my being forever. *Anything* that can affect me the way those simple little tunes still do just proves how wrong a mere mortal can be. I did decide, however, that before going to bed, I would snap that particular CD up in its little plastic box and file it away under…"yesterday."

* *

Christmas day came and went. I couldn't keep my mind where it belonged, in spite of the presence of all three of my sons, and the wives of the two who are still married. There was a Christmas feast fit for royalty (and I didn't have to cook it). Friends came by and even Santa visited (Dave Marshall in a rented suit, for the occasion). He and his ladylove Suzanne Lassiter had joined us for coffee and dessert before going to regale other of their friends. All in all, I guess, it was a lovely day. I just wasn't there, in spirit, to *enjoy it*.

God, help me.

7

There was a nasty, little worm crawling around in the nether regions of my mind. The shadow of a creature, so vile, that God must have a special fate in store for him. Why else would such a scab on the butt of society have ever been born? I couldn't imagine. I just knew that he was out there, somewhere, lying in wait for his next victim, his next opportunity to rape, maim, and murder. God knows what other miscreantic deeds he might be up to. He wasn't finished. This I knew to be true, not unless he was caught and put away where he could no longer get his filthy hands on other children like Marie Zhou.

I wondered if he had a family. Did he have a wife and children? I wondered if he were misogynistic, or just plain crazy as a shithouse rat. At some point in time he had had two parents, and I prayed, for their sakes, they were no longer around when he was exposed for what he was—and is. Being a mother, I could not imagine the panic, guilt and self-recrimination that would come from knowing your child's life had been taken with the savagery that not even the wildest of beasts would commit unless it were starving or its progeny were in mortal danger.

I had lain awake for most of the night, light slumber tippy-toeing in and out like Carl Sandburg's venerable "Fog." Worn out from lack of sleep and the reasons I couldn't sleep, I rolled over and looked at the clock. Its gleaming, pulsating, green numerals told me it was seven o'clock, Sunday morning. It was the day after Christmas. The alarm would blast me back into the real world in just under thirty minutes. Mr. Coffee would perk to life in about fifteen minutes. Apparently, I had been so restless that Hillary, my calico cat, had gone to find more restful digs. Her usual spot beside me was empty and cool to the touch. "Hell," I thought, "I can't sleep with me either."

I lay there, semi cognizant, but already lolling around in a mental funk. My mind was haphazardly snatching at glazed-over memories, trying to discern where to store what. I didn't want to be doing this, lying in my bed, reliving times gone by, times never to return. What's the use? I thought I had made my peace with the past, but apparently I had not done a very thorough job of it. Was Jerry trying to tell me something, something beyond the painfully obvious void that was creeping in and out of my daily and nightly existence, eating me from the inside out?

* *

Felix had called last night, and after the hubbub of Christmas, my children (and the whole holiday fracas in general), I had enjoyed our quiet conversation. We had made plans to have dinner together the following Saturday night, and, now I think, I was beginning to feel little snatches of guilt or remorse. I couldn't decide if I actually felt I would be dishonoring Jerry's memory by going out with another man or if I just didn't want to go and was looking for some enigmatic excuse to bail out. No, I knew it wasn't the latter because I *did* want to go out with Felix. I was looking forward to it—he is a warm and entertaining man. I knew it would be a very pleasant evening, nothing more, nothing less. He is the very epitome of the "southern gentleman." Hell, maybe I would feel flattered if he tried to put the moves on me. Disappointed and disillusioned, but flattered, nevertheless. Damn, I didn't know what my problem was, and wished to hell I didn't care. Why was I wrestling with these ridiculous minutiae? Because I'm Dare Murphy, that's why. I worry today about what I'm going to worry about tomorrow. My late husband Tim used to tell me that I would make the perfect Jewish mother. I guess he was more accurate than I had given him credit for. I dozed.

* *

The alarm stung my senses and snatched me, more or less, back to the realm of the alive and mostly conscious. After hitting the "off" button, I reached for the phone on my bedside table. I pushed the speed dial number for Lee's home phone.

"Brrrrr and hello," Lee shuddered, sounding wide-eyed and bushy-tailed after her morning's five-mile walk.

63

"My God, how cold is it?" I had my head, along with the receiver, under the covers, putting off the inevitable for a little while longer.

I heard her flip her Zippo and afterwards blow a long slow satisfying breath past the mouthpiece and into my immediate frame of reference. *Pavlov lives.* Dragging on my terrycloth robe and slippers, I got up and stumbled toward the kitchen, carrying the cordless phone and Lee along with me.

I could hear her blow across the surface of a cup of hot coffee, "I checked the thermometer before I left, and it was 29 degrees. I damned near froze my tushie before I got cranked up to my pace. Why?"

"Oh Lord," I groaned, "it took all my energy just to haul my butt out of the bed. I just don't know how you do it."

"Perseverance darlin', perseverance."

"Yeah, right, and the horse your perseverance rode in on."

"Are we just a little out of sorts this beautiful, sunshiney morning?" She teased.

"Yeah, I guess we are. Are you coming over here, or do you want me to pick you up?"

"I'll be over as soon as I load the dishwasher and take a quick shower. Joe had breakfast cooked when I got back from my walk. I guess he felt sorry for me because my Sunday will be spent knee-deep in rape and murder, while we scour the frozen countryside in search of that poor child's body. I didn't even think to tell him last night that Calhoun had invited us to breakfast. But, anyway, I'll be there in about forty-five minutes. Is that soon enough?"

"Lee, I haven't even had my first cup of coffee yet. I probably wouldn't be out of bed, except I heard you light a cigarette, and *voilà*, my feet hit the floor like a pair of trained seals." I coughed as the first drag of the day stung my sensitive, unprepared lungs. Smoke whirled toward the frost-brushed window that over-looked the lake. "Forty five minutes will be fine. Just come on in, I'll leave the back door open." It was then that I noticed the lone, Canada goose making her way through the dimness, gliding effortlessly across the cove. Her stately head was aimed directly toward the freshly pinked horizon. She could very well have been a carved and painted decoy, for there was no visible movement above her watermark. Only the slightest surface wake trailed her gracefully tufted body through the ripples.

"See you then," she promised. I listened to the fiber-optic silence after she hung up the phone.

I poured steaming coffee into my favorite mug. It sports a drawing of Maxine, the adorably frowzy and cranky, slippered character made famous by Shoebox Greeting Cards. She's standing poised beside her Harley Davidson, clad in her ubiquitous bunny slippers and a leather motorcycle jacket. The caption reads "Born to be riled." *Now, ain't that just the God's honest truth?*

8

My innards felt leaden with the unaccustomed weight of an early morning breakfast, as I trudged through the snow incrusted mud. The sun, at its almost exact forty-five degree angle, was stabbing at my eyes like infinitesimal solar needles. The sheltered area where we were poking around made the wearing of sunglasses impractical, so when I stepped into the clearing, it was painful indeed. Lee wore the flip-up type, which were in constant motion, due to the movement from bright sun to mottled shade and back again. I think they are *tres* tacky, but I could see the prudence in owning such a pair if one wore glasses.

I motioned for Lee to come closer.

"What?" She was digging in her jacket pocket for her cigarettes, pulling out cell phone, Kleenex, and cough drops before finally locating the pack in the opposite pocket.

"This is not the place. It's similar and looks as I think it should. It corresponds with the map pretty well, but it's not the place I'm looking for. Marie Zhou is not here, and my guess is that she never has been...dead *or* alive."

Lee's exhaled cigarette smoke met the brisk breeze and dissolved before becoming one with the elements. "Do you want me to tell them it's time to move on?"

I lit up, having a difficult time with the Bic, gloves, and windy conditions. I knew God was telling me I was treading on thin ice (both literally and figuratively), and I knew I had to quit...but not today.

"No, I'll talk to them. But first tell me, how goes it with Glinda the Good witch?"

"Dare Murphy, I can't believe you said that." She, nevertheless, nearly choked on covert laughter, or maybe on the cigarette smoke as it recycled itself inside her lungs. "Tacky, tacky."

"Yeah, like you hadn't come up with it yourself. Well?" I questioned.

"How the hell would I know? I'm up here riding point with you. You want I should drop back into the herd and reconnoiter?"

"Could you do that? I just don't know about her. And I really would hate to see her send the troops off on a snipe hunt. Anyway, I'm going to circle the perimeter one more time, just to make sure I haven't missed anything, then we can go."

Lee peeled off like an F16 on a mission and headed for the rest of the group.

* *

Glinda Güdwich had entered my life amidst exuberant breakfast conversation at Clarksville's, inimitable Sharkey's Diner. Cops, wherever they may be, seem to have an innate sense of separation of "time on" and "time off." I think if they didn't have that "safety valve," there would be more suicides and malfeasances among their numbers than there are. I also think Duncan Hines never dined at Sharkey's. I could be wrong. However, once upon a time he had lived just up the road in Bowling Green, Kentucky. What I meant to say was, "I doubt that the old sycophant would have given Sharkey's his *seal of approval*. My food was good, but what could possibly go wrong with oatmeal and dry toast? I watched as everyone else's fare swam in grease, but the looks of satiation, afterwards, spoke for themselves.

Glinda's father was, indeed, a former member of the U. S. Army. She had grown up on and around military bases, spending the last few years of her father's active duty in Clarksville, where he wrapped up his thirty-year career at Fort Campbell: the massive, sprawling home of the infamous "Screaming Eagles," the 101st Airborne. Her family was, in fact, acquainted with Chief Warrant Officer and Mrs. Zhou *and* Marie. And she was very eager to help find the wretched creature who had taken Marie from her car on the night in question.

All of this told me very little. However, not for one moment did I doubt the sincerity exhibited by the young woman who had come along with Will and Rolanda Bealer on this snipe hunt.

* *

Glinda leaned against the fender of Will Bealer's official car: a mud-caked, battered-looking, albeit, super-charged Chevy Blazer of indeterminate vintage. Lee and I were sharing the contents of our king-sized, coffee-filled Thermos with her. Our gloved hands, further warmed by the styrofoam cups containing the steaming cream-colored liquid, held onto those cups as if they were our only tethers to the civilized world of normalcy. The cops were gathered in a clutch, off to the side, waiting while the three of us talked, and *felt each other out.*

"Where are you coming from, Glinda?" I asked in my inimitably, tactful fashion.

"I'm not really sure, Dare. I just know that I have to be out here. I know that I'll *feel* something when we're near."

"That's rather enigmatic, don't you think?" I knew exactly what she meant and exactly where she was coming from. The whole psychic world is enigmatic, for God's sake. I just needed for her to be more forthcoming—to expose more of her esoteric self if I were to be expected to work with her. However, I wasn't at all sure that I wanted to. I feel rather jealous of my turf, if I may be permitted the luxury, which I'm not at all sure I may, or even should be. But, hey!

"She continued, haltingly, "I woke up crying in the middle of the night…you know…the night Marie disappeared. I didn't know a thing about what had happened to her. She hadn't even been reported missing, as far as I know. I just felt this intensely nagging sensation that something was terribly wrong. So I got up and paced the floor. Finally, I tried to read. Forget it, I couldn't concentrate. I *nuked* a cup of leftover coffee, and of course, that just made matters worse. I tried to lie back down, but I felt as if electrodes were imbedded inside my brain. It was terrible. I've never felt anything like it before, and I hope I never do again." She rummaged through her purse in search of a cigarette, finally coming up with a tattered package of Merit Lights. I could tell by observing the scenario that she was not a *real* smoker. Why in hell would anyone want to play at such a dreadful habit? It beats the hell out of me. She was too young to associate smoking with the glamour of films *noire,* but hey, so am I.

"Here." Lee offered a light from her Zippo, shielding the tenuous flame from the elements with her cupped hands. It took a couple of tries before the operation was successful. Glinda coughed non-inhaled fumes into the crisp morning breeze.

Crap a daisy, I thought, *give me a freakin' break.*

* *

Clarksville was a blur: wooded areas all running together like a jigsaw puzzle with the occasional piece missing. Not the tiniest clue or trace was evident indicating that Marie Zhou had passed that way before. Nowhere we went that day brought me any closer to my goal, and I knew it. But I had to give each location a fair shot. I was waiting for some internal mechanism to set off bells and whistles, which wouldn't happen until we found the specific location where Marie Zhou had been discarded, like the shoe I would know, when I saw it. Her sneaker would guide me to her sweater, which in turn would guide me to her body, or whatever was left of it by this time. I remembered my dream: dogs howling in the distance. There were some surprisingly remote stretches in rural Montgomery County, plenty of places where hungry four-legged predators roamed the woods. I shook off a chill. There went that metaphorical goose running across my grave.

We tramped through frozen thickets until my jeans were covered with winter-browned stick tights, and my boots were caked with frozen mud. By the last time we had crawled wearily into the seat behind the lieutenant and his partner, in spite of our efforts to scrape off the *out-of-doors,* the floorboard of the Taurus looked like a mud-wresting pit.

Lee nudged me. We were sitting in the backseat, and I was absent-mindedly opening my second package of cigarettes of the day. "What?" I looked at her to see what had possessed her to poke me like that.

She nodded toward the front seat. I looked up to meet the lieutenant's eyes in the rearview mirror. God knows what he was saying or how long he had been saying it.

"I beg your pardon?" I feebly offered.

"I said, do you think there's any point in going any further with the search this afternoon?"

The low-slung, icy-white sun made me shiver just to look at it. All the warmth seemed to have been sucked out of it as the western horizon beckoned it home. I scanned the sky outside the window, remembering an old Hoagy Carmichael tune, *Buttermilk Skies.* Snow was going to revisit us before long, and it made me ache just to think about it. "No, I don't, Emmett, it's getting late. Why don't we try again tomorrow? I don't work on Mondays, so if you're game, so are we."

He was obviously tracking along the same wavelength as I, for his reply was, "That'll be great—if it doesn't snow."

"I won't be here if it snows heavily, it would be pointless. But if it doesn't, what time would you like us to be here?"

"Ten o'clock would be early enough, if that's okay with you."

I looked at Lee sitting next to me. She nodded, blowing smoke up and down as she did so.

"That'll be fine." Grateful as hell that my feet wouldn't have to hit the floor tomorrow morning before the sun had had its coffee.

* *

"Godammit!" Ricky-Dino was having a time trying to fumble the cigarette out of the package with his bandaged hand. He had been to the infirmary where the *circuit-riding* medic had confirmed Cobra's diagnosis: there were no broken bones. Doc had smeared antibiotic salve on the back of the throbbing hand, then across the knuckles before wrapping it with gauze. All was anchored with adhesive tape. He had given the patient a brown bottle containing several ibuprofen tablets for his pain.

"Godammit," Ricky-Dino reiterated, waiting as Cobra disgustedly yanked the Lucky out of the ratty looking pack and crammed it between Ricky-Dino's waiting lips. He raked his thumbnail across the flint wheel of the Zippo. Cobra held the lighter to the tip of his fellow trustee's cigarette. The wick flamed like a blowtorch. "I might have to give up smokin' if this fucker stays bandaged up much longer." The consummate whiner, Ricky-Dino plucked the cigarette from between his lips with his good hand and blew smoke obligingly at Cobra.

"Not to mentioned bangin' ghosts and concrete walls."

"Hey, asshole, I got one good hand left, and as long as he's got that, ol' Dino can jerk-off 'til the cows come home'."

"Cows? You didn't tell me you was raised up on a farm, Dino. I bet you learned how on a goat though, 'cause cows are too pretty to stand still for an ugly bastard like you." Cobra bent double in laughter, choking on the cold and his own cigarette smoke. The guard had let the trustees outside to smoke after the sheriff had left for the day. Ricky-Dino and Cobra always smoked four or five in a row to make up for their forced abstinence while "the man" was around. The heatless sun was making its way home for the night, and the wind was kicking up in its wake.

"You're a reg'lar Jerry Lewis ain't cha? You sombitch."

Cobra lit a fresh Pall Mall from the butt of the one he was presently smoking. Flicking the used-up butt off the end of his middle finger, he watched as it sailed across the yard, landing in a pile of dirty snow, *psssssting* it's way through the surface and disappearing from sight. Its soggy remains would lie hidden there until the thaw. "I'm gettin' out next week, anybody you want me to talk to for ya?"

"Shit no, you motherfucker, you'll be back before you can talk to anybody. Quick as you can lay your sticky fingers on a gun, you'll be out there in some ol' Hadji market waving it around in some goddam A-rab's face. Next thing I know your snakey dick'll be right back in here on another *attempted while carryin'*. And just how long you think it'll take you to get back to bein' a trustee again, after that? Like a hun'derd years? You're a goddam habitual, and if you're not careful, your ass is going to end up down in Nashville in the the fuckin' big-house."

"I ain't gonna get caught next time. Anyhow, that gun I used was a water pistol."

"Yeah, I hear ya." Ricky-Dino choked on the last drag of his Lucky Strike, and he threw it on the ground, walking away from Cobra with his shoulders hunched against the frigid gust that leached its way down his collar, past his neck and shoulders. "See you in the funny papers, asshole."

"Not if I see you first," Cobra words were tossed across the yard by the blustering wind. Lost to Ricky-Dino's ears: *"You godammed, baby fucker. Not if I see you first."*

71

9

The sky hung heavy. Ponderous, gray clouds rolled, *en mass*, like puppies do before they find their legs. The wind was hiding in the trees along the banks of the brown, muddy stream that Montgomery countians simply called "the river."

My back was stiff from sheer inactivity, as much as the damp cold that held me in its icy grip. I looked at Lee, who sat beside me. Our backs rested against the windshield of my Lexus. It had been no easy feat for us to mount that perch, but we planned to watch every move as the Montgomery County Mounties made fools of themselves: damming portions of that river, diving, partially draining, then dragging for the body that wasn't there.

Jack Catcher, TV psychic, whose public career had headed south a few years ago, had come to Tennessee, claiming that Marie Zhou's body lay tangled in brush at the bottom of that river. I will always believe that his main objective was to rescue his public personae as much as it was to find that unfortunate child.

Cops, and all manners of public officials, dressed like Eskimos, were lining the frozen riverbank where cold-suited divers were presently slipping and sliding their way out of chocolate-colored water. We could see them shaking their heads and hunching their shoulders in dismay. Lee looked at me and grinned. Somehow, the prospective failure of Jack Catcher didn't give me the kick-in-the-head high that it would have under different circumstances. I knew in my heart that Marie was not in that nasty, half-frozen stream. And if they drained it dry, and swept the bottom till hell itself froze over, they were working in vain. They were sidetracking valuable search time, but I wasn't paid to give logistical advice.

* *

After I had spent a long and exhausting Sunday out in the field, Emmett Calhoun had called me that evening. "I'm sorry to bother you at home," he apologized. "I hope I didn't interrupt anything." He had proceeded to tell me about the impending arrival of the world famous psychic.

"Yes," I had told him, I knew who Jack Catcher was, and yes, he had been on the Oprah Show the same day that "The Amazing Randy," professional *nay-sayer,* had tried to debunk me, along with several other "self-proclaimed" psychics. He had finally given up on me, and had shaken my hand at the end of the show. He didn't, however, seek out Brother Jack, I might add.

Were they going to parade every *wannabe,* who was seeking his or her fifteen minutes of fame, through the county? I didn't know, but I sure as hell hoped not, not unless someone out there actually had a clue. I suspected, however, they did not.

"Hey, Dare…you still in there?" Lee shook me out of my self-induced stupor. "Are we going to sit out here till dark? My ass is an ice cube. If you'd crank-up the motor in this *mother,* it might make it a little more hospitable— a little warmer under the butt, anyway."

I looked at her sitting there all wrapped up like a mummy. I lifted her earmuff and said, "No. Let's drive into Clarksville and get some lunch. I don't think we'll miss much while we're gone. Let's go."

I slid off the driver's side of the hood. The front of my SUV was aimed directly at the muddy river. Restless bloodhounds, infinitely smarter than their human counterparts, (when it came to finding bodies) sat on their haunches on the riverbank. Occasionally, one would set off the entire pack in a cacophony of howling and baying—it was spooky as hell.

I turned the key in the ignition, and the engine hummed to life. Public Radio filled the interior with the initial strains of *Un bel di vedremo* from *Madama Butterfly.* I hit the remote control and banished Cho-Cho-San to the netherworld, remembering how after a brief honeymoon, her Lieutenant had left her too. I surfed for something less acutely nostalgic. I landed on Louis Armstrong crooning "It's A Wonderful World." How damned ironic could it get?

The ruts (that served as the road to the river) were iced-packed and slicker than owl shit. "Whoa!" Lee was bouncing inside her safety harness, and hanging on for dear life. "Watch it, will you? First you freeze my ass, then you shake it like a maraca. If you want to get rid of me, just drop me off at the bus station."

I didn't dare take my eyes off the pitiful excuse for a road, but I could sense her sarcastic grin bearing down on me. "Yeah, okay, first chance I get," I teased. I glanced at the rearview mirror just in time to catch sight of a mud-caked Chevy Blazer top the hill behind me. "Hey, Lee, turn around and see if that's who I think it is."

She craned her neck toward the rear window. "Looks like Will and Rolanda Bealer...that who you think it is?"

"Yeah, I wonder why he would be leaving *the scene* at what could be a crucial juncture, even though you and I know it isn't."

"Beats the hell out of me," she offered, "maybe he's got business elsewhere. He is the chief co-ordinator, you know."

"Yeah, I know, but still...." He stayed on my tail until I pulled up to the stop sign where I prepared to turn left at the highway. From there on it was onward to Sharkey's, where I knew cholesterol-on-a-plate was waiting with my name on it. The blazer slid to a stop right behind me. The driver's door flew open and Will Bealer jumped out, his feet already in full gear when they hit the ground.

"Where you two running off to?" I had my window down by the time his cold-reddened face appeared at the opening.

"We're going to Sharkey's to get a bite to eat, why?"

"Do you mind if Rolanda and I tag along?" He looked rather sheepishly, then grinned.

"Of course not, you guys are buying. Remember?" I accept no remuneration when working with law enforcement or families of victims. I do, however, request expenses for Lee and me: that includes food *and* lodging (if the latter becomes necessary).

He nodded, and returned to the Blazer. I watched as he climbed back into the driver's seat. He had left his door open when he jumped out. No doubt, now, Rolanda Bealer was sitting inside with her teeth chattering. "*Men!*" I heard myself say, before dropping the shift lever into drive. I checked the deserted highway before turning left. I could see Sharkey's warm, red and blue neon beacon just up the road. Will Bealer pulled out directly behind me.

Lee, my *Socratic* sidekick, patted my knee and proffered, "Don't worry about it, nothing's going to be okay anyhow."

"You've got that right, Mrs. Kennedy, and by the way, how was Dallas?" I spied a parking spot close to the door.

* *

"When you getting' out, anyhow?" Ricky-Dino was bent over, trying to shield himself from the full brunt of the wind and trying to sound as disinterested as he knew how.

"Tuesday, tomorrow evenin' around six, why? I thought you didn't care."

"Can't I be a little sociable? Shit, you don't have to make a federal case out of it, but that's exactly what's gonna happen if you don't keep that goddam pistola in your pocket and out of folks' faces."

Cobra smirked as he hunkered down to light another cigarette off the butt that he had smoked almost too short to be useful. "If I was you, I wouldn't throw stones at anybody. Look at you sitting there with that hand of yours all bandaged up. You—the masterbatin' baby-banger—tellin' me all about your "wild-ass-tales." You take the cake, Dino. You know that? How can you stand there and talk to me like I was the idiot in this group?"

"You callin' me a idiot? I ain't no idiot, and don't you never forget it. I told you about what happened that night 'cause you wanted to hear all about it. If I'd knowed you was gonna preach and pass judgment, I'd never opened my yap."

"I ain't passin' judgment, Dino, you just fret me, that's all. If anybody else in here finds out what you did, your asshole won't hold shucks, if you catch my drift."

"I got your goddam drift, ain't nobody never gonna know, less you tell em. You ain't that stupid are you?"

"No, asshole, I told you I'd never tell it, didn't I? I may be a lot of stuff, but I ain't no fuckin' snitch. Now, why'd you want to know when I was gettin' out?"

"Well," Ricky-Dino took a deep drag off his Lucky Strike, and wiped his sleeve under his nose (from his wrist to his elbow) leaving a little snail-trail everywhere his nose had touched.

"Jesus, Dino, you make me plumb sick wipin' your snotty nose like that, can't you find a rag somewhere? I'm surprised you can even bend them sleeves they're so stiffed up."

"Godammit, don't interrupt me when I'm talking. I'll wipe my nose when I get ready, how I want to…get over it, dickhead. Now, where was I? Oh, yeah, I thought mayhaps you might want to go out and check around and see what that Dare Murphy bitch is up to. I seen her on TV last night. She's out looking for Missy Poon Tang, or what ever her gook name was. I heard that they was going to drain some river up there in Clarksville—goddam stupid cops."

"Hey, Dino, if she's got them lookin' for that little girl in the river, you ain't got nothing to worry about."

"She ain't the one. Some queer from up north has convinced 'em to try lookin' in the river. The TV showed Murphy and her lezzie buddy, that's always with her, sittin' up on some big, old fancy car out at the river. You could tell by looking at them all huddled up there together that it wadn't her idea. Once they showed her with her eyes closed, like she was sleepin'. Didn't look none too interested to me. Naw, it's that queer with that sissy little beard that's got them all tore up about the river."

"What makes you think the guy's queer? And where'd you ever get the idea that Murphy and her sidekick are lezzies?"

"Shit, you stupid asshole, I can tell by looking—can't you? This place is crawling with them"

"Dino, most of these guys are straighter'n sticks. They're just horny and'll fuck anything that'll stand still long enough. I don't think you'd know a queer if it bit you on your pecker. Have you ever made nice with a girl before? Or can't you get your rocks off in the normal way? I bet you gotta hurt a woman, or ought I say little girl, before you can even get it up. Ain't that so?"

"What are you now, the shithouse shrink? Just how damn normal would you call yourself? You're forgetting that I've seen that big, old snake crawling around your dick."

"Would you like to see him spit his venom?" Cobra grabbed his crotch with his left hand and squeezed it a couple of times, laughing like a wild-man the whole time.

Ricky-Dino spun on his heel and almost fell down on the icy exercise yard. Cobra lurched forward, forgetting about his *viper*, and grabbed his pal from the rear. "Watch out there, Dino, next thing we know your little head'll be doing all your thinking for you, cause your big un's gonna be cracked open from fallin' down on this goddam ice."

"Thanks, Cobra, but don't think this makes me behold'n enough to let you get near me with your snakey schlong."

"Dino, I hate to be the one to bust your bubble, but you ain't exactly my type. But, if you want I should take a look at what that Murphy dame is doing, I'll do it. It's gonna cost you though."

"What's it gonna cost me, you mercenary bastard? I just asked you for a little favor, that's all. What's it gonna cost me?"

"Dino, just keep your dick in your drawers. I ain't never seen a man get so het-up, over nothin', in my whole life. 'Bout what it's gonna to cost you, I ain't decided yet. But I'll let you know when I see her up close and personal."

"Goddam you, Cobra, you ain't gonna talk to her are you? You ain't gonna tell her what I told to you, are you?" His eyes were pleading with Cobra, who was lighting another cigarette and just as unconcerned as he could be.

"Dino, I told you I wadn't gonna do that, now didn't I? You keep havin' these fits and spells, and not trustin' me, maybe I'll change my mind. Now just calm down. I ain't gonna talk to the bitch. I just want to get a good look at her, watch her and see how close she's getting' to the big prize. Hell, maybe I'll be a volunteer, and go out with her while she's huntin' for your little babycakes. You want me to find out for sure if she's a lezzie, good buddy?"

"Cobra, I'm asking you as nice as I know how. Just please stay away from 'er. She's a goddam psychic, you stupid sumbitch. She'd spot you quick as a wink. Then she'd trail me through you. You gotta promise you'll stay away from 'er, okay?"

"Dino, you been in this place so much, it's done sucked your sense of humor right out the end'a your dick. I didn't fall off no turnip truck. I ain't gonna get you in no trouble, I swear."

"That's real good to hear, Cobe, and I'll be looking forward to seeing you when you come back."

"I done told you I ain't getting caught next time, didn't I?"

"Yeah, I reck'n you did. Let's get our asses inside out of this bitchin' cold, what you say, Cobra?

They picked their way carefully across the ice. Cigarette smoke melded with their frosty breath, even after they had arced their spent butts over the fence where freedom lurked—like the proverbial butterfly.

* *

"Dare, what do you think of Jack Catcher?" Rolanda Bealer was unoffically picking my brain, and subtlety was not her strong suit.

"To be perfectly honest, Rolanda, I try *not* to think about Jack Catcher. I don't know him well enough to have an unbiased opinion. He and I met under rather unorthodox circumstances, and I have nothing further to offer on the subject." I detected unexpected consternation at my reply, but hey, ask me a question and I just take for granted you want an honest answer. "By the way, I see you don't have Glinda in tow. Where is she?"

Will spoke up, looking to head his wife off the subject, "She wanted to stay around there and watch them drag the river. I saw her talking with Jack Catcher a little earlier. I don't mind telling you, that guy gives me the creeps."

"He looks like a Satan prototype to me." Lee was dabbing at the corners of her mouth with a paper napkin. She looked at the two faces across the table, enjoying the reactions her pronouncement had created. She motioned the timeworn waitress to our table, and requested another cup of decaf, making sure that we were all offered the opportunity to refill our cups. "That little widow's peak, the one bushy eyebrow—and that Van Dyke looks like it was trimmed by Mrs. Beelzebub herself. That says it all for me." She was playing this small gathering for all it was worth, giving the Bealers time to digest her observation before continuing. "I think he's a cocky, publicity-seeking pariah." She stirred the half and half into her coffee, while taking a long satisfying drag on her after-lunch cigarette.

I spoke up, "Now Lee, tell us how you *really* feel."

She grinned as she took a sip from the cup. "Now that's coffee." Setting the cup in front of her, she retrieved her cigarette from the ashtray and gave it her full attention.

Will looked at me with something akin to panic in his eyes. "Do you think Glinda will be all right back there with him?"

"For God's sake, Will," It was my turn to add my two cents, "half the cops in this part of the world are back there on that river bank. If he *were* Satan, which he is *not*, he wouldn't be able to drag her through the gates of Sheol without a police escort. Don't worry about him. He's just a little weird, but harmless. He's just trying to boost his ratings, and the "new look" certainly doesn't seem to be hurting the image he apparently hopes to purvey."

* *

The rest of the afternoon was spent watching Jack Catcher choreograph the river dance. He walked the bank from one operation to the next. He directed the pumping and dragging, stopping occasionally to talk to mud-encrusted divers, who had amassed a pile of old car tires, a fishing boat with a hole the size of Rhode Island in the bottom of it, and the bloated and putrefying corpse of a German shepherd. I thought I was going to lose Lee when they dragged up the dog's body; her heart bleeds for animals as well as children. She jumped off the hood of my car, and made a dash for the woods. When she came strolling back, neither of us mentioned it.

By four-thirty the sun had that flat, sucked-out winter look. We received no warmth from its core and very little illumination from its surface. What little blue had occupied the heavens earlier had bled to the color of lead and cold, corrugated clouds hung like saturated cotton rows awaiting their turn.

The divers were packing their tanks, flippers and masks into dun colored duffel bags, while the county engineers released the foam-riddled, mud-choked water back into the riverbed where it belonged. Unless a major break came in the case, I would not be back to Clarksville before next Monday—one week from today. I had told Will Bealer and Emmett Calhoun that I would be at their disposal on my days off. For a while, anyway. I knew if they would dispense with all the *pseudo-psychics* that were crawling out of the woodwork, and get down to business, we would find that child's body (but that was not my call to make). With any luck, I prayed, we would find sufficient clues to crucify the bastard who had killed her. *Hell*, I thought, *that might be one execution I'd stand in line for*.

"Let's go, Lee." It was cold as a well digger's knee, and I was chilled to the bone. By the time we got home, darkness would have become complete, and at the moment my prime objective was to beat the snow down the plateau.

Lee dug her cell phone out of one of her multitudinous pockets. I knew she was stabbing in her home number, hoping Joe would answer. He did. She explained that we were on our way home, and he told her that he had made a gigantic pot of vegetable soup, salad and cornbread. He invited me to dinner. I graciously declined. My butt was dragging, and all I wanted to do was take a bath and fall into bed. Maybe I would read for a little while, maybe not.

"There's Pearl," I said, referring to her precious automobile, as we rounded the last curve at the top of my driveway.

"I'm going to crank her over, and while she warms up, I'll come in and have a cup of coffee with you. You don't have a hot date lurking inside do you?"

"If I did, would I tell you?"

She grinned and bailed out, heading for her car. By the time my antiquated garage door had wheezed its way up the tracks, and I had pulled quickly inside (I'm never really sure when that familiar creaking wheeze will be its last) the Mazda's twin exhaust pipes were burping thin smoke rings into the icy twilight. I hauled my purse out of the back seat and found the key. I left the garage door up so Lee could follow me inside. I unlocked the deadbolt and stepped into my kitchen.

"I left my muddy boots and the other junk in the car, what about you?" Whereupon, she announced that she had already taken hers to her car and would endeavor to clean them up before she had to wear them again. The first thing that caught my eye was the flashing light on my answering machine.

Lee was right behind me. "Hey, if that's somebody in Clarksville wanting you to come back up there, tell them to take a hike. That is, unless they've found Marie."

"It's not," I said, putting my purse on the table, and plugging my cell phone into its charger on the countertop. I sat down and lit a cigarette. I drew the smoke deeply into my lungs and held it there for what seemed minutes. First, the head-rush, then the calm, as I slowly expelled the leftovers. God, what a feeling, I didn't think I could ever quit. I simply enjoyed it too much.

"Well, O, Spookette," Lee used the nickname that never ceased to amuse me, "are you going to share with me who the mysterious call is from?" She got up and strolled to the fridge. Opening the door, she stared into its cavernous emptiness. "This thing is so sterile you could do open heart surgery in here."

"No, and I'm on a diet."

"For God's sakes Dare, if you weren't so smug about it, I wouldn't care, but you know I can't stand it when you get all mysterious on me."

"I know," I teased, "isn't it fun?"

"Dare!....."

Oh, for God's sake, Lee, it's probably Katie or MaryBea...hell, it could be anyone."

"But it's not just anyone, is it?"

"Remember what they said about curiosity and the cat? Would it make you happy to hit the button so we can be surprised together?"

"Yes, it would, but I doubt that either of us will be surprised."

Surprise, I must admit, was an understatement. We had both expected the caller to be Felix Walker, simply because he had said he would call sometime after my return from Clarksville. But it was not Felix. The voice on the answering was the familiar, sweet man I had known and grown so fond of, when he and Jerry Collins were partners on the Nashville Metropolitan Police Department.

"Dare, this is Dave. I just got a call from a Sheriff Horace Whitfield from down in Houston County. He's been looking for you. Apparently Katie just gave him my number when he explained what he wanted. I'll be home by seven thirty. So why don't you give me a ring about then and we can talk about this? Hug Lee for me, and tell her I have a joke for her the next time I see her. I look forward to talking to you later. Bye."

Suddenly, I was very tired, my bones felt like jelly, and the weight of my body was almost more than I could bear. Lee watched as I sank into my shell. "Dammit, Dare, every time you talk to Dave you can't puddle up. I know he makes you think of Jerry, but hell, as long as you and he are friends…

"Lee, darlin', get a grip, I'm just tired. No, I'm absolutely exhausted…I'm not thinking about Jerry, I'm just wondering what some jerk-water sheriff from Houston County could possibly want with me and why Dave would consider it important enough to deliver the message himself?"…*Yes, I was thinking about Jerry. Just a little.*

"Pardon?" Lee had just scooped the decaf into Mr. Coffee and was pouring water into the reservoir. It was as if she had actually heard my *quasi* confession.

I said, "Sure I miss Jerry. Even after all this time, sometimes, at night, I roll over to put my arms around him…and then I may wake up in a mood. Sometimes I'm sad. Then other times I'm pissed off enough to kill him for dying on me in the first place. Sometimes I just feel empty, You know what? Yeah, I miss him, but I'm beginning to wonder if it's not *just* loneliness— which I'm almost sure it is. I've got to get on with my life."

She finished her coffee-making chores, walked to the table, gathered me up in her arms and held me like a child. I let go. I was so tired and concerned for the parents of Marie Zhou that I broke down and sobbed. All the while Lee patted my back and talked to me. She couldn't go long without cracking wise about one thing or another. "Do you remember the time he and Dave had the flat tire somewhere out off Brick Church Pike? Remember Dave telling us how Jerry was standing there watching, while Dave did all the work? God forbid he should have gotten his hands, much less his Gucci's, dirty. Wouldn't you have loved to have been a gnat in a tree when that eighteen-wheeler came barreling around that curve and blew that mud all over Jerry, leaving Dave high *and* dry, where he was changing that damned flat?"

Soon I was laughing over past memories, instead of moldering in them. We drank coffee, smoked, and I managed at long last to put a whole lot of things into perspective. I told her that I knew the past was suffocating my present and possibly even my future. I felt as though a great weight had lifted from my shoulders. Sometimes it takes me awhile, but once I make a decision, that's it.

"You have no idea how happy that makes me. You want me to stay til Dave calls?"

"No, no, you go on home. Joe must wonder what's happened to you. Besides, that old Mazda's probably warmed its way through a tank of gas by now. I'm fine. My God, Lee, I don't know what I would do without you. You've been saving my emotional bacon with regularity for years, but hopefully that too is in the past. You'll never know how happy I am that you stopped in tonight."

"Hey, Joe knows where I am, no problemo. And Pearl just sips gas, unlike that beast you drive. You couldn't get rid of me if you tried. Dare, I'm your friend, and I love you—that's what friends are for."

"I realize that, and I love you too. I appreciate you more that you'll ever know."

She grinned. "...*and I say to myself, it's a won-der-ful world,*" she crooned, while grinding out her cigarette and reaching for her coat. "Say "yo" to Dave for me, and tell him I'm waiting with bated breath 'til I hear that joke."

"Will do. Call me when you get back from your five-miler in the morning, and for God's sake, be careful out there in all that snow and ice!"

"Didn't you notice that the streets in the neighborhood been cleared? Nary a scrap of ice or snow on the pavement."

"No, I guess not," I said, "we got home, I guess that's all that was important at the time."

* *

No lobster would have survived the bath I had immersed myself into. Hot baths and aroma-therapeutic candles are one of my great weaknesses.

I watched the reflections from the candle-flames dance about the ceiling, down the walls and back to their origins. The fatigue slipped from my body and lay in the bottom of the tub, until I would pull the plug. Not just yet. My muscles relaxed, and the tension and general crappiness followed the fatigue. I thought I might live after all.

I stepped from the tub and dried myself before rubbing lotion onto my elbows and knees. I wrapped myself in my old, tattered terrycloth robe and was comfortable. I would fix myself a sandwich before getting into bed, leaving time to spare before I was to call Dave.

* *

Barely able to stay awake, at seven-thirty I placed the call.
Dave, this is Dare. I got your message. What can I do for you?"
"They've found her purse."
"Whose purse?" Teetering on the edge of unconsciousness, I was not up for Trivial Pursuit.
"Dare, listen to me. A hunter found Marie Zhou's purse."

10

Did you talk to Felix" Lee had phoned as early as she dared.

"Yeah, he called just after I hung up from talking with Dave."

"Well?"

"Same deep hole in the ground."

"Dammit, are you two still on for Saturday night?"

"We're still on."

"Dare."

"Yes, darlin', we had a lovely conversation, or rather he did. I nearly fell asleep on him a couple of times."

"*Oh, that was nice*. What did you talk about? That is when you could manage to keep your eyes open."

"I told him I was horny, and did he want to come right over? He turned me down."

"Jesus, you're crass."

"*Me*? You're not going to give up are you?"

"Nope."

"He just wanted to confirm our date for Saturday night, and he asked me if I would like to go to the Bar Association's black tie dinner with him Saturday week."

"Well, what did you say?"

"I said, 'Not if I live to be a million.'"

"Do you want to sit on your butt for the rest of your days and let me watch you and that cat grow old together?"

"Not necessarily, I just don't wish to rub elbows with Nashville's legal sub-culture. Excuse me, but I don't need to go anywhere that desperately."

"I'll bet that made a good impression on Felix. Wait. We can't go on calling him Felix."

"What would you suggest we call him? Oswald?"

"No, but we've got to give him a nickname."

"Why, if you'll excuse my asking?"

"Let's just suppose this gets a little serious, and the time comes when you two wild, impetuous creatures decide to jump into bed together. What the hell are you going to call him in the throes of passion?" I can just hear it now. 'Oooooooh, Feeeeelix.'

Get my drift?"

"What the fuck are you talking about?"

"Exactly."

"Okay, then, just what would you suggest? Assuming this ever takes place, and if I were you, I wouldn't give odds."

"What's his middle name?"

"Henry."

"Jesus, what kind of name is Felix Henry Walker?"

"An old one. Ask me how I know."

"Well?"

"He told me he's the fourth or the fifth, and also the last. He said if he had ever had a son, or if he ever should, he certainly wouldn't hang a moniker like that on him. He also told me that his friends call him Phil, except it's spelled F-e-l; he seemed compelled to point that out. Now does that paint a prettier picture for madam?"

"Infinitely, thank you very much."

* *

I had broken one of my cardinal rules, or rather one of Katie's. I had taken a workday off to do police business. That meant Katie had to spend Tuesday clearing my calendar for Wednesday by rescheduling appointments. And she did so with remarkable restraint.

Lee had come over bright and early and was sitting at my kitchen table drinking coffee and reading the newspaper when I got out of the shower. "Now that we've gotten your potential passion problems all worked out, where is it we're going again?"

"Erin."

"As in go *braugh*?"

"Something like that. The sheriff wants me to see the purse."

"Have you worked with that county mountie before?"

"No. I'd never even heard of him until Dave told me about him."

"Do you know what he wants you to do?"

"He wants us to go out with him and a deputy to where the hunter found the purse. The sheriff's still got the purse, so maybe I can pick up something there. The longer this goes on, the more complicated it becomes. You know how it gets when different municipal and county departments are involved. It can, and usually does become a jurisdictional nightmare. They all get their knickers in a knot, don't want to share evidence or even communicate. They remind me of a bunch of kids."

"But you get to see it all, Sherlock."

"You got it, Doctor Watson. Let's go."

* *

The deputy parked the patrol car on the shoulder of the highway. Actually, it was a macadamized county road, little more than a paved path. The four of us got out of the car, and the sheriff continued with his narration about how Herman Sayers had come in on Monday afternoon with the purse stuffed inside his hunting jacket. They hadn't thought too much about it until they dug out the driver's license, and there, "bigger'n Pete," they'd seen Marie Zhou's picture. It had been undamaged by the elements because it was laminated in plastic. He continued on about how they had also discovered a nearly empty Kent cigarette package that was a little worse for wear and containing little more than shredded tobacco strands and torn bits of paper. I raked through the clutter with the eraser end of a pencil. A tube of lipstick had broken inside its tube. The remaining items were just run of the mill teenage dross. A painful picture began to emerge. The sheriff had called me because he had seen me on TV sometime in the past, and then he had read about my connection to the current search in the newspaper. Not exactly proper protocol, but like we had talked about earlier, nobody wants to share anything with another jurisdiction. It was getting curiouser and curiouser.

* *

"Sheriff Whitfield, answer me this one question if you can. What was a hunter doing out here in the open so close to the road?"

"Well, Ms. Murphy, old Herman had pulled his pickup onto the berm there, and left it while he went on foot into that little patch of woods over yonder. It's not the kind of place most men would go to do any serious hunting, but Herman ain't a serious hunter. He don't even load his 22. He just

86

goes out there to get some peaceful time away from Edna. Anyhow, that's another story. He told me that he was walking along that little beaten-down path over yonder, when he looked across the road and seen that shiny, little plastic-looking purse, all hunched up in that bed of pine needles. God only knows how long it'd been there. See up there on top of that bank?"

"See what Sheriff?" I searched the muddy horizon and saw nothing.

"That's the highway up there. This little old road down here just carries local traffic. That's Route 13 up there. You can get to Clarksville that way," he said, pointing somewhere beyond the trees, "or if you go the other way, you'll come to Waverly. The way I got it figured is somebody just chucked that pocketbook out a car window. If it was dark, whoever threwed it out probably figured nobody would ever find it 'cause it is sort of out in the sticks around here. He wouldn't see no lights close by or nothin', less somebody was coon-huntin' under lights. But then it ain't coon season. That, Ms. Murphy, tells me we're dealing with a stranger to these parts."

I ventured into the cloudy waters of this incredible…I was hesitant to call it an investigation. "I think you're probably right about it being a stranger, sheriff. Tell me, has your forensics team been out here, checking for footprints or any other type of evidence?"

"Ma'am, we got no *frenzics* in Houston County. I only got six deputies to cover the whole county, and the mayor says we're gonna have to cut that back to five. Basically, Ms. Murphy, when a homicide happens, and that ain't often, mind you, it's me and Hershel here that takes care of things. Hershel's my wife's little brother."

"Well, Sheriff, let me ask you this, have you notified the chief in Clarksville or the sheriff of Montgomery County that you've found Marie Zhou's purse?"

"No, I wanted to talk to you first before they got their hands on it. I did call that detective in Nashville that your secretary told me about. He seemed to think I should call everybody and his brother, but I thought better of it. Now, if you think it's time I make the call, then I will."

I dug in my pocket for my cigarettes, then waited while Lee searched for her Zippo. I bent my head, cigarette in mouth to the flame, while shielding it from the raggedy breeze. I took a long drag while exchanging incredulous glances with Lee.

"Well, Sheriff, it is my considered opinion that you should call the proper authorities, just as soon as we get back to your office."

"First, ma'am, I want to know what you've *picked up.* I've read all about you in the papers and seen you on the TV. Seems like a lot of folks think mighty highly of you."

"Thank you for your kind assessment, Sheriff. I'll let you know more after I've examined the purse."

"All right, let's go then." He turned toward his county car and yelled at his brother-in-law, "Hershel, get on the stick; we're gonna head back to headquarters."

The sheriff and his deputy/brother-in-law had met us at Shoney's, just outside the town limits (where I had left my locked car in the parking lot). So we hadn't actually laid eyes on either headquarters *or* the purse. When we pulled up to the clapboard building, I wouldn't have been at all surprised if Chester Good had met us at the door (with his old, gray, granite-ware coffee pot with the chunk of glaze missing at the bottom), shouting over his shoulder, *Mister Dillon, we got company. Ye 'ont me to call Miz Kitty?*

"Come on in, ladies," the sheriff took off his hat and held the squeaky screen door open for Lee and me. He dusted off two old reprobatic-looking chairs with that same hat before he tossed it, *James Bondishly,* onto a hat rack behind his littered desk. I was impressed by his dead-on aim. He was then forced to evict a pair of longhaired felines, who grumbled indignantly as they skulked from the room before we sat down. *Talk about getting hair in your teeth.* "Ya'll have a seat while Hershel (*Chester*) here gets us a cup of coffee. *God, please don't let it have been steeping on a wood stove all morning.*

"Sheriff, if you don't mind, could I see the purse?"

"Oh, yeah, I'm sorry, I reck'n I'd forget my head"...*ya da ya da ya da...*

If I didn't soon get my wacky appreciation for the absurd under control, I was going to get Lee and me thrown out on our ears, then we'd have to hire a guide to lead us back to Shoney's and my car. The sheriff opened his desk drawer and withdrew the small red patent leather handbag. He had left the desk unlocked and the purse unattended, but *had* stuffed it into a Ziplock bag. Upon closer examination, I determined the patent leather was actually plastic, and the inside of the Ziplock bag was peppered with crumbs. What I was looking at was a casebook example of ludicrousness: a missing handbag that had been fingered by at least two ungloved persons before it had been *bagged* and stashed. It wouldn't interfere with what I needed it for, but Clarksville and Montgomery County law enforcement officials would collectively *shit in their new shoes,* to put it euphemistically.

"Lee, are you ready?" I knew before asking that she would have her micro-recorder at the ready. I extracted the purse from the bag and blew a stray crumb from the zipper-track before I looked inside. *Hummmmm.*

** **

My answering machine was flashing, and the phone was ringing when I entered my kitchen. I had let Lee out at her car before pulling mine into the garage. Watching her descend my driveway, I waited for the antiquated, wooden door to crawl its way laboriously up then back down the tracks before keying my way into my kitchen. I turned the key in the inside deadbolt lock, twisting the doorknob to make sure it was secured tightly. Whoever was on the other end of the phone line had waited this long. They could wait a little bit longer. As I took my cell phone out of my purse and plugged it into the re-charger, I heard my own voice giving the same-old-same-old *wait 'till you hear the beep* instructions before the angry-sounding voice of Emmett Calhoun invaded my private space. God only knows what he had said to Sheriff Whitfield because he was reading me the riot act, with no uncertainty. I listened to him rail, and after his tantrum abated a bit, I picked up the receiver. "Hello, Emmett, so nice of you to call. May I help you?" I disarmed him, just as I knew I would. He could yell indiscriminately at dead air, but not to an actual female person.

"Dare, how could you aid and abet that country bumpkin Whitfield?

"Emmett, I cooed (I can coo when necessity dictates), I don't know what you're talking about. Sheriff Whitfield called and I agreed to help him, just as I agreed to help you. I take it Marie's body hasn't turned up in the river yet." I was hoping to head his tirade off in another direction.

"Hell, no. We sent Jack Catcher packing this morning. Jesus H. Christ, I'd hate to be the one paying for that little operation."

"You are, Emmett. You're a tax-paying citizen living in Montgomery County, remember? Sorry Jack didn't work out."

"Yeah, well, it wasn't my idea in the first place. Listen, Dare, can you come up here tomorrow, so we can get back to our search?"

"No, Emmett, I've got to work sometime. I've still got to earn a living, you know. I told you and everyone else that I would work with you on Mondays, and if it's really, really imperative, I will work on an occasional Sunday. But, all God's children gotta rest once in awhile."

"You went to Erin today, and I might add that today is Wednesday."

"Chalk it up to insatiable curiosity and the unreasonable desire to find that child's body."

"Okay, I'm sorry for losing my temper, but you should have known better, Dare."

"Maybe, Emmett, but if the state would put more into educating and training its rural law enforcement officials, then we wouldn't be having this conversation. Talk to our illustrious legislators instead of jumping all over me. And by the way, I'll see you Monday morning at ten o'clock. Shall we meet you at Sharkey's or your office?"

"I'll meet you and Lee for breakfast at Sharkey's at ten."

"Good, Emmett, see you then....oh, by the way, have a nice rest of the week." He hung up without further comment. I rolled through the messages on my machine. Six were from Calhoun, one each from my sons (when it rains it pours), one from Dave and one from Felix...my, my, he was becoming a persistent cuss. I checked the clock over my oven. It was four-thirty. I would wait until later. I didn't want to call his office.

I sat at the kitchen table smoking, having a cup of coffee and musing over the day, when suddenly the phone rang. I nearly fell off my chair. I must have been deeply ensconced in *la la* land. "Hello?"

"Hey, Dare, I called earlier, I was just going to leave you another message telling you I was on my way home and to ask you to call me there later." It was Felix Henry Walker IV or V, whichever.

"Hello, Felix."(Suddenly Lee's earlier admonition occurred to me.) "*Fel*, how are you? I just got home. I was going to call you later." I was babbling mindlessly...just exactly why, I didn't have a clue.

"Dare, I was just wondering...I've got a meeting downtown tonight...I was just wondering if...if you're not busy...would you mind if I dropped by later?"

Drop by? He lives twenty miles on the other side of Nashville and I live twenty miles on this side of Nashville. "No, I don't mind. I'm not doing anything tonight. What time can I expect you?"

"How's a couple of hours."

"I thought you said you had a meeting downtown?"

"I lied. How about some Chinese takeout?"

"I love Chinese." *Did I say I loved Chinese? I'm deathly allergic to MSG.* "Wait a minute, Fel"...*there, I said it...again,* "I was thinking about grabbing some of my wonderous, homemade marinara sauce out of the freezer. Forget the Chinese. I'll cook pasta, make a salad, and we shall feast. I even have a loaf of garlic bread in the freezer.

"Are you sure? I don't want to put you to any trouble. Can I, at least, bring a bottle of wine?"

"No trouble at all...and you can always bring wine to my house. We'll eat at eight, so if you're hungry, just cinch in your belt."

I'm wearing suspenders."

"Whatever."

"Thanks, Dare. I'll see you soon."

What could possibly have possessed me to invite this man that I hardly knew to dinner? I probably would have opened a can of soup for myself, if that.

* *

I lay in the tub, occasionally reaching for my tumbler of Jameson and club soda. The magic-bath-time-elixir had virtually drained the day from my mind. It would come crawling back at the most inopportune times, of that I was sure. *Bang!* It hit me. Did the Sheriff say he had put the purse in the plastic bag? Could it be that the killer had done it? And if so why?

I heard my cat Hillary Rodham Kitten as she scurried between the ball and clawed feet under the antique tub as I stood up suddenly. I jumped, well, shall we say, I moved expeditiously, out of the bath. I swiped at my flesh with a bath towel before stepping into gray sweat pants and matching sweatshirt…not exactly first date attire, but let's stack priorities where they fall. I had to get to the phone and call Lee. I generally bring the cordless into the bathroom because just let me get settled and it'll start to ring without fail. This time, however, it was the other way round. When I needed to call, the phone was in the kitchen where I had left it so I could relax…*let the machine get it* had been my logic.

"Lee, I gotta talk to you right now."

"Hang onto your pony there, girlfriend. What seems to be the trouble?" She was *John Wayneing* me, which is usually quite amusing, but not this night.

"Hey, bury the *pilgrim* shit and let me ask you a question."

"What's so important that it's got to interrupt my cooking?" She feigned exasperation.

"Lee, think real carefully, okay? Now, listen to me. Did Sheriff Whitfield ever mention where the Ziplock bag came from? You know, the one the purse was in."

"Wait a minute while I go get my tape recorder out of my jacket pocket." Silence pierced my ear like a dog whistle. No ears but mine could hear it. I waited for what seemed like long crippled minutes while Lee fetched her recorder. I could hear it distantly unwind toward my interview with *the gang from Dodge City.* "Here it is." She placed the tiny speaker to her mouthpiece while I listened.

"He never did say. Lee, am I reaching here? It just occurred to me that maybe, just maybe, the killer stuffed the purse into the baggie. What do you think?

"I guess he could have, but why?"

"I don't have a clue, but I think it must be checked into. Don't you agree?"

"I agree. Are you going back to Erin tomorrow?"

"No, I'm going to call that Sheriff the first thing in the morning...then depending upon his answers, I'll call Calhoun and Bealer."

"Do I foresee another trip up the plateau?"

"Could be, let's wait 'til morning. Call me after your walk, okay?"

"Sure. What's on your front burner tonight? You want to come take potluck with us?"

"Thanks, but no. Felix, er...Fel is coming over. Marinara sauce is simmering on the stove, even as we speak. Never mind that now. I was lolling in a bubble bath when that bit about the baggie hit me up side the head. I couldn't wait to get your take on it."

"Never mind? Are you crazy? Look, you can't do anything about the baggie situation tonight, so drop it. Have a nice dinner and enjoy yourself for a change. I'll be expecting to hear all about this event in the morning. If there's a Jag parked out front when I walk by in the morning, I promise I won't come in."

"Lee, for crying out loud, it's dinner, not a slumber party."

"See that you keep it that way. You don't know where he's been."

I could see her throw her head back as she laughed at her own joke. She said a quick bye and made a *kissy* sound in my general direction. The line went dead. I put the phone down and poured myself another Irish whiskey over the rocks with just a *skosh* of soda added for interest. As I walked into my bedroom, I caught sight of my disheveled reflection in the antique floor mirror, which loomed before me. *Oh, shit, the way I look I can't even sit across the table from Felix without making him retch.* I pulled the sweatshirt over my head and pushed the sweatpants over my bare feet and started afresh. I wasn't really all that interested, but still, I didn't want to ruin the poor man's appetite. I am Irish by birth and by marriage. However, I love to cook and eat good Italian food. Mine is good, if I do say so myself.

I pulled on gray wool slacks along with trousers socks before stepping into a pair of comfy black Aigner flats. I plowed through my closet until I found a navy cashmere pullover. I retraced my steps to the bathroom, where I bent over to see if Hillary was still lurking under the tub. She wasn't, but she came padding in and jumped upon the commode seat to watch the transformation.

I applied my make-up, blotted my lipstick and blew my still damp hair into the proverbial *Dare-do*. I scoured the tub, mindful not to get any residue on my clothes. I wiped the inside with my towel then chucked it into the laundry hamper. *It'll probably mildew Murphy.* I turned my attention back toward the kitchen.

I stirred sauce and put together an endive, romaine and radicchio masterpiece. No onions. By the time the doorbell rang I was just seriously beginning to look forward to this evening.

* *

The lights in the rearview mirror appeared to come out of nowhere. The flashing blues followed on their heels. She pulled over onto to the narrow shoulder and braked to a halting stop. She didn't feel comfortable. Her head spun with indecision about stopping at all out here in this godforsaken wilderness...but it was a police car...you stopped when the police said so.

* *

The night hung languid in the cold. Yesterday, Thanksgiving, celebrated a day early—since she had studying to do back at school—had fairly crackled with holiday fun and frolic. The family had gathered around the dinner table, and after they had feasted, nothing was left of the turkey's carcass except a plate of stringy bones and chunk or two of gelatinous cartilage. The leftover mashed potatoes and gravy had been stowed away in the refrigerator, along side the stuffing and cranberry sauce. Crusted rings inside serving dishes had loosened in Mama's sink while Chester the pit bull waited patiently, hoping to be on the receiving end of a wayward morsel. Lillie Hammer and Sara Jevo, the twin Siamese ankle-rubbers, had howled at the top of their feline lungs while picking paths stealthily among the remaining clutter on the dining table. Mama's dishtowel had ripped through the air like a sling blade as she swiped at the pair. They were entirely too agile to be caught that easily. Daddy, along with her brother and nephews had all stuffed themselves before retiring to the den where the big-screen TV loomed like an altar in its place of honor. She, Mama, her sister and her brother's latest girl friend had busied themselves with the chores of cleaning up the after-dinner debris. She had checked periodically to see if the men had wanted anything. College football game followed college football game. Channels changed with precise regularity. Picture in picture was utilized to keep abreast of every game being played, even as they discussed the upcoming evening NCAA schedule and tomorrow's even fuller lineup. "Men," she had said to her mother, "can't live with them, and can't live without them." She was anticipating going back to Austin Peay University. After the holidays she would see Charlie, the boy she'd been dating for the last few weeks. He had gone home to Paducah, Kentucky to spend Thanksgiving with his family. She liked him even more than she had suspected she would before their holiday-forced separation.

* *

Earlier she had left her parents' home in Bowling Green, Kentucky hoping to get back to Clarksville before dark. She had studying to do then she had to get her clothes ready for work on Saturday. She worked part-time at the costume jewelry counter at Penney's, which took more time out of her busy schedule than she had anticipated. She knew she would have to make some changes before next semester. She had failed to factor in the heavy Thanksgiving weekend traffic and had decided to take a short cut several miles before she reached Clarksville. Before she had gone more than a mile, she saw the lights that had almost blinded her with fear.

* *

"Let me see your driver's license and registration, please." The officer's flashlight was trained directly at her eyes, but the glow puddled in her lap as she dug her wallet from her purse. She reached over to fumble in the glove compartment for the registration card that always accompanied the car that her daddy had furnished her and her siblings, when each of them went away to college. It had gone to Trevecca Nazarene College in Nashville with her sister, and would spend another two years in Nashville when her younger brother goes away to study to be a diesel mechanic the year after she graduates. She handed the documents to the officer. He aimed the flashlight in their direction before handing them back to her. "You got any dope in there, girlie?" When the harsh light was deflected away from her eyes, she could see the blue cotton shirt underneath his unzipped jacket. **It wasn't a uniform. It looked more like a Wal-Mart work-shirt.** The headlights from an oncoming vehicle loomed in the distance. "Go on," he said, pressing his face inside the open window, "get on out of here!" She didn't look at him, but she smelled the syrupy fetidness of his breath close to her ear. He turned and ran back toward the patrol car. She heard the gravel peppering the undercarriage as he peeled out and sped around her on his way into the deepening night. She rolled up her window and threw her car into gear, heading with new purpose toward her small efficiency apartment near the campus.

* *

When I had fallen asleep, I was content. A good meal and several glasses of the excellent Merlot that Felix brought had relaxed me completely. We had feasted and then sipped wine long into the night. He was an engaging conversationalist and a remarkably nice guy…for a lawyer. He was tall, with dark, curly hair and eyes the color of Canadian whiskey. I liked him and now I wished I hadn't been so impetuous in turning down his invitation to the Bar Association's *do.* But, he seemed to enjoy my company as well, so perhaps we would spend other evenings together. If not, nothing ventured, nothing gained.

* *

By the time my sleep swathed eyes acclimated to the dark, I looked at the clock on my bedside table and realized it was four AM. My body was a-sheen with oily sweat. The dream was ricocheting around inside my skull like a stray bullet. I was having a difficult time separating what actually was from what was merely part of the nightmarish experience from which I had just awaken. My guts were curdled and my heart was doing push-ups somewhere between my throat and my diaphragm. I lay there shaking like a dog shitting peach seeds. I couldn't seem to get myself under control. Slowly, I began to differentiate between the two worlds. The dream was from whence my fear emanated. The real world was where the glow of a very enjoyable evening lay, waiting to be dreamed about, but shoved aside by something too terrible for words to describe. The former is one of those things I have learned to live with…reluctantly.

* *

The Ziplock bag…what was it about that damned bag that was doing the fandango inside my cerebrum? It made absolutely no sense that a maniac would stuff his victim's purse inside a plastic bag before disposing of it. *Let's face it, Murphy, this time you've gone 'round the bend.*

Something was tugging at my innards so subtly that I couldn't figure out what it was. My little Filipinos were receiving and processing data, but it weren't spitting it out the other end so I could decipher it. Speaking in the vernacular, I guess my systems had crashed and needed to be rebooted before I could access the damage. Sleep would do it…I hoped.

* *

"COOKIES?"

"Yes, ma'am, they was oatmeal-raisin, best I can recollect. It was all I had around here. We got no budget for such as evidence bags, so we use what we got on hand." I could tell by the timbre of the sheriff's voice on the other end of the line that my questions were as confusing to him as they were to me. To add insult to injury, he had never experienced anyone quite like me before. I thought he was doing pretty well…all things considered.

"Cookies," I repeated rhetorically. I don't know why I was so surprised. I've run across stranger stuff in my career. It still didn't explain why I had such a nagging sensation about that bag. "Okay, and thanks for your help, Sheriff Whitfield."

"Thank you, missy, for taking your time to come up here to help us out."

I hung up the phone and turned around just in time to see Lee's smiling face at my kitchen window.

* *

"Cookies?" Her expression told me she wanted to giggle, but that situation wasn't quite ripe yet.

"My reaction exactly."

"You're telling me that that old geezer bagged up Marie's purse in a Ziplocker that his wife had packed cookies in?" It was getting closer.

"Oatmeal-raisin."

"Oh, well, that makes it all right." The ludicrousness of the situation, no matter how grave, gave her permission for a couple of good sniggers.

"Help me, Lee" I guess my tone failed to belie my exasperation.

"You're the spook, what the hell do you expect me to do?"

"I don't know...but if I have to take this quandary to bed with me again tonight, I may call you sometime before dawn's early light...."

"So, what else is new?"

* *

Mr. Coffee had performed his duties while I was in the shower. My conversation with Sheriff Whitfield had scattered my brain cells, so I hadn't even had my first cup of the day. Lee and I each drank a cup and smoked a couple of cigarettes. I was silent and introspective. I could tell she was about to burst to inquire into my dating experience last evening, but she knew my mind was otherwise occupied. She contained her curiosity admirably.

"Lee!"

"Huh?"

"It's not the baggie. It's the cookies...damn! I was picking up some weird, extraneous piece of information about the killer—something that caused those crumbs to strike a chord in my brain."

"Hold it a minute. let me grab my tape-recorder."

"Hurry it up!"

She reached for her jacket, which she had draped over the chair and pulled her micro-recorder from one of the pockets. I lit a cigarette and blew smoke rings at the ceiling while I waited. "Okay, ready. You mean like we're dealing with the *Cookie Monster*?" She made a wry face at her own black humor.

"I don't know; sounds pretty good though, doesn't it? Her purse, which we know *he* handled, coupled with the contents of that bag just triggered a series of cryptic mega-synapses."

"You're serious, aren't you?"

"Lee, I don't know exactly what I'm serious about, but yes, indeedy, I am. Maybe our killer has a cookie fetish...maybe an oatmeal-raisin cookie fetish...I don't know. What I do know is that those cookie crumbs in that plastic bag that Sheriff Whitfield had crammed Marie's purse in are significant. Of that much I am sure."

"Do you suppose he was eating cookies when he pulled Marie over in that school parking lot?"

"*Oh, Holy Mary!* That's it, Lee...I *saw* him...and the asshole *had been* eating something with a sweet odor."

"You what? When? What the hell are you talking about?"

JOY M. JAMISON AND CAROLE KENNEDY

I started at the beginning and didn't stop until I had told her about waking up in a cold sweat. "I know it was him and he had that nasty aura of poor dental hygiene compounded by *raisin breath*. The bastard was eating raisins...he had taken the time to buy a box of raisins...I *hate* raisins...but they are unmistakable. *I smelled them in my dream.*"

"Uh, Dare..." she apparently thought better of what she was about to say; nevertheless, I hesitated a moment before continuing.

"I know he was driving a police car of some description...but he's not a cop...yet he obviously has access to vehicles, clothing, flashlights and other accoutrements." I stopped my dissertation and looked at my *partner-in-crime*. "Lee, think about it for a moment...who would have that kind of access to law-enforcement toys?"

As she sat there deep in thought, I could almost see the light bulb brighten when it hit her. "Maybe a trustee, someone that a local mountie might feel comfortable letting out without his leash." She looked at me and beamed. Then the smile melted off her face like icing on a hot cake. "It all fits, Dare. Everything you've said about him fits. I'll be a son of a bitch. He's a freakin' convict...probably sitting around enjoying three hots and a cot, not to mention a big screen TV in some jail out there. Obviously some damned Sheriff isn't keeping a real close eye on his charges. Talk about somebody having his ass in a sling when all of this comes out...oh, my."

"I've got to call Emmett Calhoun and Will Bealer and tell them what I know. This puts a whole new coat of wax on this stinking case. They're going to have to check every jail in every county in Tennessee...maybe even southwestern Kentucky. This is large, baby, large."

"Yo, Dare, I got every bit of that on tape. Thank God, I carry that damned thing everywhere I go, anymore, that is except to bed. I guess we've been together too long, dear heart. There are very few surprises anymore."

"Bless your little pea-pickin' heart. Now I won't have to scrape the floorboards of my memory to piece together what little we've got so far." I couldn't imagine trying to work a case like this one without Lee's support.

"Now," she said, "Dare, can we get down to tass bracks? Her vernacular is very often seasoned with dashes of spoonerisms, along with various and other idiosyncratical *Lee-isms.*

"Like what?" Playing dumb is one of my natural talents. I grinned, "But first just let me make a couple of phone calls to the guys up in Clarksville. We don't want them stumbling around in the dark any longer that necessary. This ought to keep them occupied for a little while at least."

* *

"Damn it, Dare, I'm in pain. Tell me about last night. I've been patient entirely long enough…now tell me, darlin', did you get laid?"

"Just exactly what do you think I am?"

She grinned, "Next question?"

"Okay, I guess I owe you this…I had a very nice evening. When he got here, we had a couple of drinks. Then we ate a late supper. I think I told you I made pasta Marinara. I even fixed up a small tray of antipasto to hold us until the entrée was ready. I discovered that he loves artichoke hearts. Well, let me see, what else? He insisted on helping me clear the table. He even rinsed the dishes before I put them in the dishwasher. I had fired up the gas logs earlier, so we sat in front of the fireplace and had a few glasses of wine and talked."

"Talked about what?"

"He asked me about the case, and I filled him in on what we had come up with so far."

"Jesus, that must have curled his toes."

"Well, you must remember that was before my dream. He's interested in what I do, apparently."

"That's good, what else did you talk about? Did he mention anything else about going to the Bar Association *dog and pony show*?"

"No, I think I was a little too emphatic the first time he asked. Oh, well. No shit, though, he's a really nice guy, not the least bit lawyerly."

Lee chuckled, "Oh, but if we could say the same for the rest of his breed. I guess you two are still going out Saturday night…but apparently he just couldn't bear to wait that long for your charming company. My God, you get some of the best looking men in town…I think they sense you're not really interested, so they go after you like you've got a pork chop hung around your neck."

"Delightful analogy, but maybe you have a point there. I'm not interested…at least I wasn't until last night. Lee, have you ever taken a good look at Fel's eyes?"

"*Fel's eyes*? Can't say that I have. The opportunity has never presented itself. Why?"

"They're liquid…you've heard the term 'whiskey voice', well, he has 'whiskey eyes'."

"How utterly intoxicating."

"You want to know everything, then your ass makes fun of everything I try to tell you. I don't know why I put up with your incessant bullshit." I put on my best scowl.

"Cause I'm your best friend, that's why. If I didn't push your buttons, you'd think I didn't care."

"The pathetic thing about it, dear heart, is you're probably correct in your, oh, so, astute observation. You know me entirely too well."

"Dare! I think I just borrowed one of your epiphanies! How 'bout you invite the Esquire over to dine at our house one night next week? Saturday would be ideal, but he is otherwise occupied that evening. You want to ask him, or would you rather I do it?"

"What do you think? I guess I could ask him. Any other particular night or will any do?"

"Well, since we can't do Saturday, how about Friday or Sunday?"

"He said he would call this evening, I'll ask him then. Thanks, Lee."

"They calls me Dolly Levi."

"I've heard that somewhere before, but thanks anyway."

"Well, I've got to go home now and take a bath. I'm offensive even to my self after that five-miler. Tell Katie I'll probably see her later."

* *

My Saturday morning and early afternoon were filled with clients, for which I was truly grateful. I have found that the best way to clear the personal dross out of my head is to sit across the desk from a living, breathing person, one who has come to me, seeking advice. That's when I'm truly in my element. I can't imagine the day will come when I no longer work, one on one, with my clients. That's when I truly feel that I'm doing what God has called me to do. The investigative work, along with other related activities, is merely a byproduct of what I started out to do, and I feel, for the most part, I've done relatively well.

Saturday morning was busy. The time flew by, as it always does when I'm busy. I had a thirty-minute lull around lunchtime, when I took the time to call Emmett Calhoun at Clarksville police headquarters. He was out, but when I told the dispatcher who I was, he patched me right through to the detective's cellular.

"Calhoun, here," he snapped at the mouthpiece, and consequently, at me.

"Emmett? This is Dare Murphy, how's it going? You found anything yet?"

"Dare, when are you coming back up here? We need you to follow up on the map you've drawn. We can't make heads or tails of it."

Emmett, I told you that Lee and I will be up there Monday morning at ten o'clock. In fact, it was your idea to meet us at Sharkey's, instead of your office. Remember?"

"Yeah, I remember. I've stuck post-it notes all to hell over the place. That's why I haven't called you. However, when I heard your voice, I thought maybe you had changed your mind."

"'Fraid not, Emmett. I just wanted to check in with you. I'll be out of pocket tonight. I won't even be carrying my cell phone. I may be busy tomorrow, as well. If anything turns up, just leave a message on my answering machine. Otherwise, we'll see you on Monday morning."

"That's fine. The weather is supposed to be very uncooperative the whole weekend, anyway. I just hope you'll be able to make it up the plateau on Monday."

"Don't worry about us, Emmett. I've got an all-wheel-drive SUV, remember?"

"Yeah, I remember. Just be careful and don't get cocky."

I hung up the receiver just as Katie ushered my one o'clock client into my office.

She wanted her palms read, which I rarely do anymore since my close vision went south. I turned on the powerful halogen lamp that sits on my desk, dug out my reading glasses, as well as my hand-held magnifying glass and went to work. After nearly an hour of tracing lines, explaining their meanings, how they related to that particular individual and their consequences, I finished. My client, with traces of ballpoint ink in her palm, where I had emphasized faint, but important, markings, left my office satisfied, and with a promise to make an appointment for a psychic reading at a later date. I thanked her, and told her I looked forward to seeing her again.

* *

"That was it." Katie leaned into my office before going upstairs to search for something to eat.

"No more today?" I queried, looking up from my desk.

"No more, you've got the rest of the afternoon to get ready for Felix."

"Katie, is that all you think I have on my mind?"

"Like I said, you've got the rest of the afternoon. I'm going to dig around and try to find the fixins' for a sandwich. Then I'll stop by the bank to make your deposit on my way home."

"Hey, kiddo, just put the phones on voice mail and take the rest of the afternoon off."

"Are you sure, Dare, or is that just your libido talking?"

"Katie, you've been around Lee entirely too long, you're beginning to sound just like her."

"She's my mother-in-law, remember?" Katie was referring to her short-lived marriage to Lee and Joe's son. "Wade and I may be a thing of the distant past, but Lee will always be my mother-in-law."

* *

Maybe it was my libido after all. It had been awhile since a long, leisurely soak in the tub has been so relaxing. I lay there in the dimness, candle-flames dancing and casting shadows like tiny specters silhouetted on the wall. They trembled on updrafts as piano tones crept their way through steam, homing in on my highly-attuned senses, where, at the moment, *Murphy mellowed 'midst Mozart.* I knew that next on the agenda was Chopin's *Piano Concerto # 2*, and if I didn't get out before that started, I might sit there for the rest of the evening.

* *

I hadn't even picked out anything to wear. Everyone had voiced prognostications about how "ready" I was. Well, right about now I wished they hadn't been so wrong. We were going downtown to Caffé Milano, a relatively new establishment that had been owned by Chet Atkins before his death, and where fine dining takes on new meaning. I have no idea where they find their help, but they are the most courteous, conciliatory, customer-oriented bunch that it's ever been my pleasure to deal with. We are talking "white-glove" service personified. The *maître d'* Alfonso is second-generation Sicilian, all the way from his pencil moustache to his patent-leather slippers. His looks and demeanor are very *Rudolf Valentinoish.*

Murphy, mush...get it in gear...dig out something appropriate and get dressed. I have a terrible tendency toward wool gathering at the most inopportune times. Felix would arrive in less than an hour and I had nothing on except my make-up. I had done my hair. Thank God for small favors. I scanned my closet until I spied a little, basic-black, wool/silk number. I pulled it off the hanger and over my head, trying unsuccessfully to avoid mussing my coif. Oh, well, a couple of brush strokes and it would be good as new. God and my parents had blessed me with good hair.

The doorbell rang. I swallowed my gum and almost choked. *Good move Murphy.*

11

The *Dom Pèrignon* was chilled to perfection, the Shrimp Alfredo was superb, but I managed a very regrettable and weak-willed, "no thank you," as the tiramisu smiled up at me from the dessert cart. However, Felix had a man-sized slab of cheesecake while I sipped an Irish coffee. The string quartet had run the gamut from Mozart to Mancini, and Felix was, once again, a wonderful conversationalist and most attentive dinner companion.

* *

"Have you been to the Frist Gallery at the old Post Office Building?" He was referring to the newest in a series of cultural establishments that had appeared recently in the downtown area.

"No, I haven't, but I understand they are showing Erté and a collection of Toulouse-Lautrec serigraphs."

"They are, are you a fan of either?"

"I'm crazy about Erté. As a matter of fact, I love the whole Art Deco concept. Toulouse-Lautrec was no slouch, himself."

"You want to go take a look?"

"I would love to, thank you," I couldn't remember the last time I had visited an art gallery on a whim. One of those things, I guess, we let slip by when we are so preoccupied with the mundane. "I wasn't aware they were open this late."

"Well, they're not usually, but tonight is the opening of those two exhibits, and I just happen to have two tickets. Let's go."

* *

Talk about sensory overload. The vibrancy and sensuality of Toulouse-Lautrec perfectly countered by the cool intensity of Erté was almost a schizophrenic experience. I was so incredibly entertained by the whole evening that not only did I not miss my after dinner smoke (Caffé Milano is a smoke-free environment), but I didn't even think about a cigarette until we were walking back to Felix's car. I glanced back at the beautiful old, Greek Revival building that had once housed Nashville's downtown Post Office since year one. The Postal Service had vacated it a few years before, and the building had sat fallow until the Frist family had contributed enough money to get it up and running. For a while our brilliant city fathers had seriously considered razing it to the ground to make room for another parking lot. Not that downtown couldn't use the parking space, but there're plenty of derelict structures to choose from without robbing Nashville of one more example of her classic architectural past. After all we are known as the *Athens of the South.*

Felix pulled a pack of Marlboro lights from his pocket and offered me one. He held his slim, gold lighter while I lit up and took the first long drag. He touched the flame to the tip of his own cigarette, and we continued the trek to the parking lot where his antique Jaguar XKE awaited. "The hood of this baby is long enough for a 747 to take off," I quipped.

"Just an F16, that is if I cock the rubber band just right." He grinned, and ran through the gears like a NASCAR driver. "It takes a lot of room for a V-twelve with duel overhead cams."

"Home, James."

"As you wish, m'lady."

* *

"What would you like to drink?" I was putting our coats away in the closet. He threw his suit coat over the back of a chair and loosened his tie.

"Do you have brandy?"

"Yes, I do. As a matter of fact, I got a lovely bottle for Christmas." I hadn't wanted to break the seal for just me, so now I was digging behind the bar looking for the elusive bottle of Christian Brothers XO *Rare Reserve.* What I know about Brandy, one could put in the eye of a needle, but the bottle was pretty, and it had come packed in a lovely tin. I rummaged around until I found the snifters and I poured out two healthy shots.

He cradled the glass in his hand, transferring the heat from his body to the amber liquid, lolling it around in a lazy, circular motion with the subtle movement of his wrist.

"How 'bout some music?" I asked, more for something to say than anything else.

"Sure, what you got?" His eyes met mine as I got up to go to the stereo.

"What do you want?" I expected the surge from the unintentional double-entendre to cause a brownout.

He grinned; it wasn't lost on him. "How 'bout Sinatra. You got Sinatra?"

"Is a pig's butt pork?" I countered. We both laughed and he brought his glass along and sat down on the floor beside me while I searched for one CD in particular, the classic *Only the Lonely*. Now that I knew the type of music he was in the mood for, I loaded the carousel with one CD after another, watching him nod in agreement with each of my choices.

"I saw him once in Philadelphia when I was a kid." Felix had lit the gas logs and we were sitting on the floor propped against the hearth among the plethora of cushions and pillows thrown there for that very purpose. "My parents and I were visiting relatives; my uncle took me."

"I've always loved his voice, but I never saw him in person—and now he's gone. I took a sip of brandy and continued. "My father used to buy me Sinatra's records when I wasn't old enough to know him from Adam's off ox. He bought me swing, jazz, and the pop of the day, whatever it was he happened to be interested in at the time. As a result, by the time I was ten years old, I loved Ella, Sarah, Satchmo, Woody Herman, Stan Kenton...the list is as long as it is tall. Not only that, but because he taught me the love of baseball, I could figure batting averages and ERA's long before I went to school and discovered that math was actually a pain in the ass. After that point, numbers and I never *gee-hawed*, as it were. I've often wondered if the teachers had slapped Yankee's stats on the reading problems, would I have figured them out. That will remain one of the great mysteries of the universe, I suppose."

"Your dad must have been a remarkable man."

"I don't know, I suppose. He just loved music, books, art and sports of all kinds. And since my mother was busy trying to keep hearth and home together, he had more time to expose me to the things that I now can't imagine living without."

"And you don't think that makes him remarkable?"

"Maybe so, I just never looked at it that way. Perhaps in his own way he was very remarkable...but let's not talk about my father."

"Fine, what do you want to talk about?" He touched my hand, smiled and took a sip of brandy.

"I have nothing in particular on my mind. Do you?" I picked up my glass from where it sat on the hearth. The radiant heat from the flames had warmed the contents. The sip flowed smooth as warmed, liquid glass before it burst in a tiny explosion when it found my stomach.

He sat his drink down, leaned over and kissed me sweetly on the lips. Another tiny explosion. I was mute...nothing would come out, and I'm entirely too old to start stuttering, so I didn't say anything. I had not expected his kiss, not that I hadn't welcomed it, but I hadn't expected it...not yet, anyway. I guess he took my silence as approval, which of course it was, and he kissed me again. Only this time it was more than a mere brush of his lips against mine. I joined in.

"Nice." He looked into my eyes, the fire was warm against my face. It had been a long time since I cared whether or not I ever kissed, much less went to bed with another man...tonight I cared.

"Yes, very nice." Peggy Lee's sultry *Is That All There Is?* spilled across the room with all the warmth of the brandy at the bottom of my glass.

* *

"Come here, please." I couldn't believe my ears...*did I say that*?
"Ummm."

I couldn't very well put out a retraction, nor did I wish to. He put his arm around me and pulled me gently to him.

"Fel, I've got to get out of this dress...I mean I've got to change. This actually isn't loungewear."

"Yeah, I noticed," he smiled and his smoky, amber eyes twinkled.
"No, I mean it."
"I know you do...but so do I...here, let me help you."

I caved. He unzipped the back of my dress, and with a modicum of help from *moi*, he slipped it over my head. His gaze was intense. He smiled.

"May I return the favor?" My heart was pumping *high-test* for the first time in a long time.

"I was certainly hoping you would."

I couldn't help myself. I was undressing him with my eyes. Why do men think they're the only ones who can do that? "Do you always wear suspenders?"

"Except when I'm in bed or the shower."

"Does that mean I have a choice?" *Did I say that?*

"Well, you could make the choice by ignoring your choices. You know, decision by indecision."

"God, I love lawyers, you're always so ready with the clever comeback," I teased.

"I certainly hope so. Tonight especially."

I ran my fingertips down the front of his white silk shirt. His eyes never wavered from mine. I carefully unknotted his already loosened tie, unbuttoned his shirt and leaned over and brushed his lips with mine. My innards were firing off warning shots.

"Ummm." He kissed me back.

He slipped his suspenders under his arms, where they hung loose, still attached to the buttons inside his waistband. I undid the waist button on his trousers and eased down the zipper. He pulled off his shoes and socks and slipped out of his slacks and laid them beside his suit coat, on the back of the chair. He had on the sexiest boxer shorts I'd ever seen. They looked tailor-made; and probably were, for everything else he had on was. And like everything else they ended up on the chair. He was beautiful. In the firelight, his smooth, olive skin took on a burnished glow. With gentle fingers he finished undressing me and lay my head on a pillow, looked straight into my soul and whispered, "My God, you're beautiful."

"Thank you, you're no slouch yourself." *Shit, Murphy, curb the repartee.*

"Does that mean you put me in the same class with Toulouse-Lautrec? You said the same about him."

"You're much taller...do you paint whores too?" *Murphy!*

"Never whores, and...never with a brush."

"Oh, my."

He put his arms around me and I could feel his heart against mine. Letting him make the moves, I found myself responding involuntarily; my body making its own choices, and oh, they were exemplary choices. We took each other, not with the appetites of hungry puppies, with all their nipping and tugging, but with the maturity of two adults who knew what they wanted and exactly how to go about getting it.

"Dare..." He whispered my name, again and again, between searching, passionate kisses. I heard somewhere that the tongue is almost wholly muscle, and is one of the most acutely tactile organs in the animal kingdom. Whether or not it's true is no longer in question. With my fingers tangled in his curly hair, I pulled his mouth back to mine. This was *my* kiss. He played my body like a finely tuned violin, and his was a tautly strung bow. I felt the subtle increase in momentum as I was being drawn toward the ultimate. Every muscle vibrated. I surrendered to Fel's kisses as they stroked my soul, just as surely as his fingertips stroked my flesh. He filled me completely, both physically and emotionally. I felt that if I could hold him tightly enough we could go on forever. The law, obviously, wasn't his only area of expertise. I felt sensations stirring within the depths of me—beginning with the slow sweet swell of anticipation. Each move was like waves nudging at the shore—each one gaining in intensity. When the dam burst the tide came pouring in. Every nerve ending dragged me toward that invisible portal separating human reason from animalistic sensuality. That place where otherwise erudite folk are reduced to drooling bundles of pure lust. It's when one's innards explode like roman candles and burn uncontrollably until that last spark has vanished. His timing was impeccable. We crossed the line together. It was an intense, gut-wrenching, teeth-rattling experience. We collapsed in a gasping, sweaty, tangled heap. What can I say? Old Blue Eyes was singing *I Did It My Way*, and this man I was with, in front of the fireplace, on the floor in my great room, was nothing less than a *fucking god.*

* *

The telephone jarred me awake.
It was Lee. "Well?"
"Same deep hole in the ground."
"Damn it, Dare."
"What, Lee? Please don't jerk me around this morning; I'm still half-asleep. Just tell me what you want in as few words as possible...please. "
"Whatta you think I want? Did Monica smoke Clinton's stogie? Who gives a flying fuck? What I want to know is did you get laid?"
It was Sunday morning and I had been asleep, for what seemed like only minutes when the phone had rung. I could smell coffee brewing and the wonderfully deceptive fragrance of turkey bacon wafting from the kitchen. I smiled, and she could hear it.
"Yes, as a matter of fact, I did...several times. Did you?"

* *

Orgasmic satiation can jump-start one's appetite like nothing short of cocaine (or so I've heard). Personally, I don't go there, thank you very much.

After a thorough tooth brushing and a cursory hair brushing, I donned my terry cloth robe, which wasn't designed to win me sexual favors, but, hey, there's a lot to be said for staying warm.

Felix stood at the stove. His back was to back to me. He was wearing my apron and nothing else except his sexy boxers and Gucci loafers, sans socks. It was a sight to behold. This was a stretch for even my imagination; the fashion statement alone was more than noteworthy.

I walked up behind him and slid my arms around his waist. He carefully turned down the gas flame and laid the spatula on the spoon-rest before turning around. He tipped my chin slightly with his forefinger. His parted lips met mine, and after a few teasing passes our tongues embraced. That familiar weakness in my lower abdomen was followed by a colossal adrenaline rush.

"Hey, you're distracting me, lady. Can't this wait till after breakfast? You've seen me without my suspenders in bed—want to go two for two?"

Hormonal backlash. "I guess I could probably handle that."

* *

Hillary R. Kitten was sitting in the bathroom sink. She glared at me as if to say, "*Just who the hell was that stranger in **my** bed?*" I had to pick her up, bodily, and remove her from the bathroom. She was royally pissed at what she considered to be the usurpation of her personal territory. She snagged at the hem of my robe, and I scolded her. She padded across the carpet. Gauging the distance with mathematical exactness, she leapt to the center of the pillow where Fel's sleeping head had lain. She sniffed with all the feline disdain she could muster, before sidestepping to my pillow where she stretched, then folded into a furry ball, peeking surreptitiously to make sure I was watching. She meowed a warning and went to sleep.

* *

The steaming water beat down on our bodies with an intensity surpassed only by the activity within. A bar of soap can be the most effective of all aphrodisiacs when in the hands of gorgeous, sweet and skillful lover. He pulled me close, reached around and eased the *Caress* slowly up and down my spine, rubbing my lower back gently with his free hand. He massaged the nape of my neck, and I leaned my head back in order to kiss him. When I took the soap from him, he gently kneaded my back, teasing me unmercifully. I pressed the *Caress* between our lubricious bodies; he leaned forward, enabling me to ease the soap in lazy circles over his neck and shoulders. I slathered his chest and stomach before centering my concentration on his lower abdomen. He knelt down, and what came out of my mouth was, *"Beam me up, Scotty."* His shoulders shook, and I could feel his laughter, but thank God, he didn't let it distract him. When it was my turn, if I do say so myself, I felt that I brought out the very best in him. As they say, *no good deed goes unpunished,* and I was afraid I was going to take a plug out of him when he announced, *"Take us home, Scotty...warp speed!"* I, however, had no intention of going that far...at the moment. As odd as it might seem to some people, humor, too, can be a powerfully, suggestive stimulant.

I don't think of myself, shall we say, as vocally demonstrative, but I must have been there in the shower because afterwards, the first cognitive impression I recall was Hillary squalling outside the bathroom door. Perhaps she thought "that stranger" was killing her mama. Well, if you have to die before you get to heaven...maybe we just did.

12

"You look like you just won the lottery, or should I say, like the cat who swallowed the canary?" Lee was nursing a cup of coffee and smoking a cigarette when I came into the kitchen. "I've finished reading the paper, and I was beginning to wonder if you still had Felix stashed back there somewhere."

I wasn't expecting her to be sitting there quite so early. "You startled me, Lee...I didn't hear you come in. Watch that or I'll take your key away."

"Jesus, Dare, You actually look like you're glad to be alive. I haven't seen you so...so...I don't know...anyhow, not since...."

"Enough! Let's not compare them...okay?"

"Now, how in the hell could I compare them? In the first place, I barely know Felix, and as you know, I never knew Jerry...like that."

I looked at her impish grin and couldn't help but smile in return. "Just drink your coffee, smoke your cigarette and use your imagination, 'cause you're not getting any info out of me."

"What? You're not going to describe your weekend in lurid detail? What's a girl to do?"

"Go home and make out with your own husband and not try to live vicariously through my, you wouldn't believe it anyway, experience. Anyhow, girlfriend, your heart couldn't take it. Mine barely could. Now shut up, I'm just out here to get a cup of coffee; I've got to get dressed. You ready to head out for Clarksville?" I was stirring my four sugars and sprinkle of Coffee Mate into my coffee when I looked out the window over the sink. "Hey, I didn't know it snowed."

"My God, didn't you two come up for air long enough to look out a window? Didn't you even walk him to the door when he left? What the hell kind of hostess are you anyway?"

"Well, let's just say precipitation wasn't a topic of conversation, and, no, I didn't walk him to the door. He kissed me goodbye and left me in bed this morning. As for the rest of your question…I'm a fucking *good* hostess if his reactions are any indication."

"I don't believe you, and yes, it snowed. It's ass deep on a giraffe. I didn't dare drive Pearl this morning." Lee was referring to her sports car, which she loves like a member of her family. Not as much as some, more than others.

"Surely you didn't walk over here."

"Not hardly. I didn't even go for my regular walk. It may be only two blocks from there to here, but it's entirely too cold this morning. Joe dropped me off in the Explorer. No problem, he drove all the way around and let me out at your kitchen door.

"Well, I should hope so, I would've hated to hitch Hillary up and gone mushing through the neighborhood searching for a *Leecicle.*

"Yada yada yada. If you're not going to share with me, just go get dressed. If you can get your crotchety, old garage door up past the snow, we got places to go and people to see."

"Has it actually drifted up against the garage door?" Jeez, it must have really snowed big time. Why don't you do us a favor and go out with a shovel?" I teased.

"Screw you!"

"Don't try to get on my good side."

* *

Being a cop hangout, Sharkey's interior is perpetually enshrouded in clouds of cigarette smoke. The only thing lacking may be the clacking of billiard balls against each other and the occasional rip of green felt to round out its ambiance. Other than Lee and me, the only women evident were the sweet young cross-eyed waitress Geraldine, the pathetic over-the-hill cop hustler, Cora, and what appeared to be (to these virginal eyes) a uniformed dyke, straddling the seat of a chair turned backward. It was a veritable vignette taken directly from the pages of *Geek Love*. The cop was leaning her arms on the back of the chair while half-heartedly listening to a group of her breakfast-gobbling, patrol-car-jockeying peers. She was oddly fascinating. I couldn't figure out who she was "eyeballing" with such intensity. Finally, I spied Geraldine grinning, coyly in the general direction of the masculine-looking female cop. *Oh, please.* I felt oddly sad for the optically challenged Geraldine. I scooted my chair around to get out of the line of "make-out" glances, almost ending up in Lee's lap. Typically, she was quick with the repartee, a little too quick for the present situation.

"Not now, Dare, we've got work to do," she innocently quipped. I couldn't believe no one else had noticed the budding lust-fest besides me. *Come on, Murphy. Different strokes for different folks.*

* *

Lieutenant Ernest Calhoun was digging through his over-stuffed briefcase, pulling out papers, then cramming them back in again. His good-looking sidekick Harold Riggens sat watching. "Damn it, Harold, where's that FBI release?"

"I saw you stick it in your jacket pocket...I think."

"Well, hell, if it'd been a snake, it'd bit me." He looked through every one of his jacket pockets before coming up with the multi-folded sheet of paper, which he handed to me. I carefully unfolded the page, stopping midway when a blast of arctic air roared through the door. I looked up just in time to see Will Bealer come strolling in, red-faced from the extreme cold. He pulled off his gloves, stamped his feet and yanked off his cap, all in a series of animated gestures. With his cap in hand, his sparse gray hair was standing at attention. He rubbed his fingers across the top of his head as if to say, *at ease.* He sidestepped his way through clutches of cops on his way to our table.

"Where's Yolanda?" I heard myself ask.

"Oh, she's home. I didn't want her out in this weather. She's kinda got a cold."

"Well, you be sure and tell her we asked about her."

Lee looked at me as if I had lost my mind. I guessed my newly resurrected happy-face was going to take a bit of getting used to.

Without bothering to rise, Ernest reached across the table and shook Will Bealer's out stretched hand. Bealer was aimlessly looking around for a vacant seat when he asked, "You tell Dare yet?" Harold got up and got him a chair.

Calhoun was zipping the myriad of pockets and compartments in his briefcase while explaining that it had been a Christmas present from his wife. "Not yet, Will, I was waiting on you, as a matter of fact."

"Sorry I'm late, but I had to stop by the drug store to get some cough medicine for Yolanda."

"Tell me what?" I was getting back with the program after having watched the progressive game of cat and mouse between the two, not so surreptitious women. "What, Ernest?"

"We just got a release from the TBI (referring to the Tennessee Bureau of Investigation). They're through with Marie's car."

"My God, I could have built another one just like it in the length of time they've had it," I sniped, knowing full well it was official courtesy that was going to get me access to that automobile. That was a fact, and no one on the case seemed to have a clue, with the possible exception of Will Bealer, husband of Yolanda and close personal friend of Glinda Güdwich, *psychic nouveau.*

"The weather's too bad to go tramping around the countryside. You feel like crawling around inside the Cavalier instead?" Calhoun looked up as he completed his packing.

"God, I reckon." I couldn't believe that I was actually going to get my hands on the car that had eluded me for so long. "When?"

"Now, if you're ready." The three men were pushing chairs back, as wood squealed against wood. "Let's go." Ernest threw tip money on the table, and that caught Geraldine's good eye. She waved and mouthed thanks somewhere in our general direction. Big Bertha had sidled up beside her and was putting the moves on left and right. *Whatever blows your skirt up.*

Outside, frigid wind slapped me with an open fist.

* *

The white Chevy Cavalier sat alone in an unheated corner of the city garage. It had been tucked in behind yellow crime scene tape to discourage indiscriminant touching and feeling. The entire length of the passenger's side bore a long, narrow, jagged streak where nothing but gray primer paint showed through. It looked as if during one of its lives the old crate had been side swiped by something bigger…something that had kicked its ass in passing. Plated chrome had flaked and peeled. The radio antennae hung at half-mast, and the windshield still bore the smear marks where someone had wiped the inside of the glass with gloved hands or some other rough fabric. Perhaps that had been one of Marie's final acts on her way home that fateful night. November 23. My birthday.

I opened the driver's door and eased myself onto the cracked vinyl seat. The interior was a washed-out blue, otherwise, ratty as the exterior. "How big was she?" I asked no one in particular.

"Small, she weighed about a hundred pounds soaking wet." Will was leaning on the top of the open driver's door, looking inside and speaking directly to me, "She was about your height."

Now, I'm five three on a good day, but it's been decades since I weighed but a hundred.

"Why?"

"Oh, nothing, I was just noticing that the seat is seriously "butt-sprung. " I guess because it old and well-worn."

"Nothing, including a seat, gets in that condition over night. That took years and somebody's broad ass to break it down like that." Will was speaking to me as if no one else were around.

"Yeah, or a succession of broad asses." The door to the glove compartment was lying in the floorboard on the passenger side. It, and everything else, wore a fine layer of black fingerprint powder. I hate the stuff. It's like getting a hair in your teeth; once it's there, it's there. I swiped my index finger inside the ashtray...dust and a trace of ash from a bygone era, nothing recent. "If I recall correctly, there were cigarettes in her purse, weren't there?" My eyes were seeking Ernest, since he's the one who had gotten the purse from that cowboy sheriff who had called me from Houston County to come check it out.

"Yeah, there were, but maybe she snuck around and smoked. You know, scared her aunt and uncle would smell it if she smoked in the car."

"I guess," I said, Bealer stepped back as I reached to close the car door. "Hey, Lee, how 'bout getting in here with me." Walking around back of the car, she gave it a quick once-over before slipping through the passenger's door and onto the bench seat beside me. She closed the door behind her. "You got it?" I inquired. She held her micro-recorder where I could see it. With each spoken word I could hear the tape whispering quietly inside. I grimaced as that infernal, metaphorical goose danced across my grave one more time.

"Lee, can you smell it?"

"Smell what?" She had laid the voice-activated tape recorder on the dash in front of me.

"The fear."

"No, Dare, but even if I could, I'm not sure I would recognize it. That's your bailiwick, remember?"

I continued, almost as if in a trance. "It's like old sweat socks that have been left in a gym locker over the summer."

"My, that sounds appetizing."

I ignored her sarcasm and continued. "It's putrid."

"Oh, that clarifies it nicely."

Once again I ignored her, just as she knew I would. She's my sounding board. I bounce my ideas and perceptions off her before they get near anyone else. "Fear crawls out of one's pores like something on its way back from hell. It winds around its victim like a shroud, lingering like rotting carrion. When we find that child's body, the odor of fear will still be with her."

"Hey, Dare, are you speaking literally or figuratively? I mean what if it's like you and the cops have speculated, and the wild creatures have torn her apart and her bones are scattered all over hell and half of Georgia? What then?"

If there is one scrap of her found, even if it's just a hank of her hair, and there will be, that odor will still be with her. I will smell her fear *and* his animal excitement. His insanity."

"Oh, Jesus, girlfriend, I'm glad it's you and not me."

"Hey," I lightened, "It's nasty work, but somebody's got to do it." I reached over and tapped her on the shoulder with my knuckles. "I'd sure as hell hate to do this if your weren't my partner-in-crime. Thanks again, Lee, and I really mean it."

"I know you do, but I live to hear it anyway. I guess you think there's enough money in your bank account to haul my ass out to these ungodly places if you didn't throw me a bone once in awhile. In fact, I don't even mind buying new boots, after losing the sole of one of the old ones in a mud-hole. Have you ever heard me bitch about dry cleaning bills, not to mention my valuable and precious time?

"Sometimes I think maybe I take your good nature for granted. I haul your butt to places I know you don't want to go, anymore than I do. Maybe I should start making it worth your while.

"Didn't you just hear me? There's not that much money in the world. No, dear heart, I just like to think that maybe we can make a difference. Anyway, Joe's always told me I'm a cheap date. "

I grinned and playfully sucker-punched her, which wasn't easy (nor apropos) considering we were in the cramped front seat of a crime scene. "Bitch," I whispered affectionately through the grin.

"Always happy to oblige," she retrieved her micro-recorder as we exited the Cavalier.

I stood facing Ernest Calhoun and Will Bealer. Handsome Harold hung on the perimeter, as usual. "Call me when you think we can get out onto the back roads again. She's out there. We've just got to find her."

"Dare," Will Bealer was looking very intently at me, his face chapped from too much outdoors. "One of my deputies suggested we look in a place that never would have crossed my mind."

"Where's that?" An unaccountable spurt of adrenaline raced up my spine.

"A place I would never have thought of because it's too close to civilization."

"Okay, but that doesn't matter, where is it?"

"There's an old washed out rarely, used pig trail off State Route 149. It used to be a logging road up until some time during the late seventies when the hardwood played out. There's nothing much left now, but some white pine and a few scrawny oak and maple saplings trying to get a foothold. There may be a few so-so maples left, but not enough to make it worth anyone's while. There's still a circle of big old cedars out there, but they're not fit for anything, so there they stand. Some of us used to play out there when we were kids. It was a real forest back then." He sighed, as if taking a momentary dip into childhood. "Not long ago a trailer or two popped up in the vicinity, but they're on the other side of the woods from the old road. Civilization is creeping deeper and deeper into the county."

"Does it fit the map?" I knew in my bones that it did.

"Yeah, best I recall, it's a pretty good match."

"You call me as soon as you think we can get into the area, okay?"

"Sure will. Now, let's go get some dinner before you ladies head back to Nashville."

"I hesitated, "Do we have to go back to Sharkey's?"

"What's the matter, Dare? You're not going to let a little thing like the romance of the century keep you from good food are you?" Will Bealer laughed into his gloves, trying to breathe a little warmth into his hands.

"You noticed?"

"Notice? They're our newest alternative item. Clarksville may be provincial, but I don't care where you are, nowadays, if there's more'n ten or fifteen people gathered around, at least one of 'em's probably queer."

I was amazed at the seemingly unbiased candor among these police types. "How did what's-her-name get on the force if she's a known homosexual?"

"Clarice is her name and she's the product of EEOC, ACLU, attrition, and not the least of all, her daddy's the mayor of our fair city. And by the way, she's a hell of a cop."

Lee couldn't let the situation die without adding her two cents worth. "Does Jerry Falwell know there's a gay cop fighting crime in your streets?"

Bealer blew his nose on a crusty old handkerchief. "That's what I think of

Jerry Falwell and his kind. Maybe if he'd get back behind the pulpit and preach like he's supposed to and quit telling the rest of us how degenerate we are, maybe he wouldn't piss me off so bad."

Lee and I silently applauded him in the cold, hollow, dampness of the old, draft-ridden city garage.

* *

I focused all my energies on the highway. The horizon melted into opaque grayness up ahead. It seemed as though the pale winter sun had pulled the covers over its head and planned to nap at least until spring. The grim sky spit grainy pellets of snow that appeared to be well on their way to becoming sleet. God, I hoped not. Snow is bad enough. My SUV was crunching right along like its tires had teeth. There were seemingly abandoned cars dotting the median and shoulders, like toys that had been tossed aside after a day of hard play. The inside lane of I-24 south was temporarily shut down while a massive wrecker attempted, somewhat tentatively, to haul the tractor end of an eighteen-wheel rig up the steeply banked median. The over-turned trailer lay in its own smoke, as if it had been shot down on the run. Traffic crept along at the proverbial snail's pace. Blue lights were flashing up and down both sides of the highway. There would be no rest for the weary badge-bearers this night. When I got to the precipice of the plateau, I knew immediately what the holdup had been. Lack of sufficient snow removal equipment is hazardous unto itself, but this was ridiculous. The hill looming before us was the toboggan run from hell. A solid sheet of frozen snow wound its way down the curvature of the mountain as far as the eye could see. After that it melted into fog and blowing snow. My windshield wipers were slapping time in a futile attempt to keep up with the heavy precipitation, the result was like *pissing into the wind.* The weather, on the whole, was deteriorating at an ever-increasing rate.

"Oh, shit." My vocabulary suffers considerably under stress.

"I concur." Lee was hanging on to the overhead strap with her right hand and puffing on a Benson & Hedges 100 that she held with her left. She cracked her window just milliseconds before I asked her to. "You okay, Dare? Do you think maybe we should pull off at the next exit and wait?"

"Wait for what?"

"I don't know," she answered, "how 'bout wait for *awhile?*"

"Shit," I laughed. Her attempt at snow-humor had loosened the constriction in my chest muscles, and suddenly I felt better. I have the best bad-weather car on the market, and I'm an excellent driver, if I may be permitted to brag, so I saw no reason not to keep plugging. "Let's keep going unless it gets worse. You game?"

"Sure, but I think I better call Joe." No sooner had the words left her lips, her cell phone began to sing somewhere inside a coat pocket. She dug around until she found and retrieved it. "Hi Sugar." She held the tiny apparatus to her ear. I glanced at her just in time to see the tension melt from her shoulders. "Yeah, sure, honey…we will…I'll tell her…me too…see you later, sweetheart…bye, now." She stabbed the "end" button and folded the phone back into its miniature self and dropped it into her jacket pocket. "That was Joe."

"Naaaawwww."

"Smart-ass. He was just worried about us being out in this weather. He said he wished we'd stayed the night in Clarksville."

"Do you, Lee?"

"Not really, but it's rather a moot point now, don't you think? Anyway, if I've got to be out in this shit, I'd rather be with you, in this tank, than anyone else. Except Joe."

"Yeah, well, I must admit, he'd be infinitely more fun to be marooned with. Did he say anything else?"

"No, just for us to be careful and take it easy. You know, the same old same old. Husband's at home in front of the fire, while wife and partner-in-crime are out braving a snow storm…oh, and he loves me."

"That's nice," I mused, taking advantage of a momentary lull in the conversation, thinking about yesterday and the night before. *Wow!*

"Dare? Where are you, girlfriend? Back in the sack with Felix?"

"As a matter of fact…" I had been woolgathering at the Olympic level.

"Did you remember to ask him when you two can come to dinner at the *Palais Graham*?"

"Uh huh, how 'bout Saturday night?"

"I thought he was all gung-ho about going to the Bar Association do."

"He was, but he said if I didn't want to go, then neither did he."

"Jesus, the boy's smitten, I reck'n."

"I reckon."

"Are you?"

"Ummmm."

"Good for you, it's about time you crawled out of your cave and turned your face toward the sunshine for a change. I was beginning to worry about you, what with this Marie Zhou business, and all. You need to get out of the past and get on with your life. Now maybe I can get a good night's sleep for a change. Consequently, so can Joe. He'll be so happy for you."

"Thanks for caring. Here again, you two are my best buds."

"What shall I cook for the big occasion?"

"I'll leave that up to you. I'm sure whatever you decide will be wonderful."

The snow abated somewhat as we neared the Old Hickory exit, which was a good thing, for the ramp was bumper-to-bumper as drivers eased onto the boulevard. We had managed to beat the ordinarily mad traffic hours, but who could tell? It had been this way ever since we'd left Clarksville, hadn't it?

"God willing and the creeks don't rise, we should be home in the next half hour or so. Shall I drop you off at your house or do you want to come home with me and have some hot chocolate, a hot toddy or something?"

"Thanks, but you can just drop me off. Odds are your message light will be blinking itself to death."

"Maybe. I think I'll jump in the tub and let my tired cold muscles soak for about an hour. I have some leftover pasta that I may nuke. Then I think I'll hit the sack. I have a full day's worth of clients tomorrow since I've put the radio show on hold 'til this Zhou business is behind us. However, I may sleep till Katie comes in. God, that sounds good."

"Hard weekend, huh?"

"Yeah, dear heart."

* *

The snow crunched beneath the tires as I pulled into my driveway. That would be my final weather-related hurdle for the day. After negotiating the long, narrow, curvy tract, I tapped the brake and came to a rest at exactly the correct spot in front of my garage door. I reached over the sun-visor and retrieved the remote control. I aimed it, and between swipes of the windshield wipers, I heard the bump and grind of the antiquated motor hum into life. When it had raised just enough for me to pull the car through safely. I eased the big vehicle inside. I switched off the ignition and leaned back and waited while the garage door crawled back down its rusty tracks and made contact with the floor, locking itself for the night. The snow had slowed considerably, and the deep quiet of flakes upon flakes had been replaced by rolling thunder and lightning melding with the last sagging vestiges of daylight.

I crammed my key into the deadbolt lock and turned it, twisting the doorknob simultaneously. I was home. *Thank you, Jesus.*

After retrieving my cell phone, I tossed my purse on the countertop and then immediately plugged the phone into the re-charger. I pulled out a cigarette and lit it, pulling the acrid smoke deeply into my lungs, savoring its calming effect. The phone rang and I almost choked to death. I dropped my cigarette, picked it up, knocking my purse onto the floor in my haste to reach the cordless phone before the answering machine kicked in. I could see it's tiny, red beacon announcing I had multiple messages awaiting answers.

"Hello?" I croaked.

"Is that you, Dare?"

"Yeah," I answered, trying to clear the cigarette smoke out of my throat. "Who's this?"

"It's Fel. You forgotten me already?"

"Oh, hi, Fel. No, I haven't forgotten you, not by a long shot. I just got in from Clarksville and got on a coughing jag, excuse me."

"You're excused…you busy tonight?"

I couldn't believe my ears. "Well…no, but have you looked outside lately?"

"Believe it or not, the Jag's not the only car I own. I almost never got that sucker home this morning. I drove the Blazer back to work, so I'm in good shape. I'm just about ready to leave the office…you want to go out for a bite to eat?"

"No, I don't think so, not tonight. I would love to, but to tell you the truth, I'm just too tired to change clothes. And besides, I think it's getting ready to rain on top of all this snow, if you can imagine that. It's a lot warmer here than it was up on the plateau." I was babbling.

"I understand…maybe another time." There was a pregnant pause while he awaited my reply.

"But, hey…" I stumbled, "I'm not too tired to grill a couple of cheese sandwiches and heat up some homemade split-pea soup, if you're game." I heard the offer at the exact same moment he did.

"I love grilled cheese sandwiches and homemade split-pea soup. When…?"

"How soon can you get here?"

* *

"*Jeeezus*," Ricky-Dino thought as he sat alone under the aluminum-roofed shed where he had gone to smoke his cherished, elicit cigarettes. The sheriff had gone off the premises, so the guards turned their backs, as usual. "This weather sucks, and if I don't get outta here and get me some pussy soon, I'm gonna bust wide open." Ricky-Dino was alone out in the storage shed. He was cold, horny and miserable. Jerkin' off out there was out of the question, even if his un-gloved hand wouldn't have thrown his dick into shock and made it shrink-up like wool-in-hot-water. If that pansy guard was to turn around and catch him, ole Ricky-Dino wouldn't have to worry about his *family jewels* for awhile. No siree, he'd heard that fairy could suck the chrome off a trailer hitch. "Not really my idea of a good time," he mused to himself between drags off his Lucky Strike. He subconsciously rubbed his hand across his heavy crotch, feeling a noticeable response, "but damned if it ain't lookin' better all the time." He flipped the butt into the snow-turned-to-rain and climbed down from the fifty-five gallon barrel where he'd been sitting, ready to make his way back inside the lock-up. He paused just short of the concrete apron where the quasi-shelter of the roof gave way to the full brunt of the incessant downpour. One more step and cold rain would be crawling down the collar of his county-issue jumper. He watched as the newly arrived transport bus pulled to a grinding halt outside the cyclone fence that separated him from the civilized world. He would wait and see what kind of trash the goons had drug in this go round. The gate rolled back on time worn tracks and complained metallically as its mechanism labored automatically through its cycle. Ricky-Dino thought about counting *one Mississippi, two Mississippi*...to see how many seconds would elapse before the damned thing made its journey from closed to open. He decided he wasn't that bored. Not yet. The big, rain-washed Department of Corrections transport bus, with its cage-like barred windows and security guards, pulled through the gate and came to a rest in the slush-infested mud-wallow, that only yesterday had been slicker'n owl shit with ice. Now it was slicker'n the same ol' owl shit, but now with ice *and* muddy slush. Last night Ricky-Dino had slipped and busted his ass after smoking five cigarettes in a row. He couldn't decide which he hated more, snow or rain. He turned his attention away from the bus to the mush where he was about to put his sneaker-clad foot. "Don't fall down again, asshole," he chided himself.

"Hey, Dino!" He looked up to see his pal Cobra waving madly at him as he stepped off the bus.

"Holy Shit, Cobra," he shouted into the frigid rain, "what the hell you doing back here so soon? You've broke your own record this time." Cobra, waving Ricky-Dino off, strode across the familiar yard toward the lock-up, unmindful of either the slimy ground or the rain that pelted his head and shoulders like tiny rocks. Ricky-Dino knew he would have to wait 'til after the recidivist from hell was properly processed before they could talk. That wouldn't take long cause the fairy on the door "liked" Cobra, and he would see to it that the papers were signed, sealed and delivered to the admissions officer, quick as a *wink*. Ricky-Dino decided to light another cigarette. He huddled against the wall of the makeshift storage shed and waited for Cobra, the closest thing he had on earth to a best friend. The wind whipped around the corner, whining a sad lamenting melody as it sucked the cigarette smoke into the soggy nothingness. He waited.

* *

"Here I am, you sonabitch, you." Cobra was splashing through the ice-laced mud, heading for the relative dryness of the shed where his friend awaited. Dino had watched as *fairy boy* slipped Cobra a pack of Pall Malls. He couldn't help but wonder why? *Just who was doing what to who and when and where?* If they were, he knew *why*. He decided he didn't give a shit. He was just glad to have someone to talk to again. Besides he was a little weary of Cobra running around on the outside knowing everything that Ricky-Dino had bragged to him in a very weak moment. Cobra stepped onto the concrete apron and out of the pounding rainstorm, just as a neon lightning bolt split the early evening sky, spitting watery, stinking ozone in its wake. "Dino, good to see you, you sorry piece a shit."

"I thought you said you wouldn't be back?" Ricky-Dino playfully punched his pal on the shoulder.

"Hell, you fool, I hadn't meant to, but you know how it is. A goddam A-rab pulled out a .45 Magnum. What the hell was I supposed to do? Shoot him before he could shoot me? Fuck that, I ain't no fuckin' murderer, and ain't gonna be, for a fuckin' six-pack o' Icehouse and o' fuckin' carton a smokes. Hell, the sonabitch didn't have but fifty-five dollars and change in the fuckin' cash register. I ask you, Dino, what's a guy to do in a case like that?" He stuck out his hand.

Ricky-Dino grabbed Cobra's outstretched hand, pumping it with genuine *glad to see you.* "Goddam if I know, I don't stick up no Seven-'levens. Never did."

"Yeah, I know, but if you ever get caught for what you did do, it's gonna take more'n a 45 to get your busy little prick out of that big ol' fuck-up. They'll fry your sorry ass like it was a big juicy steak set out to sizzle on the grill." He laughed at his analogy.

"They ain't gonna catch me, less'n you talk, and I can tell you for sure, you don't want to do that. Anyhow, asshole, they don't smoke 'em no more, Tennessee's got all civilized now, or ain't you heard? They shoot you up with dope now before they kiss your ass good-bye. Anyhow, that's what they'd do if they ever got around to startin' back up with the death penalty. And if you want my opinion, there's too goddam many pansy do-gooders out there to ever let that happen again. You can mark my word—I ain't worried. It'll be a cold day in hell 'fore anybody walks that last mile down at Nashville again. A *real* cold day."

"You mean like the one we're havin' today in this here hell?"

"Ha ha, you comical sombitch…welcome back. I ain't had me a good laugh since you left here."

* *

I pulled a quart Tupperware container out of the freezer and I pried the top off and stared at the inhospitable-looking, ice-crystal infested, glob of pea-green goo. How could anything that looks so god-awful taste so scrumptious?

The newest chapter in the storm caught my attention. I watched the lightning as it repeatedly stabbed the earth with multitudinous electrical pitchforks. Thunder reverberated in the distance like feral growls. The snow had given up the ghost. A massive warm front was plowing in from the southwest and was dragging in rain by the buckets full. Just a few degrees had changed the storm from a blizzard to a typhoon in what had seemed like only seconds. I flipped off the weather band and concentrated on my make-shift dinner for two.

I ran a table knife between the frozen soup and its container, loosening it sufficiently to allow it to *plop*, unimpeded, into a heavy pan, whereupon I placed it on the gas burner. I turned to flame to low, allowing the heat to slowly melt the split pea *ambrosia.* I checked to make sure I had plenty of cheese and bread before setting out a stick of butter to soften.

I knew I had at least an hour and probably more, due to traffic and weather conditions, before Felix would come knocking on my door. I mixed myself a Jack Daniels and water and carried it with me to the bathroom, flipping on the receiver and CD player as I passed through the great room. I ran my bath, complete with aromatic bath salts. I dropped my jeans and sweatshirt on the bathroom floor. Tossing my bra and panties on the heap, I topped the whole thing off with my clammy boot-socks. I had left my boots just inside the kitchen door, and knew I must remember to towel them off good and move them to my closet as soon as I got out of the tub. I didn't take the time for candles; I just wanted to wash off the stench of the day's experience and warm my bones at the same time. No time to wash my hair. That would have to wait, as would a lot of other things. I did allow myself a few uninterrupted moments of pure soaking pleasure, while listening to a CD of favorite, quiet jazz classics. Astrid Gilberto strolled along the white sandy beach at Ipenema, accompanied by Stan Getz's soulfully haunting saxophone. I thought about the coming evening.

* *

"Tell me about it." Ricky-Dino was starved for conversation, besides he was hoping Cobra would drop a hint about himself and that curly headed guard on the door.

"I done told you. I was stickin' up this 7-11 or Kwik Sack or one of them places. Shit, they all look just alike after awhile. This big ol' hairy A-rab with a goddam rag on his head had a Magnum .45 hid under the counter, I reck'n. He pulled that thing out on me. Shit, I ain't never looked at the busy end of a fuckin' cannon that big before. Shit, it like to scared me to death. The sonabitch held that motherfucker on me while he dialed 911. Then the little asshole had the balls to show me that he didn't have but fifty-five fuckin' dollars in the motherfuckin' cash register. Can you fuckin' believe that? I just stood there all hung-dog like. 'Cause, shit, he had me. I waited real peaceable for the cops. Shit, like I said, I weren't going shoot no fuckin' A-rab and spend the rest of my days talkin' to James Earl Ray wannabes. Can't ya just hear it now? '*Whad you do, Cobra? How come you're down here on death row with all us badass throat slashers and baby killers?*' No disrespect there, Dino. '*Oh, hell I just blowed me a A-rab off the fuckin' planet for fifty-five dollars.*' Now I ask you Dino, what the hell kinda story would that make? Telling them death-rowers a tale like that? Shit, I ain't got no intentions of spending my last days fuckin' with some public defender. Naw, I'll just serve my eleven-twenty-nine right here with you, you warped little shit. Hey, you been out and got you any real live pussy since I been gone, or you still just whackin' your weenie?"

"Why? Like that's some more of your fuckin' business, you ig'nert sumbitch."

"Well, I wouldn't want to see you go blind, little buddy. Besides, I got me some low friends in even lower places. *Comprende, amigo?*"

* *

I had gotten myself together by the time Felix arrived. I had slipped into a pair of soft jeans and a cotton pullover. I hadn't gotten around to putting on shoes; I padded to the door in my sock-feet.

"Here, Darlin', he quipped," handing me a brown paper bag which I recognized immediately as having come from the liquor store.

"Well, Fel, to what do I owe this sack of whatever?" I reached into the bag and pulled out a bottle of *Dom Pèrignon* . "Felix, what's this?"

"Champagne."

"I know its champagne, I mean what are we supposed to do with it?"

"Well, we can either drink it or pour it in the bathtub…I hear the latter can be quite stimulating," He grinned.

"Felix Walker, you are incorrigible, but other than that, what on earth were you thinking of? I told you we're having grilled cheese sandwiches and split-pea soup…did you think I was pulling your leg?"

"No, but that's a thought. What would you have had me bring? Buttermilk? Chardonnay or Petite Sirah would have done for the sandwiches, depending upon what kind of cheese you're planning to use, but I didn't have a clue about split pea. I knew we'd put it to good use…one way or the other."

I stood on my tiptoes. He tipped his face toward mine, and I kissed him on the lips. "Thank you, sir, I'm sure we will." All of a sudden the snow, rain, death and destruction were forgotten. I sat the wine bottle on the countertop, and put my arms around Fel's neck. Our mouths met in a mind-bending, toe-curling, *forget supper* kiss.

* *

The clouds scrolled across the yolk of a moon that hung suspended on an invisible tether from the dome of the universe. The night was bright as noon, then black as the maw of death. No rhyme, no reason. Time compressed to the *nth. The darkness enveloped me in its cloak. I heard the dogs. Sensing the slight taint of decay as they yelped and bayed in the distance, I followed their malevolent barking until I was as close as I dared to be, not particularly fearful for my safety, only for what I might find. The blackness abated somewhat as abbreviated dawn crept in to replace the night. I saw the beasts for the first time: a pack of rabid hounds shat from the bowels of Old Scratch himself. Luminescent eyes married to massive, serrated fangs, slobbery ichor oozing from between black, quivering lips. Grinning performers, they danced the circle around where I stood. At last, the leader of the pack, a huge mastiff the color of raw midnight made his presence known. In its mouth was a long bone. Perhaps, I thought, a human femur. I tried to speak, "Nice doggy." He responded with a feral growl that jarred my teeth in their sockets and chilled my bones to the marrow. My blood pressure dropped appreciably and it was all I could do to keep from retching. I perceived them to be some sort of canine committee. This gathering I had stumbled upon bore all the earmarks of a ritualistic celebration. The vile participants displayed their treasures for my perusal, but I understood, innately, I was not permitted to touch. These were their woods and I was the interloper. Tears stung my eyes. Yet, I feared any movement to wipe them away would incite my hosts to react. One by one they brought forth their trophies, placing them at my bare feet. Atop the femur, an ancient, white, milky-eyed German Shepherd dropped a length of long, dark hair. It was still attached to a ripped and shriveled cap of scalp. My own scalp crawled as the shepherd bared his aged yellow teeth and pale gums, in what I surmised to be a canine grimace. Next, in this necromantic marathon, came a Golden Retriever bearing clavicles and a bit of a partially articulated spine. On and on they came, a parade of scavengers returning osseous treasures to their point of origin, as if by primeval preordination. From underneath the sacrificial stack of bones, a fire sprang, crackling and whistling, issuing forth as hot gasses vaporized putrefying marrow. The stench was unbearable. I watched, mesmerized, as the beasts gathered Marie Zhou from the forest floor, transporting her, piece by piece, bone by bone, to the makeshift altar. Each animal looked directly into my eyes as it passed. Bone, sinew, scraps of snow-stiffened, rain-drenched clothing protruded from gaping mouths. Where was I? I knew in my gut...and I knew why I was there. I screamed, **sans voix**, in supplication for the lost, the forgotten and the hopeless. The licking flames exploded into full-blown conflagration. My legs were paralyzed as if they had been double-dipped in Quikrete. I was going to burn along with Marie. I could not forgive myself for not having found the* *poor child sooner, nor would I plead for divine dispensation. I but wailed the silent moan of abject failure. Standing in the midst of the carnage, I was an inescapable part of the horror, an integral piece of the action, yet unable to make myself heard, even to my own ears. Only mute self-recriminations could be wrung from my anguished heart.*

* *

"Dare!...Dare!...What's wrong?...Wake up!...Are you all right?"

I could hear Felix somewhere out there beyond the wild dogs. I tried very hard to answer him, but I couldn't speak. He kept repeating my name. I could hear him but obviously he couldn't hear my unarticulated implorations. *Oh, God, help me!* Get me out of here before I choke on my own fear. Its fist had a death grip on my vocal cords. Slimy fingers squeezed my chest. I couldn't breath. Out of the deepest recesses of my subconscious boomed, *"Cave canem!"* Phosphorescent, the words burned across the backside of my memory, caroming raucously inside my skull like a handball around the court. *"Beware the dog."* Sister Mary Angelica, my tenth grade Latin teacher, would have been so proud.

* *

"Dare! Please wake up...if you don't wake up *right now*, I'm callin' 911!"

"No...don't...please." I was crawling hand-over-hand, scratching my way out of that black pit where such dreams are born. "Don't call anyone...give me a minute...I'm all right..."

"Damn it, woman, you nearly scared me to death. What happened?" Felix was sitting on the side of the bed, holding my hand and brushing damp strands of hair from my clammy forehead. I must have looked like death incarnate, all wild-eyed, like a deer caught in headlights, or worse.

"I'm sorry. Maybe I should have warned you. This can happen when you sleep with a psychic who gets a lot of information through her dreams." It's just that it doesn't happen very often. Well, anyway, if you grab your pants and go running into the night, I'll understand."

"No, I don't want to go anywhere." He didn't let go of my hand. Instead, he reached over and kissed me gently, as if to reaffirm what he had said. "Do you want to tell me about the dream?" He continued to touch my face, wiping away the mortal fear that had vomited me out of that satanic slumber.

"I can't, not now. What time is it?"

He glanced over my shoulder at the alarm clock that was perpetually set for seven thirty AM. "It's four o'clock. Can I get you something? Hot chocolate, tea, something that will help you get back to sleep?" He had eased down beside me. Propped on his elbow, he looked directly into my eyes.

My pulse and respiration were almost back to normal, allowing me to think of something other than the hideous place my *Id* had dragged me earlier.

"Yes, there is. Hold me, please."

13

I had called Katie at seven o'clock and rousted her out of bed, and she was not a happy camper. She promised to be in by eight-thirty to start calling and rescheduling clients. I knew she would be grumpy so I was glad I wouldn't be around when she came in.

* *

"Jesus, Dare, you look like you've been rode hard and put away wet."

I had called Lee at six thirty, right after Felix had kissed me goodbye and given me the good news about the weather. It was doing nothing for a change.

Thank you, Lee, you're looking quite lovely as well.

"What's this about the nasty dream you spoke about when you called? And by the way, thanks for the untimely *coitus interruptus.*"

Regardless of how ridiculous the comparison may have seemed, the Latin phrase stung the lining of my cerebrum. *Cave canem* loomed back. The words "rebooted" the hideous dream experience. I banished it. I quipped, "That's a redundancy if ever I heard one. Anyway, I'm sorry, but it couldn't be helped. Maybe you should leave your answering machine on, that way I, or any other unsuspecting caller, wouldn't interrupt your coitus. Suddenly realizing the banality of this conversation, I balked. "For crying out loud, Lee, give me a fucking break…"

"Exactly, my point!" She continued, "That's all I'm asking. Why in hell would I be expecting you or anyone else to call at that hour? Only strangers don't know I walk every morning, and generally speaking, strangers don't call."

"Well," I conceded, "I knew you'd be back."

"You have an uncanny ability to catch us with our pants down."

"My God, Lee, you guys are like rabbits."

"Go on, continue to bolster my defense. You know perfectly well that Joe falls asleep during the ten o'clock news, so occasionally we warm the sheets before breakfast." She threw back her head and blew a long stream of cigarette smoke toward the kitchen ceiling, hiccuping staccatoed laughter in the process. She scooted back her chair and walked toward the countertop where Mr. Coffee sat. "I miss Jolt'n Joe." Notorious for changing the subject mid-stream, Lee referred to the deceased Joe Dimaggio, long-time, New York Yankee outfielder, turned spokesman for Mr. Coffee for a while. *The Yankee Clipper* (as he was almost reverently known) had, sometime ago, struck out in the ninth inning of the final game. Metaphorically speaking.

"Me too," I agreed, "It's kinda like a little piece of America's pastime died with him. You know?"

She nodded, stubbing out her cigarette, "Maybe Don MacLean will write a song."

* *

It was a gray flannel day. It was daylight but that was about all that could be said for it. Night had taken the wind with it, now only a timid breeze danced in the treetops. I-24 glistened darkly against washed-out landscape. No snow, no rain, no sun, just a gray flannel day.

* *

"Holy Toledo! That's the worst one ever, isn't it?"

I had told her the dream, every minute detail from the beginning to the mind-bending conclusion. I told her how I had almost scared Felix out of his skin. "I couldn't speak," I told her, "hell, I could barely breathe. In fact, until Fel touched, me I couldn't fight my way out of it. I could hear him calling my name, but until he touched me, I couldn't break loose from that awful place inside my head...Lee, sometimes I think I've gone 'round the proverbial bend."

She tapped my shoulder with her knuckles and laughed, "That's what gives you that little something special—that slightly tilted edge."

"Screw you and the horse you rode in on!"

"Do you talk that way to Felix? Poor soul probably thinks you're just issuing orders. My next question is, is he up to it?"

"That's some more of your business."

"Well?"

"You're incorrigible. Not only is he up to it. But...Lee, I don't want to jive about this...I'm too superstitious."

"Wow! I do believe you're blushing. I've never seen you blush before. Well, that's all right, darlin', go for the gusto!"

* *

I wheeled the Lexus into the parking lot at Sharkeys' *Barf and Gargle,* driving all the way around back before finding a vacanct slot. "Lot's packed this morning, every cop in town must be scarfing down the breakfast buffet."

"Either that or Jeopardy's on." *Lee Graham, the irony maiden.*

* *

Where cops hang out smoke is generally abundant, and coffee is usually strong enough to corrode the digestive tract. Nerves strung like piano wires need plenty of nicotine, caffeine, and in some cases, the occasional amphetamine to keep in fine tune. Not all cops use drugs; they don't all smoke cigarettes or even drink coffee. Some go to church, teach Sunday school and coach little league. But by and large, uniforms on the street and not just a few plain-clothes detectives indulge in at least two of the three vices—four if you count beer, which is a given. Once in a while one of these law-enforcers will flip out, go on a rampage, maiming or even killing someone—perhaps because he's embittered at the injustice of it all. It becomes very difficult for the families of those who walk the tight rope over a landscape strewn with death, destruction, murder and mayhem—a landscape populated by murderers, rapists, arsonists and thieves. When such a person (for whatever reason) snaps out of reality's grasp, then he may or may not be held accountable for those actions, and generally speaking, cops have a higher incidence of going over the edge than most other professionals. As a whole, they are trained to react in a manner that is diametrically opposed to societal mores. The world loves a brave crime-fighting police officer, but God forbid he should behave like a regular run-of-the-mill citizen and react to any given incident with basic human instinct. He would be castigated to the hilt. Some cops have been known to leave their human compassion at home in the dresser drawer, along with their morality and manners. And as a result, there are a few who are unequivocal creeps. Or worse. With the possible exception of school teachers, no other profession is held to higher standards, paid less for their efforts and demeaned more critically by the tax-paying public. Is it any wonder crime never takes a holiday? Then there are those who, for— whatever reason—"get-off" by dressing up and just pretending to be cops.

* *

"Dare, Lee, over here!" Will Bealer stood waving his hand from behind a small table that had been butted up against another to make room for several of us to sit around without feeling crowded. Emmett Calhoun, Harold Riggens and Will had already ordered breakfast by the time we arrived. Lee, spying him first, waved back before taking me by the sleeve. She plowed her way though the humanity in between.

"Dare, I don't mind telling you your phone call surprised me. I didn't think you would be back till next weekend at the soonest." Lieutenant Calhoun tapped the filtered tip of his cigarette aimlessly against his thumbnail. A hangover from the time when he smoked non-filters, I reckoned.

"To tell you the truth, Emmett, I had no intention of coming back up here today, that is until about four o'clock this morning." I looked up to see Geraldine standing over me with her order pad in one hand and pencil in the other. Her good eye fixed on me, she popped her gum with a vengeance. "Just coffee, and bring the sugar bowl, please." I sounded apologetic, even to myself. Lee ordered a three-minute egg and toast. My stomach did a roll. I turned my attention to Will Bealer. "How's Rolanda this morning?"

"She's feeling better, thank you. Oh! That reminds me, Dare. Rolanda sends you a message from Glinda. It seems that she called the house at the crack of dawn this morning crying and going on about her corns hurting something fierce." I guess he could tell by the look on my face that I was totally without a clue as to what he was talking about. "She explained it to Rolanda. It seems that when something big is about to happen her corns pain her like the devil. Do you think there could possibly be anything to that?"

"Well, Will, do you know how I think Shakespeare might address that question?"

"Hell, I never took much to that kinda stuff. What do you think he would say?"

"I believe he just might say, '*He jests at scars, that never felt a wound.*'"

He looked at me for a moment then he grinned. "In other words, you're saying I shouldn't doubt her ability just cause I don't understand *it*, cause I don't have *it*."

"That's a pretty good analogy. Hey, I've got it and I don't claim to understand it. I just accept it as a gift from God, and you know what they say about looking gift horses in the mouth."

Well, anyhow, Rolanda told me to tell you and Lee that she and Glinda both send their best and hope to see you soon."

"Well, you tell them the same from us." I didn't have to look at Lee to know she thought I was as full of shit as a Christmas turkey about that last statement. "Will, you mentioned a place where you used to play when you were a kid—a patch of woods somewhere."

"Yeah, it used to be a logging area. There's still the remnants of an old road leading into what used to be quite a stand of timber. It quite literally used to be out in the sticks, but not anymore. If it's used for anything these days, my guess is it's a lover's lane. The thick woods that used to be out there were an ideal place to play cowboys and Indians, when we were kids. I didn't live very far from there. Back in those days parents didn't worry too much if their kids roamed a bit away from home. Not like now…too many crazies out there anymore. We won't have any trouble getting back up in there in my Blazer."

I lit a cigarette and watched as Geraldine appeared, from out of nowhere, to top off my coffee. "I surely hope so. I have some very strong feelings about today. Very strong, indeed." I glanced at Lee, then at the eggcup. She was dabbing at the corners of her mouth with a paper napkin, and thankfully the shell was as clean as a picked bird. She knows soft-boiled eggs turn my stomach.

Will tossed a quarter and caught it in midair. He called heads before slapping the coin on the back of his hand. Emmett lost and picked up the breakfast check, dropping two crumpled ones on the table for Geraldine. *Maybe with that windfall, she could afford to buy Clarice an ice cream cone later.*

* *

We had all piled into Will Bealer's ageless Chevy Blazer and were transported through the streets of downtown Clarksville. We wound through suburbs and finally onto a rural side road that bore toward a wooded area. A stand of mature pines and gnarled cedars towered over a fledgling forest. I doubted, in my heart, that it would be long before suburbia crept up to this peaceful spot. Will braked the Blazer to an easy halt. Pointing ahead where sheltered snow had managed to hold on by the skin of its teeth and rain had bunched into puddles, he said, "There it is."

Two barely distinguishable, mud-impacted tracks crawled innocuously into Will Bealer's former playground. It looked ordinary enough, but I knew it was anything but. "Now what?" I queried, "Do we walk through the muck, or do you really think you can drive that road without miring us up to our axels?"

"Old Paint'll get us in there just fine." He locked and loaded into four-wheel drive and eased forward. Initially, spinning wheels threw liquid mud past windows before grabbing a purchase. The old Blazer did just what its owner had promised. It got us to a circle of ancient cedars where winter soaked leaves lay ankle-deep on the spongy earth. We crawled out of the Blazer where everyone stood waiting for me to make the first move. I leaned over and whispered into Lee's ear. *"Will's as crazy as you are—he names his wheels."*

* *

The atmosphere was so sodden with residual humidity that I could feel my sinus cavities shutting down. I dug through my pockets, frantically searching for my nasal mist. Finding it, I sprayed and snorted my way back toward relatively unimpeded breathing. Capping the tiny spray-mist atomizer, I dropped it back into my jacket pocket. "Ah, that's better." I hadn't realized they were all standing around watching me as if I were a sideshow geek. "Sorry about that. Sinus congestion," I felt compelled to explain. That *goose* was cutting back and forth across my grave like a broken field runner. I knew this was it. "Lee." She turned toward me showing me that she did, indeed, have her trusty tape recorder and it was, in fact, cranking away. I nodded and smiled. "Let's go around this way first." I headed east. I knew it was east because we were walking directly into the face of the dull, cloud-enshrouded mid-morning sun. Lee stayed at my side. I stopped suddenly, and the clutch of cops almost ran over me *en masse*. I took a deep breath, closed my eyes and announced *"She was...is...here."*

* *

A stray twig stabbed the tender flesh just below his bushy eyebrow He didn't take the time to stop and check his wound, nurse his pain, or even wipe the tiny trickle of blood that traced a crooked line to his ear. He had spent entirely too much time with little Miss what-ever-her-name-was. He had to get his carcass back to the jailhouse on the double. He didn't think anybody would even care, not yet, anyway. He had permission to be out—just not this late.

"What a night," he laughed to himself, "I shot off more rockets than Cape Kennedy. He grabbed his crotch and proclaimed, "Good boys!" He sensed a stirring in his jeans, but this time he felt compelled to ignore it. He crammed his hand into his pocket for the car keys. Nothing. He patted himself down, touching every spot where the keys to the patrol car might be. Nothing. "Oh, Jesus Christ, where'd them keys get to? Oh, boy, talk about bein' up Shit Creek without a paddle." He ran back to the circle where earlier he'd gotten down on his knees and preformed cunnilingus on the girl. He'd heard that word down at the jail, and he liked the way it sounded and especially the way it felt on his tongue. But like the act itself, the word meant just plain ol' eatin' pussy. After he'd done that to her, he'd yanked down his zipper and taken her right on that very spot. But his pants had stayed with him.

He raked the frost-rimed leaves with his hand. Shivers of dread were beginning to crawl up and down his spine. He stood up and kicked leaves like a kid after his dad had raked them into a pile. Nothing. He turned around and around several times, searching the disarray at his feet. He raised his fists to heaven, cursing God for letting him lose his goddam keys.

The moon had slipped a little. The woods were no longer illuminated as if by a klieg light. The shadows had muddied and melted into the dank mist that was oozing from decaying leaves. Fear was as strong an emotion as was lust, and it enveloped all the spare space that Ricky Dean (Dino) Harris had in his bleak heart. Fear—pure and simple—of losing his tenuous tether to freedom. Never mind that if he couldn't get that car out of there, but eventually someone would find it and the girl. Talk about having your ass in a sling.

He stumbled to where the girl's body hung by her wrists and ankles. Her bloody head hung limply—her chin rested on her chest. The blow that had crushed her skull had snapped her neck as well. He didn't know that. If he had, it might have blown his dick clean off. He stood for a moment, quietly looking at the battered remains of the teenager that he had abused so savagely and repeatedly before bashing her brains in. He forced himself to look away. He had to find those keys, get back to Dickson County and into the jailhouse before shift change. He didn't trust any of them cocksuckers on days, no siree. He had to get back while Billy Weathers was still on the gate. Billy would let him in with a wave and a howdy, never asking any questions.

He had permission to be out but knew full well, he should have been back hours ago. He was just supposed to drive some clown to the airport down in Nashville and then come right on back. "Oh, well," Billy Weathers would think, "boys will be boys—even if they are jail birds."

"Oh, Jesus, please let me find them keys." He figured the prayer would fall on deaf ears because he didn't profess to have any type of relationship with the Lord or anyone else who couldn't be bullied into submission. That didn't keep him from trying several more times. Nothing.

He figured he'd kicked every leaf within a square mile, to no avail. He decided to check the car one more time. "Maybe them damned ol' keys fell down in the floorboard or under the seat. Can't hurt to look one more time." He glanced over his shoulder at the limp body hanging spread-eagled between the two saplings, straining under their burden. His pants grew tight around his zipper. He didn't have a clue that the reaction was anything but normal. He turned, forcing the image from his mind, trying to concentrate on finding the missing car keys.

He sat in the driver's seat whining to himself. "Where the fuck can them sombitchin' keys be at? I ain't been nowhere but right here. Where the fuck could they've gotten off to?" He stepped out of the car and slammed the door. The reverberation caused a scurrying in the treetops. He didn't know if it were little furry things that had their sleep disturbed or if the few remaining leaves had let go. He didn't care. Nothing in those woods scared him. Nothing scared him, but the thought of having his trustee privileges yanked away. He only survived in that goddam lockup because he always knew that sooner or later, he'd be let out to run some kind of errand for that prick of a sheriff. He could always find himself a little pussy, even though it might not be the young stuff he hankered after—like he'd lucked across tonight. Sometimes a man just had to settle for what he could get. If it made that terrible pain away, then it had to do. But he knew there weren't no pussy in the death house—young or otherwise.

He walked all the way around the car before realizing that the back door, on the passenger side, had been left ajar, "Must of left it open after I screwed the little missy back yonder in the backseat." He flung the door back on its hinges, creating another flurry of activity far up in the treetops. He dropped to his knees, grabbing the official police-issue flashlight that he had left in the floorboard along with the girl's tennis shoe. He shined the halogen beam across the floor and swept every inch of the back seat with its brightness. "Oh, shit!" There they lay, crammed almost entirely between the seat and its back. If he had brushed against them in the dark, they might have dropped into the netherworld without him ever knowing they were there. "Must a lost them babies when I opened up my britches so's she could go down on me. Jesus, I gotta be more careful next time."

The thought of what she had done to him earlier painted vivid pictures in his head. He slammed the rear door, but not before grabbing the tennis shoe from where it lay on the floorboard. Walking around the car and opening the driver's door, he slid into the seat just long enough to cram the key into the ignition, making sure it was anchored in its slot. Getting out, he kicked the door shut then hauled off and flung the shoe over-handed, sending it crashing into the underbrush some distance away from where the girl's body hung suspended. Striding across the clearing, he unzipped his jeans. His penis, fully engorged and eager, jumped out of his pants. He ripped open the waist button to give himself more freedom of movement. He stood with his sneakers planted wide apart, fondling himself for a couple of minutes before getting down to serious business. He knew he was still flirting with the loss of his freedom, but he couldn't reason beyond purely unadulterated, animalistic sexual release. Or as he would put it, "Gettin' my rocks off." His fist pumped like a well-oiled piston, bringing him closer and closer with each stroke. He never took his eyes off the girl. A loud groan pierced the night, sending a third and final flurry though the foliage. His throat constricted around the next sound, stifling what he wouldn't contain between his legs for long. His thigh muscles knotted and cramped from his hips to his knees, and his abdominal muscles bunched to the verge of spasming. The sounds coming from his throat were low, guttural moans. The only other sound in the woods was the hollow slap of the heel of his right hand against his empty belly. He focused increasingly on the screaming in his groin. His breathing broke raggedly as the burgeoning orgasm snaked its way through his gut, and finally, between his legs, where it grabbed his balls, kneading them viciously in its fist. His shuddering penis hawked up its load and spat it between the tethered feet of the dead girl.

She didn't care anymore.

* *

"Dino! Goddam it, wake up! You're havin' a fuckin' nightmare. If you don't knock it off you're going to wake up the dead."

"*Fuck that!*" Jerking wide awake, Ricky-Dino lay sweating and trying to catch his breath, while considering the picture-show his mind had conjured up. It was almost more than even Ricky-Dino wanted to consider. He wiped his hand on his boxer shorts, told Cobra to go fuck himself, rolled over and went back to sleep. In thirty seconds his snores were cutting through puddled drool on the crusty pillow ticking.

Cobra contemplated what Dino had just said. He had lain awake watching and listening to his crony building up to and pulling off yet another monstrous, self-induced orgasm. And on top of that, ol' Dino had been sound asleep. He just didn't understand it. Dino seemed to have better climaxes by just jerkin' himself off than anything Cobra had ever got from even the most talented *fellatio* experts. When given a choice, a bang-up blowjob had always been his preference.

He stuck his last Pall Mall between his lips, sucking the taste of unlit tobacco across his tongue. He allowed his fingers to slip through the opening in the front of his shorts. The snake was primed for a strike.

He threw the covers back and swung his bony legs over the side of his bunk, pulled on his county issue dungarees, carefully situating his gigantic, snake-festooned erection inside the britches. He poked his tube-socked feet into sneakers and grabbed his denim jacket. He strode, as best he could (considering the boner he was sporting was almost as big a woman's forearm), around the corner to the corridor leading out to the yard. "Curly," He whispered. The guard on the door looked up from his *Playgirl* magazine. Cobra noticed the bulge in the sharply creased uniform pants. A result, Cobra figured, of Curly's fascination with the muscular, young hunks in the magazine. "Let's you, me and the snake take a walk out to the maintenance shed. Gimme a pack a smokes, and I'll let you give me some head. Then gimme a carton, and I'll suck your skinny dick 'til your head caves in."

Deputy Jon Peterman, better known as Curly by almost everybody, showed the *Playgirl* centerfold to Cobra. It was a popular Hispanic actor, the star of his own prime time detective show on TV. In the photo he wore his make-believe detective's shield draped around his neck on a chain—and nothing else. His bare foot was propped on the bumper of a squad car, and he was posed in such a way that his *schlong* hung, tantalizingly, almost to the popular actor's knee. "Shit, and he ain't even got a hard on!" Cobra was incredulous. "Would you just look at the size a that motherfucker?" He could only reiterate disbelief, "I can't believe that guy! Sonabitch could throw a blanket over that pole and go campin'."

Curly concurred, "It's damned near as big as your old anaconda there. Let's get on out to the shed. With that he closed his magazine and locked it in his desk drawer.

Cobra hadn't lost an inch, not that anyone would have noticed. If anything, that centerfold had beefed him up a notch. He fingered his erection through his pants pockets as he followed Curly out to the shed. Once inside, Curly inserted a key in a metal cabinet door and withdrew a bright red carton of Pall Mall non-filtered cigarettes: Cobra's brand. He laid them on the table before taking an unopened package of the same brand from his shirt pocket, and he slid it deftly into Cobra's grasp. Cobra peeled the red tape from the cellophane, broke the foil and tapped the package across his left forefinger. He snatched the precious weed as it poked its tiny, unfiltered head from the package. Firing up his trusty Zippo, he teased the tip of the cigarette until it pulsed brightly in the dimness. He inhaled the full hit of acrid smoke, savoring the effects before expelling it in a series of slow, lazy smoke rings. Making the most of the guard's obvious oral fixation, Cobra made quite a show of the ritual. *That was the only thing that wasn't hard.*

* *

By the time the shifts changed Cobra had his cigarettes safely duct-taped to the wall under his bunk. He lay on his back listening to that creepy asshole Dino blow slobber bubbles in his sleep, until he couldn't stand it any longer. He stuck a Pall Mall behind his ear, where he liked to carry a spare, and strolled out toward the yard.

After changing his clothes in preparation for heading home to his unsuspecting wife and three kids, Curly surprised the restless trustee. Walking up behind Cobra in the shadows, the jailer spoke just above a whisper, "Hey, man, It'll be a cold day in hell before I forget your ugly face *or* that fancy tattooed dick of yours.

"What the hell you talkin' about, motherfucker? You plannin'on jumpin'ship or somethin'? Anyhow, it ain't many that forgets the snake once they been bit."

"Hell no, I'm got going anywhere. I may just have to take disability…what with my head caved in and all." He snickered and left Cobra shaking his head while lighting his spare. There wasn't much of the night left for sleeping. So he prayed to whatever gods might be listening that by the time he finished his cancer-stick, Dino and the rest of the skanks would be done snoring and yankin' off.

14

The oxygen was sucked from my lungs and my blood as surely as I stood there. I felt like a cartoon character who had been on the receiving end of a falling anvil and was anticipating the inevitable crumble into tiny, fragile pieces. I tried to silently swear that I would never allow myself to stumble into another situation like I was in at that moment. Oh, but if I could.

Lee touched my sleeve and I took a breath. She took my hand and I looked at her; her face was a puzzle. "Shit Dare, what's the matter with you? Is she here or isn't she?"

"*She is...somewhere*. Lee, keep the guys away until you and I look around a bit."

She left my side and I could sense her behind me spinning some yarn to keep them off my back. Just as silently she returned. "Okay, they're going to hang back, and they promised to stay out of your way."

"That's perfect, but do think they understand they're not to speak to me? I'm afraid things are about to become crucial, and I sure as hell don't want to lose it at this point."

"Well, you've told them before and I told them just now. What do you think?"

"Okay, let's just hope they've been paying attention. Let's go."

The ground debris was soggy and slippery. Winter had sneezed all over these woods. Last year's leaves clung to my ankles and whispered wetly beneath my boots. Jagged rotting sticks snagged at my pants legs. Long, brown, sticky fingered pine needles longed to warm themselves inside my collar.

The weather was temporarily on hold. Precipitation was holding in abeyance, while the temperature had seemingly made up its mind. No sound came from the heavens, and rancid clouds slipped greasily by overhead. My knees screamed at me. I knew it was just a matter of time until the lull was enveloped by the storm.

I trudged around the perimeter of the copse of beautiful old strong cedars. "Look at those magnificent trees, Lee."

"Are they significant?"

"I believe so, let's go take a look." I glanced over my shoulder to see the three cops in a clutch of winter-stripped saplings, attempting to stave off the cold. Cigarette smoke hung about their heads, disturbed only by their collective frigid breaths. We picked our way through the ground cover and came to stand inside the circle of trees. An invisible fist shot into my gut. "He brought her here...he raped her. Oh, for God's sake Lee, it's worse that I imagined...it's my worse nightmares. He's a fucking maniac, and I mean that both figuratively and literally. He's out there somewhere passing for sane, but he's a crazy as a blind dog in a meat house.

"Is this where he killed her?" Lee was right in my ear. She knew I wasn't ready to share my findings with the police because the clues were still "bare bones"—that's known as *Galgenhumor* or (gallows humor), in professions where once in awhile one must smile to keep from crying.

"Maybe, I don't know yet. But he didn't he might as well have. He forced oral sex on her and then he finished off whatever crazed fantasy he was having by raping her repeatedly."

"A real boy scout, huh?"

"Wait just a minute! Lee, you may have just stumbled onto it without realizing it."

"What?"

"Follow me."

I walked around the circle of cedars, taking careful note of a wad of scraggly maple saplings nestled in a stand of much older maples and other hardwoods. I would guess there was probably a quarter of an acre of the hardwood fledglings in the area. "Let's go," I whispered, "I think we'll find something over there in that patch of wannabe woods."

Lee was beside me, step for step. "Do you think there's enough cover here for a man to commit rape and murder and not be seen or heard?"

"Oh, yeah, there are no houses in sight, just those mobile homes that Will mentioned. But he said they were way over there." I nodded in the direction of the unseen trailer park. "Anyway it was night. Even if he were not familiar with the location, but I seriously doubt that, he wouldn't have needed a flashlight to find his way around out here. There was a full moon, November 23. If, for whatever reason, she didn't scream, and he did nothing else to draw anyone's attention, he could have done what ever he wanted to and no one would have been the wiser."

"What about the car?" She was *interviewing me* for the tape recorder that was so I wouldn't have to repeat every single word a hundred times later.

"He could have pulled off the road far enough to have called no attention to it. As a matter of fact, the night she disappeared the ground would have been dry as a bone. It hadn't rained for days. He could have driven up that old logging road and almost all the way to those cedars, *no problemo.* Hey, let's keep looking." I had stopped to light a cigarette and prepare myself for what I was afraid I might find next. I blew smoke and stalled.

"Dare, look!" Lee was emphatic but almost totally voiceless. The words caught in her throat like a hiccup.

I followed her gaze to two spindly maples just to the left and about ten paces from us. *"Holy Mere!"* I looked Lee squarely in the eye and knew we both, indeed, had seen the same thing. "Let's check the ground as unobtrusively as we can between here and there, and let's try not to disturb anything or stir up the guys' curiosity, if we can avoid it. But, by God, this time I'm going to get there first. Protocol be damned. We found it, let's check it out."

Suddenly, the weather played very little part in my chill. My gut was wound up in a hangman's knot and I wished there was a restroom handy. My knees had forgotten to ache, but were shaking like a dog shitting peach seeds in the snow. My body hair stood erect due to adrenaline and apprehension. Even a fresh cigarette couldn't calm my jagged nerves. I gave up and crushed it into a bare spot of earth with the toe of my boot. I picked it up, wrapped it in a used tissue before cramming it into my pocket, so as not to corrupt the scene.

We inched unhurriedly to the spot where the two small trees leaned toward each other, like sisters sharing secrets. Trying so very hard to appear calm and unconcerned, we inspected the smooth, tight bark of the two wiry trees. They had both suffered trauma, and I knew that when the sap rose in the spring those two saplings would bleed their juices just as surely as their hostage had.

"Look at these little knotted bits of string, Dare." Lee was nodding toward a wind and snow washed tangle of what looked like the remnants of binding twine. "Oh shit, Dare look down there at the trunks, just above the ground, the scars are there too.

"Lee, he had her tied up spread eagle between these two trees." I squatted in the rotting leaves to get a closer look at what Lee had pointed out. "This is the place Marie Zhou breathed her last."

Lee put her arm around my shoulder and spoke softly. "Dare, if you hadn't had those hideous dreams, no one would have ever found her."

"Remember, Lee, this place was Will's idea, not mine."

"Yeah, but he said it fit the map *you* drew."

"I'm not going to argue with you. We haven't found her, but you can bet the farm that this is where he killed her."

"Next question, O Sage. Where is she?"

"Now, that's a hard one, Lee. But, I'll wager she's around here somewhere—at least parts of her. My guess is he just piled leaves or stones on top of her, 'cause once he'd sated his sexual demons and killed her, he was probably anxious as a whore in church to get the hell out of this place. If she's here, by damn, we'll find her sooner or later. Look, can you see these faint dark stains along the side of this tree?"

"Where?"...Oh, yeah, now I do...do you think that may be blood?"

"My guess is yes, in triplicate. Forensics will answer that one for us. And see the scars in the bark where it looks as though something rubbed against it? Well, look closer. See these marks? They look like little cuts...like maybe they were made with a razor blade."

"Or a pocket knife." she fumbled for her cigarettes Taking her time she brought her Zippo to the tip and inhaled a double lung full of the biting smoke, "Maybe that's where the blade slipped when he cut her body down."

"Lee, he brought her out here, and either dragged her to that spot in the circle of the cedars, or maybe even convinced her he would let her go if she cooperated with him. She was, after all, only sixteen and probably scared enough to believe anything he told her. He demanded oral sex, probably both ways at various times during the evening. He had sexual intercourse with her more than once. And God only knows what he did to her in the car. If we could only find that car, we'd have his sorry balls in a vise."

"Dare, have the cops come up with any information about whether or not a trustee from anywhere around here might have been out prowling that night?"

"Not yet, and it's not likely any county mountie is going to willingly volunteer any such information. No matter how much confidence a law-boss might have in an individual, he wouldn't likely come forward and state that an inmate was out in an official car and unaccounted for after ten o'clock at night, particularly not on the night in question. You know how I think this will finally come down?"

"I don't have a clue in hell. How?"

"Some equally squalid piece of shit will use it as a bargaining chip. Some cellmate or fellow yard jockey is out there somewhere, just waiting to make a deal. Mark my words. You know that old honor among thieves crap—it's bullshit. Lee, you can go get the three stooges now. Let's see if they can figure what we're about to put directly under their noses."

* *

The flurry of evidence bags was on hold while Will Bealer called the forensics lab. "They'll be here soon, but Captain Halprin said they'd probably want to call the state lab in Nashville.

Lieutenant Calhoun volunteered, "Dare, you and Lee can go on back to Sharkey's where it's warm, or even on home if you want to. This may take quite awhile."

"Not on your life, Emmett Calhoun. You people brought me into this, and Lee and I are staying right here 'til the fat lady sings. Oh, no, you won't get rid of us that easily."

"We're not trying to get rid of you—I just thought."

"Fine, let's just understand one another. You stay, we stay." I trusted Will implicitly, however, even though I had known Emmett Calhoun longer, I wasn't so sure about him. I felt he would claim sole credit, even to Will's exclusion, if he were given half a chance. Police types are strange creatures. I knew in my head that we were physically within Will's jurisdiction, but just the same, one can never be too careful. I sat on the rotted stump of a long gone oak tree and chain-smoked until my pockets were crammed with tissue-wrapped Raleigh butts. It was becoming more apparent as the day wore on that in the battle of dry vs. wet, wet would eventually be the victor. Viscous clouds were coagulating behind the furry cedars. The barometric pressure plummeted, and I gouged though my pockets in search of my sinus atomizer. The first tendril of lightning sent shivers crawling like spiders under my skin.

"It breaks my heart." Lee was sucking on a Benson & Hedges for all it was worth.

"What does?" I knew perfectly well what she was talking about, but I also knew she wanted to talk.

"That son of a bitch doing what he did, then just pulling up stakes and splittin' like he'd been to a goddamned picnic. What kind of a heartless bastard could do a thing like that?"

146

"Lee, some people are in this life for pure self-gratification. They have no concept of the 'do unto to others…' concept. It's inconceivable to most people, thank God, but to others, it's just take, take, then take some more. Remember the old saying from our hippy youth? *If it feels good…do it?* Well, *your* hippy youth, I should say."

Lee sat pensively, watching the smoke wind itself on torpid air. "Yeah, but it sounded good at the time. Some people just take things just too fucking literally, I guess." She inhaled so deeply and held it for so long that I coughed en proxy.

* *

The forensics crew arrived along with the first drops of rain. I recognized Charlie Nickens from another time I had worked in Clarksville. He spoke to Lee and me as he unpacked his traveling lab. He introduced us to Heather Lafferty, his photographer and gofer. She was young and eager to please. In part, I guessed, to impress Charlie, who certainly had the where-with-all to help her get a position with CSI in Nashville. Not everyone is content to work in their hometown for the rest of their lives. The other part is that Charlie has the ability to make female knees go weak with the most innocent glance. He's one of those really nice guys who is totally unaware of his potential powers of persuasion. What I know, that apparently nobody has bothered to tell Heather, is that Charlie is gay. S*ans gene,* or in other words, his closet door is wide open, and he doesn't care who knows it. But he's so good at his job, the department looks the other way.

Charlie's tweezers are like a paintbrush in the fingers of a painter. He never misses a stroke. He picked up numerous particles of debris, and bagged not only bits of twine, but a tiny scrap of material, several wads of what looked like caked, cigarette tobacco. He actually found a footprint that had been preserved from the elements under layers of protective leaves. "We can't be sure about this," he warned, "could belong to just about anybody, but I'll make a plaster impression if this rain will hold off a little longer." He turned to Heather and she immediately began to photograph the shoe from every conceivable angle, with her 35 mm and then her Polaroid—taking notes after every few shots. She stood by, waiting for further instructions.

After the first few languid drops had fallen, Mother Nature cinched up her girdle and held on to her downpour, giving the plaster of Paris mold just enough time to set before she let go in full force.

"Pictures taken, evidence gathered, scene swept, Charlie announced. These trees are evidence—let's cut 'em down."

* *

"Them goddam dreams ain't as much fun as they used to be." Ricky-Dino was sucking on the soggy stub of a Lucky Strike. "They used to be like going to a pitcher show. I could get my rocks off, then go right back to sleep for the rest of the night. Not no more. They leave me with a splittin' headache and another hard-on. What good's a boner if it just hurts? My balls feel like they've been squoze in a warshin' machine wringer."

Cobra squinted into the cloud-shrouded afternoon. The sun was hiding out up there somewhere, and its masqueraded glare hurt his eyes. "I don't see how you got any meat left on that *night-stick* a yours. Hell, all you do anymore is jerk-off. It used to be once in awhile like the rest of us. But lately its like that's your job or somethin'. I don't mind tellin' you that all them moanin' and groanin' noises you make are about to get on my nerves. It used to make me horny, but not anymore. It just makes me want to kick you in the nuts. Anything to shut you up so's the rest of us can sleep without a play-by-play of your fuckin' wet dreams."

"Do you think I can help it? Well, I can't…I dream about that fuckin' little slanty-eyed bitch ever night. It's like she's fuckin' moved inside my brains or something. It's about to wreck me."

"Wreck you hell…its about to kill me. Maybe you ought to go out and bump off somebody else. That would at least give you some new dreamin' material."

"You think this is fuckin' funny, don't you?" Ricky-Dino was whiny and looking for a little sympathy. He didn't think that was too much to ask.

"Do I look like I'm laughin'? I just got through tellin' you that you better quit this shit. Hell, no, I don't think it's one little bit funny. I'm probably not going to get another solid night's sleep 'til I get outta here. I'm not the only one you're keepin' awake either. If I was you I would try to put a lid on it. Do you want everyone in here to find out who you're screwin' ever night in your fucked-up dreams?"

"Course I don't!" Ricky-Dino lit another bent and wrinkled Lucky Strike from the stub he held between his nicotine-tinted fingers. He dropped the used up butt into the slush between his sneakers. It had been so long since his feet were warm that he had forgotten. Trips out into the yard on smoking forays took him through mud, slush and even hard-packed snow, where the shade was a permanent resident. He kicked the side of the storage shed in a feeble attempt to jump-start the blood circulation to his extremities. "Shit, the fuckers hurt."

"Hey, Dino, is there anything on you that don't hurt?" Cobra was getting restless and tired of hearing the whining and complaining. "Why don't you put in a request to see the fuckin' skull doctor? Maybe he could scoop that "gook" outta your brain."

"Fuck you, Snake Dick. If you can't come up with something better than a head-fuck just keep your shitty ideas under your goddam cap. You do want me to spend the rest of my days in the fuckin' big house, don't you?" Ricky-Dino hauled off and was just about ready to hit Cobra up side the head when Cobra raised his own hand and caught Ricky-Dino's balled-up fist in mid-air.

"You know something, you fuckin' weird sonabitch?" Cobra's big yellow teeth glowered like a beaver's.

Ricky-Dino already knew he'd made a near-fatal error. "What's that?" He was making a feeble attempt to slough off his actions as a joke.

"If I was you, I would try and remember that ol' Cobra knows what you did, and then do my best to not rile him." Cobra took his leave and strode toward the lock-up where Ricky-Dino knew Curly sat behind his desk just inside the door. Ricky Dino also figured Curly had his head in one of those muscle men's "look-books." Cobra and his snake could be in one of them books, he thought...sure could.

God knows what that cocksucker's libel to say to that faggy guard. Worrying with that, Ricky-Dino forgot about his icy feet and even the beast between his legs.

* *

Lee and I stood by while Charlie and Ernest wrapped the two thin tree trunks in sheets of clear plastic and then taped their ends firmly in place. Ernest stood spread eagle between them, with a hand on each one—*almost as Marie had done*. Charlie sawed the saplings, almost even with the ground. Afterwards they carefully placed the pertinent portions into the backend of the forensics van. A huge lump grew in my throat as a cloudy vision brushed the backside of my eyeballs. I saw her suffering. I felt her pain in the pit of my own stomach. My gut ached and I wanted to scream. Lee glanced at me just in time to see a tear trickle down the track made by its predecessor. She put her arm around my shoulder, and the pressure of her fingers spoke volumes.

* *

"Hey, Lieutenant, come here. I've found something over here! Dare, you better come too."

Harold Riggins was excited, to say the least, and in my heart of hearts I knew why. "Come on, Lee," I whispered, "I think he's found her shoe."

"This way!" Harold was guiding us with his voice. He wasn't that far into the woods, however, the underbrush was a tangle of frostbitten honeysuckle vines and God knows what other wild growth that grabbed at our ankles with every step.

No one offered to touch it. The winter-warped shoe lay shrouded loosely in a cloudy chunk of semi-frozen snow. Only the vamp and forward was free of the icy grip. We stood in a piece of a circle, just gazing upon the one piece of evidence that would tell us what we had come looking for—where to find what remained of Marie Zhou. A dog howled menacingly somewhere in the distance. The dream. I almost wet my pants.

15

The trail was as cold as the ground we stood on. I picked my way around the thicket, and without disturbing its perch, I got just as close to the heel of the lone sneaker as I could. With practiced eyes, I followed the direction the toe was pointing, which was away from the crown of cedars. This meant going deeper into the woods. The cops, forensics experts and Lee stood perfectly still, as if awaiting my confirmation. *Not yet.* "May I pick it up?" I had already been told I could have the first crack at touching any of Marie's personal belongings because after other people have handled an item, I would be unable to *pick up* any residual vibes.

Charlie spoke up and said, "Let us get some shots of it first." Heather placed a ruler beside the shoe (for perspective) and proceeded to take photographs from every conceivable angle, making marks in a spiral notebook after every four or five clicks of the shutter. Finally, after satisfying herself and Charlie that every square millimeter of the sneaker, and its surroundings, had been photographed thoroughly, she stepped back and cased her Canon 35 mm. She then proceeded to take twenty or thirty Polaroid shots of the immediate area before indicating to Charlie that *that was that.* She stepped back to the periphery so I could move up and get a better look, and she handed me a pair of latex gloves. I pulled off my leather gloves and replaced them with the latex ones before reaching out to touch the soggy, white leather sneaker. As soon as I touched the rubber sole I experienced a flash of adrenaline and almost knocked the sneaker from the thicket, and onto the mud caked snow underneath. I caught it with a *whoosh* and a sigh. I held it in my hands, looking it over for anything that might have clung to it during Marie's encounter with that piece of garbage on that fateful night of November 23. As if there was a doubt in the world, I felt compelled to announce to the clutch of cops, forensics and friend, "This shoe did, in fact, belong to Marie Zhou, and she was wearing it the night she disappeared." We stood in awe, as if we were modern-day explorers who had stumbled upon

Ponce de León's elusive Fountain of Youth. *Now what?* I cradled the footwear in my gloved hands. Ripping one glove off with my teeth, I rubbed the side of the shoe—much as I think one would rub a genie's lamp. With a little luck one could be as equally effective as the other. The leather had drawn tight and the sole had warped into "V" shape, causing the entire shoe to take on the look of a convoluted boomerang. It had been a good shoe; I wore the same brand, and I knew the leather had not easily relinquished its innate suppleness. It told me a lot about the young lady who had worn it. She had good taste, and knew how to judge sneakers…obviously better than she knew how to judge her human counterparts.

Beyond my physical perspective, I *saw* a discernable mound of earth and leaves protruding from the slush and mud. I knew that somewhere under its moist surface lay a moldering, long white cardigan sweater and other things I'd just as soon not think about. With sneaker in tow, I picked my way through the honeysuckle and grapevine infested trail, past brown hollow, but nonetheless lethal barbs of last summer's blackberry thorns. They tugged at my jacket and jeans. I followed my intuition, as well as my eyes, to guide me to my objective. I had just stepped over a discarded Styrofoam cooler when I spied it. It looked like a huge nest married to the ground. Decaying leaves, dried and rotted tree limbs, mud and string (or perhaps unraveled yarn from a white cardigan sweater) had been fashioned—maybe by man—but probably by beast. I picked up a stick from the path and poked a broken end into the pile. It put me in mind of an Alligator's nest. *That friggin' goose was doing a tap dance across my grave.* A breeze shot up out of the southeast— the first thermal movement of the day. Leaves trembled in its wake. Brush tugged at its moorings and begrudgingly gave up a portion of its treasure. I spied the knobby end of a discolored bone. "Careful where you step," I warned…like I was in charge. "There may be all kinds of stuff in that heap of leaves and underbrush—maybe something taking a nap." I stopped in my tracks motioning to Heather and her trusty Canon 35 and Polaroid. She stepped up beside me. From there I guided her to the bone. She stepped forward then dropped to one knee and aimed her camera.

"What's you got there Heather?" Charlie was eager to get in there and see what there was to see.

"Spoor."

"Just exactly what kind of spoor?" Charlie was becoming apprehensive. He was an experienced forensic scientist, not easily perturbed nor disturbed, but right at that moment he was feeling none too confident. I think my methods spooked him—he wasn't the first. He knew the three officers were packing weapons, but he wasn't sure that could take care of what had shriveled his balls into a tight little package. Everyone is psychic to a certain degree—we just *know* when something terrible is about to happen.

"Well, there are some very large canine tracks. They're dog prints as opposed to wolf or coyote."

"Okay, anything else?" Charlie wanted to get on with this and get back to the office where he could pick through his bonanza under the glare of lab lights.

"Dog shit," she announced matter-of-factly. "Tons of it."

"Lee had been silent just about as long as the law allowed, "My mama always told me that a dog never shits where he eats."

"Lee," I proffered, "these are not canines your mama would have been philosophizing about in her spare time."

Heather took nearly another ten minutes getting various shots of piles of dog defecation. She aimed her cameras at the mounds and then, last but not least, she hunkered over the bone that was peeking out of the heap of rotten organic matter. *Someone else could scoop the poop for the lab techs to go through.*

"Now?" I was champing at the bit to get hold of the bone, not to mention that my feet had lost all feeling within my sturdy hiking boots. I couldn't decide if they were cold, too constricted or just tired. Maybe all of the above.

"Okay, I'm done." The photographer had finished her chores, and Charlie stepped up beside me, where he would wait until I fondled the bone and made the pronouncement that it was, indeed, a bone from the body of Marie Zhou. It was a long bone, and even before it could be positively identified, I knew it was the femur I had seen so clearly in my nightmare. I passed it to Charlie, and he slipped it carefully into a large plastic sleeve to haul back to the lab, along with a sample from each of the piles of doggy doo, wads of what could be tobacco, twine, yarn, shoe impression and saplings.

What a job, I mused to myself, while looking at my partner-in-crime. She nodded as though she too had had a similar thought. *What a shitty job.*

* *

Supper was canned mushroom soup and a chicken salad sandwich. I sat at the kitchen table where I perused the day old *Tennessean,* and half watched the news on Channel 5. Chris Clark droned on about the proposed state income tax and other unwelcome tidbits. Meteorologist Ron Howes promised that it wouldn't snow tomorrow; however, he added that the probability that the sun would make an appearance before the end of the week was dim. I didn't care. I glanced through the kitchen window where my eyes were met by a solid curtain of fog. There was a faint smudge of luminescence where I knew the moon patiently waited for the weather to clear. From all indications she would have quite a wait.

I hit the remote and banished the toothy news team into the cosmos. I flipped on the Bose and was met by the mellifluous Roberta Flack—one of the few pop-singers in the world who has the ability to make me wish I had a live in-lover. I closed the paper, shut my eyes and floated in my own little dream world. Then Earl Sheib, the king of the cheap automobile-paint job, destroyed my mood. He was hawking a $139.99 offer to rejuvenate somebody's worn-out old jalopy. I cut him off at the knees.

I pushed back my chair, folded the newspaper and placed it on the pile with its predecessors. I put my bowl, spoon and plate in the sink; put the crackers back into the tin and placed them high on the shelf in the pantry. "Now," I said aloud. Hillary looked up from the chair where she's taken up residence while I ate. "Let's go, Girl." I turned off the radio, the overhead light, and left the kitchen in darkness.

There had been a message from Felix on my answering machine when I came in. He had called to invite me to attend the symphony with him Wednesday night. I had called him back to say I would love to go if I didn't get bogged down in Clarksville. I had begun to explain how things were going when he asked if he could come over and listen in person, rather than over the phone lines. I was actually too tired, but did feel a little tingle at the base of my spine when he asked. So, of course, I said, "Sure...come on over."

He was still at his office when he called. He would be here as soon as he cleared his desk, he had said. Yes, he had eaten a sandwich, and wasn't coming for food. Just exactly what was he coming for? I conjectured—like I didn't know. At this point the answer to my question wasn't too important. I enjoyed his company immensely, and not to be crass, he was quite a lay.

I figured I had a least an hour before Fel would show up at my door, so I could take my time and get myself presentable at the same time. I decided on a bath rather than a shower. I had fired up the gas logs, turned on the stereo, and I was working my way into quite a mood. I ran my bath and sprinkled in a favorite bubble bath. I lit candles and turned off the overhead light. As I eased my tired body into the tub, I could feel the weariness leach from my bones. Oh, it felt so good. I lay there, my mind wandering aimlessly when I found myself really looking forward to the coming evening. Marie Zhou was nowhere in my frame of reference. Clarksville was a little town to the northwest that held no special meaning for me. Calhoun, Bealer and Riggins were but names. The whole hateful tragedy was laid to rest like another bad dream that I would be forced to deal with when the sun came up in the morning—but not tonight.

* *

The night air sometimes creeps though the pores in an old house like mine. I had saved it from demolition a few years before and had done major renovations. But nevertheless, it was as though it remembered its early life before R19 insulation, and I was part of that memory. Before my bath I had checked the carousel in the CD player and checked the ice supply behind the bar.

I brushed my teeth, wiped the tub down with my bath towel and straightened up the bathroom before moving on to my bedroom. I hung my terry cloth robe on the hook inside my closet door, before even thinking about what I would wear. I chose a nice pair of running pants and matching sweatshirt, topping the whole thing off with a tiny touch of *Eau de Joy* (which in my belief, is the sexiest perfume on the planet) behind each ear and in the hollow of my throat. Felix would come in wearing his lawyer persona, but that couldn't be helped. He would just have to get used to the real me if there were to be an honest relationship between us.

I did condescend to makeup. I blew my hair into my regular soft fluff: what Lee calls the Dare-do. I was ready when the doorbell rang.

* *

"You buttfuckin' Curly or is it the other way 'round?" Ricky-Dino had the delicacy of a runaway freight train.

"You askin' me if I'm queer?"

"No, I'm just askin' who's doin' it to who?"

"You know that ain't none o' your bidness, don't you?"

"Hey, asshole, I done told you ever thing there is to know about me…you tellin' me you can't tell me one little thing about your love life?"

"It ain't my fuckin' love life, shit-face. It's the means to an end—you know what that means?"

Ricky-Dino was no rocket scientist, but then neither was Cobra. "Can't you just talk English? I reck'n it means it's an easy enough way to get your rocks off."

"Exactly, Boy Wonder. But dammit, we don't buttfuck."

"You mean you suck-off a goddam deputy dawg? Jesus H. Christ, Cobra. What does the screw think about your big old snaky dick? I'll bet he gets so tore up at the very sight of that monster that he cain't hardly hold his load back, don't he? Ya'll 69 it too?"

"You're a nosy little sonabitch for a baby-fucker. Does the ol' adder make you horny too?"

"I ain't no baby-fucker, you faggot cocksucker you. And no, for your sorry information, it *don't* make me horny. It's just the biggest, decoratedest up prick I ever seen, that's all."

"Dino, if I was you, I would watch my nasty tongue. That's what I would do if I was you. You get my drift?"

"You threatenin' me?"

"Like I said, asshole, you don't need me to threaten you. Them dreams you have are all the threatenin' you need. One o' these nights somebody's gonna hear your babblin' about rapin' and bashin' in that girlie's brains, and then your ass is gonna be grass and that somebody's apt to mow you down. I told you what you need is to go visit the head doctor and get rid of them dreams."

"I ain't! Now shut up about it," Ricky-Dino whined.

"And you quit pokin' your nose in my private bidness." Cobra warned.

"Pokin's right, but I ain't puttin' my nose there. Okay, you just stay outta my stuff, and I don't care who you fuck…just don't do it where I am."

"Now if that ain't the goddam pot callin' the goddam kettle black. "Cobra turned his head and sucked on his Pall Mall while Ricky-Dino, his balls shuddering as his overly active imagination got the better of him, looked on. Cobra tossed the butt into the slush, turned around and stood virtually toe-to-toe with his fellow trustee. "You know what Dino? If Curly got your scrawny, wore-out, nub-of-dick between his jaws, just once, you'd never dream about that *gook* ever again."

"You have turned queer, ain't you?"

"No, asshole, I ain't turned nothin'. I just happen to be enterprisin'. Make the most of what you got. That's my motto. Make the most of what you got. Shut your eyes and head's head, my man. Exspecially if it's got nice curls to grab holt of.

**

The sour mash whiskey set off a series of tiny explosions when it hit my stomach. Whatever weariness that survived the bath, was expunged by good old Jack Daniels. Felix had stripped off his jacket and tie before sitting down, and I poured him a brandy, before easing down beside him on the floor in front of the fireplace. He put his arm around me and eased closer. His tongue, slick with the pungent potable, embraced mine in a passion-laced kiss—I responded eagerly. He smelled good enough to eat. I asked him if he were hungry—he said yeah, and grinned evilly as I unbuttoned his dress shirt; he shucked out of his suspenders. He wore no undershirt, just smooth, hairless, olive skin met my lips.

"Dare," he nuzzled my neck, "ummm, what's that perfume you're wearing?" He was obviously ready, and I like to think my *Joy* had a little something to do with it. We made exquisitely, unhurried love among the cushions in front of the fire, while Andrea Bocelli sang quietly in the background—enhancing the already heightened mood. I'm not sure just how apropos it was, but we finished together just as Sarah Brightman joined Bocelli in "The Prayer."

We lay in semi-darkness as the reflected flames danced around the walls and onto our naked bodies. My head rested on Fel's firm bicep. His other arm rested across my breasts. He was on his side, facing me in the firelight. His brown eyes, so pale and clear, reflected the golden hues as if they were mirrors in the night. He smiled and pulled me to him, kissed me deeply and asked me if I wanted another drink.

"Why not?" I answered, rolling up in the throw that I pulled from the chair beside me. I propped myself against the hearth and lit a cigarette. I decided it couldn't get much better than this.

Felix, in his birthday suit, was across the room pouring drinks for the two of us. He stood in near darkness. "Mine's in the square bottle." I directed.

"I know, you don't mix your liquors, neither do I. Your Christmas brandy hits the spot."

"Something surely does," I teased.

**

I was hungry. Nothing whets my appetite like wonderfully satisfying sex. Felix was dozing, and I hated to disturb his rest. I thought to myself, *you're the best looking man I've ever looked at,* as my fingers traced lazy circles across his chest. He opened one eye, as if reading my thoughts. He grinned and playfully stuck out his tongue at me. I responded in kind. He grabbed me and pulled me on top of him. Food was soon the farthest thing from my mind. The next thing I knew we were in my bed. Fel had found my "on" switch, and I loved every minute of it. John Tesh's melodic piano tones were winding through my bedroom speakers when once more my muscles bunched up in a collective knot, waiting for my neural connectors' signal that it was time for another orgasmic festival. We came together, and it was deliciously exhausting. They were just getting better and better each time. *What is the apex in such matters?* I wondered.

We lay in a heap among the knotted bed covers. "Are you hungry?" I ventured again.

"Yeah, I am, kinda. How bout I make us an omelet?" He was volunteering for kitchen duty.

"I'll do it, but you can make a pot of coffee if you want to, or is it too late for caffine?"

"Caffine is a stimulant, remember?" He stretched his gym-firm body with feline grace. I had often watched Hillary Kitten make those same selective moves. He propped himself on one elbow, leaned over and kissed me. I was beginning to get back into the mood when he announced, "Eggscuse me...time for chow."

I grabbed my terry cloth robe from the hook in the closet and padded barefoot in his wake. He turned around in the great room and asked me to start the music over again on the CD player. He held me against the door facing and kissed my mouth before nuzzling inside my robe, where he kissed my breasts. He returned to my mouth for one more searching kiss before backing off and raising his hands. "I give up," he said, "you've got me where you want me."

Did I?

* *

"Cobra...you awake? Ricky-Dino was scared to shut his eyes after what his fellow inmate has told him. What if he really had been talking in his sleep? He didn't know if Cobra was bullshitting him or not. He couldn't always tell. He never could tell, as a matter of fact. All he knew was that he couldn't take any further chances. But he didn't have the slightest notion of what to do about it. "Cobra...hey, snake dick...you awake? No answer seemed forthcoming, so Ricky-Dino slid his scrawny body off his bunk and eased over to where Cobra lay nude in the semi-darkness. The huge tattooed penis lay heavy on his stomach. Ricky-Dino became almost mesmerized, watching as it twitched like it had a mind of its own. *Shit,* he thought to himself, *anything with a head that big's got to have its own mind.* He was musing thus, when Cobra opened his eyes and saw Ricky-Dino watching his snake.

"What the fuck you think you're doin'?" He raised up on his elbows, the sudden movement caused the flaccid penis to hit the mattress between his legs and just lie there like a big ol' decorated summer sausage. "I said what the fuck you think you're doin?" Cobra repeated, not caring who he might be disturbing. "You little fish-eyed bastard, don't you even think about it. You hear me? You think you're gonna slobber all over me you go another think comin!"

"Wait a minute, Cobra…it ain't what you think…I just come over here to get your advice and a little help…that is, if you're willin'. I need some help bad…I'm scared I might do what you said…you know…talk in my sleep about what I done."

"Whatta you want outta me? I ain't easin' your pain, if that's what you're after, you greasy-dicked little pecker spit."

"That ain't it. You said earlier Curly might could help me. He might get my mind off all that other shit…you think you might ask him for me?"

"Dino, what do I look like? Your fuckin' pimp?"

"Cobra, no, but you gotta help me…I told you everything…you know what kind of a fix I'm in…can I count on you, buddy?"

Dino, first of all, I ain't your buddy. Second of all, you got your ownself into this fix, I didn't, and Curly sure as hell didn't. Anyhow, even if he is a fuckin' AC/DC, I don't know that his tastes don't run higher'n you. He'd probably floss his teeth with your pencil dick. But even if he did, it'd be the best damned flossin' you're ever apt to get."

"Will you just talk to him?"

"Well, I reck'n I will if it'll shut your yap. He's gettin' ready to go off duty about now, and he won't be back 'til Friday at four. Hell, you got me wide awake. I'll go ask him now if you promise to either go to sleep, or lay over there in your bunk and keep your yap shut. If you feel the need to jerk-off, go to the can and do it. Got it?" Cobra crawled out of his bunk, pulled on his raggedy drawers and started toward the hall where Deputy Curly was gathering up his magazines in preparation for shift change. Cobra seemed to change his mind and headed back in Ricky-Dino's direction. "Wait a minute, weasel dick, I forgot to ask. Whatta you want?"

"Whatcha mean?"

"I mean just what I said. Do you want him to give you head, do you want to give him head or do you want to buttfuck him…or him buttfuck you? Just what the hell you want…or do you want a sample of each…like a buffet?"

"Dino was twisting his hands in his lap. His penis stirred under his touch. Head I reck'n…ain't that what he done to you?"

Ignoring the question, Cobra replied, "It's the best you'll ever get. Might even ruin your hankering for under-age females."

Dino flinched, but ignored the verbal jab. "Okay, Cobra, you ask him and I'll be obliged."

Cobra rounded the corner just in time to catch Curly before he left the building. They talked for a moment, and Curly grimaced but eventually nodded his head in agreement. He turned his back on Cobra and walked toward the locker room where his personal items lay waiting for him in his locker. Cobra's veiled blackmail threat had unnerved him.

"Okay, Dino it's all set up…Friday after dark out in the maintenance shed. Tell him you'll let him suck you off for a pack of Lucky Strikes, then if he goes for that, tell him you'll suck him off for a carton of the same."

"Yeah?"

"Yeah. Now you want o' go out for a smoke? If you do then get your scrawny ass up and let's get some clothes on. If you don't, then get your weenie whack'n done while I'm outside." Cobra sat on the side of his bunk and shoved his shoes though his pants legs. He stood up, zipped his britches and pulled on his jacket, knit cap and gloves. Ricky-Dino waved him off with a fishy grin. Thanks, Cobra…you won't be sorry."

Cobra already was sorry, but he said, "Yeah, I heard you." He followed the yellow glow to the hallway, pulled a Pall Mall out of the pack, and stuck it behind his ear. He hoped Dino would be fast asleep when he got back inside. Oh, God, how he hoped he would be asleep.

* *

Sated, I walked Felix to the door where I kissed him. He responded with a low growl in his throat. He took my face in his hands and smiled so sweetly that I wanted to hold him tightly and not let him slip away into the night. "Do you have to go?"

"Yeah, unfortunately I do. I have to be in court at 8:30 in the morning, and I've got briefs to go over. Is it okay if I come back tomorrow night…or would you like to come to my house?"

"I don't know," I teased, "maybe...what's the incentive?"

"I'll cook dinner. How 'bout a couple of inch and a half thick porterhouse steaks? We'll have baked potatoes oozing with butter and sour cream. And baby peas with mushrooms, salad...then we'll slather each other with whipped cream for dessert! How's that sound?"

"Sticky, besides I don't eat red meat...maybe another time would be better."

"You're not getting off that easy. How about crab and shrimp gumbo or maybe you'd prefer crawfish *etouffeé*? Name your poison, m'lady."

I was amazed at his culinary offerings, "Sounds like maybe you've spent some time in south Lousiana (rolling the word around on my tongue 'til it came out Looozyannna).

"Make fun of me will you? As a matter of fact, I taught contract law at LSU for a few semesters. You know, Louisiana State University in Baton Rouge" (which he pronounced Ba-tawn Roouzz in the manner of the Cajun dialect).

"Crab gumbo does wonderful things for my disposition. What time?"

"If your disposition gets any better, I'm not sure I can take it. How about 6:30? I should be home before then. I'll tell you what, though." He pulled his key ring out of his pocket and fumbled to release a sturdy brass house key. "If court runs long, and I get behind at the office, you take this and let yourself in. Fix yourself a drink, and I'll be right along behind you. I promise. He closed my hand over the key and gave me a kiss on the lips.

"I don't know where you live," I rationalized. "I don't even know your address." He took a gold-trimmed tortoiseshell Waterman fountain pen from his inside jacket pocket. I grabbed a scrap of paper and he wrote. He capped his pen, handed me the paper and kissed me again.

"See you at 6:30. He closed the door behind him. I was too tired to think tonight—or this morning—whatever it was. I fell back into my bed, plunging, almost immediately, into a mindless, dreamless shadowland. *To sleep, perchance **not** to dream.*

* *

I was jerked to awareness by the coldest, most penetrating scream I'd ever heard. It was my voice, inside my head. My blood stopped dead in my veins while my senses grappled with what seemed nothing akin to reality. I listened until my ears throbbed. Silence pounded around me. I gathered my wrap about me in an effort to stave off the dankness that seemed to have swallowed me whole. I ventured a step into the dark unknown. There was not a trace of natural or artificial light to guide me on my way. I could see nothing, but I sensed I was not alone. I felt, rather than heard, an ominous palpitation in the vast void. I knew no sense of time, up or down, right or left, hot or cold—only tepid sweat-laced consternation. There it was again. The sensation Jonah must of felt when he found himself in the belly of the great fish. A part of some huge beast's life force, breathing another's fetid, secondhand air. I felt the bitterness of bile rising in the back of my throat. I swallowed deeply several times to tamp my runaway emotions. As my eyes became increasingly accustomed to my caliginous surroundings, the mist and the dark added to my discomfort. And as I endeavored to divine where I was, I felt my psyche banging on the back door of rationality in a valiant effort to get a grip on some semblance of reality. There was no logical, but every physical reason for me to feel trepidation—overwhelming unfamiliarity being but one. That was not all; the place exuded certain formidability, just nothing I could put my finger on—exactly.

Then there was the odor! The place reeked of soured gym socks that had been left to molder over the summer on the floor of a XXX movie theatre. I couldn't remember the last time my olfactory system had been so violently assailed. I knew the surroundings, but yet I didn't. I ventured forth tenuously…eyes slowly adjusting, yet still unable to see more than a step or two in front of my face. Where was the moon?

The subtle cracking sound was as if something awash in the congealed dimness were munching on a dry stick—or bone. Oh, Holy Mary, Mother of God! My consternation seemed to stir the creatures that inhabited that evil place. Feral growls penetrated my immediate surroundings, renewing the stench that perhaps emanated from the bowels of hell itself. I heard her muffled scream. I turned to run. My own fear-stricken muscles held me locked in place. My lungs were constricting against the filth they were attempting to filter. I was desperately trying to breathe, but there seemed to be no clear, uncontaminated oxygen around me.

She screamed, or rather moaned, again. Once more I tried to run. "She's dead. I can't help her now. I may not be able to help myself if I don't get back home. Home? Where is home?"

"Who the fuck's there?"

A frightened, tremulous, wrapped in madness, masculine voice intruded upon the palpable silence like a spring-loaded switchblade…then it was gone.

"Who want's to know?" I queried with much more bravado than I actually felt.

Nothing. Not another word. I felt as though I had been sucked into a vacuum, and my blood couldn't decide whether to boil or freeze solid.

There was the agonizing moan again. This time, I got a bearing. I turned, and like a blind person, gingerly edged my way in the general direction from whence the sound had emanated. If I couldn't make my escape circumspectly, then maybe the direct approach would furnish the answer to my dilemma. I rarely perspire, or not until recently. My underarms were damp, and the hair on the back of my head lay plastered against my skull. My tongue felt as though it had been crammed into a jar of peanut butter then pushed up against the roof of my mouth and left to dry. My nose was parched as the Sahara in August and felt as though it might hemorrhage bloody flames at any moment.

Heavy breathing. A voice reached out across the expanse to me. **"Who's there, goddammit?!"**

I knew I was infringing on his territory, whoever he was, and I knew from the sound of him that he would prove to be a viperous adversary. At best, I had no business being here...wherever here was.

More heavy breathing. Sobbing, moaning. A gallimaufry of vocalizations blending in pleasure/pain.

"Marie?" Nothing ventured, nothing gained.

"I ain't askin' again after this...who the fuck's there? One more sound out of whoever you are, and I'm comin' to get your ass!" The voice rose in craze-tinged vibrato.

Who's more frightened of whom? I wondered silently—no real doubt in my mind.

Sobbing again...grunting, moaning...the slap of flesh against flesh. The reek of animal sensuality rode the night like wood-smoke in winter. I heard him hit his peak. The expulsion of unconsciously held breath that had gathered in his lungs during those last anticipatory moments before what sounded like animalist orgasm had grabbed his reason (or lack thereof) by the tail and flung it headlong into uncontrollable, ecstatical frenzy.

* *

Violent cursing and the sound of wet kissing slipped between the tree branches that had become increasingly visible as the darkness de-coagulated, easing its grip on my senses. I could see the two of them: her, a lost soul, him, her self-appointed tormentor. I was reasonably sure he could see me. There was naught but dead air and cold sweat between us. I could go no further. I could only watch as he zipped up his jeans and paraded around her like a cock-of-the-walk. I could see, even in his deranged state of mind, that he too realized I was but a hapless bystander in his world. I watched, without recourse, as he dragged her out of my focus. They were gone for some time, and for a while I thought the whole episode had vanished as quickly as it had appeared. No such luck. I saw them re-emerge from the mist. She was bound and tethered. Her hands were twisted behind her back. She still wore no clothes, save for a long cardigan, and it was not buttoned. Her nakedness was exposed to the frigid elements. He threw her down on the carpet of leaves in the midst of several majestic cedar trees that formed a near perfect circle. She winced as her arms were pinioned beneath the weight of her body. He unzipped his jeans and exposed himself to her. He fondled himself before savagely dropping down on top of her slender body. Again I tried to turn away, but my head would not move, nor could I shut my eyes. I looked on while his animal lust diminished her once again. He was like a wild rabbit. It took him no time to reach his lecherous climax and zip up again. He jerked her up by her long ebony hair that glistened despite the clinging leaves and debris. She was no longer wearing the sweater. He ripped the binding from her wrists. Pulling another length of twine from his back pocket, he strung her up between two saplings. First, he bound each wrist tightly to a tree. Then, he spread her ankles wide apart and bound each, in turn, to the saplings, leaving the soles of her feet—one shod, the other bare—pressed into the cold dry leaves. She was strung up spread-eagle for his demented self-gratification. Her eyes were covered with a makeshift blindfold, and something had been cruelly stuffed into her mouth. For all intents and purposes, she was blind and mute. Finished with this chore, and apparently satisfied with his labor, he disappeared from the scene. A few minutes passed before I smelled the pungent odor of stale cigarette tobacco smoldering somewhere beyond my sight. It triggered my urge to smoke which, all things considered, made me feel ashamed of myself.

There was no sensation of time in this place, but it seemed that he was gone for more than just a few minutes. I saw him reappear through the curtain of time, space or whatever. He approached the girl with the stealth of a cat. I couldn't determine whether or not she knew he was nearby. He had his hand on his swollen crotch. What a horny bastard was he. He rubbed himself through the denim material of his britches before he apparently decided there was no quelling the tide. He unzipped his fly, jerked open the button and his ready penis jumped into his waiting palm. He curled the fingers of his right hand around it and caressed it like a long lost loved one. He stroked himself while silently closing the distance between himself and the girl. A few feet from where she was hanged in a quasi-crucifixional pose, he bent to the ground and picked up something in his left hand. I could see it was a medium-sized rock that he clasped in his fist. As he grew closer, he raised the rock higher and worked more vigorously on his erection. I watched gaped-jawed, helpless in the midst of a mute scream, as he brought the stone down forcefully on the back of the girl's bowed head. Blood and brain matter exploded from her skull. Simultaneously, the man's penis exploded in ejaculated fury. He kneaded it affectionately, long after the sensation had dissipated. He allowed it to hang limply between his legs, as he raised his clenched fists above his head in an unmistakable exhibition of self-exultation. After a few stupefying moments, he pulled up his jeans from where they hung on his bony hips, and stuffed his flaccid penis back home, before zipping his fly. He spread his legs and with his right hand, he adjusted himself from the outside.

He no longer seemed cognizant of my presence as he went about the business of cutting the girl's bloodied remains from between the trees. He had pulled a small penknife from his pants pocket and sawed through the heavy twine that had held her so effectively. First her ankles, then her arms. He allowed her lifeless body to drop to the ground, not bothering to stem her fall. He dragged her like a felled deer, her head bouncing silently over the hard winter ground. His left hand brushed his crotch just before they disappeared into the murk.

* *

The groaning and sobbing of lust and pain gave way to the mewling grumbles of beasts, not of any earthly plane—restless whining of the canine variety, impatient creatures of the night waiting their turn. I saw nothing, but I knew they lay in those ethereal woods, licking their chops and biding their time. There was no hurry in that place of perpetual darkness.

* *

The scream returned. It pierced the night like a blade through chocolate pudding. Dear God, it was my voice. My own ravings were dragging me back from where the dead and the undead dine as couples—a place where creatures foul and vile shoot craps on the souls of newcomers. A grave dug in the side of every human mind since Adam—hell to the believer.

16

My bed was a wreck. Sheets had been ripped from their elasticized moorings, and the bedspread and pillows were thrown asunder on the floor. My heartbeat was off the chart, and my blood pressure would have to be peeled off the ceiling. My body was so drenched with cold sweat that I felt the chill radiating from the windowpanes across my bedroom. I knew I was going to be sick, so I struggled from my barren mattress and made my way toward the bathroom, barely in time to retch away the dream.

Face washed and teeth brushed, I was truly grateful to be alone. *Thank you, Jesus that Fel didn't stay the night; otherwise, I probably would have never seen him again.* The explanation of my bizarre, phantasmal dream—and after effects—would have most likely put the kibosh on any meaningful future relationship. No matter how much we had in common in bed—ghoulish nightmares do not engender permanent bonding.

I carefully retraced my path through the dream in which I'd been entrapped only a short while before. I had subliminally ventured into an uncharted netherworld, and although most of my dreams can by no means be classified as normal, this one defied even unconventional interpretation. Even more frightening was the fact that I had not been alone in this hellish venture. I had been transported psychically, or by some other esoteric means, into the nocturnal foray of another…into the nightmarish exploits of the creature who had wrenched the life from Marie Zhou's body. Cross dreaming is relatively virginal territory. I shuddered, and my skin crawled with revulsion for that beast that crawled on his belly in his own slime. And I had seen him this night. I had seen him commit his murderous debauchery—seen him rip life's blood from the veins of an innocent teenager he had never seen before. I had seen him gloat and revel in the rape and devastation of the young woman: crimes of the most heinous, lowest order. If there is any retributive justice, that flagitious piece of offal will spend eternity in hell, swimming in the pustulant vomit of his fellow demons. I would turn it over to my little Filipinos.

Lying back down, I dragged the sheet off the floor and across my body, while attempting to find a comfortable spot to rest my throbbing head. I glanced at the alarm clock; its green pulsating numerals only added to my discomfiture. It was 3:30 a.m. I had several hours before the winter sun would crawl laboriously out of the east. Plenty of time to either try to go back to sleep or *think*. The latter seemed inevitable. My mind was swimming in a sea of mental trash, and I wanted more than anything to eradicate it. In exasperation, I hauled my feet over the side of the bed and headed back toward the bathroom, then the familiar goose grabbed me by the shirttail and spun me on my heel. *You saw him!* Mind and body were not in sync—neither was awake enough to catch the other's drift. *Murphy, pay attention! You saw him! Now, all you've go to do is figure out who the son of a bitch is. Where were those little **Tagalogs** when I needed them most?* Stunned by the realization that the culprit's physical appearance had been made known to me, I sagged heavily against the doorframe. Then feeling completely hollow inside, I shook my head in denial. I couldn't deal with the enormity of it all. *Hell, Miss Scarlet, worry about it tomorrow—no sense in waking anybody at this ungodly hour.*

I washed my hands and made my way toward the kitchen. I thought about flipping on the Bose but decided against it. I pulled open the refrigerator door and stared into the gleaming porcelain cave, as I had watched all my sons do at one time or another—like something deliciously appetizing would magically appear before my eyes. Nothing did, so I poured myself a glass of skim milk. Perhaps the milk would settle me down so I could catch a few more winks before the sun—as in the words of an old song—caught me crying. Or whatever.

I rinsed my glass and put it on the top shelf of the dishwasher. Studying the washer's interior, I recognized that I nearly always ran out of clean dishes before this thing was full enough to wash a load. I sometimes wondered why I bothered to use it—*maybe because I'm lazy?* To keep my mind occupied (and out of the woods) I debated the question, as I headed back toward my bedroom. *God, I'm rambling...I'm discombobulated!* I went to the bathroom one more time, just to assure myself of the uninterrupted passing of what was left of this ragged night and early morning. I brushed my teeth for the second time, trying diligently to scrub away the bad taste left in my mouth by that hideous dream. Exhausted, I drifted into a troubled slumber...*please, dear God, don't let me go back...*

* *

The night-cloaked woods were alive with winter's hidden, skulking, night creatures. The dogs, of course, then there were other beasts, as well as a mélange of domestic animals gone feral. It seems all God's children must have a place to call home. Also to be counted were the various house-cats that bargained their souls, flesh and bones every time they took a shortcut through these woods. Did children play here anymore? God, I could only pray they did not.

The entire forest smelled sweet with the crispness of new winter. That would soon be a thing of the past. Evil was about to evacuate its bowels in this glade; in this long ago picnic spot, this former children's land of pretend. Once spring comes, I suspected not even the scrubbiest weeds would grow within the crown of cedars.

"W-Who's…t-there?" The hesitant words trembled as they garbled from his mouth. He thought he had heard the forest groan. "I said, who the fuck's there?!" Madness lurked at the corners of his lips, and sprang full-blown from his hooded eyes. His breathing was labored, as he lay reclining on his elbows with his legs spread apart. A young woman's face was buried in his lap. His apprehension over an unknown presence, could not override the sensation that was growing in his loins. One thing at a time. He grabbed the head in his lap and roughly pushed it down on his organ in an effort to expedite the overwhelming release he was birthing—it ripened into a scream as it clawed its way through his belly and toward his testicles. His mind dissolved into flashing-neon exclamation as the throbbing explosion culminated between his legs. Choking, gurgling sounds came from the girl's throat, and she pulled her mouth away from his body in order to gasp for air. He drew back his hand as if to hit her, then seemed to change his mind, as some post-coital goodwill temporarily tapped into his black heart. "Okay, girlie, you can quit now…you done good. You want I should do you now?"

She answered by raising her haggard, semen-smeared face and spit his own pleasure back at him—it landed with a splat between his outstretched legs. She wiped her mouth on her bare arm, grimaced, and spat again.

"Okay, girlie, you ain't got no idee what you're missin'—I reck'n you can go back to suckin' on your own nasty sock…see if you like that better'n my

169

cock. If you change your mind just raise your hand." He heard the forest moan again, and without the distraction of animalistic blindness, he gave it his full attention.

He cocked his head, as if that would give him an auditory advantage. He held the girl loosely by the wrist and inched backwards, searching the moonlit glade and straining to pierce the darkness beyond. The girl, wearing one shoe and standing beside the preoccupied man, drew back her foot and kicked weakly at him, striking a glancing blow to his groin area— momentarily he faltered. She stumbled forward, but her getaway was abruptly aborted. He tightened his grip considerably, turned, and dragging the girl, he made his way toward the patrol car. Using the ignition key, he opened the trunk where he found a spool of binding twine.

"Look girlie, you give pretty good head, but that don't mean I can have you running around loose out here, so I'm gonna hav'ta tie you up. I ain't gonna hurt you, so just be still. You try another stunt like kickin' me in the nuts again, and I'm goin' to carve out your pussy and feed it to you for breakfast. Whatta you think about that? Bet you'd rather eat me, wouldn't you? Yeah, that's the ticket"

Suddenly it was as though I was inside her head, looking out. He sat her down beside the patrol car and watched as tears tracked their way down her soiled, yet pretty face—leaking their way from under the blindfold he had wound around her eyes. She pursed her lips in defiance, sensing that it infuriated him. He jumped up, grabbed the twine and twisted it around her wrists in several tight loops. She could feel the blood deserting her fingers. She thought she heard the sound of his hand rubbing denim (as if he were feeling himself though his jeans). Perhaps he was just checking it see if everything were still in place. I could "feel" her mind run amok. She wondered what kind of perverted maniac this was who had pulled her over and lured her from her car—erasing any semblance of civilized life that she had previously known. She decided then and there, if she were given the chance, she would never stop for anyone ever again. Cop or not—she would welcome arrest for evading a police officer, rather than go through anything like this again. She would never again stop for anyone, unless she found a brightly lit area with lots of people bustling about. Suddenly she thought about her mother and father. They were here for the holidays. Would she ever see them again? Her heart ached in her chest. She thought about her aunt and uncle who had been so generous to let her live with them while she got her education in the United States. And Terry—she did love Terry—or she thought she did. Otherwise, how could anything as sweet and exciting as they had experienced together, be so ugly and hurt so bad with this animal who had savaged her? She had never reached a climax like Terry always did, but he had promised her with a little patience she would. She had looked forward to that. Now she was sure she never would—not with anyone.

"Hey, girlie!" his voice cut though her contemplative haze and jerked her back to vicious reality. "Let's go, I gotta figure out what to do with you... 'til I'm ready to go." He grabbed her long sweater off the ground and tossed it around her shoulders. They made their way back to the opening in the midst of cedar trees. Off to the side, he spied a pair of saplings—and made his decision. He pulled twine from his pocket before cutting the bindings on the girl's wrists. He spread her arms, then her legs between the infant trees, tying her spread-eagle between them. Her wrists and ankles were bound tightly and uncomfortably against the rough bark. Her feet, only one of which had a shoe on, were pressed into the rough, cold leaves. He paced around in the tree-dappled moonlight, eyeing his trophy while caressing his crotch. He walked up to her, exaggeratedly rubbing his bulging jeans against her shivering, nude body. "Lookie here, girlie! Did you ever see anything good as this before? Oh, s'cuse me, I forgot you can't see, but you already know how good it is, don't you? I reck'n you gotta a boyfriend you been lettin' bang you—ain't that right?" Pretty little thang like you gotta be fucked reg'lar or else dry up on the vine. I bet some ol' boy gets in your britches might near ever night—ain't that right?"

By the time he had his jeans unzipped and the button yanked open, his penis was swollen to the point of pleasurable pain. He continued to talk to his captive, even though her mind (as well as her blindfolded eyes) was closed to the crazy man who stood caressing what was apparently the most important thing in his life...his stiff penis. He stroked it like a man in love—albeit a sick and demented Narcissistic, self-obsessed love. Though she couldn't see his face, she could hear the madness in his voice as he made love to himself. She heard him tremble ecstatically as his orgasm racked his being and splashed on the leaves between his sneakered feet. She heard him zip his jeans and stomp off somewhere out of earshot.

* *

"What the fuck am I gonna do now?" He heard the woods come alive again, and he was worried about the girl. His wretched, demented mind was in a quandary.

171

He cocked his head and listened to the night. *"I ain't askin' again...who the fuck's out there anyhow...show your yella self, if you ain't scared to."* Nothing. Then he saw something. A form appeared in the distance—across the woods in the moonlight. A woman—someone he couldn't quite recognize—her face was in shadows. He thought there was something familiar there, but he just couldn't put the pieces together in the right order. Besides, it made his head hurt to think too hard. She was doing nothing...just watching him. *"Who are you bitch? You wanta good fuckin' too? Come on over here...there's a plenty to go around. Come on, bitch! You scared you might like it too much? Betcha ain't never had no real man before. Come on over here. Let a real man show you what it's all about!"* She didn't move. She just stood watching him make a further fool of himself.

"I bet you ain't really there. I bet you're just a fuckin' fig-newton of my imagination...that's it, ain't it? I'm sleepin' in my bunk, and this is just another one of my fuckin' dreams...ain't that right?"

She answered—to his surprise and dismay. *"Yes, it is, you crazy son of a bitch. It's just a dream, but now I know where you are...don't hold your breath, you worthless piece of drek...I'll see you soon."* She silently read the words on the side of the patrol car. Then she added pointedly and directly, *"Watch your back, asshole...watch your back...'til we meet again."*

* *

The man stood in a daze. He shook the irritating voice from his head then looked around to see if he could find the interloper. She was gone. Her voice was replaced by low, feral growls and stealthy, creeping footsteps that he knew belonged to nothing that walked upright—but he didn't fear the night or its denizens. The spectral woman worried him briefly; then he remembered she had told him it was just a dream. *"One more jerk-off 'fore breakfast cain't hurt."* He laughed and rummaged through the front seat of the squad car. Finding nothing, he tried the ignition key in the glove compartment lock; nothing, it wouldn't fit. He opened his penknife and pried the door open—*Nary a scratch, you fuckin' genius!* Ahh, a bent and stale package of Kool cigarettes. He pushed in the dash lighter and lit up, inhaling voraciously, like a dying man suddenly finding oxygen. The menthol bit at his ragged lungs, but he didn't care. He smoked the cigarette to the filter and lit another from its dying ash, before tossing the first one aside. He smoked three in a row, while making up his mind that he had no alternative but to kill little Missy

Gookie Girlie. Having made that decision, he was prepared to take action, but his gonads were sending him an urgent message.

* *

"Oh, Jesus H. Christ...Cobra, you awake?"

"Goddammit, Dino, what does it take to get a good night's sleep around here? You're either runnin' off at the mouth or whackin' off your weenie. You're drivin' me slap dab crazy with your carryin' on. What the fuck's it now? You dreamin' about your babycakes again? I told you that after Friday you won't never think about that sweet young thing again. Now, dammit, put your scrawny itch on hold so's I can get some sleep."

"Cobra, *please* wake up!" Ricky-Dino was now hunched on his knees beside Cobra's bunk. "Somebody knows I done it, Cobra! It's a woman, I seen her, but I just didn't see her good enough to know who she is. You didn't talk to no one about me while you was out on the street, did you?"

"What the hell you talkin' about, you friggin' little pecker drool? If you're goin' to grill me, at least let me get my eyes open and my feet on the floor before you start in. But if I was you, I'd be real careful what I accused ol' Cobra of. Mind you, Dino, that's just a little piece of friendly advice you might want to hang on to."

I dreamed about it again, but this time that woman was in it. I tried to remember who she was after I woke up, but I cain't...she talked to me...she told me she knew where I was at, and she was comin' after for me."

Cobra clearly was not amused by the revelation. "Your baby-fuckin' conscience has just finally grabbed you by your busy little balls...got to be, 'cause you ain't got no brains. It was a fuckin' dream—you said so your own self. What do you want me to do? I ain't going to hold your stinkin' hand or sing you no lullaby. I'd tell you to go fuck yourself, but you might just take me up on it, and then I'd never get back to sleep. Take my advice...go to the can...bend over, and maybe your fairy godfather will stroll up behind you and make all your problems disappear. But right now, asshole, just shut the fuck up and let me get back to sleep.

"*But, Cobra!*" Ricky-Dino's whiney little voice cut though Cobra's brain like a bullet through Jello.

"Dino, I ain't talkin' n'more tonight. We'll think about all this in the morning. Now...shut up!"

Ricky-Dino crawled back into his bunk. Fear laced tears ran down his cheeks, resting in his ears—pooling with cold sweat before silently morphing into crystalline salt patches in the rusty darkness of the lockup. *Oh, Jesus, help me remember who that bitch is…Cobra talked, I know he did…what'm I gonna do, sweet Jesus? My ass is in a sling, and somebody's gonna sneak up and snatch me by my ass…and I ain't got no idee who it is. It's got to be that prick Cobra that yapped his head off while he was outside. Shit, you cain't trust no fuckin' convenience store sticker-upper. I'm gonna have to find somebody to take care of that snaky bastard. How the hell does he live with that snake hangin' outta his belly? Shee-it, looking that thing in the eye would drive me crazy, much less grabbin' holt a them colored-up scales. Well, I reck'n if my dick was as big as that'n, I probably could just close my eyes and not think on what it looks like…I cain't remember who that woman is…I reck'n I'll just worry about it tomorrow. Please, Jesus, if you can remember who I am, help me out a little, will you?*

He squeezed his eyes shut and tried unsuccessfully to block out the night. *I wonder if she'll track me down before Friday…I'd hate to miss that head job I'm supposed to get from Deputy Curly…a carton o Lucky's too, hell, I'd suck off that prick of a sheriff for a carton o' Lucky's.* He tried to turn over onto his belly, only to find he had the ever-present hard-on. Lately they were slipping up on him with no warning. He slipped his drawers down around his knees, trying to be real quiet while he set about alleviating his problem. He didn't want to piss off Cobra any more than he already had. He just wasn't real sure if he could trust the Snake anymore. It didn't take him long to reach his climax, and soon he had the solution well in hand, which, in turn, he wiped on the underside of his sagging mattress. That taken care of, he rolled over and drifted into a dreamless unconsciousness, until the overhead lights came on with the dawn.

17

Before my bare feet had hit the floor, even before the alarm had gone off, I had called Lee. My mind was so muddied up from the night's dreams that I didn't trust myself to make an intelligent decision on which coffee beans to grind for my morning jolt, much less what to do with the grit I had gleaned from my latest necromantic foray. I had just returned from a mind-boggling tour into the twilight zone.

Lee came.

* *

I sat scrutinizing the smoke rising from my cigarette as Lee let herself into the kitchen with her own key, poured herself a cup of coffee, and sat down. I aimlessly stirred my coffee while attempting to explain the dream—and my dilemma. "Lee, I just don't know what to do next. I don't want to screw things up, but I want to get the information into the right hands as soon as possible."

"I've got a suggestion. It's the same song, second verse."

"What?"

"Call Dave." She was referred again to David Marshall: Metro-Nashville homicide detective par excellence and friend to boot.

"Lee, he's Metro. I told you what I saw, plain as day, in the dream. The side of that police car was painted in bright, green letters—*DICKSON COUNTY SHERIFF.*"

"Well, let me ask you this, O sage, do you intend to confront that sheriff on your own—on his turf?"

"Hell, no, he would probably throw me out on my ass—or worse—for false accusation or some such nonsense."

"Well, let me ask you something else, do you think there's a possibility that it could be the sheriff himself, or a deputy or some other county employee, or are you still thinking it might be a convict?"

"Everything I trust and believe in tells me it is an inmate…a trustee who has access to county vehicles and the time and opportunity to use and abuse his privileges to his advantage. I'm almost positive that I'll know him the moment I set eyes on him, but I also believe he may recognize me as well. This has got to be handled with kid gloves. Maybe we could get Dave to cook up some cock and bull story…something that would entail his checking out patrol cars for some reason or other. Who knows how thoroughly they clean the interiors of those cars when they put them away? Shit! That's just a pipe dream. A Metro cop couldn't get to those cars, even if he had the proverbial *keys to the kingdom.* I just don't know, Lee. All I know for sure is that the clock is ticking, and that piece of shit will be out on the streets. What's to keep him from doing it again?"

"Do you really think he's going right out and do it again? Not a candidate for the rocket scientist award is he?"

"Lee, I know how weird and unbelievable it sounds, but believe me, he will do just that. I somehow crawled into his dream—if one could call it that. Actually, it was the vilest nightmare I ever hope to be a part of. No sane person could conjure up such scenes…not even in the wildest recreational S&M dream."

"What are you talking about…a recreational dream? I mean sadistic-masochism not withstanding. Is there really such a thing?

"Oh, yeah, with practice one can program oneself to dream whatever is desirable for that individual at a particular time."

"Dare, you're bullshitting me, right?"

"Would I do that?"

"Hell, yeah, and it wouldn't be the first time. I remember when you had me convinced…"

"Lee," I interrupted her diatribe to nowhere, "I'm not bullshitting you. Dream programming takes a lot of time and patience to get it even passably satisfactory. Obsession, however, is the most potent dream inducement of all."

"Can you do it?" She had her back up, and wasn't totally convinced I wasn't pulling her leg.

"I have, but I don't—not on purpose, anyway."

"Why not, pray tell?"

"Because that's one more manipulation that I feel should be left alone, unless one is willing to take precautions and not just screw around. Presently my brain is mucked up enough without my adding extra strain to it. We can try it later if you want to; however, I hope you'll settle for a nice pastoral setting. Something unobtrusive..."

"Hey, I'm game. But what I want to know is how do you account for the fact that you found yourself in a wannabe *Nightmare on Elm Street* with a crazy man who was raping, maiming and murdering before your very eyes?"

"He stopped short of murder the second time around. She was still alive when he apparently woke up. After that, it just vaporized...I found myself back in bed shaking like an aspen leaf. I can't account for any of it—just a psychic *phenom*, I guess. That, dear heart, is when I called you."

"Well, spook-o-mine, do you really think he got a good look at you?"

"I don't know."

"Oh, shit, do you think actually he may have recognized you—I mean for who you really are?"

"I don't know—he didn't show any real light behind those windows."

"Well, anyhow, Dare, I think we must assume that he did recognize you. I mean if the crazy prick gets out to run an errand or something, what's to keep him from looking you up?"

"Nothing, I guess. I've got the security system. Maybe I'll have to get a man-eating dog to sleep with me."

"Hillary would certainly be thrilled at that prospect...not to mention your current *stud muffin*."

I knew what she was doing. Trying to lighten my mood by teasing me out of my funk. "Lee, watch your mouth! I happened to be very fond of Fel, and...and..."

"And he is your stud muffin...right? Or is the term too imposing?"

"Lee, you're incorrigible—he's imposing alright..."

"Curls your tiny toes, does he?"

"My dear, he curls more than my tiny toes...now enough about my sex life. We've got a stinking little twerp down there in the jail in Dickson County, but I don't know what to do about it. But the last time I checked, intuition wasn't acceptable as evidence in court for anything...much less murder."

"I told you to call Dave. What's wrong with that? You know that he knows everybody in the state. I don't care what you say; I'll bet he can get into that place and never raise an eyebrow. I also wouldn't be a bit surprised if he could get a Metro police sketch artist to draw a picture of your prey...if you remember enough about him to describe..."

"Not to worry, I'll never forget that scrawny asshole if I live to be a hundred. I could probably identify him by his pathetic dick. He waved it around enough."

"Call Dave, Dare. It's the only thing that makes any sense...please?"

"Okay, maybe I will, but let's get this on tape. Do you have your tape recorder with you?

She reached over the back of the chair, dug in the pocket of her ever-present Vanderbilt jacket, and withdrew her mini-recorder on the first try. "Fire when ready, Gridley." Lee grinned. She was at the ready.

"He's about five-nine or ten...he probably weighs around 130 to 135— he's just plain skinny. His hair is shaggy...almost shoulder length. It looked greasy, so I have no idea what the actual color is...probably a dishwater blond. He pulls a knit cap down over his forehead, but those eyes are always visible. They are deep-set and cautious...*hooded*, I think, is the word I'm looking for...and they're dark. I wasn't close enough to determine the actual color. I will tell you that they have looked on more evil than your average person would in a lifetime."

"Yo! You be *very* careful, Dare! Sounds to me like your dealing with a certifiable crankcase here. You're not going to do anything foolish are you? I mean before you call Dave you're not going to do anything alone, are you?"

"No, darlin', I plan to take you with me.

"Oh, great! Where?

"Back to the woods outside Clarksville where we found the bone. Lee, that's where all these dreams have occurred, and quite obviously, where his are taking place also. We virtually met there, face to face. Don't worry, we'll go this morning...while the sun is shining."

"Dare, the sun isn't shining...nor is it supposed to."

"Well, it's daylight. Just as soon as I take a shower, I'll be ready to go. You better call Joe and tell him you may be gone all day."

"Joe's in Atlanta 'til tomorrow night. Oh, shit! I guess your mind is made up, so just go take your shower and I'll make a fresh pot of coffee and pour you some V-8. Hey, isn't that place still cordoned off...you know...yellow-taped for police purposes? It's a bona fide crime scene still...isn't it?"

"Yeah, but we're still a part of the team, Lee, it'll be fine, don't worry...and thanks for making the coffee. Don't get your knickers in a knot, darlin', everything will be copacetic...okay?

"*Yeah right.*" Lee poured water from the Brita Pitcher into Mr. Coffee's reservoir, measured the Macadamia infused grounds into the filter and flipped the switch. After a couple of false starts, it burped, and the steady stream of mahogany-hued liquid began to fill the glass carafe. Lee stared mesmerically at its steady progress. *Yeah, right,* she mused silently.

* *

"Dare, I'm freezing my butt off, don't you think we've raked through these skanky leaves long enough for one day? Maybe if you could give me some idea of what I'm looking for I could be more help to you."

"Lee, if I knew what I was looking for, then I would tell you. I'm just not sure…but it's here all right…I know something is lying here just waiting for us to find it. That's the way the universe works. *He* did something despicable, and in turn he left something behind to hang himself with. All we've got to do is find it. Now keep looking. Soon it will be getting dusk, and I don't think either of us wants to be rambling around out here after dark."

"You got that right, spook-o-mine…wait, Dare, come here! What's this way over here off the beaten path? Do you suppose this is where the sleaze parked the patrol car? Jesus…why didn't the Keystones find this? Look here…down here…look…under this pile of debris."

"What you got there, Lee?" She waited while I looked around and walked up and down a bit, "I think you may very well be right about the car being parked here. How would you like a job?" I teased. "Now, let's see what you've dug up."

"Petrified looking cigarette filters. *The son of a bitch smokes Kools!* That shouldn't be too difficult to trace once we get started checking out the guests at the Dickson County lockup. Just how many Kool smokers can there possibly be in that hellhole?"

I pressed closer to get a better look. "Let me see." She moved aside and showed me where she had systematically raked the individual layers of last fall's leaves into quadrants. She pulled her trusty Polaroid camera out of her bag and began photographing the area. "My, you've been watching *CSI* on TV haven't you?" I spoofed. She had separated the piles in such a way that it would expedite our search for any other evidence that might still be lurking about.

"*Bite me*, will you?" She retorted. She had been working hard, wasn't entirely comfortable out in those woods, and apparently had misplaced her sense of humor. She looked over her shoulder at me and asked, "Hey—you got any Baggies on you?" She cracked a feeble grin.

"As a matter of fact I do. What size do you want—and I suppose you want the tweezers too?"

"Just give me one, I guess the smallest will be sufficient, and yeah, I need the tweezers to pick up these freeze-dried filters. Maybe since they've been protected under these leaves, the lab will be able to extract a DNA profile. Wow! Wouldn't it be a hoot to plaster that bastard to the wall with his own spit? Dare...do you know if there's a precedent for you to identify him through a dream...or should I say, a mutual dream?"

"I hardly think so...it's hard enough to convince most folks that I, or anyone, have any extra-sensory abilities at all...people are hesitant to take a psychic's word when a person's life may hang on what may be considered, in some circles, as *zoom dweeby* testimony. I can't say that I blame them...if we don't understand something, then generally we don't trust it. That's just human nature."

"Doesn't your crime-solving record stand for anything? What about when you and Dave followed your psychically inspired map and found that lawyer's body buried down by the Cumberland River? What about when you dug out all that child sacrificial evidence during the Atlanta child murders? And who was it that tracked down Mama Santini, the biggest old Voodoo priestess in Georgia? Oh, and let's not forget the drowning victim you led that sheriff to...the guy who had on the red shorts and gold watch, just as you had described, and was exactly where you said he would be?"

"Lee, what we're doing here falls under the guise of the occult—that very word makes some people's skin crawl...people who haven't taken a few minutes to check the meaning of the word. It means *hidden,* as you are well aware...but it conjures up all sorts of spooky connotations to the uninformed. Quite frankly, my dear, I haven't the time or the inclination to educate the populace, thank you, very much. Desperate police departments will try almost anything—including calling in a psychic now and again. Desperate people are not hard to convince, but judges and juries don't tend to be desperate. I do what I can and then hope some legal eagle will be able to show cause and then convince what I cannot not—that's not my job."

"Hey, Dare, what about Felix?"

"What about Felix...other than the obvious?"

"He certainly fits the description."

"Just what description are you referring to?"

"Hey, wake up and smell the coffee...l-e-g-a-l-e-a-g-l-e...Felix Walker...*duh.*

"I don't know, Lee, I've found it difficult to work with someone I'm romantically interested in."

"You did okay with Jerry, I would say."

"And directly due to our involvement with each other, both on the case *and* personally…he died…in my car…" I had to take a deep breath.

"Dare…shit happens. What if I had picked up your car instead of Jerry? Then I would have been blown-up instead of him…right?"

The very thought stunned me. "Correct, now tell me who's my right hand in these investigations? You are…what's the difference? A best friend is irreplaceable."

"Okay, Dare, anyone—involved or not—would have been vaporized in that explosion. You can't protect everyone. Anyway, I think Felix would be ideal. You trust him don't you?"

"Implicitly!"

"Okay, there you go…an in-house attorney could be very handy, not to mention prudent. He could advise you every step of the way, and some slick-tongue devil of a defense lawyer won't be able to trip you up when it all comes down. What do you think?"

"I'll think about it. Maybe I'll talk to him about it tonight. I'm going to his house for dinner."

"My, my, it is getting serious for you to drive all the way to Bellevue. But take my advice, don't talk business tonight, make an appointment if you have to, but don't talk about this horrible stuff tonight. That, my dear, would very definitely mess up your happy streak. You really are happy about this new *thang* with him, aren't you?"

"I've already told you that I like him very much. He's sweet without being condescending…you know…that lawyer thing."

"God forbid he be condescending." She cocked her eyebrow, letting me know that I shouldn't take myself or anything else too seriously. *"He's one fine lookin' genlemens,"* she drawled.

"You've got that right, Sidekick. He makes me go weak in the knees. I just don't know what to make of this whole thing."

"Why don't you go with the flow for awhile? If you float too far off course I'll grab you with a hook and drag you back to reality…how 'bout it? Hey, let's get this baggie of cigarette filters out of here. If you want to take it to Ernest we can drop it off on our way out of town, or maybe you'd rather leave it with Will Bealer instead.

"I know we should take them to Ernest or Will, but what the hell? You found the butts, so let's just hang on to the baggie for now. I'll call Ernest first thing in the morning."

"Look, I don't care where you take it or what you do with it. Let's just get the hell out of Dodge and get you back home—you've got places to go and people to see. My, my…and I've got to spend tonight alone. Ya'll think about me will you?"

"Oh, yeah, we might even light a candle for you—between courses."

"Dare, watch your tongue. Bragging is unbecoming…not to mention disconcerting…I just told you I'm spending the night alone. What if I should have a dream?"

"Trust me, Lee, you won't have *that* dream."

* *

After Lee left I turned on the stereo. The CD player came on, and very relaxing *New Age* music wound its way throughout my speaker system. I listened aimlessly as I undressed and then tucked fresh lingerie under my arm before heading to the bathroom. I had poured myself a Black Jack on the rocks and had lit the proverbial candles around my tub when the phone rang. I picked up the cordless, standing naked as the day I was born. "Hello?" I answered tenuously, half fearing something—or someone—was about to drop an anvil on my evening.

"Dare? Is that you? You sound down-in-the-mouth."

"Oh, Fel, I'm just tired. Lee and I have been tramping through the woods in Montgomery County today. Is there anything wrong?" I couldn't imagine why he would be calling me when I would be seeing him shortly—I hoped.

"No, nothing's wrong, on the contrary. I just wanted to tell you that I'm home. I simply said, 'To hell with it,' and took the afternoon off. I wanted to make sure I had the time to get the gumbo just right. Besides, I deserve it. I've been told I'm a workaholic—maybe I need some treatment—think you can help me out?"

"Oh, I think maybe I can figure something out that might make you feel better." I stepped over the side of the old-fashioned ball and claw tub and settled into the steaming, bubble-infused water. "*Aaaaahhhhh.*"

Hillary Kitten chose that particular moment to make her presence known. Rearing up on her hind legs, she peered over the side of the tub, as if to check things out. Giving me a disdainful look, she moved on—without making a sound.

"Hey, who was that sigh of pleasure for—you or me? What the hell are you doing over there?"

"Let's just say it's for both of us. I just slid into a steaming, hot bubble bath—it doesn't take a whole lot to entertain me."

"Obviously, if a mere bath can elicit a reaction like that."

"Ah ha, I can see there is a major aesthetic difference between us."

"And just what might that be?"

"Apparently the lowly bath, to you, is purely utilitarian."

"Well, I haven't given much thought to bathing, per se, except for that enlightening shower we took together. I generally take showers...do they count?"

"I'm going to ignore that bit about the shower together. I don't think either of us was thinking about cleanliness being next to Godliness at the time. But as far as showers being satisfactory—utilitarian wise, I certainly hope so, particularly if one is alone."

"I heard that! And to you, dear Dare, utilitarianism is not the goal?"

"Not when it comes to taking a bath. For instance, I'm reclining, at this moment, almost neck-deep in nice, fragrant, warm-as-toast bubble bath. I'm relaxing my tired bones and muscles...thinking about the drive to Bellevue and what's waiting for me there."

"And what might that be?" I heard a slight hitch in his voice.

"Crab and shrimp gumbo!" I teased. And if I don't get off this phone soon, I'll never get there—traffic you know."

"By all means get back to your bath...and enjoy. Hey, keep thinking about what's waiting for you, I mean besides the gumbo. I think I better go take a cool shower. Please drive carefully...I'll see you soon."

I hit the off button and laid the receiver on the commode lid, noticing the *new age* music had vacated the speakers. I eased back into my reclining position and discovered that my breathing too was a little more rapid than usual. I took a sip of sour mash and closed my eyes while Tony Bennett messaged my psyche with *The Shadow of Your Smile*.

18

I got off the interstate at the Bellvue/Newsome Station exit. Pulling in at the first liquor store I came to, I eased to a stop and went inside. I strolled the wine aisles until I came upon what I was looking for, a lovely *Fumé Blanc*. I paid the clerk and carried the brown-papered treasure back to my car. Checking Fel's written directions one more time, I headed up Sawyer Brown Road and wound my way through the unfamiliar streets until I found myself in front of a beautiful, long, low, *tres* contemporary home. Its sleek lines melded so beautifully with the landscape that each became one with the other—the effect was stunning. I parked at the end of the driveway, which just happened to be around back, adjacent to a lovely glass-enclosed sun-porch. No sooner had I turned off the key, Fel appeared outside my car. He opened the driver's door for me, and I stepped down from my perch, holding purse in one hand and wine in the other. He put his arm around me and brushing my lips with his own, he led me inside. I must admit...I truly felt welcome.

"You have a lovely home, Fel." I was genuinely impressed. He had an original Jackson Pollack hanging over the fireplace in the den. *Jesus, what must be hanging in the living room?* He must have read my expression, because he grinned.

Would you like to see the rest of the house now, or would you rather wait until later?

"Whichever is more convenient to the chef," I chuckled—*checked* by an expert.

"I would hardly call myself a chef. I just hung around with a bunch of Cajuns down around the bayous on weekends when I was teaching at LSU. Cooking, to them, is the next thing to religion, or is it the other way around? All you need is a string with an ol' hunk of *baloney* tied on the end, and those damned crabs will climb right up that string and into your hand. Actually, the crabs don't eat the baloney, but the Cajuns do...after they get all the crabs they want. I had the time of my life down there, but I really didn't care to take up full time residence in a place that has "Gator Crossing" signs along the highway. You do know that the mosquito is the state bird of Louisiana, don't you?"

"I've heard that…I've also heard that a Cajun will eat—by God—anything that *don'* eat him first…i.e. used baloney."

"That's the rumor." He set the wine, along with my purse, on the countertop. Unencumbered, we each turned to the other. He took me in his arms and kissed me as though he had truly missed me, and was, indeed, happy to see me. I felt the same. I couldn't get close enough. I was falling in lust.

"Are you hungry?" He asked through his trademark grin.

"Yeah, but not too, will dinner be trashed if we don't eat right now?"

"No, I haven't added the crabs and shrimp yet. They only take a short time. So…?

I smiled.

He took my hand and led me down a hall, past soft pastel walls, to his bedroom. It was huge, big enough to roller-skate in. "So this is your *ballroom?*" I laughed, surreptitiously checking the ceiling for mirrors.

He grinned, making an exaggerated "*tsk tsk*" sound—he had read my mind. He slowly began to unbutton my blouse. I touched his silk tee shirt and had a classic hot flash. I put my hands under the back of his shirt and pressed my warm palms against his cool flesh. He let go of my buttons just long enough to pull his shirt over his head. His dark hair fell askew across his forehead, and I felt compelled to kiss him. My blouse hit the chair behind me, and my bra followed shortly. I kicked off my shoes, stepped out of my slacks and peeled off pantyhose, while he dropped his trousers and boxers, in one fell swoop. He lifted me to him, and I received him with unbridled anticipation. He reached inside of me and touched my core. He laid me on his bed and came to me with the gentleness of a man whose aim is to give nothing but unvarnished pleasure. His fingertips traced invisible circles on my breasts, preparing them for the touch of his lips, which could be classified as national treasures. After teasing my nipples to erection, his lips kissed their way to my navel and beyond. By the time he took me into his arms and his lips found mine, I was way past ready, but I was determined to hold off as long as he did. Our tongues were so busy with each other that I could barely gasp when I felt the ribbons of my impending orgasm tightening their little knots, one by one. Fel was with me. He placed his hand on my buttocks, and we rolled over onto our sides, never missing a beat. He pulled me to him, and with legs thrown askew, we gripped each other in an ecstatical explosion that left us both breathing hoarsely, long after our nerves and muscles had unwound and found their proper places. The heat receded—but it had branded my brain indelibly. Not to be crass, but as I had thought to myself after the first time we were together, *this man is a regular, fucking, love machine—sweet and gorgeous, to boot.*" We kissed deeply and lay entwined for a long time.

* *

"You hungry for gumbo yet?" He was propped on his elbow.

I looked him up and down before answering his question. "Yeah, I think I am." I brushed the stray hairs from his forehead and he grinned. Using his fingers as a comb, he raked the loose hairs back into a semblance of order. "Let's go drop those little crustaceans into the pot," I added.

"Sounds good to me," he winked, but you must realize if we get any on ourselves we'll have to take a shower."

* *

Dinner was superb. We stuffed ourselves. It appeared as though neither of us had much control when it came to certain aspects of life's spicy sustenance.

The thick walnut-colored *roux*, rich with *filé*, cayenne pepper and the other delights *cuisine Cajun*, was awash with okra, crabmeat and succulent pink shrimp. This exotic concoction was ladled over beds of fluffy white rice, which immediately absorbed the flavors and aromas that are so classically reminiscent of south Louisiana. He had toasted baguettes to their supreme crunchiness, to accompany both the gumbo and the lovely salad he had prepared in advance. Raddiccio and Bibb lettuces with a trace of sweet, red onion, kissed discreetly by an olive oil and balsamic vinaigrette. I was just thinking how grateful I was that nobody tried to put me on the spot as to which I had enjoyed more—the *appetizer* or the *entrée*...when Fel brought forth a cheesecake to die for. "You did this?"

He grinned, "I'd like to take the credit but I can't. Becker's gets all the accolades." Now, as every native knows, Becker's Bakery is a Nashville treasure. I dare say, one doesn't live anywhere in the vicinity of Nashville-Davidson County for very long without learning about the sumptuousness of pastries, cakes, pies and breads from Becker's magical ovens. "Hey, the baguettes came from there too," he admitted.

* *

A nap is exactly what we neither of us needed for our figures, but hey, it couldn't be helped. We lay in each other's arms, heads resting on cushions from the sofa. The gas logs flickered silently while we dozed. Visions of recent lovemaking danced in my head.

"Hey, how 'bout we jump in the hot tub?"

I looked sleepily into those whiskey-brown eyes, and at that moment, I would have followed him anywhere.

"Do you have a spare tooth brush?"

"No, but you can use mine."

"Oh, Jesus, no! Swappin' spit is one thing, but putting someone else's toothbrush into my mouth is tantamount to…to…I can't think of anything so ghastly. My mother told me back in the dark ages that that's how I'd know when I was really in love—when I could use a man's toothbrush. If that were the case, I would have ended up an old maid. Yecchhh!"

"Now that I know your oral hang ups, allow me to explain. I use an electric toothbrush but I do have spare heads—unsullied, I might add."

"*Touché*—now, after a good teeth scrubbing, I think the hot tub will be delightful, and you're right, I do have oral hang-ups.

* *

"Ohhhhhhh…outside is it? Can't be more than thirty degrees out here."

"Actually, it's 36—here, let me have your robe."

I tentatively removed the terrycloth wrap from my bare shoulders and handed it to my host. He held my hand while I stepped into the swirling, steaming water. He tossed the robe—along with the one he was wearing—onto a wrought iron chair beside our cigarettes and his lighter. His hot tub was built into a deck off the end of the sun-porch. The frost dusted redwood glistened like silver in the moonlight. The *wooshing* of the heated spa was symphonic to my ears. If I became anymore contented, I would probably melt from sheer pleasure.

"This should be just the ticket for an old bath-worshipper like you—how is it?" He kicked his slippers aside and stepped into the spa, sitting down very close to me.

"Devine." I watched his expressions through the roiling vapors. My hair was going to hell in a hand-basket, but I would worry about it later. His thigh touched mine and he put his arms around my waist.

"You want to see how long I can hold my breath?"

Before I could answer, he had ducked under the water—a new hot tub experience for me. When he came up he kissed me, and I was more than delighted to show my appreciation. Thanks be to California Spas that his hot tub was a large one—plenty of space for maneuverability—oh, my! I was hot, sapped and completely sated when he helped me climb from the tub and into the frigid night air. His nude body, cloaked in an aura of misty steam, was ever so distracting as I tried to get my arms into the correct sleeves of the borrowed robe. Throwing his wrap around his shoulders, he slipped his feet into the slippers, and we walked, arm in arm, back into the house. Here he poured each of us a snifter of cognac. We sipped the nectar of the gods in front of the fire.

The most incredible jazz was playing in the background—it reminded me of a smoky jazz club I had been to years ago. "What's that fabulous music? I don't recognize it?"

"Do you like it?

"Very much."

"Would you believe the title of the CD is "Sample This?" He rolled over and took me in his arms.

"Oh, yeah, I believe it." I brushed his lips in the shadowy darkness. "You're bad."

"That's cause you bring out the worst in me," he grinned impishly.

"I believe that also." I smiled at him—I felt closer to Felix than I had felt to any man in a long time. I lay watching the reflected firelight dance across the ceiling, my thoughts a secret even from myself.

Hey, Murph," he pulled me close, "please don't go home."

He had never called me Murph before—I liked it.

* *

Early morning has never been a particular inspirational part of my day, especially when the sky is overcast and a fine drizzle is crawling down the bedroom windows when I awake. Today was an exception. I awoke to breakfast in bed; then we got up and had something to eat. I listened to Fel's arteries clog to the tune of Canadian bacon, scrambled eggs and buttered toast...I enjoyed corn flakes with skim milk and no sugar.

I left his house with my blouse un-tucked and my pantyhose wrong side out. However, I did have my shoes on the right feet. He kissed me goodbye before opening the car-door and helping me inside, where he kissed me again. "Hey, cut it out, I've got a long way to drive, and I don't want to be pulled over by some under-quota, ticket-happy, county mountie who might think I look too happy, especially after I get to Wilson County."

"Yeah, I must admit I've heard tales about them, but they're your *homies*. Are you telling me they'd give you, the infamous Dare Murphy, a ticket?"

"Homies, my ass, they'd give Jesus Christ a ticket if he looked sideways at one of 'em. I'm sure there are a few upstanding officers on the force. It's just that I haven't met them yet—nor do I ever hope to, thank you very much."

"I'm sorry to say that they do have sort of a reputation…"

"Sort of?" I was incredulous, "Remember, I had three sons who grew up driving in Wilson County. When Scotty joined the Air Force, I figured some of the deputies would hang a wreath on the door of the Justice Building in Lebanon." Suddenly, I realized this was neither the time nor the place to discuss the locally notorious, sheriff's department where I made my home. Mt Juliet and Wilson County are bursting at the seams with new growth, and our small-town law enforcement cadre is suddenly faced with a whole new source of income.

The outside air was galloping through my rolled down window. He touched my lips with his and said he would call me when he got home from work.

"Now, go home and please drive carefully…especially when you cross the county line."

"I shall," I replied, raising the power window. "*I promise,* " I mouthed to the smiling man who stood shivering, *sans* coat, in the cold pre-dawn. I thought of last night—his steaming body hovering beside the hot tub. Wow! What an excellent way to kick-start one's self early in the morning.

* *

Traffic was light, and I hoped the sky would soon brighten. By the time I exited I-40 in favor of I-440, I was heading almost due east. The sun sent word she would again be spending the day under the covers, when the first huge snowflakes attached themselves like Velcro to my windshield. One at exactly eye-level was, indeed, six-sided and looked just like one of the hundreds of doilies my maternal grandmother used to crochet when I was a kid. I blinked, and it was gone—replaced by a myriad of others, until finally I was forced to turn on the wipers. *The sun will come up tomorrow…*I mused—knowing full well that I lied to myself one more time. I didn't care. I love dreary days. When the sun is shining, work is the last thing on my mind. Solar heat seemingly shorts out my brain cells—some congenital *quark* of fate. A cold, snowy or even rainy day makes me feel alive and ready to take on the world, which was exactly what I expected I might be doing before long. My mind swiped at the latest dream/vision I had had only night before last…it was engraved firmly into my consciousness, by way of my sub-consciousness. I wondered if I would ever be able to flush those abhorrent sequences from my memory. I sincerely hoped so. I thought I could if we caught the filthy bastard who had invaded my private space. My private space—how selfish I felt. I thought about Marie Zhou hanging between those trees—all dignity dismantled—only fear for her life, clinging like frost to her shattered spirit. How many lives had he destroyed? How many more would he plow through before he was caught?

* *

It was six-thirty a.m. as I sat in my car, inside my garage, woolgathering. I waited for my antiquated garage door to grind it's way back down the tracks—in its own good time—to what I feared soon would be its final resting-place. I opened the car door before gathering my purse and jacket in my arms. Slamming the car door with my hip, I fumbled with a myriad of keys before stuffing the right one in the hole and unlocking the deadbolt. Finagling the door open with my knee, I dispatched the security code. Inside the house wasn't exactly cold, but it was by no means hospitably warm either. Dropping my purse and keys on the countertop, I plugged my cell phone into its outlet. I lit a cigarette, nervously drawing the warm fumes into my lungs. Blue smoke, mingling with my breath, hit the kitchen air with frightening clarity. Had my furnace met its maker? It certainly shouldn't be a circuit breaker, not after all the money I had spent upgrading the furnace, rewiring and all those other expense devouring home improvements. I remembered setting the innovative, electronic thermostat at exactly 68 degrees just before I left home the night before. The furnace people had convinced me that I could not live without this new miracle in environmental control. The security people had their turn at bat and sold me on their state-of-the-art alarm system which, together with the furnace, could be remotely controlled from anywhere via my cell phone keypad...or perhaps some hacker's pocket calculator. Who the hell could figure out all this high-tech rigmarole? Something was amiss. Had someone been in my house while I was away—or had my sanctum sanctorum been electronically violated? *Murphy, grab hold of yourself, get a grip, then go check the thermostat.* I did—it was 60 degrees and dropping. If someone had, in fact, been in my house and screwed with my furnace, it had been very recently—and might still be around. *Oh, shit!* I wasn't ready for this— someone was trying to mess up my happy streak—and they were doing an admirable job, I might add. I punched Lee's preprogrammed number into my cordless phone.

"Hello?"

"Have you walked this morning already?"

"Who is this?" *Smart-ass, no matter what the time of day.*

"Please, have you?" I plead.

"Yeah, as a matter of fact, I just walked in the door. I thought you were still in bed or I would have stopped by for coffee. It was snowing. Now it's just a fine, cold mist out there. Why are you wide-awake so early?"

"I just got home. Lee?"

"Still a little wired, huh? Nothing like a good lay to get you all bright-eyed and—pardon the expression—*bushy-tailed.*"

"Lee!" I felt like yanking her through the telephone and shaking her into paying attention to my plight.

"What the hell is wrong with you? You lose your sense of humor between here and Bellevue? Not hard to do, especially if you make the swing by Antioch..." she babbled.

"Lee, did you see anyone around my house when you walked by the lake? Anyone?

"No—what's wrong?"

"My house is cold as the proverbial well-digger's knee. I left the thermostat on 68 and now its 60 degrees—no, wait—now its 58. Lee?"

"Look, there's bound to be a logical explanation. You wait right where you are; I haven't even taken my sweats off yet...I'll be right there. Hey, try not to panic before I get there. You're probably too tired to get it right anyhow."

"Bet you smell good."

"Well, at least your sense of the obtuse seems to still be intact. Don't move—I'll be right there."

I did move, however, I picked up a bread knife. What was I going to do—

saw him to death? Him? Who? A temporary reaction to fanciful stimuli, I sincerely hoped. I crept through the kitchen, the great-room, down the hall and beyond. The farther I went, the colder it seemed. I felt as though I were crawling toward a great, gaping, clammy maw—instead of my bedroom. Where the hell was my psychic ability when I really needed it? Blank...nada—but it's never been a beacon in my own life's troubled waters. Why should it make an appearance now? I peeked around the door into my bedroom. There on my pillow lay Hillary Rodham Kitten all wound up in a tight little ball. I could see her back and shoulders rise and fall, indicating peaceful slumber. Unlike a snarly dog, a cat will lie peacefully while a house is being dismantled around it...at least I'm sure Miss Hillary would. I'm also sure she would figure it to be for her benefit, and let it go on, with nothing more than a switch of her tail. I passed the bed. She half opened one eye, then yawning, went back to sleep—nary a welcome home. I eased into my bathroom, flipping the light switch as I passed the door—pure reflex. Nothing...no one—*thank you, Jesus*. I heard a key in my backdoor, and I almost wet my pants before remembering that Lee was coming over.

"Dare, where the hell are you? I thought I told you not to move!"

"I'm back here...how do you know I did move?" I headed back toward the kitchen.

"Because," she reasoned—in a loud voice—"your cell phone is plugged in, and the cordless is right beside it. Am I to believe you strolled all the way to the back of the house before calling me?" Then she changed tracks, "The infamous thermostat is not more than ten feet from where I stand. Hey, you may be Sherlock but I'm Watson, the chronicler. I've picked up a little along the way, you know. Get out here—now!" She shouted. "What the hell possessed you to go roaming through this big ol' barn after calling me and sounding as though you were half scared to death?"

"Watch it, this is my home you're denigrating here...and I was—sort of scared." I walked back into the kitchen, on the tail end of my own raised voice.

"Are you all right?" She grabbed my shoulders and glanced at my feet, as if to make sure that all my fingers and toes were accounted for.

"Yeah, I suppose I overreacted, but doesn't it seem awfully cold in here to you?"

"I don't suppose you've checked the circuit breaker box."

"Hell, no, I haven't checked the friggin' circuit breaker box. It's in the basement. You told me not to move, remember?"

"And a lot of good that did. You could have lit the gas logs while you were meandering through the great-room—bet that never occurred to you...did it?"

"Put a cork in it, Lee, and let's go down and check things out in the basement."

"Put that bread-knife away. I won't even ask the obvious." She took the serrated weapon from my hand and returned it into its slot in the knife block. She followed me grimly, as I peeked around the door and down the steps to the landing. Beyond that I could see nothing.

"Let's go," I announced, sounding braver than I felt—but infinitely more than I was before Lee came in to save the day. I crept my way along the wall, then bent over when I was on the step before the landing. I don't know what I thought I was doing—if anyone were downstairs, they would have seen my feet long before I got to the landing.

"What do you see?" Lee whispered into my back.

"Nothing...unless it's a ghost."

"*Shit!*"

I knew I had reminded her about my long-departed grandmother, who makes her presence known around my house periodically. Lee hates the thought of it. I find it rather comforting.

I reached the bottom step and still had detected nothing in the shadowy dimness that in just a few hours would be bustling with secretary, clients and me—dressed for a day at the office. But right now, it was anything but bustling.

"Looking over my shoulder, Lee announced, "Look at the computer!" A message alert was flashing in the center of the screen: "*You have one instant message on AOL.*"

"I checked this thing before I left last night. You didn't leave me a message did you?" I mumbled.

"Well, hell no, why would I do that? I knew you were off to the hinterlands to play house with the Esquire last night. Why don't you just punch it up and find out what it is before you have kittens?"

"Okay, here goes." I hit the AOL instant messenger icon at the lower left corner of the screen. The computer woke up from its nap—beeping and grinding its way to life. Nothing is more annoying than waiting for the damned thing to get its shit together while I sit waiting for the unknown. Suddenly, there it was:

"WANT TO GO TO THE DICKSON COUNTY JAIL? I MAY HAVE SOMETHING JUICY FOR YOU"

In the corner of the screen was an unknown email address. "Now just who in the hell could that be from?" Lee queried under her breath, "You don't think it could possibly be that asshole convict do you?"

"Lee, if I had the slightest inkling, I would be doing something instead of standing here spinning my wheels like a complete fool. In my dream he looked incapable of turning on a radio, much less operating a computer."

"Darlin'," she consoled, "you're not a fool. And besides, you could simply click on and reply—that is—if you want to find out right now."

"I think I'll wait a little while. I'm not ready for another major jolt before it's good and light outside, even if it turns out to be nothing, which I'm sure it is. *I was not sure of anything at that point.*

"Okay," Lee reasoned, "Let's go back upstairs, and I'll make a pot of coffee while you shower. You better hope your water-heater isn't kaput too—then again a cold shower just might do you some good. Never mind, just hurry up, then we'll both put our *thinking caps* on and try to put this puzzle together so all the pieces fit.

"I don't mind telling you, I'm not looking forward to getting undressed in this temperature, but I'll be glad to get *shed* of these pantyhose." Lee looked quizzically…then decided not to go there.

* *

The steaming water literally sucked the trepidation out of my pores—*nobody could get to me here in the sanctity of my home—could they?* I washed my hair and stood motionless, while the hot water pounded the weariness from my bones. When I opened the shower door, the fragrance of freshly ground, freshly brewed coffee met me head on. I pulled my jeans over my hips and fastened the top button. Even as I pulled a fresh, orange, UT sweatshirt over my towel-dried hair, I was heading for the kitchen and fully caffinated nectar—Pavlov lives.

"Lee, when did you say Joe would be home?"

"He drove to Atlanta, so he should be home earlier than if he flew…probably by four or five. That way he'll beat the major traffic at both ends of the spectrum. Why?"

"Well, I had a thought while I was in the shower."

"Careful, Sherlock, you don't want to weaken the nation," she teased, trying to lighten an otherwise, pretty grim situation.

"And your horse, Watson. Anyway, as I was about to say, do you think Joe would come over here tonight and see if there's any connection between the failure of my newest electronically controlled gadgets and the ominous message on the computer?"

"Oh, that, forget it. In all the hubbub of seeing that computer message, we forgot to check the circuit breaker. I went downstairs while you were in the shower. Sure enough, it had kicked off—sensory overload I guess. Can't you tell how much warmer it is already? As for your ominous message...I can't help you with that one.

"Oh, thanks, Lee. I feared that somebody might have been screwing with the controls via my computer or something. The temperature, along with the security system, can be set by a flick of the telephone—so why not a computer?" If some son of a bitch had gotten into my hearth and home through the wires (as had happened during a case in my past)...I swear I was considering dumping those damn computers into the lake and going back to a typewriter and an abacus."

"I hear you", she chuckled, "I thought Joe told you to put in passwords, and whatever else you needed, to keep the outside world out of your business...you did...didn't you?

"Well...not exactly. Joe's going to kill me, that is, if somebody else doesn't beat him to it.

19

"Cobra, don't forget your hearing is coming up Monday morning. You're looking at eleven/twenty-nine, if you can't come up with something creative to convince Judge Werthen's that you're worth giving one more chance. Hey, Cobe, you know what? You're probably better off in here than if you was out on the street. Shit, all you'd do is get put right back inside soon as you stick up the first 7-11 you come to." Deputy Jon Peterman, aka Curly, had his own agenda here. Not only did he enjoy the inmate's company, he also knew that more than likely the next time Harlan "Cobra" Merriweather was hauled in, he would surely be sent—for an indeterminate time—to the Tennessee State Prison down in Nashville, due to his recidivistic past. Curly cringed. He didn't want to think about being deprived of that incredible snake between Cobra's legs, while some asshole-of-a-cellmate down at the big house reaped all the benefits of Cobra's highly specialized talents. As it was, Cobra was sure to lose his trustee status this go round. That was going to make their getting together a hassle—that was for damn sure. Curly cringed again, thinking about his "appointment" with that skanky little shit they called Dino. He'd consented to meeting the despicable ne'er-do-well only after Cobra had "twisted his arm". Cobra knew too much.

"Yeah, I been thinkin' on that, my man. I think I figured me a way out." Cobra grinned at the deputy but offered nothing more in the way of information. He patted his crotch—just to watch Curly turn red—and walked away. Pulling the spare Pall Mall from behind his ear, he headed for the yard where he could smoke undisturbed until the sheriff decided to show up.

Deputy Curly reached inside his desk and retrieved his latest dog-eared edition of *Playgirl* magazine. Looking around surreptitiously, he ducked into the restroom and locked himself in an empty stall.

* *

"Ernest, don't ever do that to me again. Hell, if you'd had your computer raped like I did once, you'd have been a little more forthcoming with your message."

"Damn it, Dare, I just figured you would recognize the official e-mail address—I didn't know I had to leave my social security number too." He spat the words though the telephone. He was behaving like a three-year-old.

"Yeah, like *clktnpol@.gov* is a dead giveaway. Excuse me, but one of the biggest porno outfits on the internet ends in *.gov.* Give me a break." I just hoped he didn't ask me how I knew that choice piece of information. "I'm a fucking psychic—that's how I know." *Oops.*

"Did I ask?" I could hear his hostility melting at the other end of the line. I sensed his sheepish grin.

"No, but you wanted to. Sometimes in my business I need to check these things out." I was digging myself deeper and deeper.

"I understand, so do I."

We both laughed and I asked him why he had e-mailed me and why he was calling. He explained that when I didn't reply to his e-mail, he had figured I was one of those people who didn't check her messages religiously. So he had simply decided to call and check directly with me. He had been about to do just that earlier, when he had received an ominous phone call from Harlan Merriweather's Public Defender. He explained that Merriweather was a habitual, small-time punk who spent more time in jail than out—that he was harmless enough, just a constant thorn in the side of Dickson County *officialdom.*

"What did he want?" Forgetting, once again, all about the cigarette butts that Lee had picked up at the crime scene.

"Well, Rick Scarpadis, his public defender, said Merriweather wants to talk to me. You want to come along? That's what I was asking you on the internet—that's all."

"Oh, I get it "...*meet me at the jail—something juicy...*"yada yada yada. You're forgiven. Just don't be so friggin' clandestine next time—did Scarpadis say why?"

"No, just that his client wants to talk to me. He didn't ask for me by name, but the PD seemed to think it might behoove everybody concerned if *I* talked to him. I don't know, maybe Mr. Scarpadis knows something I don't know yet. Well?"

"Well, what?" I queried.

"Do you want to come with me? You can bring your friend along."

"Aren't you kind?" I bit my tongue...sometimes he just rankles me so. *Of course, I want to come—somewhere in that lock-up lurks the son of a bitch who murdered Marie Zhou, and this guy knows who he is.* "When?"

"How 'bout this afternoon?"

"Damn, I can't"

"Why?"

"I just can't today, I've got clients coming in...starting in just a few minutes—too late to start shifting them around."

"Well, how bout tomorrow afternoon? Let Merriweather stew in his own juices for a little while—can you do that?"

"Yeah, I suppose that's workable, but I have to be home by six, so I'll have to leave there by quarter to five. I won't get there until about one-thirty...that okay?"

"That's fine. I'll make the arrangements. See you at the jail at one-thirty."

I was just about to hang up when suddenly it hit me. "Wait, Ernest...I've got something for you—it could be *tres* important. First, I got your cryptic message on the computer very early in the morning—long before time for you to be in the office—then later on I got busy with clients and...I just forgot to call—good thing you called me."

"What is it?"

"Lee and I went back to the crime scene yesterday and..."

"You found something *yesterday,* and you didn't call me?!"

"Yes, I did, and no, I didn't, I'm sorry...just hold it in the road while I tell you..."

"I can't believe this, Dare."

"Damn it, Ernest, will you shut up while I tell you what we found that your investigators should have found? We found some old Kool cigarette filters. They were under layers of leaves."

"Where did you find them?"

"About two or three hundred yards from where we found the bone."

"What makes you think they belong to the perp?"

"And what makes you think they don't? Do you want me to bring them along or just flush them down the john?" I had no intention of doing such a foolish thing. I was just tired of being taken for granted. I was the one out scratching for clues.

"No! For chrissakes, don't flush them! Bring them tomorrow; I'll send them to the lab. You didn't touch them with your fingers, did you?"

"I'll ignore that—but Ernest, just in case you're paying attention—they're his."

"How do you know?"

"I'm a freakin' psychic…remember?"

"Did you ever hear me call you such a thing?"

"No."

"Then why keep bringing it up? Did someone tell you I called you that?"

"Didn't I just answer your question?"

* *

"Harlan, I called a detective, just like you asked me to." Rick Scarpadis was a squat little man of dubious Greco/Roman heritage. He had worked his way through YMCA law school (at night) while serving as a part-time bounty hunter for a relatively prominent bail-bondsman. He wore a permanently curled lip, where his big, foul-smelling cigar was usually ensconced between his tobacco-stained teeth. For a Public Defender, he had a pretty good track record. His mind was like a steel-trap. The problem was the limited time he had to spend on each case. They were stacked up like cordwood outside the office. He took his work home with him, and instead of watching television, he poured over his cases with the diligence of a Johnnie Cochran. Each case on his overflowing desk was equally important to him: he gave each client his due day in court—and then some. He wanted to get Harlan Merriweather a deal if he could—help him break the cycle—get him some counseling.

"Hey, thanks, my man," Cobra was genuinely surprised when he told him that Lieutenant Ernest Calhoun himself was dropping by to see him. Cobra knew from watching TV that he was the dude that was lookin' for ol' *num-nuts* himself. He would love to see the look on that jerk-off Dino's face when he found out that the Cobra had took him down. "When's he's comin?"

"I don't know for sure…he had to clear some time from his calendar…he said he'd call me back early this afternoon. I'll let you know just as soon as I find out. Okay?"

"Okay, Rick, I 'ppreciate everthin' you've done for me…you gonna be there with us ain'tcha?"

"You know I'll be there. You sure you don't want to let me in on this before we go into the meeting with Calhoun?"

"Look, Rick, it ain't that I don't trust you. You ain't never been nothin' but fair with me...but...well...I cain't, not yet, anyhow. This could get my ass killed deader'n a doornail. I'm hoping what I have to tell him will get me outta this place. You ain't mad are ya?"

"Of course not, Harlan, I just thought if there were anything I could do to help prepare you for this confrontation. You know I'm ready to go to bat for you."

"Thanks, just the same," Cobra wanted to get outside where he could smoke, "but there ain't nothin' to do now but wait 'til I see the "dick" hisself."

Scarpadis recognized Cobra's restlessness, and after assuring Cobra he would set up the meeting as soon as he could, he bid his client farewell—knowing nothing of the part he was about to play.

Cobra crammed a half-empty pack of Pall Malls into the hip pocket of his county-issues and stuck the spare—that had been parked behind his ear—between his lips. The morning was pregnant with overdue precipitation. Voluminous, milky-gray, hump-backed clouds hung preponderantly in the western sky. The wind was hovering just out of reach, as if awaiting word from the storm gods. Static electricity stirred Cobra's slicked-back hair.

* *

"Looks like a fuckin' tarnada, don't it?" Cobra turned his head, just in time to see Ricky-Dino walking up behind him.

"Too fuckin' cold for a tornado, Mr. Wizard. Whatta you care anyhow? It's Friday ain't it? As they say in the funny-books, 'this here's the first day of the rest of your life.' Soon as it gets dark you and ol' Curly gonna *blow* up your own private storm, ain't ya?" He chuckled at his own cleverness. "Way it's lookin', you may get your party started earlier'n you'd expected. You just better hope'n pray that damned old shed don't blow away while you 'n Curly's goin' at it. Talk about your ass hangin' out in the wind—your flag'd be flappin' too." Cobra flipped his cigarette into a shallow, oily puddle and headed back to the lock-up.

"I hope it's gonna be as good as you said it was!" Ricky-Dino sounded like a little kid about to see *STAR WARS* for the first time, as he trailed along behind Cobra.

"Oh, it is, Dino, *it is*—the best you ever had. Has ol Cobra lied to you yet?"

That was a question for which Ricky-Dino had no immediate answer.

20

Who's that?" Harlan Merriweather was just exactly what I had expected. He was bout five foot-ten, 160-65 pounds and obviously older than he looked. He had not a hint of the hollow, beaten look of the desolate, habitual criminal. He had obviously been working out with weights while serving his time. His shoulders were broad and squarely-defined, while his well-developed pecs and washboard stomach were visible through the too-tight tee shirt he wore under his unbuttoned blue county-issue jumper. I couldn't see his biceps, but I could imagine.

Rick Scarpadis was tiptoeing around the tulips. He was the self-appointed moderator of this quasi-clandestine meeting between his client and the Clarksville PD's Chief of Detectives. Why? He didn't have a clue. However, he felt in his bones that it would turn out to be an interesting day, if nothing more.

Rick spoke, "Harlan, this is Dare Murphy; she's been working with Lieutenant Calhoun on a case up in Clarksville this winter."

I nodded.

"Yeah, I know," he leered, "I seen this one on the television more'n onest." He indicated, referring to me with an insolent flip of his chin. "Hey, who's your friend there?" I surmised he was referring to Lee. "You guys lost your manners? There's another lady in this room. What's the matter? You scared I'll ast her for a date 'er somethin'?"

"Please excuse my client, ladies, he doesn't get out much anymore—he's lost what few social graces he ever had."

"This is my associate Lee Graham, and I wouldn't advise it, if I were you." I nodded in Lee's direction.

"I didn't mean nothin' by it."

"And nothing taken," Lee said, as if he had asked her the time.

"Well," Ernest said, interrupting the little *tête-à-tête*. "Shall we get down to brass tacks?

JOY M. JAMISON AND CAROLE KENNEDY

I watched the prisoner, who was wearing ill fitting, recycled jailhouse garb. His shoulders strained at the seams of his jumper, and the sleeves quit abruptly at his mid-forearm. He sat complacently on a straight-backed chair across a small table from Ernest. Merriweather's public defender, Rick Scarpadis' presence was unobtrusive—for the moment. I sat slightly to Ernest's left with Lee close by. Merriweather had a cigarette balanced behind his ear and an open package of unfiltered Pall Malls, sitting on the table in front of him. Occasionally he would pick up the red pack and rub his fingers against the cellophane covering, before setting them down again. His random actions were unhurried, and his hands were steady. He wasn't the least bit nervous. I was, but he wasn't. Jails always give me the willies—as do hospital emergency rooms. He just wanted to smoke—everyone in the room wanted to smoke. Signs on all four walls forbade smoking, dipping, chewing and spitting. *Well, that pretty much takes care of my habits.* I was beginning to feel giddy. Perhaps I could chalk it up to claustrophobia…

After thumbing through the prisoner's considerable file, Ernest laid it aside, pulled his chair closer to the table, and looked directly into the eyes opposite his own. Merriweather did the same. "Merriweather, I hope I didn't drive all the way down here to Dickson County for a dog and pony show." One could tell by the questioning expression that befell Merriweather's face that he didn't understand the meaning of the Lieutenant's metaphorical license. "What I mean to say is, I hope we didn't make this trip for nothing. I hope you have something positive to tell us. I still don't have any idea why you felt it necessary to talk with one of us from Clarksville." Ernest was secretly hoping for some bit of information about Marie Zhou's disappearance, but he didn't hold out too much hope for such a break. Still, because of the circumstances, he held out a modicum of optimism.

"Do you reck'n they'd clamp us in chains if we smoked one cigarette?" This could be Merriwether's Achilles heel—it surely would be one of mine.

"Can't you read?" Ernest too would have liked a cigarette, and he knew he could get away with smoking—but wouldn't.

"Just thought I'd ast…ain't no law agin asting, is there?"

Ernest ignored the question. "Okay, Merriweather, what's going on here? What is it you want to talk about?"

"Hold your horses, there, detective. I don't get much civilized conversation in here. I'd just like to talk to you and the ladies for a while before I get down to the bad stuff. Like you can probably guess, we don't get many pretty ladies in here, Oh, onest in awhile some homely bull-dyke guard's assigned here for a bit, but, shit, that don't count. Excuse my language, ladies. He doffed an imaginary cap and went back to fingering the package of Pall Malls."

"Merriweather, *can* the shit and cut to the chase. We can't stay here all day. You got something to say, then say it. If you don't, then say so and we'll be on our way. We've all got better places to be than here. If you think we came down here to look at your sorry face, then you go another think coming. Now, if you want to jawbone with pretty ladies, maybe you just better watch your p's and q's, if you ever get out of here again. From the looks of your rap sheet here," he poked his rigid forefinger at the file on the table before him, "you'd rather stick up convenience stores than spend time with anyone— even pretty ladies."

Merriweather's expression clouded slightly, but before he could speak Rick Scarpadis stepped forward. "Lieutenant Calhoun, I don't know what my client wants to talk to you about, but I do know that he thinks it might help him with his present situation."

"And just what in the name of God makes him think that?" Ernest was tiring of the song and dance he had allowed himself to become a part of. He was seriously thinking about just getting out of his chair and calling for the guard to release us back into civilization. I definitely did not want that to happen—not yet anyway. This reprobate knew what I wanted to know, and I had every intention of finding out what that was before I left the premises. I leaned toward Ernest's left ear and asked him if I could ask the prisoner some questions. He shrugged and said, "Merriweather, you got any objections to answering a question or two for Ms. Murphy?"

"Oh, hell no...sorry ma'am," he made me feel in my dotage with that *ma'am* stuff, "I'll be happy to answer anything you wanta ast me—fire at will."

"Mr. Merriweather..."

"Please ma'am, would you just call me Cobra? That's what everbody calls me..."

"Okay...Cobra...I know you hear things in here...the question is are you willing to talk about those things?"

"Well, you ask and we'll just see what you receive...okay, ma'am?"

I held my breath for a moment, trying to formulate the question in just the right way...a way that wouldn't scare this man into total silence. "Mer...Cobra, do you know of anyone in here who smokes Kool cigarettes?"

He cocked his head at a peculiar angle as if to allow his gears and cogs ample room to grind. "No ma'am, not in here." I must have shown my disappointment because I had been so sure. "But, Mz. Murphy…I know a deputy that does…smokes Kools, I mean." I looked at Lee, Ernest, then back at Merriweather. Scarpadis bent down and whispered something in his ear, but Merriweather brushed him off with a wave of his hand. What makes you ask that ma'am?"

"We're the ones who'll ask the questions, Merriweather." Ernest wasn't about to let this interrogation become a familiar discussion.

"No disrespect, detective, but I was talkin' to Mz. Murphy here…maybe if you'll let us be for awhile, we might just come to some good stuff for all of us."

I looked at Ernest with what I hoped was a confident, yet a tad bit pleading countenance. "Let's see what he has to say, Ernest. If you don't mind I'd like to talk to Mer…Cobra for a few minutes." He begrudgingly deferred to me.

"Okay, for starters, why do they call you Cobra?" I was trying to lighten the atmosphere, hoping to loosen his tongue."

"You sure you want to know?"

From the grin on his lips, I really wasn't sure whether I did or not; however, my insatiable curiosity got the best of me. "Sure."

"Well, you see, ma'am…I got this tattoo…"

Right here, Ernest and Rick Scarpadis caught his drift and signaled for him to stop.

I shook my head, "Let him talk, if he wants to." I was hoping to gain his trust, and then perhaps he would get diarrhea of the mouth.

"Well, like I said, I got this tattoo…on my penis." I could sense Lee's eyes rolling back in her head. I, Ms. Cool, Calm and Collected, felt my face flush. It's not like I wouldn't have reveled in this story under other circumstances. But not here, in this room with these men: Ernest, along with a recidivistic nightmare and the nightmare's lawyer. Neither of the latter had I even met before today.

"Yeah?" I was doing my best off-handed act.

"Yeah, and it's a bigg'n."

I hated myself for having started down this road, but I would be damned if I would stop then. "The tattoo?"

"Yeah, that too. It's a snake…wrapped all the way around my pecker from start to finish. His fangs are bared at the very tip." He was definitely going for shock and awe. "A pretty, little tattoo artist from down around New Orleans done it. A good lookin' woman—with a slow hand—had to do it…or else it wouldn't a…"

"That's all right, Cobra, I get the picture. Now, please, let's get back to the Kools."

* *

Gun cleaning to Festus Arbuckle was like house cleaning to his wife Mary Magdelene. Festus had already cleaned and oiled his 2-10, his 12 gauge, and his 16 gauge shotguns. They were all laid out like little soldiers on the front porch along side the twenty-two rifle he had given to his boy on his 12th birthday. He had the rest of his hunting arsenal, including a 30-0-6 and a 30-30, laid out just waiting their turn at the bore rag and gun oil. He was just about to disassemble his .44 magnum handgun when he heard his prized blue tick hound begin to yelp. "Hey, Jeff Davis, shut your cake-hole and get on up here to the porch. Where the hell you been at all day?" The dog paid no attention. Soon Festus recognized the bark of his neighbor's dog. Soon a strange canine voice joined in, making it a trio. Soon the barking turned to growls and whining—a full-fledged, teeth-snapping, neck-gnawing fray ensued. "Mary Magdelene! Bring me some of them 16 gauge shotgun shells that I loaded up with rock salt! And be quick about it, woman! Jeff Davis may lose this war too, if'n you don't get a move on!

* *

The rock salt stung the hides of the slick-haired dogs, but they weren't ready to give up whatever it was they were quarreling over. Festus fired one more shot before he picked up his cane and headed off toward the ditch where the dogs were going at it. "Git on outta here, Horace," he yelled at his neighbor's dog, as he poked him in the flank with the rubber tip of his walking stick. Shoo! You too! He shouted as he took a healthy swipe at the strange dog in the pack. "What the hell's wrong with you varmits? Cain't a man clean his weapons in peace no more? Ya'll act like a bunch a them panty-waists up there in Washington. Ya'll ain't under-coverin' for the democrats are you?" He laughed out loud as the dogs finally scattered toward to woods. *What the hell is this?* He prodded at the nasty looking, grime and slobber encrusted—whatever it was—with his the toe of his brogan. Bending over—best he could—he looked closely at what had been the object of the dogs' rabid attention. Standing up shakily, he shouted, "Mary Magdelene! Get on the horn and call 911, then git out here to the yard...down here by the ditch...quick!

205

* *

"It ain't no jailhouse guard that smokes them nasty, menthol cancer sticks; it's a cruiser-jockey. You know…he patrols around the county lookin' for bad guys like me." Merriweather laughed out loud. "Them guys generally don't even come around the inmates. But I'm a trustee, you know, and I've seen that one light up, right inside the building…when the sheriff ain't around. I've seen his leavin's. They're Kools all right."

"What's his name?" Ernest had taken a whole new interest in the conversation.

Merriweather never missed a beat, nor indicated that he had even heard the question. He continued to look me directly in the eyes. "His name is Deputy Rupert Head. He works the third shift. He don't get off 'til six in the morning."

"Did you happen to see him come in on the morning of November 24th?" I knew I was spitting into the wind on this one.

"Jesus H. Christ, woman, what do you think I am? I ain't even sure I was in here then." He closed his eyes for a moment, when he opened them they were clear and bright. "Yeah, I was—I was here alright." He smiled—almost as if to himself—before he spoke. "That was right before Thanksgivin'…yeah, I was here then. But I don't remember seein' Deputy Head come in that mornin' or any other mornin, far as that goes. That's about the time we go to the chow-hall for breakfast. If you can call fried baloney with grits and grease, breakfast."

"Is he the only one who smokes Kools?" I was sure disappointment ran down my face like rain.

"Yeah, 'fraid so. But lookie here…he ain't the only one that drives that car neither."

* *

"I called the 911, Daddy, and they said that they'd be out drek'ly." Mary Magdelene had called Festus *Daddy* since the day their only child had been born. That child, a son, had been killed in a hunting accident, over twenty years ago, when he was just sixteen. Mary Magelene had never dropped the term of endearment. Festus still answered, not even thinking anymore about how the Arbuckle family tree had been chopped down to a stump the day Buddy died. "Whatcha got there on the ground, Daddy?" She came a little closer. Then she screamed and grabbed her apron, twisting it into a knot before hightailing it back to the trailer. She heard the Montgomery County Sheriff's Department, the fire department and rescue squad—all with sirens blaring—even before they turned off the blacktop down at Bubba Dye's Seafood Shack and Bait Shop. She also knew that had been no wild animal's skull she had seen lying on the ground at her husband's feet. She slammed the trailer door so hard that (had there been one, the back door would have rattled). She turned on the brand-new twenty-seven inch color television set and ran the volume up as high as it would go. Sirens scared Mary Magdelene Arbuckle worse than rattlesnakes or even cottonmouths did.

* *

"Who else drives the car?" I held my breath, trying to stem the anticipation that jumped rope inside my chest.

"Lots a guys. They don't always drive the same car..."

"Oh, I see." I felt myself deflate like a balloon that someone had poked with a straight pin.

"I don't think you do, Mz. Murphy."

"Just what the hell are you getting at, Merriweather?" Ernest was getting tired of Merriweather's little cat and mouse games.

This time both of us ignored the lieutenant. "What do you mean, Cobra?"

"I mean that the fuzz, s'cuse me, Lieutenant Calhoun, ain't the only ones that drive them cars. Trustees do too...sometimes."

I was taken aback in my naivete, even though Lee and I had discussed the possibility weeks ago. "What about you, Cobra?"

"Onest in awhile, but never on no long stretch. I just pick up shit for the sheriff and run piddly little errands around town. I never got one of them trips to Nashville or Memphis, like some of the guys do."

"Cobra," I ventured, "just why do you want to talk to someone from Clarksville law-enforcement?"

"I *don't* want to no more."

Once again I was crestfallen. "Why not? Obviously you have some important information. Why won't you help us?"

"I didn't say I wouldn't help *you.*"

I looked at Ernest. If looks could kill, I would have fallen dead on the spot.

"I want to make a deal." He had put his cards on the table; now it was time for someone to up the ante.

Ernest stood up. "I can't offer you anything. You only got a few months left on your sentence. What the hell do you need a deal for anyway?"

By this time Rick Scarpadis was sweating profusely. "Harlan, are you sure you don't want to talk about this before you go making statements to the authorities?"

"I ain't makin' no statements to the authorities. I want to talk to Mz. Murphy alone, then she can make me a deal with whoever'll come through for me. She'll understand how important what I have to say is. You won't...nobody won't but Mz. Murphy here. She'll be able to make everybody else understand. Look Rick, all of you, if I don't get outta here soon, my life ain't gonna be worth a plug nickel."

"Well, shit, come on Lee, let's go grab a cigarette while these two get up close and personal." Ernest was livid...rightly so.

"No, lieutenant, Mz. Murphy's friend don't have to go. They'll be just fine with me and Rick here. Don't worry. Go smoke your weed. Hey, smoke one for me while'st you're at it."

Ernest glared around the room, then without further ado, he called for the guard. The four of us sat silently while we waited—with bated breath—for Merriweather's prophetic words.

* *

"Whatcha got there, sonny?" Festus was back to himself and more than willing to lend a hand to the crowd of officials who had gathered down by the ditch. No one paid him any attention. So he watched as the gloved coroner picked up the human skull with what looked to Festus like a big ol' set of salad tongs. Festus was mesmerized by the myriad of flashbulb explosions. He thought they looked like tiny displays of fireworks—celebrating what exactly, he couldn't fathom. He looked on amazedly at the precision and gentle quickness with which the men and women dispatched their work individually, as well as members of a well-trained team. After a few minutes of being ignored, he strolled back toward the trailer. He was cold and didn't have his gloves with him. His chill seemed to emanate from within.

A uniformed county deputy was cordoning off the perimeter with yellow crime tape when a mud-spattered, red Blazer pulled up and nosed into a narrow spot at the edge of the soggy gravel road. The door opened and a cloud of acrid cigar smoke preceded the driver out the door. Will Bealer stepped out onto the mud-slicked grass.

"What they got, Piggy?" He spoke to the deputy who was still holding the roll of yellow tape in his hand.

"Looks like some kind of skull to me. My guess (now remember, I only saw it from a distance) is that it's human. We called the coroner just as soon as we got here and saw what it was. He's over there bagging it up now, getting it ready to take back to the lab. Then the boys from forensics showed up and have been scratching around this yard like a flock of chickens ever since."

"Well, then," Will drolled, "I guess I'll go up and check with Dracula."

"You better not let Doc hear you call him that. He just might invite you up to his castle for supper some dark and stormy night." The deputy giggled at their private joke about the coroner.

Will Bealer laughed and walked away, thinking about the conversation he had just had with the deputy. Will had known P.G. Henry, a twenty-year veteran of the Clarksville Sheriff's Department, since Will had retired from the Army and begun his job as Deputy Chief Inspector with the department. When Will had asked Piggy why he answered to that ridiculous nickname, he'd simply replied, "I can't rightly say. My mama called me Piggy, and my papa called me Piggy, so I reckon when I growed-up and haired-over, I just stayed Piggy." Will figured the deputy had told that story a thousand times. He laughed again.

The coroner looked up just as Will stepped to his side. "How's it hangin', Doc?"

"Not so good today. Take a look at this." The coroner held the clear plastic bag so Will could get an unobstructed view of the grisly contents. "See this trauma?" He said, pointing toward the left, rear quadrant of the skull. "There's a piece missing."

"Yeah, what do you suppose happened?"

"My professional opinion is the former owner of this cranium suffered a severe blow with a blunt instrument. I'll take a good look at it when I get back to the lab. I'm going to put in a call to Dr. Bass up at UT before I do anything else."

"Why you going to call him?" Will asked, knowing full well the reason.

"Dr. Bass is the best there is. He's the granddaddy of anthropological forensics."

"Aren't you 'fraid he'll steal your thunder?" Will was baiting the good doctor.

"*Will* !" The sheriff had spotted him and was trying to gain his attention. "Will!"

"Yeah, Sheriff? Be right there!" He nodded at the coroner and strode through the mucky, gummy remains of mud-tracked grass. He was on his way to the trailer's make shift front porch, where the sheriff was having a conversation with an elderly man wearing overalls and a World War II army field jacket. He could see a woman frantically peering from behind a diamond shaped window in the scuffed front door.

"Yo, Sheriff, I see you got quite a find down there. What happened?"

"Will, this is the owner of the property, Festus Arbuckle. His dog, along with his neighbor's dog, apparently dragged a skull up out of those woods over yonder." The sheriff pointed up the gravel road and across the highway towards the woods where Will Bealer had played as child. The woods where he had been a few short days ago with Ernest Calhoun, Harold Riggins, Dare Murphy and Lee Graham. He nodded in acknowledgment of Mr. Arbuckle's presence. Will pulled off his Massey-Ferguson baseball cap and crossed himself. *"Holy Mary, mother of God,"* he whispered into his gloved fists— *"Holy Mary, mother of God."* Totally unaccustomed tears stung his eyes as he turned to head back to his Blazer and his mobile phone. "Sorry, Sheriff...Mr. Arbuckle—I'll be back as soon as I call my wife. He would make the one, possibly two more calls before rejoining the others. He yanked open the driver's door. Sliding onto the front seat, he hurriedly searched through his "Daytimer" for the number listings for Lieutenant Ernest Calhoun and Dare Murphy. He punched in numbers, before rubbing his nose with the back of his glove.

* *

I was just getting into what I thought was a "mood conducive" with the prisoner. He was lightening up a little. In addition, he was an incorrigible flirt. His time inside, however, had dulled whatever such skills he might have possessed at one time. If it hadn't been such a tragedy, it would have been hilarious. Lee and I could have laughed over the situation for days. But, alas, it was tragic, and I tried desperately to comprehend what living in a place like that might do to one's psyche. Harlan Merriweather was a victim of all that can go wrong in one's life. And lacking the where-with-all—or the ambition—to remedy his situation, he would probably spend at least half of the rest of his life incarcerated in one penal facility or another. Perhaps in the end, some department of corrections would ship his body home in a corrugated box. That is, if there were a home to ship him to. Otherwise, at the rate this young hoodlum was going, it stood to reason he might eventually end up in a grave in a potter's field somewhere. He might even become the victim of one of his own 7-11 fiascoes. Either way—what a waste.

* *

"Merriweather...I mean Cobra...what is it?" I knew he detected the concern in my eyes. He had seen me on television. He knew I was helping in the search for Marie Zhou. We—those of us working on the case—had battled the media when they began to suggest murder hypotheses, hoping against dwindling hope to keep optimism up, especially for her family's sake. In this case, as in a lot of other such cases, local law enforcement agents become somewhat emotionally involved. Everyone except the FBI, and they come across as cold-hearted bastards. *But who knows what really lurks in the hearts and minds of men?*

"Mz. Murphy, do you think the Lieutenant gives a rat's ass if I live or die?"

"Cobra, Lieutenant Calhoun is a compassionate man. But first and foremost, he's a cop who has spent a great deal of this miserable winter looking for a young girl whose been missing since November 23rd. She was only sixteen years old. She was on her way home after spending the day with her boyfriend and his family. Someone lured her out of her car—under false pretenses—and she was dragged to some dark woods out off Cole's Road. She was repeatedly raped and was subjected to such degradation that no one of any age should ever have to face. He tied her between two trees, where he left her hanging naked, for only God knows how long, before he bashed her skull in with a rock."

By the time I finished my oration, Harlan "Cobra" Merriweather was sitting in slack-jawed amazement. "How'd you know all that? They ain't found her yet, that I've heard—only one bone, and that ain't even been identified yet...accordin' to the tube.

"You're correct, Cobra, but let us just suffice it to say, *I do know.*"

"The dream...you're the one in the dream, ain't you?"

My stomach grabbed itself from the inside and tied itself into a ragged little knot. "What dream are you talking about?" Lee, God love her, hadn't even breathed hard. Rick Scarpadis, on the other hand, was sweating the proverbial bullets.

"*You know! It was you!* You was there, he told me—but the stupid little shit couldn't place your face or remember your name. But by God, it was you—*wadn't it?*

"Cobra, I think it's time we called Lieutenant Calhoun back in here. Mr. Scarpadis, if Cobra is in agreement, we need to get a court reporter in here *tout de suite*. Can you do that for us?"

He stared at his client for a moment before he could get his tongue in gear. "Merriweather?"

"Rick, just do what Mz. Murphy says. Let's get this shit over with." He looked into to my eyes, never twitching an eyelash. "What now, Mz. Murphy, you think they'll help me?"

For an instant I wanted to hug him. I got over that in a hurry. "Cobra, I'll do everything I can to help you. All things considered, I'd be a bit surprised if you didn't get your request. But, I have no authority to make such a statement. I'll do my best for you".

21

The traffic wasn't bumper-to-bumper at four o'clock, as it would be at six, but it was bad enough. Driving toward Nashville from the west is a beautiful, scenic drive when conditions are good. However, clouds were circling—as if charting a landing. Not being a meteorologist, or even a fair judge of weather conditions, I couldn't discern whether they boded rain or snow. It really didn't matter, provided I got home before they ripened and produced. I was shaken by the results of my afternoon in the company of Harlan "Cobra" Merriweather and his *pro bono* lawyer. I knew Ernest was fit to be tied, having been excluded from the big finale, but I couldn't help it. We got more than we had hoped for.

Lee was ruminating. The whisper of cigarette smoke, as it escaped from her lips was the only sound I had heard from her since shortly after we had left Dickson County, and I didn't wish to disturb her reverie. Suddenly she ground out her cigarette and looked in my direction. "I'll be glad to get home and take a shower. I feel like I've been wallowing with the hogs."

"Yeah, me too. Maybe I do believe what the prognosticators of doom and gloom are predicting."

She lowered her window and took a gulp of near-frozen air. "Like what? She queried.

"That the world is going to hell in the proverbial hand-basket," I replied.

"I refuse to believe that," she defended.

"Then how the hell do you account for the dregs of the earth that are camping out in that den of iniquity?"

"Dare, it's a jail, what the hell would you expect to find in a jail?"

"Not that...can you believe what Harlan Merriweather told us?"

"Why not, Love? You had the dream—you *saw* it—he merely related what he'd been told."

"No, not just the part about Marie Zhou's tortuous murder. That I believe. I have no reason to doubt a word of it. You're right, I saw that happen in my own mind's eye, and I lived the whole episode in my sleep."

"Then what in hell can't you believe?"

"That ludicrous part about his *dick*."

"Oh, that…yeah. I can't picture that even in this fertile mind. You think we should ask the court to see the evidence?"

I took my eyes off the road just long enough to confirm it was sarcasm that had leaked out. It was. "Sure, Lee, and what should we have put on the warrant—*herpetological research?*"

She bent double in laughter and I reveled in her glee. I needed to flush the trash from my mind and soul, and Lee Graham was the medicine I needed. She lit fresh cigarettes for both of us. I took one from her fingers without taking my eyes from the road. The weather was deteriorating, but my mood was lifting.

"Looks like we're in for a bumpy night. Think we'll get home before the bottom falls out?" I knew she was anxious to get home to Joe. "You going out with Felix?"

"I surely plan to…I'm supposed to call him when I get home."

"Shall I dial him up now so you can inform him of our location and estimated time of arrival?"

I surprised myself as well as my passenger by replying, "Yeah, why don't you do that? I surely would hate to miss even a moment of Sebelius."

* *

I lay in the bathtub. In the twilight darkness of candlelight, shadows dancing the minuet playfully around the walls, their distorted reflections bowing back to themselves in the steamy mirror. Tiny bubbles crackled around my neck and shoulders as I relaxed deeper into the fragrant water. I couldn't get the afternoon's interview with Cobra out of my mind. What happened? Where do such people come from? What genetic or environmental crapshoot produces such creatures? I knew this was a problem that had plagued mankind since its inception, but that didn't make it any easier for me, as I soaked in the twilight. Nor could I help but be concerned that Lieutenant Calhoun was pissed off at me. Nor could I be responsible that Cobra didn't trust the *fuzz*. I didn't blame either one of them. I was in the middle and I would have to find my own way out. The phone rang.

"Dare, I'm on my way." It was Fel. He was calling from his car. "I'll be there in about thirty minutes. I thought we could stop by the Green Hills Grill for a late supper after the concert, then maybe go back to my place for the night. How does that sound to you?"

214

"Fel, that would mean I would be stuck all the way out in the hinterlands without my car. If you want to come back here, we could do that."

"Hey, Murph," *he called me that again*, "You sound down, what's wrong?"

"Oh, shit, Fel, I just had the most horrendous interview today with a guy who's locked up in the Dickson County Jail. God, it was hideous. I had to come home and try to scrub myself clean."

"Do you want to stay home? If you don't feel like going out, it won't take me five minutes to get rid of these symphony tickets..."

"No, no, don't do that. I think going out is the best thing for me tonight. I just think it would be better if you spend the night here rather than the other way around."

"Fine with me...if you're sure you feel like it."

"Look, Fel, if staying away from the concert would be the worst thing for me...you spending the night with me would be the best."

"That's very nice to hear."

"Now," I said quickly, "I've got to get out of the tub. I'll leave the backdoor open. Come in and fix yourself a drink. I'll try to be ready on time."

"Don't hurry, *Finlandia* is after the intermission. We've got time without your hurrying."

"Good...Fel, I would like to discuss what happened today, if you don't mind—later, I mean—after the concert."

"I don't mind...this can be your night to pick the topic of conversation...just remember the next time it'll be my turn."

"I hear you. Now get off the phone so I can concentrate on getting ready."

"Later, Murph."

"Why do you call me Murph?"

"Cause it's a cute name and you're a cute lady...does it bother you?"

"No, it's just that no one's ever called me that before. It *is* kinda cute, isn't it?"

I stepped out the tub, wrapping myself in a bath-sheet and waited for the last dregs of the bubbles to wind down the drain. Picking up a towel from the hamper I wiped down the tub. I felt better already. I rubbed myself pink and dabbed a touch of Joy behind each ear and in the hollow of my throat. *Ah! Mustn't forget the bends of my knees. Not tonight.*

* *

The symphony was brilliant under the baton of maestro Kenneth Shermerhorn. The weather had held, and occasionally even a few stars peeked from behind the clouds. The Green Hills Grill was crowded, but a path was cleared for us when Felix surreptitiously passed the *maitre d'* a greenback. The place was filled with everyone from Belle Meade blue noses and West End yuppies, to the rest of us—eclectisism personified.

For an appetizer we shared a delightful artichoke, spinach and garlic dip, complete with home made corn chips. The Angel Hair pasta was as its name implies. Piled high with fat, pink shrimp sauteed in garlic and butter, and tossed lightly in Alfredo sauce. Dessert was to die for—Crème Brulée so rich and creamy I could almost hear feel my arteries sweating.

"I swear I don't think I'll ever eat again," I moaned as we waited for the attendant to bring around the car.

"Yeah, I've heard that somewhere before," he grinned, opening the passenger door for me. "Maybe we better go to your house and take a brisk walk around the lake."

"I hear you, but if you think I'm going to stumble around out there in the dark just to work off a pound or two, you have another think coming. You can ride my stationary bicycle or go nowhere on my rowing machine if you want to." I winked at him.

"That sounds entirely like too much work. Anyhow, don't you know you're not supposed to do strenuous exercise after a heavy meal?" He looked pseudosly stern at me.

"If that's the case, perhaps you should just let me out at my door, and then you can just run on back to Bellevue so you don't hurt yourself."

"Hey, it's you I'm worried about as well. Anyway, why do you need to exercise when you already look so great?" He pulled onto I-40 and we headed east toward Mt. Juliet—and home. I felt my face flush with pleasure in the darkness.

* *

We had joked and laughed when suddenly he grew serious. "What was it you wanted to talk about?"

You're familiar with the Marie Zhou case being investigated in Clarksville, aren't you?"

"My God, yes, one doesn't have to be a lawyer to know about that one." He reached over and touched my hand. "Is that what you're working on?"

"Yeah, and I've got to tell you, this is about the worst thing I've ever dealt with—other than the Atlanta murders."

"What about it?" He continued to rest his hand on mine.

"Do you remember the nightmare I had the other night?" I looked at his profile in the glare of passing headlights.

"How could I ever forget it? Did that have something to do with the case?"

"Uh huh, unequivocally."

"Well, fire when you're ready—I'm all ears."

"Well," I stammered, "I dreamed I was at the scene of the crime…crime seems such an impersonal term for what happened." He waited patiently while I gathered my thoughts and words. "I dreamed I saw the whole debacle take place. I *saw* the beast, after he had stripped her naked on that God-awful cold night and forced her to perform fellatio on him." I paused and Fel squeezed my hand.

"You sure you want to talk about this?"

"No, I'm not…but I have to." I continued, "Well, after he'd done his dirty deed, he zipped up and strutted around like a "banty" rooster. It seemed like only a matter of a few minutes 'til he was ready to go again. He pushed her down on the ground, unzipped again and raped her like a crazed animal. When he was finished, she apparently caught him at a weak moment—she made a half-assed attempt to kick him in the gonads, but all that did was piss him off. He jerked her up and dragged her off somewhere out of my *sight*. I know now, that he took her back to the car and tied her hands behind her. They reappeared after a few minutes, and he pitched her back to the ground. It must have hurt her arms and shoulders terribly to fall on them like that, but I never heard her make a sound. I could hear him mumbling, but I couldn't make out what he was saying. He raped her again. Felix I couldn't…can't begin to believe that a fellow human being could be so heartless and cruel. Nothing I've seen in my professional life could have prepared me for that."

"Dare, some people aren't human; they're mad, demented beasts. I've run across a few in my time—not many, thank God—but a few."

"I guess after he had sated himself one more time and decided that she might seriously try to escape from him, he tied her between two small trees. He threw her sweater around her shoulders and took off back toward the car. He was gone for about twenty minutes or so. I could smell cigarette smoke so I knew he was still nearby…he hadn't just left her there. When he came back—you're not going to believe this—he was rubbing his crotch. The son of a bitch was working up another hard-on. Oh, I forgot to tell you, he had fashioned some sort of blindfold out of what must have been a piece of her clothing so she couldn't see him. But she had to have seen him when he picked her up...I don't understand...he's just fuckin' crazy, is all I can figure out."

"More ways than one, I would say."

I glared at him because I thought he was making a pun, but I quickly saw otherwise.

"Fel, he was walking stealthily out of the trees when he unzipped his jeans one last time...ripped open his waist button and went to work on himself. At first he just touched himself, then he fondled himself into a full erection. She never gave any indication that she heard him; I could *see* that she had just given up. He picked up a rock, and all the while he was pumping his handle, he was sneaking up behind her...then I woke up. This indicates to me that he must have awakened too." I looked at the sweet man behind the wheel, "Fel, he saw me too."

"My God...what do you mean? How could he see you? How do you know?" His voice was laced with alarm.

I told him what Merriweather had told us. "He saw me all right." I felt immeasurably better for having told him—a catharsis of sorts, I supposed.

"Jesus Christ, Dare, this whole episode would constitute a nightmare in anyone's lexicon." He pulled off the interstate at Stewart's Ferry Pike and drove across Percy Priest Dam. His tires crunched the gravel of the parking lot as he pulled to a stop.

"Fel, you do know we could be mugged while sitting here, don't you? This is a notorious spot." I grinned beyond the memory of the horror tale I had just told him.

"I'm only going to stop for a minute...I have an uncontrollable urge to hold you." He put his arms around me and pulled me close. This would have been the perfect opportunity to sob, but the tears wouldn't come. Instead, I felt warm and safe in this terrific man's arms. He held me close and kissed my hair, while repeating my name. Lust was still rearing its delightful head but I felt something else catching up fast. We sat for a few, short minutes before he kissed me and reluctantly moved away. He put the Jaguar in gear and pulled out of the parking lot. He held my hand. "Feel better?" He asked.

I squeezed his fingers; that was answer enough.

* *

I awoke, as always, when we slept together, to the aroma of fresh coffee and other culinary delights. Here was a man who loved to cook too. What more could a woman ask for? There had been no dreams. Only slow, measured lovemaking before the blessed peace of uninterrupted sleep had overtaken us. Harlan Merriweather and his snakebite kit were a world apart. Then there was his slimy cohort who had invaded my life from the inside out. But now I could handle it. I would find that lowly piece of trash soon. He, who had caused me such nocturnal grief, would live to regret he had crossed paths with Dare Murphy. *Count on it, asshole.*

* *

There is a great deal to be said for sitting across the breakfast table from a great-looking man with no newspaper to block the view. The thought fleetingly passed my train of consciousness: *How long would that last?*

"Well, Murph," he took my hand and grinned at me, "I gotta be going. I have a meeting at nine, and I don't want to rush in with a smirk on my face."

"You have a meeting on Sunday morning?"

"Well, not exactly a meeting, I have a foursome at Belle Meade Country club with Fred Thompson, Jack Lowry and Judge Tatum from Lebanon."

"Jesus, don't they have a golf course in Lebanon? That would be closer for everyone but Fred. But if you must know the truth, I feel safer with him at Belle Meade swinging a golf club than I did when he was in Washington swinging a gavel."

He grinned and reached for my hand. "Ah, Fred's okay—he's just a little zealous. Besides, you know he's back in Hollywood playing the D.A. on *Law and Order.* Want to come to my house tonight?"

"Yeah, I would love to, but if I don't get a few things done around here, the health department may condemn the place."

"Now, what could be more pressing than spending the night with me?"

"Well, I've got clothes to wash, then clothes to iron. I've got to dust, vacuum and all the other little things that make life worth living. You know, all the fun stuff."

"Why don't you hire someone to do all those fun things? That would leave you more time to play with me."

"Because, believe it or not, I enjoy doing some things for myself. I have the miracle girls once a week—they do the heavy stuff—but no one else can please me when it comes to certain things."

He grinned, "I do okay, don't I?"

"Can you iron?"

"You'd be surprised what I can do," he laughed, "I'll call you when I get home."

22

Dare, where the hell have you been? I've been trying to get hold of you since yesterday afternoon."

No sooner had I turned on my private phone it started ringing. "Good morning to you too, Ernest. *Who peed in your Wheaties?*

"You should leave word when you're going to be out of pocket."

"Well, *excuse me*, I do have a private life you know. What's got you so fired up?"

"It may just interest you to know that they've found a skull not far from the woods where we found the bone."

We? "Who found a skull?

"Several dogs dragged it up to some old geezer's trailer. They had a regular game of soccer going with it out in the yard. It seems that one of the dogs belonged to the owner of the place. The guy went out to see what was going on, figuring on breaking up a fight among 'em—and there it was. You know what they say about a dog with a bone."

"Damn! Did you by chance leave a message on my voice mail? I turned off my private number so I could get some rest. Believe it or not, I was bone tired when I got home yesterday. *No pun intended.* When I'm out of the office, I always leave my business line on voicemail."

"No, I figured if you didn't answer your private line, you wouldn't be likely to answer anything."

I heaved a sigh of relief because, of course, I hadn't checked my voice mail. Right after I had talked to Fel yesterday I turned off my private phone— one never knows who might call at an inopportune time. Lee has a penchant for doing so.

"Listen, Ernest, I'm sorry, but there's nothing to be gained by recriminations. Have they identified the skull yet?"

"No, it's being gone over by forensics, even as we speak. The mandible is missing, as would be expected—but Will Bealer's boys are searching the entire area where we were the other day. Will's with them. They're going over every inch of ground with a fine-tooth-comb. I've been trying to locate Marie Zhou's dentist so we can compare dental charts with the teeth in the skull. Go try to find any kind of doctor on the weekend—it's damned near impossible. Dare...there is very severe trauma evident. Looks like you were right all along."

"About what?" I queried.

"Someone bashed her head in, but good—from behind."

"Oh, my God." I felt my knees go weak, and I needed to sit down. My stomach did a flip and all the happiness I had felt only a short time ago drained from my heart like tepid dishwater. "I'll be right there."

"Good, I'll be in my office."

"Ernest, I want to go back to the woods."

"I figured as much."

"I'll see you. I've got to call Lee now."

I pushed the off button on my portable and laid it on the kitchen counter. I poured myself another cup of coffee, lit a cigarette and cried.

* *

"What the hell's he yelling at you for? He's the one that called you for help in the first place. Anyhow, it's Sunday. Is there to be no rest for the weary?"

"He just got frustrated when he couldn't reach me. I had turned off my private line before I went out last night. I'm not blaming him. You know how he gets when he's stymied."

"Yeah, nuts." Lee had pretty well summed it up.

The day was overcast but crisp. "Not a very good day for golf," I muttered, half to myself.

"You got a golf game planned for later?" Lee looked at me like I had lost my marbles. "You must have been taking lessons when I wasn't looking."

"No, you know perfectly well I don't play. It's an insipid game for people who'd rather knock a ball around than use their brains." Knowing perfectly well that was not the truth, if for no other reason than Felix was on the course even as we spoke.

"Whoa, there," she defended, "I know a lot of people who could find fault with that premise...Joe for one."

"Lee, I'm just discombobulated, what can I say? That poor child's parents are going to hear—if they haven't already—about the skull. Just as soon as the dental records are compared with the teeth, they're going to know that there is no hope. Give it up, get on with it, chop chop."

"Yeah, I know," she mused, "Jesus, can you imagine what they've been going through all this time—not to mention her aunt and uncle. I believe I would slit my wrists if I were in their place."

"No, you would not! I might, but you wouldn't. You're one of the most level-headed individuals I've ever known, Lee Graham."

"Bullshit! Yeah, fluff me and stroke me. You know how to get a full day's work out of me, don't you?" She lit a cigarette and lowered her window, blowing smoke into the frigid out-of-doors.

I watched her out of the corner of my eye. She was off in the cosmos somewhere. Where was I supposed to meet Ernest? His office, or the woods? I decided to bypass the woods and do what I should, for a change. Don't pass go, don't collect $200, go directly to jail. Well, the Chief of Detectives office would be close enough. We passed the Acme Boot Company, and I roused Lee from her woolgathering. "Hey, we're here. We'll be at Ernest's office in about five minutes."

"I'm with you," she grinned, scratching the cobwebs out of her brain.

* *

A young, peach-fuzz faced rookie, who looked barely old enough to be a Boy Scout, led us into Lieutenant Calhoun's office. Apparently Ernest had left word with whomever, that we were to be shown in immediately upon arrival. Ernest was talking on the telephone. He was pacing behind his desk while scratching his head with the point of a yellow pencil. I hoped he didn't lose his rhythm, perhaps stabbing himself on the up-step. Lee and I sat down in the only spare chairs in the room—two familiar old-fashioned straight-back chairs. They looked as though someone had lifted them from their mates at a garage sale. I lost interest in watching Ernest pace and scratch, and began to look around. The window behind him was in dire want of washing—cobwebs decorated the sills and corners like lace on *Miss Haversham's wedding cake*. The dingy daylight leaking through the panes made my mood even bleaker. I reached inside my jacket pocket for my cigarettes and lighter. There was a new "No Smoking" sign neatly tacked to the corkboard, where the Lieutenant kept various scraps of paper taped, pinned, tacked and stuck behind the wood of the frame. It was like the rest of his domain—a mess. The overflowing ashtray on his desk was more that I could stand. I picked it up and dumped it into the wastepaper basket, banging it noisily against the side of container, in an attempt to flush out the grime that coated the aluminum receptacle that had been filched from a McDonald's fast food restaurant.

Ernest looked up and gave me a grave expression before forgetting once more that I was there. My eyes continued to wander around the room—this home-away-from-home, this sanctum sanctorum, shrine to justice—seemed the antithesis of detective Lieutenant Ernest Calhoun, a man I suddenly realized that I barely knew. Nor was I sure how I felt about him. Sometimes I liked him okay, but most of the time he had a way of stripping the insulation from my neural connectors. Lee liked him and he seemed to genuinely like her. Just goes to show you, I reckoned.

Ernest hung up the phone. "I've been talking to the chief. It's Sunday—his mother-in-law is in from Nashville. He's got to drive her home. How fuckin' convenient."

I added my two cents worth, "Ernest, when you get to be chief, you'll get to drive your mother-in-law around while some grunt crawls around in the mud gathering evidence. Your knees will never get dirty again. Just think about it." My sarcasm was not lost on him, but he ignored me while his mind churned ahead, gathering his scattered thoughts about him like a wrap.

"Well ladies, ya'll ready to go to the woods?"

I held my tongue. I swallowed my smart-ass answer and answered civilly.

"Do you want to ride out with me and Riggens or do you want to drive your own vehicle?"

"I'll drive, if you don't mind. Lee and I will meet you there shortly." We left his office and headed toward the side door. I could see my grimy Lexus sitting next to the curb outside. "I've got to get my car washed," I mused aloud, "before that damned road salt eats holes though it."

Lee ignored my comment and asked instead, "Any particular reason you would rather drive than ride?"

"Yeah, I just want to walk around for a few minutes without Ernest sniffing my trail. You have your mini-recorder, don't you?"

"Of course I do, you know I never leave the house without it. I've told you the only place it never goes, is to bed with me."

"I'm not going there, thank you, very much."

* *

I drove slowly through the mist. Not enough precipitation for the wipers to be effective, just enough to muck up the windshield. My mood was as gray as the morning: thick and damp with no improvement in sight.

"Hey, watch out there! Your turn is coming up shortly." Lee warned me just in time.

"Thanks, I must have been in *zoom dweeby land*. I probably would have passed it by. Hey, I wonder if there's a back way into these woods?"

"I don't know!" Lee was excited, "But instead of turning here, why don't you drive up the road a little ways and see if there's another turn off. If so, that should take us to the backside. At least we can check and see if there's a road back there."

I kept driving—past the Cole's Creek Road turnoff and further. After I had driven a quarter of a mile or so, Lee noticed a double rutted path cutting through the roadside weeds. "There!" she shouted, pointing into the windshield. I slowed to a crawl and eased the Lexus's heavy-duty tires onto the side of the road. Finding the ruts I followed them into the trees.

I announced to the universe, "This is where the fucker brought Marie. He came in this way and parked the squad car where it couldn't be seen from either road. He was definitely familiar with the terrain. If he didn't live here, he's hung around here with somebody—probably some of the ne'er-do-well trash he runs with. Creeps like that tattooed freak.

I pulled the SUV into the woods, and parked approximately where I thought I had seen the squad car in my dream. I unbuckled my safety harness, sliding off the seat, landing firmly on the clammy leaves that covered everything. "Lee, you out?" I called through the open door.

"Yeah, I stepped on my boot-string. I've got to sit here on the running board and lace them up tighter—hold on a minute."

I heard dogs howling in the distance. That damned goose was jumping up and down on my grave. It looked as if any moment the blizzard of the century was due to blow in. However, cold sweat was sliding down my skin beneath my clothes. My biological clock needed winding more ways than one.

Lee stood up and looked around. "Where the hell is Bealer and his boys? I thought Ernest said they were crawling over every inch of ground out here."

"Let's go through this underbrush, and I'll bet you we'll come up right behind them, past those trees over there. You can see the tops of that ring of cedars in the distance." After about twenty yards or so, we heard muffled voices, as the wind picked up and carried their words our way. I put my hand out to halt Lee—not wishing to embarrass the deputy, who was marking his territory on a tree just ahead. After he had zipped up, we continued forward. I saw Will Bealer down on one knee. He appeared to be scratching through the leaves on the floor of the woods. He turned around when he heard our soggy footsteps.

"Hey, Dare, Lee, where the hell did you come from? Where's Ernest?"

"We came in the back way, Will. Ernest should be here before long. However, betcha he'll come in the same way you did."

"I didn't even know there was a back way. The road didn't go that far when I was a kid, and I haven't paid much attention since. Show me where you came in, will you?"

"Surely, lets go." We retraced our footsteps through snaggle-toothed briars and stringy undergrowth, toward the place where my car sat like a beacon in the dingy afternoon.

"Shit!" Lee tripped. "What the hell is this?"

"You should have stayed on the path, dear heart," I teased.

"Look at this, would you?" She bent over and touched something before jumping back as though she'd been shot. "Jesus H. Christ! Dare, Will, come here!

She had stepped in the midst of a pile of bones, several ribs, along with a portion of partially articulated spinal column that lay beside them. No flesh clung to the ribs or the backbone. From the looks of things, they had been long ago dinner for beasts of the field. They had been gnawed almost through in places. Lee gagged and leaned her head against a tree. I just looked...and wept inside.

"Wallace, come here and bring the big bag!" Will bellowed at his deputy, who after a moment came crashing through the trees like a water buffalo. I hoped he wouldn't trample any further evidence in his wake. "Slow down, Wallace, before you kill yourself or somebody else. Now, hand me the bag." Will, after pulling on latex gloves, pulled out his trusty Polaroid and clicked pictures from every angle, before picking up each bone, one at a time with the over-sized tweezers. The chunk of spine disarticulated at the first touch. Disintegrating cartilage and what could have been petrified ligaments clung for the briefest moment before disappearing into the wetness. They had waited, since before Thanksgiving, to be discovered.

"Dare." I looked up to see Ernest hovering over me. "Rick Scarpadis just called my office—Merriweather wants to see you—says it's important."

"Well, Merriweather can take an number and get in line—there's just so much of me to go around. When you get back to your office or wherever you go when you leave here, please call Mr. Scarpadis and ask him to call me at me tomorrow. Give him my office number, please. If he wants to see me badly enough, he can come to me. I'm sick and tired of being at everyone's beck and call. I *do* have a life." I had never spoken to anyone I was working with in such a manner before. I was hanging out on the ragged edge, and I could only hope everyone understood. *Of course they wouldn't understand, why should they? I needed Cobra Merriweather as much as he needed me.* "Ernest, I'm sorry for my outburst, it was totally uncalled for. Tell Mr. Scarpadis I'll call him.

"Okay, 'cause he sounded like it was something really improtant. What the hell's all this?" His attention had been diverted to the bones that Will was harvesting from the weeds.

"Marie Zhou," I answered blandly. "Lee just found these ribs and bits of spinal column." For the time being, I mentally 86ed the request from Harlan Merriweather's public defender, and thought of nothing except the bones of the poor child that were being placed into a heavy plastic bag, not three feet away. "I hope we find the rest of her for her family's sake." My words washed away on a sudden gust of wind.

23

While I sat in my car waiting for the garage door to creep up it's ancient tracks, I watched Lee climb into her adored RX-7 and head down the driveway and out of sight. I was about half ashamed of myself for sounding off at Ernest the way I had. It wasn't his fault that I was exhausted and worn out with this case. I'm sure he was too, in addition to whatever else might be cluttering up his desk. I supposed he might even have a wife and children— I'd never asked. I even talked to Lee about it on the way home, and she had given me her stock answer, "Screw it, there's just so much of you to go around. You apologized, now get over it." Somehow, that hadn't made me feel better. I just hate to lose my cool in the company of people that I'm supposed to be helping.

As soon as I deduced that I had ample headroom, I drove under the groaning antique door and turned off the ignition. I sat in the car long enough to determine that the door was, in fact, on its way back down. Key in hand I unlocked the deadbolt and kneed the door to my kitchen open. I dropped my muddy boots and field jacket outside the door, stepped inside and reset the security alarm. I tossed my purse on the counter, after digging through its depths looking for my cell phone. I must have left it in the car. Oh, well, it wasn't going anywhere; I'd fetch it later. The red light on my private number's answering machine was blinking like a beacon in the half-light of the dying afternoon. I flipped on the overhead light and made my way to the great room, where I went behind the bar and poured myself a double shot of Jack Daniels neat—ice would only take up valuable space. I took a gulp and almost choked on it. *Mustn't get in a hurry when imbibing firewater,* I reminded myself.

Back in the kitchen, I pulled up a stool and lit a cigarette before checking my messages. I didn't want to talk to anyone but Felix, but I knew he was marching up and down the fairways with a senator, a judge and a lawyer/construction magnate.

There were several messages—all from Rick Scarpadis. After the first one, I no longer cared how he got my private number—my privacy was not all that was being threatened, it seemed.

1. *"Ms. Murphy, I hope you don't mind me calling you at home, but Lt. Calhoun gave me this number so I guess it's all right. Ms. Murphy, Harlan told me that his contact, you know, **the suspect**, told him that he was driving an official to the Nashville International Airport sometime today. Harlan just thought you should be forewarned. I, however, don't think there is any indication for concern."*

2. *"Ms. Murphy, Harlan wanted me to tell you he thinks he heard **the suspect** mention your name before he left the facility. That in itself doesn't seem tantamount to undo speculation, I wouldn't think."*

3. *"Ms. Murphy, Harlan insists that **the suspect**, whose name he will not disclose to me, is less than well-balanced, and he wants you to take whatever precautions you think might be necessary to avoid contact with him. Harlan suggests you leave. That's, of course, up to you. I'm merely passing on a message from my client. Have a good day."*

That's the direction all the messages took. "Ms. Murphy…yada, yada, yada…" Well, I did take the situation seriously. *Less than well balanced?* Now that was an understatement. There was a maniac out there somewhere with my name on his rotten lips. I left the messages on the machine so I would have some sort of concrete evidence if ever it were needed. I yanked up my portable phone from its cradle to return Mr. Scarpadis' call, after that I would call Sergeant David Marshall, Metro-Nashville PD detective par excellence. When in trouble, call the real police I always say. I was nowhere near his jurisdiction, but I knew he could and would get something done *tout de suite.* I put the phone to my ear to hear nothing but ominous silence. I must have failed to turn it on. No, the red light glowed under the "on" button. I listened again. Nothing! Don't panic, Murphy, it's certainly not unheard of for the Tennessee Telephone Company to take the afternoon off. This was the company, that when I first moved to the area, would go into the dumper every time it rained. Times, indeed, had changed, but reliable? Well, most of the time—but they still had their moments. Try again. Nothing.

I took my drink and headed for my bedroom to try the phone at my bedside. Perhaps it was just the portable that was on the blink—nothing. Taking a discreet sip of the Black Jack, I decided to look at this situation logically and orderly. I made my way back to the kitchen. Stopping by the freezer, I grabbed a couple of ice cubes. Dropping them into my glass, I sat down to think. I lit another cigarette and dropped the pack, along with my lighter, into my cardigan pocket. I drew deeply upon the tobacco for calmness and comfort, blowing recycled smoke across the counter. I grabbed my drink and took my cigarette to the next logical place—downstairs—where I had two business lines, a fax and the Internet at my disposal. I stopped at my personal office and sat down behind my desk, flipping on the lamp before picking up the receiver. I punched in line 1. Nothing. I punched line 2. Nothing. Line three: the fax and computer line. Nothing. I ground out my cigarette in the ashtray and left my glass, with only the dregs of my drink, resting on a coaster on my desk. I rounded the desk and almost ran to the computer that's connected to the Internet. I went directly to Internet Explorer—nothing. Shit! I went to the front desk, where tomorrow Katie would normally be sitting and doing her job with incredible efficiency. Today her chair was empty and suddenly a cold chill crawled up my spine. I tried all three lines on Katie's phone—nothing. My last hope—in my dreams—was the fax. Get over it, Murphy—no phone—no fax.

No point in staying down here in this cave, I thought, *not a fucking thing down here works anyway.* That wasn't exactly the truth; the computer worked fine—just not the Internet. I decided to return to the upstairs where at least I didn't feel the chill quite so acutely. I would go out to my car and get my cell phone, just as soon as I lit the gas logs.

Logs lit, hands warmed, I got up to go out to the garage. The dingy day had evolved into an even dingier twilight. The golf game would be over, and the guys would be strategizing at the nineteenth hole, as the clubhouse bar was known. It looked as if snow was contemplating making an appearance, but who could tell anymore. It had been so long since I had felt the sunshine on my body, I felt as though my world might begin to mold. I went out to the garage and opened my car door—no phone. Well, shit, I'll bet Lee stuck it in her pocket thinking it was hers. Great, now she has two and I have none. How the hell am I supposed to let anyone know that I just may be being stalked by a lunatic who's running around on work release from the Dickson County jailhouse? Damn you, Cobra, you tattooed freak and your prospective deals. The very least you could have done was whisper his name to me. Hell, I'm the one he's after.

I closed the car door and was almost to the kitchen door when the light in the garage went out. A scream died in my paralyzed throat. *Get hold of yourself, Murphy,* I mentally cautioned myself. *Peeing your pants in this cold garage will only contribute to extreme discomfort and possible pneumonia.* My God, what weird thoughts were running amok through my skull.

My throat was constricted to the point that nothing would come out beyond a pathetic squeak. *Relax, Murphy, relax. Hey, and while you're relaxing, kiddo, you better feel around here and find a hammer or something.* A pale, pathetic strip of light dribbled through the side window: the remnants of the security light out front. *Fat lot of good that damned light does with the garage door closed* Suddenly, and without warning, the security alarm blasted its way into my reality. Screaming horns and a siren whooped their way into the night outside—not to mention rattling the garage window and me along with it. *Well, you surely got all the bells and whistles you paid for.* The brain is a wonderful organ. I felt as though mine was in my pocket.

My voice found me—I scared myself—I guess I had never heard me scream for real before.

Once I gathered my wits about me I could imagine what my neighbors were probably doing...peering out their windows, stepping out onto their decks and patios, wondering what the hell was going on in this normally calm and serene neighborhood. None of them has a clear visual shot at my house. I live at the end of a long winding driveway. My house is situated on a rise surrounded on three sides by massive oaks, maples and black walnut trees. The back of the house faces the lake. I could visualize the binoculars coming out of cases on the other side of the cove.

I crammed my fist into first one jeans' pocket then the other—my keys were there—I hadn't dropped them on the counter or into my purse, which was my usual habit upon entering the house. Suddenly the overhead light blinked on. Its sudden glare temporarily blinded my gloom-accustomed eyes. Perhaps the end of my quandary. Before the lights had so serendipitously sprung to life, I had toyed with the idea of starting my car and backing the SOB through the wooden garage door. Now I wasn't at all sure that was a good idea...especially since there was a switch on the wall. But here again, the damn thing takes so long to lumber up its tracks anything could happen before...unless I rolled out from under the door and ran...no, I would not be run off my own property. But, if my space had truly been invaded, would the perpetrator turn the lights off again and murder me after I got back inside the house, and while the alarm system screamed in the background? I didn't think so. I found the proper key to unlock the deadbolt and was prepared to push it home when my attention was slammed. The door was not shut all the way. Of course it wasn't. I had merely come out to look for my cell phone. Had I failed to disarm the alarm system before I came out? "*No*," I remembered. I pushed open the door and rechecked the control panel. It had not been reset...the red light glared at me like a mocking cyclops. Why had it gone off? And why did it take its own sweet time about doing so? *Shit*!

* *

I heard the official vehicles long before they rounded the curve, and their drivers discovered they must slow to a crawl, to make it without incident up my curvy driveway. Somewhere in the distance I heard the hiccuping whoop of a fire engine. I didn't think that one was headed my way. The deafening scream of a police siren enveloped me like a storm. After what seemed like long minutes, it ground to a whining halt. Doorbells rang at both the front and back doors. I could see the beige, polyester shirt of a Wilson County mountie through the window. He had his face pressed up against the glass like a little kid staring into an aquarium. I saw Lee push him aside—Joe was right behind her. The deputy didn't put up much of a fuss. It seems that Lee had heard the alarm all the way to her house, nearly two blocks away. Being the naturally interested (some would say nosy) person she is, she checked it out. Joe, being the concerned husband that he is, wouldn't let her come alone.

The phone rang—I nearly jumped out of my skin.

* *

If I said, "I don't know" once, I must have said it a hundred times. A representative from the security firm had been the voice on the phone. I told the same "I don't know" to her, I said the phones weren't working, that's why she couldn't reach me. I explained everything I knew to the sheriff's deputies, and to countless others including Lee and Joe. Thank God, they had sent in the infantry before asking why. I would feel safer in the future. Hell, I'd always felt safe. My world had been impenetrable to the evil daring-dos of the likes of whomever it was that I feared had had me in his sights this night. Only once before had I felt so vulnerable. It had been when my computer had been broken into and potentially could have been sucked dry. That time I had, quite by accident, interrupted the surreptitious transmission by picking up on line three, which had disrupted the connection. But that was a whole 'nother lifetime ago.

* *

I had Lee call Dave—he had shown up by the time that the last of the deputies had tracked though my domain. Only then did Joe consent to go home—extracting a promise from Lee that she would call him right before she left my house. "Bring Dare with you," he tossed over his shoulder as he closed the back door behind him, knowing full well that I wouldn't leave home.

Later, after Sergeant David Marshall had arrived, Hillary Kitten peeked around the door to see who was left of the noisy crowd. She came into the kitchen and wove a figure eight in and around the Metro detective's legs. He was allergic to cat dander—cats seem to know those things and hone-in instinctively on the sufferer. I scolded her, and Dave sneezed, but she rubbed all the more diligently, before finally strolling off toward my bedroom— twitching her tail insolently over her back.

Dave had stood perfectly still until Hillary had finished with him. Then he bent over and fruitlessly picked at the downy cat hairs that sprinkled his trouser legs from his shoe tops to almost his knees—sneezing only occasionally—now that Hillary had vacated the premises.

"Send me the cleaning bill," I offered, handing him a tissue to wipe his watery eyes. Then I told him everything that had happened: from the bones we had found, to the tale that the inveterate *snake charmer* had spun.

The detective seemed nonplussed. "For some foul reason, the alarm system malfunctioned...probably due to the power-outage," Dave went on, "an eighteen-wheeler plowed into the power station down on Lebanon Road. Everything between here and Stones River was dark when I drove out from town."

"Screw the power-outage; my alarm system shouldn't malfunction for any reason. Isn't it on a battery backup?"

"Yeah, but sometimes shit happens."

"Not to me it doesn't—the sonofabitch goes off for no reason again, and you'll have to pull me out of somebody's throat with a come-along."

"A tech will be out here first thing in the morning to recalibrate the thing and check all your windows and doors—upstairs as well as downstairs. I made a well-placed call."

"And in the mean time?" I queried.

"I'll stay with you or you can go home with Lee."

"Oh, shit, now I've got to have a freakin' babysitter."

"Fine, Lee can go home and I'll stop by the FOP for a couple of beers." He referred to The Fraternal Order of Police, a service organization, which, incidentally, served as a watering hole frequented exclusively by off duty police officers and their guests. "And meanwhile you can lie in bed all night and wait for that goddamned cat to shed all over anyone who might decide to break in."

I knew he was just blowing off frustration. "Very funny," I scowled, halfway apologetically, "but only if you're sure you don't mind staying for awhile. I'd be happy if you both would stay at least until Fel calls."

"Who's Fel?"

"Felix Walker," I said, surprised that so much had happened in the past few weeks that he was totally unaware of. Not so long ago Dave had been an integral part of my life, when Jerry was alive and they were best friends and partners. How quickly things can change.

"You mean the guy who was assistant to that asshole we found buried in the mud out by the river?"

"The very same. He's in private practice now."

"Well, good for him…and good for you. I'm glad to hear you're getting on with your life, Dare."

I hugged him and kissed his cheek just as the phone rang. "Get that will you, Lee?"

She handed me the phone. "It's the Esquire, M'um."

24

We made a frantic, hungry kind of love; easing the desperation that had laced itself up inside of me. I was still frightened on some base level. An undercurrent of faceless uneasiness ran though me like low voltage electricity.

Afterwards, Fel held me hard—I know his arms must have ached, but every time he loosened his grip, I tensed. Finally, after what seemed like hours—but couldn't have been that long—tenseness began to relinquish its grip. I guess I realized that, in fact, there probably was no *bogeyman* out there with my name at the top of his list. It was with that realization that I felt a surge of unsurpassed passion for the man who lay with me.

I kissed him deeply and our tongues played hide and seek. He grew hard, and I took full advantage of the situation—we made sweet, unhurried love. I tasted the sweetness of his feverish flesh, craving to crawl inside him where I knew I would be safe forever. Finally, we left each other breathless, and needing nothing or no one else. Satisfied and gratified, we fell asleep, each in the arms of the other. I heard his tiny snores—like music in my ears—before slumber swallowed me. Rhythmic breathing lulled senses into what should have been undisturbed wonderland.

* *

Wonderland became a wasteland—a featureless landscape for as far as the eye could see. Granite-hued clouds, wandering across a cold, charcoal backdrop of sky, snowed dust and ash. Lightning sputtered like an ancient neon sign, illuminating the backside of the night. Thunder growled, sounding as if God might be fussing at his cherubs—scolding them softly for some minor indiscretion. No moon to see by. No hint of breeze. Only feeble lightning and tenuous thunder scored this phantasmal overture.

* *

The thunder and lightning quit the sky. The wads of clouds cleared and thin, pale streaks of moonlight tentatively reflected off my nude body. The curtains were drawn back against the window sashes, but my bedroom was shadowed deeply by the huge trees on the other side of the glass.

I felt rested and refreshed. I stretched longingly toward Fel, who even in sleep turned instinctively toward me. I put my arm around his shoulder and he eased closer to me. I was on my side, as was he. I kissed him, and he grew taut against me. Moving almost imperceptibly, he found his way home. We moved synchronously, as though we were joined, somehow, together. Slowly, slowly our bodies met and retreated—two souls pulsed as one. I took matters in hand and felt him gasp with pleasure. We resituated ourselves and so did the moon—the darkness quickened.

My cheek brushed against his firm, smooth belly—his breath was growing rapid but measured and controlled. I was not so self-disciplined. Tremors ran through my body. Tiny, but potent currents gripped my middle—precursor to the seismic activity on the horizon—the epicenter charging anticipatively.

I murmured against him, he understood. We resituated ourselves once again in the darkness. He kissed my breasts, as he found me without guidance. Not that I'm an expert, but he changed his tactics. He came at me with a hunger I hadn't seen or felt before; he was getting rough, which surprised, but excited me. I followed him through the door to a place I'd never been. Lights burst so brightly behind my eyes that it was almost painful—where was I? Where were we? My body convulsed spasmodically as I reached a delicious orgasm. He was with me, stroke for stroke, exploding inside me with the heat of Vesuvius. He stayed with me until there was nothing left—until we were sweat-drenched and exhausted.

*The moon peeked through the window, melting the shadows. It cast its feeble glow like a candle in the wind. I screamed—it was **him** looming over me—the phantom of my nightmares was in bed with me.*

"Hey there, Miz Murphy," he grinned, saliva dripping from his curled lips, "was it as good for you as it was for me?"

* *

I was begging God to help me hang onto what little sanity I might have left. Then implored Him to lead me to a place where I would never see that face or hear that voice again. Suddenly, I heard someone calling my name from what seemed miles away. Each call brought the faceless voice a little closer until I recognized it—it was Fel.

"Dare...wake up...what's wrong? Have you had another of those damnable dreams? *Wake up, Sugar...please."* The word sugar had come out *"suga,"* which rolled off his southern tongue like early morning dew on hollyhocks.

I opened my eyes. He was leaning over me; his dark curls dripping over his forehead. I tried to focus my eyes and my thoughts in his direction. "Did you just call me sugar?"

He gathered me in his arms and held me so tightly that I thought I might break. At that particular moment in time, I was thinking of absolutely nothing else. That would change soon enough.

"Yeah, I guess I did, he grinned before growing sober again. "Where in hell have you been? It was like you just picked up and left your body here on the bed beside me while your mind got lost in someplace none of the rest of us can go. What happened to you, Sugar?"

"There, you said it again." I tried so hard to smile but I could only manage a crooked grin.

"I did, and I'll keep saying it. But right now tell me what happened...*please!"*

"If I tell you, you'll think I've lost my mind."

"No, I won't. You've explained to me already about your precognitive dreams."

"Oh, God in heaven, I hope this one wasn't precognitive...just insightful."

"What do you mean? Are you sure you're all right?"

"Yeah, I'm okay...as long as you're here next to me...and not that beast. Oh, my God, I don't even want to think about it."

"Murph, tell me...spit it out. Don't you think you'll feel better if you get it out in the open where you can take a good, hopefully, objective look at it, instead of holding it inside?"

"Yeah, I guess it's like lancing a boil. You dread it, but once the nasty deed is done and all the goo is out, then you feel better...right?"

He grinned sardonically. "I couldn't have put it better myself." His head rested on his left arm and his right was lying across my stomach. He was on his side looking directly into my eyes. I was lying on my back, looking at him. I felt as though I were swimming in those amber eyes that beckoned so seductively. I wanted to kiss him, hold him, make love to him, and forget that god-awful dream. I knew I couldn't do any of those things until I had thought through tonight's ungodly experience. I had to spread it out where I could take a good, long, hard look at it and decide what it all meant.

"Sorry for the gory analogy, but the experience was gory as well. It's hard to describe what occurred as a dream...it was more like a *happening*."

"Well, all I can say is that it's a good thing your neighbors aren't closer. Someone would surely think you were being murdered. And here I am...in bed with the sexy victim. You know, of course, we'd be caught with our pants down." He grinned tentatively.

This time I did smile and kissed him. He kissed me back before pulling reluctantly away. "Well," I began, "all I can tell you is that it was one of the worst, most vivid and confounding nighttime experiences I've ever had."

"How so?" He smoothed the damp hair from my forehead before easing his arm back to its previous resting spot on my stomach.

"I was making love to you..."

"And I thought it was a scream of horror..."

"Ha, just wait a minute before you get all cocky..."

"Oh, you're so bad...you know it? I'm sorry, go on with your dream and I promise I'll try not to interrupt your narrative again."

"Well, like I said, I was making love to you...or rather...I thought it was you."

His eyebrows raised and his forehead furrowed with questions, but he said nothing.

"This must be what is referred to as a *wet dream*, I surmised, "cause I'm here to tell you it was vivid...just like the real thing." I ventured a little further afield, "Fel, maybe you were dreaming about me at the same time—could that be?"

"Probably was, but if I were, you scared it out of me when you started yelling and flailing about. Hey, and don't knock wet dreams. I'm a lonely bachelor, remember?"

"Lonely, huh?"

"Still a bachelor, but no longer lonely, thanks to you, lovely lady."

"That, dear heart, is two way street. *Now*, do you want to hear this somnambulistic epic or not?"

"Yeah, I do."

"Like I've said two or three times...I was making love to *someone*, and I thought, in the dream, that it was you. Speaking on a strictly physical level, it was great...but..."

"But what?"

"When it was all over, it wasn't you at all. It was *him.*"

"Him?"

"Yeah, him, the perverse sonofabitch that I've dreamed about before...the one I *saw* with Marie Zhou. I *know* he's the one that murdered her. *I just know it.*" I broke into uncontrollable sobbing. Tears ran down my cheeks, and my nose ran like a wet-weather spring. But I couldn't stop. I was horrified at what I had just told the man that I thought I was falling for—in a big way.

He turned away and came back to me with a handful of tissues. He wiped my eyes and held a tissue under my nose until I blew tenuously.

"That's not going to do it. Blow like you mean it." He stubbornly held the tissue, and I felt like a two-year-old. I blew like Mt. St. Helens. He threw the tissues into the wastepaper basket beside the bedside table. Only then did he speak again. "I'm not going to say it was *just a dream* because I know to you it wasn't. But what I am going to say is that *he* didn't make love to you...not in reality."

"Fel, after I realized who it was, the word *love* never even crossed my mind. I hope I don't shock you, but have you ever heard the term *mind-fuck?*"

"Yeah, I have. I'm a lawyer, remember? I'm sorry...no more editorializing."

I ignored his comments. "Well, that's how I feel, like he crawled inside my head and raped my subconscious. He raped me, just as surely as if he had broken into my house and done the dirty deed in person. Fel, I'm going to get him if it's the last thing I ever do. This has become a very personal vendetta. I've never felt like this before."

"Try not to worry any more tonight. We'll get him together. That's a promise, *Suga.*"

* *

No one or no thing came between us for the rest of the night. He held me tightly, yet tenderly, as he urged me to try to go back to sleep. *I was afraid. W*hat can I say? But, before long, utilizing his common sense reasoning, Fel had convinced me that I was in no immediate danger and that he was in this with me for the long haul. He would protect me, come hell or high water. I began to relax in his arms as Morpheus began to cloud my mind, carrying me off to the land of Nod...to dream no more this night.

* *

The anemic, winter sun was banging its little ray-fists against my eyelids. *Could it actually be that ol' Sol was out for a stroll after all this time?* I wondered. I was afraid that if I opened my eyes I would be disappointed. One...then the other...by golly, it *was* the sun—in all its glory. Not blindingly bright like the real spring humdinger would be, but a pale precursor of what would come before too many weeks. The glow in my heart, as well as the glow in the heavens, was short-lived. A shadow of forebodingness fell over my joy, as a cloud of impending precipitation enveloped the sky on the other side of my window. It was as if someone had lowered the curtain, heralding the end of the show.

* *

Breakfast, for the second time in as many days, was eaten across the table from the man who made my knees weak and my pulse race. How could anyone ingest so many fat grams and endless carbohydrates and still sport the body of a Greek god? I asked him, and he shot back with his razor-sharp lawyerly rhetoric, "It's all this night-time exercise I've been getting lately." He cracked an impish grin, stood up and leaning across my tiny breakfast table, he kissed me full on the lips. With a hunk of dry toast in my mouth and my glass of orange juice poised to take a sip, I was so surprised by his action that I swallowed the toast too quickly, and sloshed the juice over the side of the glass. He laughed, of course. I was just grateful that I hadn't had a mouthful of juice. I'm sure it would have come shooting out of my nose with the force of Niagara. *Wouldn't that have been attractive?*

He walked around the table and took me by the hand. "I've got to get out of here; I've got court this morning. I do, however, have time for a quick shower...that is if you'll join me."

I did. And rape, murder, nightmares and convicts were banished to the netherworld for the next thirty minutes. We came clean together.

* *

I sat smoking, sipping coffee, and thinking. The kitchen once more looked unlived in. The dishes were in the dishwasher, and the countertops and stove were wiped clean and smelling of 409. Neither a grain of sugar nor a crumb of toast had escaped my eagle eye. *One person living in a house alone, a home does not make,* I mused. But I was happy and thought nothing was going to bring me down this morning. Then the skull, ribs, and partial spine swam like a ghostly vision before my eyes. I ground out my cigarette, but not before lighting a fresh one off the butt. I got up to pour myself another cup of coffee and the phone rang. It was Lee, full of *piss and vinegar,* as she always is after her morning constitutional.

"Darlin', how you feeling this morning after all your excitement last night?"

"Well, all things considered, I guess pretty well...Fel stayed with me so nothing would get me."

"I didn't figure either one of you would let an opportunity like that get by without taking full advantage of it." She sniggered on the other end of the line.

"Glad to know you have my best interest at heart," I retorted.

"Damn, girlfriend, it's not every night you spend time in a dark garage with the alarm screaming in your ears, thinking the devil himself is after you. I take it nothing else happened after Dave and I left—I mean nothing bad. Speaking of Dave, have you heard from him this morning?"

"Nothing bad happened, and no, I haven't heard from Dave. He'll call sooner or later. I have a sneaking suspicion he's doing some checking on his own."

"I'm glad you're okay, and I figured Dave wasn't going to let any grass grow under his feet. He said as much when we left your house last night. Hey, I didn't ask, but I just assumed that Fel had already left before I called."

"He's gone. I've made the bed, cleaned up the kitchen and was just sitting here, trying to decide whether or not I want to go to back to Clarksville this morning. What about you?

"Sure, if you want to. It looks like it's going to clabber up and snow or sleet. It's too freakin' cold to rain, so dress appropriately for the weather."

"Yes, Mother."

"Back atcha, smartass. How soon will you be ready to go?"

"Well, all I have to do is dress; I've already had a shower. Why don't you just come on over, and don't forget about my screwed up security alarm. If it goes off when you come in, I'll probably have a stroke. They're coming out to check it today. Katie will be here, and they can tell her why the damned thing went off last night. Speak of the devil...she just walked in."

"Okay, Spook, I'll see you in about half an hour."

"I'll be ready by then." I put the portable phone in its cradle and hugged Katie. I told her that I would be going to Clarksville and didn't know when I'd be back. Since it was my regular day off and she wouldn't have to move clients around, she was unaffected by my decision. She followed me to the bedroom and sat on the side of my bed while I dressed and brought her up to date on all the weekend's happenings.

"Well, shit, I always miss the good stuff," she said, then added with a wry smile, "but aren't you glad nothing or nobody was really here? Can you imagine putting your life in the hands of the Wilson County Good ol' Boys?"

"Not a very comforting thought, I'll admit. If I didn't love this house so much, I would move in a heartbeat. But you know what?"

"What?" Her eyebrows raised in a question mark.

"I've worked with nearly every county law-enforcement agency around here, and basically they're all six of one and half a dozen of the other."

"Are they *all* arrogant assholes like our mounties?"

"I really don't know, 'cause when they call for my services, they're sweet as pie. But I suspect each has its share of bad apples in the barrel. Hey, not even *all* of Wilson County's mounties are obnoxious."

"Shame on me for asking." She flipped me an insolent grin before turning to leave my room. I walked out behind her. I had to fetch my boots and field jacket from the garage. I hadn't even had a chance to clean them up after yesterday's foray into the haunted forest.

"I'm going downstairs. Some of us have to work for a living, you know." She kissed my cheek before heading down to her desk."

"Oh, wait a second, Katie, did I mention that the security system people are coming out sometime today to see if they can determine why it misfired last night?"

"Yeah, you did. Hey, there's Lee, now. Tell her I said, 'Yo.'" She turned to go down the stairs, not waiting til Lee cleaned her boots on the mat. Ever vigilant, conscientious and bright, Katie had got to be one of the best secretaries...nay, best person in the world.

25

Lee had been correct about the weather. It was bitterly cold, and my poor garage door groaned like an arthritic octogenarian. I could feel the pressure change as I backed my SUV out onto the driveway. The sky was pregnant with cumbrous cumuli—the snowbirds were probably huddled under my eaves because the mercury had plummeted since last I was outside. The skeletal trees stood starkly silhouetted against the morbidly sombrous horizon. I shivered all the way to my socks.

"Last night wasn't exactly without incident," I admitted, sneaking a peek in Lee's direction.

"Why do I not doubt that?"

"Get your mind out of my bedroom, Lee—I'm talking about a dream."

"Oh, shit! You mean that after all you went through for real last night, you had to top it off with a nightmare?" She looked incredulously at me.

"You got it...and a bigg'n, I might add. The worst I've ever had—and that's going some."

"What happened?" She was lighting cigarettes for both of us, in preparation for the ensuing tale.

"First, let me ask you a question."

"Fire when ready, Gridley," she grinned.

Did you by any chance pick up my cell phone and put it in your pocket when you got out of the car yesterday afternoon?"

"No, I didn't. When I cleaned out my pockets, just the same-old-same-old was there. Cigarettes, lighter, my phone and micro-recorder...that's it. Why, have you lost yours?"

* *

I knew Ernest Calhoun would not be expecting us to show up on his doorstep. I was sure he was wishing we wouldn't make an appearance until he decided we should. He had pretty much everything he needed to solve this case, or so he thought. Sure, he had the alleged murder scene, a partial skeleton, and he thought he could get to the culprit through Harlan "Cobra" Merriweather. I supposed he could, but it would be a whole lot easier with my assistance. For some foul reason the *snake handler* had taken quite a shine to yours truly. All I had done was tell him I would try to help him cut a deal if he would help us nail the murderer of Marie Zhou. Apparently I had said the magic words. Merriweather reminded me of a starving dog eyeballing a chunk of raw meat.

The detective would be genuinely surprised, however, when I related some of what had occurred at my house the night before. If my neck were on the line, he damned well was not going to steal my thunder. I was in for the whole enchilada, and he could just get used to it. Anyway, Cobra didn't like Lt. Ernest Calhoun and vice-versa; we were all using each other. However, I thought I had the best shot at getting through to the *snake pit*. I just hoped I could accomplish my mission without fang marks. Actually, and oddly enough, Harlan Merriweather didn't really bother me all that much, but that jail-mate of his had my full-blown attention. I don't know if any murderer can be called sane, but this one was a whole 'nother ball of wax. If I could believe my dreams—and I did—whatever passed for sanity in that bastard had long ago leaked down his scrawny legs. But I would follow his trail to hell and back.

* *

"Well, Dare, Lee, I didn't expect to see you so soon." Lt. Calhoun pulled himself upright and smiled expansively. His eyes betrayed him. "To what do I owe this unexpected pleasure?" His sarcasm wasn't lost on me, but Lee smiled and shook his hand like an old war-buddy.

"Ernest, I would like to go back out to the woods, also I'm going to ask a big favor of you."

"Dare, you know I'll be happy to do whatever I can for you. Will and his boys are probably out in the woods by now. He told me last night that he would be out there most of today, if it doesn't start snowing and sleeting. From the looks of things outside, it just might just do that very thing. Is it snowing in Nashville?"

"No, or at least it wasn't when we left." I was tired of making nice with this plain-clothes cop, and I wanted to get on with it. "Ernest, the favor I want to ask is…" He looked up from a folder, his fingertips dancing antcipatively on the edge of his desk. "Will you see if you can get Lee and me into the Dickson County lockup to talk with Harlan Merriweather this afternoon? I've tried to get back with Rick Scarpadis, but we've done nothing but play telephone tag."

I knew immediately that I had pissed him off—but why? I had, more or less, asked his permission. I hadn't taken it upon myself to just go bursting in behind the detective's back—to see ol' Cobe.

"Dare, you'll have to forgive me, but the Zhou case isn't the only one I'm working on right now…I do have my priorities…"

Sometimes I forget everything my mother taught me, but I couldn't— wouldn't stand here and listen to this. "Priorities? We've got crucial parts of her remains, cigarette filters, yarn that's most likely from her sweater—what the hell more do you need? Are you planning on putting her on a shelf while you go out chasing your tail?" I knew I had *screwed the pooch*. He already resented the hell out of me—and my methods.

"No, I do not plan on going out chasing my tail. It just so happens that there is another missing child. She disappeared last night. I was up all night talking to her parents and neighbors. I have my own personal opinions, but that's not going to pay the rent on the double wide."

"Ernest, look, I'm really sorry, but I need to talk to Merriweather just as soon as I can…will you try to arrange it?"

"You mean even if I can't go with you?"

"Whatever…some son of a bitch is sending me very nasty vibes, and Harlan "Cobra" Merriweather knows who it is. Now, either you get on the horn and work out a deal with that redneck sheriff down there or I'll do it myself."

"You can't do that…you have no authority…"

"You're right, but I'll do what I have to do." You know I promised him to do what I could."

"You had no authority to do that either."

"Maybe not, but someone had to do something, Ernest, the perp knows my name, where I live, and probably even my shoe size. Now are you going to help me or not?"

He sighed, letting me know that he was going out of his way for me. "Let me see if Riggens can follow up on that missing child so I can go with you." He walked out of the room with his shoulder muscles hunched with tenseness.

"Weren't you just a little rough on him?" Lee was sitting in one of the straight back chairs, chain-smoking, from the looks of the Mickey-D's ashtray.

"Don't *you* start in." I gave her my fiercest look. "Did you hear him? Priorities?

The very idea. Who does he think he is, anyhow?"

"He knows who he is, Dare, a detective with the city of Clarksville police department, and this is not his only case. He works for the people. And the Chief-of-Detectives, whoever in hell that might be, tells him what to work on. You're the one with the priority...and the personal ax to grind. Hey, Babe, I'm with you, and I think it would behoove him to get you in to see the *illustrated man.* However, didn't your mother ever tell you that you can get more flies with honey than vinegar?"

"I stand admonished by you, but I'll be damned if I'll stand still while he tries to rake me over the coals. He's beginning to grind on my last nerve."

"Nawwww. Now, tell me how you really feel." She grinned at me and ground out her cigarette just as Detective Lieutenant Calhoun reentered the room."

"Ernest...I'm sorry I lit into you like I did."

"Forget it, Dare. Will's waiting on you out at the crime scene. Come back by here and we'll go to see Merriweather together. I talked to the sheriff down there."

"What did he say?" I queried.

"He doesn't have a clue that one of his inmates may be a cold-blooded murderer—especially one that he trusts with county transportation and spending money."

"Haven't you told him?"

"Not yet...why should I?"

"To keep him inside, you idiot."

"Harrrump!" Lee cleared her throat, being about as subtle as Sherman Tank.

"Sorry again, but have you forgotten what I just told you? That pervert knows who I am. Now what, in your expert opinion, is to keep him out of my world?"

"Your attitude, for one thing, would do it, if he takes the time to get to know you."

"*Touché*, Lieutenant." At that moment it was a toss up between this arrogant cop and Cobra's buddy.

* *

"Dare, Lee, I didn't expect to see you two out here today...want a cuppa coffee?" Will Bealer was hunkering beside his Blazer. His gloved hands cradled a cup of the steaming liquid—he sipped it tenuously. Deputies' feet and hands had raked the silver frosting that was clinging to the trampled clumps of weeds.

"Hello, Will, and no thanks to the coffee, we brought our own." Apparently, it seemed that nobody had expected us to show up today. "Have you found anything else?"

"Not yet, but if we don't find something soon we're going to have to call it a day 'cause of the weather. This breeze is like a knife blade...cuts right through to the bone."

As if I had suddenly been plugged into the great cosmic circuit in the sky, I grabbed for Lee's arm and said, "Excuse us, Will."

"What?" Lee was more surprised than I was, but she dug in her pocket for her mini-recorder and followed me like a well-trained puppy.

"I'm not sure, but there's something over there." I pointed beyond the crown of cedars—way past where we had driven in. Yesterday's mud looked like puddles of chocolate popcicle droppings, this morning. I picked my way carefully across the congealed, winter ground. "Be careful," I cautioned my partner-in-crime as I stepped across the maze of police car tire-tracks, footprints and weather-carved chuckholes. Further on we crept through the knee-high, decaying grass and wild flowers of summers past. The hair on the back of my neck suddenly prickled as if I had been shot through with a low-voltage current. Adrenaline...or was it that freaking goose again? I stopped in my tracks—Lee heeled-to. "There...look!" I pointed at the base of a massive oak tree—tangled in its ancient bark was a hank of long, dark, weather-beaten hair. Upon closer examination I saw—to my horror—that a considerable chunk of petrified-looking scalp was what was holding it all together.

"Oh, shit..." Lee rounded another tree and barfed until she had the dreaded dry heaves. On my knees, I carefully checked the pate without touching it, and waited while Lee pulled herself together. Cold sweat beaded on her forehead and under her nose. She wiped her face and made no apology. We'd been together far too long for such amenities. We made our way back across the frost-encrusted landscape, to where we had left Will Bealer and his boys, to guide them back to the latest piece of the jigsaw puzzle that once had been Marie Zhou.

* *

"I heard what you found out there today," Lt. Calhoun had no expression when he spoke. "Congratulations on finding that hair and scalp before the snow fell."

"Again." Was all that came out of my mouth. Then a feeble "Thank you" found its way past my tongue.

"Er, Dare, I've got some bad news. The Sheriff down at Dickson County just called to say they had to airlift your buddy Cobra up to Nashville. It seems they sent him over to the local emergency room, and whoever was in charge there called Vanderbilt Hospital air rescue unit. The shit's gonna hit the fan, cause he should have been sent to Maharry. They take all the cell jockeys there, because security is tight for such cases—everybody knows that."

"Ernest what the hell are you babbling about? What happened? Is he all right?"

"Well, it seems that he's had his throat cut and maybe a collapsed lung. It doesn't look good."

"Who did this to him?"

"Nobody saw anything. A guard found him in his bunk. All the other inmates were either outside or in the dayroom watching television."

"Did you find out *anything?*" Talking to this man was like pushing a chain.

"He was stabbed. They found the weapon along with a bloody towel on the floor underneath his bunk. It was your everyday, run-of-the-mill, homemade shank."

"Oh, shit, whoever killed Marie found out that he had talked to us—to me." I sat down, all the wind taken out of my sails. "Ernest, if you still want to go with us, you can, but I'm heading straight for Nashville and Vandy, as fast as my little Lexus will carry me. Now, you decide because Lee and I aren't even going to pass Go or collect $200, we're just going."

He shrugged his shoulders until they almost swallowed his neck. "I'll follow you in my car, okay?"

"Fine, how about radioing ahead, and Ernest..."

"What?"

"Keep up."

* *

Snow was splatting against my windshield like minuscule Kamikazes. Occasionally icy pellets of sleet and freezing rain would pepper the glass, only to be replaced by the silent white flakes whirling beneath the wipers. The interstate was covered, except for shiny black tire-tracks weaving into the distance. Plumes of white billowed beneath the tires of the car in front of me. Passing vehicles threw gray slush across my vision, further mucking my view of the outside world.

"Lee, if Merriweather dies, I'm in real trouble."

"Maybe he'll be all right." She was grasping at the same straws I was.

"Yeah, right, and miracles happen every day."

"It's not like you to be so pessimistic," she warmly scolded. "Do you know something that the rest of us don't?"

"No, not really. I just know that if he bites the dust, then I'm fair game, and who knows what will happen?"

"Look, even if Cobra dies, surely somebody can get a moratorium on release of all trustees at the Dickson County Jail."

"And just who might that be? The asshole who won't even tell the sheriff that he has a murderer in his care? Hell, no, I doubt that Calhoun would do anything like that...or even if he wields that much influence."

"I wasn't exactly thinking of Calhoun. Remember, Dare, you have an ace-in-the-hole. You have Dave."

"Lee, see if you can get him on the phone...please?" My inflection turned the statement into an almost prayerful request.

* *

I followed I-24 as it skirted the northern edge of downtown Nashville, then exited onto I-40 east, which I followed to I-65 south. Once on 65, I drove a couple of miles before exiting onto Wedgewood Avenue. Soon I could see the sprawling Vanderbilt University Medical complex in the distance.

Wheeling into the parking garage, directly across from the hospital's main entrance, I found a parking space on the ground level and eased the Lexus between the yellow lines. Calhoun had, in fact, kept up. Lee and I gathered our personal paraphernalia together while the detective nosed the department's confiscated red Taurus into the spot next to us, got out, and locked the doors. He double-stepped in order to keep up with us as we neared the street. "Come on," I shouted over my shoulder, my voice ricocheting around the cavernous garage. I knew he wasn't used to keeping up with anybody. He was usually the one yelling the orders.

We had to wait for automated doors to swing open before we could make our way into the enormous lobby. It looked like the reception area of an upscale corporate office building—which in essence it was—with health care thrown in for good measure. A well-groomed, matronly looking lady sat dwarfed behind the massive semi-circular desk. A *may I help you smile* was firmly plastered across her pleasant face. Ernest flashed his badge and ID, telling her only what he wanted her to know, but she was used to bigger fish than him swaggering in with badge exposed. She fingered the computer keyboard in front of her, then muttering something to Calhoun, she nodded toward a bank of shiny elevator doors behind her. I heard her tell Calhoun to stop at the desk when we got off the elevator, where, she said, there would be a security guard waiting for us. He thanked her and gave us his best *get it in gear look*. He was in charge again. We rode up through the innards of the hospital in silence. The doors slid silently open on their tracks. In the waiting room, were several worn-out looking folks. Some appeared to have been there for hours—some, maybe even for days. Open paperback books lay face down on the floor, along with magazines, plastic drinking cups and fast-food wrappers. I spied an inflated air mattress leaning against the wall behind a table. An in-house telephone stood silently on another small table. An unshaven man sat glassy-eyed, staring at the phone, as if willing it to ring.

We wound our way through a maze of corridors, before happening upon a nurse's station. Sure enough, there, on sentinel duty, stood Vanderbilt security guard. His 45 automatic rested snuggly against his overweight hip. His duty belt lay buried underneath the copious folds of his belly. *My God*, I thought, *I'd hate for him to fall on me.* The picture conjured up in my mind caused me to chuckle silently. However, it passed just as quickly as it had come. At the far end of the corridor a uniformed Metro cop spoke in hushed tones with a Dickson County Deputy. I saw Dave walk out of the room behind the two and head down the hall in our direction. He was expressionless.

26

Harlan "Cobra" Merriweather was not dead, but neither was he out of the woods. He had lost a great deal of blood, and an emergency tracheotomy had been necessary before he could be shipped out of Dickson County Memorial, where he'd been taken directly from the lockup. He was, however, bearing up *as well as could be expected* and was nearing the end of his third hour in the operating room, where surgeons were piecing him back together. There was an anesthesiologist reading dials and checking gauges. A thoracic surgeon, who cut and spread the ribs then stitched up snags in the left lung and pleural sac, while the ENT, or ear nose and throat resident, cleaned up the "trach" and inspected the patient's swollen neck.

The slit in Merriweather's throat hadn't been life threatening—no arterial damage—but the larynx had been severely damaged, and there had been some internal bleeding. The knobby adam's-apple was successfully repaired while the surgical team listened to, and reveled in, *Little Richard's Greatest Hits.* A gaggle of interns hungrily watched the procedures—still idealists at this point, they probably weren't yet figuring profit margins.

. Initially, when the report had been radioed from the helicopter, the medical team had anticipated that Cobra might be connected to a heart-lung bypass machine, but after viewing X-rays and Cat Scans, that had been deemed unnecessary. The latest official word that Dave had received expressed *cautious optimism:* the patient would not only make it through surgery but probably for many years afterward. However, Cobra Merriweather would probably never sing *Pagliacci.*

* *

Dave, in his inimitable fashion, had been on the phone with the right people and gotten the information that he knew I would want. He hadn't waited to go through diplomatic channels. When he set out to get something done, protocol be damned, he didn't particularly care if he ruffled bureaucratic feathers. He would apologize later if he felt it prudent to do so. But now he was off duty, and free to sit with me while he soothed my fevered brow—which he had always managed to do quite admirably.

Lieutenant Calhoun stood apart from the rest of us, after speaking briefly with Dave. He wanted to know if anyone had spoken with Sheriff Houston down in Dickson County. Dave didn't know. I didn't care. Calhoun wandered out of sight to call the Dickson County sheriff, I figured.

* *

"Dare, one of us will be with you at all times, 'til we question your friend in there and find out what the hell is going on. When I'm satisfied that you're safe—well, we'll go from there." Then he remembered what he'd been told about Cobra's throat wound. "The sonofabitch may have to tap once for *yes* and twice for *no*, if he can't talk. My luck will be that the pisser probably never learned to read and write. He jerked his thumb toward double doors bearing a sign: *Operating Rooms, Authorized Personnel Only.* I strolled over and took a good, long peek through the window. What I witnessed, reminded me of an ant farm I'd had when I was in grade school. Doctors, nurses and technical support of every description strode the spacious hall with military bearing: soldiers in green, blue and print smocks and head coverings (according to rank) looking as if they were ready and willing to don latex gloves at a moment's notice. A salute or two wouldn't have surprised me in the least.

I sat down to wait. Lee came and sat next to me, while Dave paced and kept an eye on the door. He walked back down the hall and spoke to the Metro cop and Dickson County Deputy, who were standing guard over the empty room that Merriweather would occupy upon deliverance from recovery. The Metro officer nodded his head and walked toward us. He stationed himself outside the double doors, where I assumed he would stay until it came time to escort the patient to his room.

Dave was nervous and wanted a cigarette. "You gals wanna go downstairs to the courtyard and grab a smoke? Maybe we could pick up a sandwich or something—that is, if you're hungry." He was hungry and he wanted to smoke, so he was being magnanimous.

I spoke up first. "Sounds good to me. I haven't coughed in over an hour, so it must be time for a cigarette and a cup of coffee."

Lee chimed in, "That does sound good. Let's get out of here for a few minutes, we all need a break." She grabbed her purse and was heading for the elevators before Dave and I even got started. By the time we reached the elevator, Lee was standing half in and half out of the car. Her finger was pressed firmly against the *door open* button. "Hurry up before this damned door gets tired of waiting and chews me in half."

By the time we hit the first floor level, all three of us had our cigarette packs and lighters in hand and were ready to fire up. That nicotine-deprived feeling makes the first drag good enough to eat. Smoking does strange things to the human brain because there were several other idiots standing around and puffing into the cold, dank afternoon.

Half-hearted snowflakes made their way to the aggregate paving before melting into mush. Heating ducts passed underneath the pavement on their journey from building to building within this massive medical complex. I assumed that the entire university was heated by the same steam. Dave volunteered to walk across the courtyard and fetch us coffee from the in-house McDonald's. "Did we want hamburgers or fried apple turnovers?" Lee and I shook our heads emphatically. I tried to donate to the cause, but he simply waved me off and strode away.

Between cigarettes, and while we waited for Dave to return, Lee and I retreated to the shelter of the entranceway—a well posted *no smoking* area. The sky was the color of tarnished pewter, and it continued to spit swirling bits of fluff. I looked at Lee looking at me. "At least I know what you'll look like in your dotage," she said.

"What the hell are you talking about?" I asked .

"Well, you're all hunched over, shaking to beat the band, and your hair is full of white."

"Hey, why don't you walk over to that glass door and take a good, long look at your reflection…you're no Gwyneth Paltrow, you know."

"Touché, Madame."

We were giggling spastically when Dave walked up with a carryout carton containing three lidded cups of Mickey D's holy water.

I opened my mouth to ask, but Dave answered before I had the chance. "Four sugars and a dash of Coffee Mate," he recited. "My God, woman, why don't you just suck on a sugar-tit and be done with it?"

I took a tentative sip of the notoriously hot coffee and asked the obvious. "What's a sugar-tit?" Lee too was all ears. I knew Dave was trying to take my mind off the present situation, so I went along with what I knew would be a colorful dissertation.

"Well, it's something my dear ol' granny used to make for us when me and my brother were little kids. She'd take a clean, white cloth, scoop up a chunk or two of butter—real home-churned country butter, mind you. She'd throw in a couple or three spoons of sugar then twist it up real tight and tie a string around it. Shit, a little kid could suck on that thing for hours…tasted real good too."

"Is that how you prefer your tits to this day?" Lee couldn't help herself.

"Naw, but I do still like 'em sweet and tasty."

"You're incorrigible, Dave," I laughed, "let's go up and check on the *snake charmer*."

I stepped from behind the massive brick pillar, and something, or someone, caught my eye: the backside of a stringy-headed individual who was about to round the corner and head toward the inner-campus shuttle bus stop. I could see the little bus puffing on its way by the time he reached it. The driver stopped, opened the bi-fold doors and watched the passenger bound onto his bus. The doors closed behind him, and the bus trundled off on its rounds. It took me a moment to process the information before my brain spat out the data—it was *him*!

I dropped my empty coffee cup and took off after the bus. I must have looked like a lunatic, with my coat flapping around my blue-jeaned legs and my boots looking like something L'l Abner had plowed in that morning. My scarf was trailing behind me, and for a split-second, the image of Isadora Duncan flashed before me. What if I caught that damned scarf on something and hanged myself? By the time I had snatched it from around my neck, I saw I wasn't going to catch the damned bus. I knew that before I started this sprint, but that hadn't stopped me. I couldn't help myself.

"Dare, what the hell are you doing?" Lee was right behind me—physically, she's in much better shape than I am.

"I just saw *him*," I puffed, trying to catch my breath in the frigid outdoors, while coughing into my gloves.

"Him who?" queried an extremely out of shape Dave Marshall, once he'd caught up with us.

"*Him…the fucker in my dreams.*" My breath plumed like clouds of smoke before me. I stood perfectly still, looking where the bus had been only a minute before. Too late, he could be anywhere by now.

Dave jerked his radio out of his belt and barked orders into it. He first of all alerted his man upstairs in the hospital, then unseen officers on the streets.

"Did you notice the number of the bus?"

"No, I did not."

He ordered units to head for the remote hospital parking lots, any public parking lots in the area and the hospital parking garage (though that seemed ludicrous) and all points in between. "Check all dormitory parking lots and the streets adjacent to them. Check up and down Broadway and West End, the areas bounding the campus and hospital, and don't forget Natchez Trace."

If the greasy little bastard didn't have too much of a head start, and he was still in the area, they might just have him boxed in. But he was gone. He'd slipped the noose, and I knew it. I could feel it in my bones. "Come on," I said to Lee, tugging her coat sleeve, "they're too late...he's gone." I took a cigarette from the pack and turned my back to the blowing snow and lit up. "Blowing smoke," I said...and did.

Lee and I walked back to the overhang that sheltered the glassed-banked entrance to the courtyard, standing with lit cigarettes where no faint-of-heart smoker would dare to be. We kept our eyes peeled for campus cops. I could see myself now, standing before a kangaroo court of undergraduate, part-time fuzz, explaining my smoking indiscretions while the criminal of the decade roamed these very streets. "Shit," I said out loud.

"What?" Lee looked at me.

"Just shit," I answered, walking to drop my spent cigarette into the container of kitty litter furnished for us damned partakers of the legal weed. "Let's go back upstairs and see how the *pit viper* is doing."

She was hesitant. "Dave said for us to wait for him. He told me not to let you go anywhere unless he was with us."

"Well, shit again." I pulled out another Raleigh and lit it. I slid down the rough, brick exterior of the building and sat on my heels. I felt like a prisoner in my own skin—better than being that creature's prisoner, I reckoned, and I closed my eyes. It was then that I *saw* him run across the backside of my mind. He was in that sheriff's patrol car, why couldn't they find him? "Dave!" I shouted, "I know where he is!"

* *

"*Goddam it!*" Ricky-Dino had nearly broken his neck several times after he had jumped off that little bus. He had slipped on the icy sidewalk as he rounded the corner heading for the squad car and had actually fallen down in the street as he was trying to jerk open the driver's door to make his getaway.

"That's all the fuck I need—break my fuckin' neck right out here by the football stadium." He knew he was too close to the action, but he felt pretty safe being in the squad car. *"Who would think to stop a cop car—even if it was from out in the boonies of Dickson County?"*

Sirens were screaming at him from every conceivable direction. Easing out into traffic and he found himself on Natchez Trace. A Metro patrol car met and passed him—blue lights were blazing and siren squalling. Ricky-Dino smiled to himself, flipping on his own blue lights and siren, he ran the red light. *This'll get me out of town without nobody lookin' at me twice.* He turned right onto Broadway and headed for I-40 west. He wanted to leave Nashville behind him, then get to highway 70 just as soon as he could; knowing that with just a little luck he could get back to the lockup unobserved. He just had to watch his ol' P's and Q's, and nobody would pay him any mind. All of a sudden he was feeling like Jessie James and John Dillinger all wrapped up in one. He felt his pants tighten in his lap—his dick strained against his zipper. *"Not now, Pedro, down, boy—we'll be back in the lockup soon—I'll let you out when we get home."* He rubbed the hump in his britches and moaned from deep in his throat. He closed his eyes for just a moment and caught sight of Dare Murphy peering into his mind—it excited him even further. *"Okay, Pedro, you win."* His lap responded. He pulled off the interstate at the next exit and drove the few short miles to Highway 70. He started looking for a deserted looking side road; it didn't take long. He drove about a half-mile down a blacktopped road to where it veered sharply. A short distance later, it evolved into a double-rutted muddy path that appeared to be headed toward a wooded area. The squad car had positraction rear-end and new snow tires. He sure as hell hoped he wouldn't get stuck, but he would take his chances.

Ricky-Dino pulled up along side a creek-bank and pushed the driver's seat back as far as it would go. He left the motor running because he didn't want to freeze to death. The radio was playing a cheatin', drinkin' and cryin' song as he unzipped his jeans. He closed his eyes and began to massage himself—his breath caught in his chest—all was right in his warped and ragged world.

* *

Ricky-Dino threw his soiled handkerchief out the driver's window and lit a Lucky Strike. He stuffed his limp penis back into his pants and zipped up. He pulled the seat forward to its former position and put the transmission in reverse. The rear tires churned into the muddy ground. *Shit*, he moaned, *car, don't fail me now.* He shifted the transmission back and forth between *reverse* and *drive,* rocking the car viciously. At last the right rear tire caught purchase on something solid, and the car heaved free of the mire. He backed up to the black top—muttering his idea of a prayer—forgetting God and everything else, as soon as he swung around and dropped the shift-lever into drive. He floor-boarded the squad car—halting only briefly before pulling onto highway 70. *Home Free.* He remembered that old lion in a movie he'd seen when he was just a kid. He too would soon be free. Next weekend he'd be saying goodbye to all the losers inside. "Short-time for good behavior," the redneck sheriff had told him. *And with a little luck, that fuckin', squealin', sonabitch Cobra would be dead as a post by now. He thought he would miss good ol 'cocksuckin' Curly though.* His crotch concurred, but Willie Nelson, croaking *On the Road Again* through the radio speakers took care of that. He grinned and cranked the volume full blast and joined in with ol' Willie "*...can't wait to get on the road again...*"

* *

Calhoun had called the Dickson County Sheriff, and after a few frustrating minutes of nagging negotiations, he had a working knowledge of what the sheriff knew—which was next to nothing.

"There were no fingerprints on the weapon...looks like the perp wrapped a towel around the handle before he attacked Merriweather. We're not sure but what it was just a random act of violence. That don't happen much, 'cause gen'ly these is a good bunch a boys in here. We don't get many violent offenders coming through these gates. Ain't got none at the moment, if you can believe their yellow sheets.

Calhoun rolled his eyes toward the ceiling, and expressed his thanks for the help the Sheriff had given him. He punched the "end" button before folding his cell phone into his inside jacket pocket. He would leave the phone "on" in case someone might call with some useable information.

* *

"They'll get him, Dare." I don't know who Dave was trying harder to convince, him or me.

"Not today they won't," I countered, "he's well on his way back to the

257

lockup. Why don't we just climb in my car and head out for Dickson County and talk to that clod-hoppin' sheriff right now? I'd like to prowl through that jailhouse and see if I see anyone that I recognize. Shit, we all know he's in there...let's go."

At that moment the elevator doors slid open and across from us—waiting for a down car—stood Lt. Ernest Calhoun. He stepped backward while we stepped out of the car. He didn't make further movement toward the elevator.

"Hey Lieutenant, you heard anything new?" I looked him straight in the eye.

"I talked to that potbellied sheriff, and he seems to think the "sticking" was intended to be nothing but a *boyish prank*, like some kind of random act of bad boy fun and games. He told me they don't have any hard-core criminals down there in his lockup. I'm heading back to Clarksville before the weather socks in the plateau. One of ya'll call me if you hear anything new, and I'll call you if I hear anything. How's that? I'll keep my scanner on.

We all nodded our heads in agreement. Dave offered his hand and they shook warmly. "Later, Ernest..." The elevator doors cut the sentence in two with knife-like finality. *A boyish prank? Jesus Christ,* I thought.

Dave motioned us to two comfy looking chairs in the waiting room and told us to stay put until he checked on Merriweather's condition. The same nervous souls as before occupied the same chairs, and more paperback books lay about in evidence. The inflatable mattress had disappeared, which more than likely meant one of two things: the patient that the owner of the mattress had been visiting had either died or gone home...or its owner had simply gotten tired and left. Interesting.

I wanted another cigarette. I had nothing to do, so I wanted to smoke. I thought of all the things that I could be doing if I were at home, but where I really wanted to be was at that pitiful excuse for a county jail, talking to that pitiful excuse for a county sheriff. I wondered just how long his head had been up his butt.

* *

"He's out of surgery and awake." I must have been woolgathering because I hadn't been aware that Dave had returned and was standing directly in front of me. "They've taken him to recovery, but they won't let me question him. The doc said he can't talk and he's too groggy to make any sense anyhow. I'm going to call that sheriff and see if any of his trustees are taking the tour today; that is if I can pull the information out of him. If there are, I wouldn't think

258

there'd be more'n one or two, at most. They've got everything under control up here and looks like we're just pissin' into the wind. Let's go downstairs and plan our attack." We rode down the elevator, each of us deep in his or her thoughts. When we reached the courtyard, we all three lit up. I asked Lee if I could use her cell phone, and she dug around in the copious pockets of her Vandy jacket, until she came up with it. I walked to a bench and sat down. I could feel the seat of my jeans bonding with the frozen wood. I had to take my glove off in order to push the tiny buttons that would connect me with Fel's private office phone.

"Hello." His voice warmed me like an August breeze.

"Fel, it's Dare."

"Where are you? I've been calling your cell phone all day. Well, damn, I just this minute remembered you've misplaced it."

"I'm at Vanderbilt Hospital with Lee and Dave. Fel, the son of a bitch stabbed Cobra Merriweather, and he's been running loose up here. I saw him with my own eyes."

"Who's up there? Who did you see?"

I rattled on, "We came just as soon as we found out that Cobra had been stabbed, and that he was airlifted up here from Dickson County Memorial Hospital. I haven't seen Cobra, but I have seen the *man of my dreams.*"

"I don't think that's funny! Okay, where did you see him—are you sure it's him?"

"Just as sure as God made little green apples. Dave's got everybody on alert. I know *he* was here one minute, and then he disappeared with no one but me seeing him. He got away undetected—slick as a whistle. He's probably on his merry way back to his home-away-from-home, if not already there and tucked in."

"Dare, you're not going to Dickson County, are you?"

"I don't know yet. It just depends on what Dave thinks we should do."

"I wish you wouldn't."

His words flew all over me. "Fel, I have to do what I have to do!" Before all the words were out I was already sorry for my outburst.

"Maybe so, but I don't want anything to happen to you…Dare, I care about you, whether you realize it or not."

"I know and I feel the same. It's just that if we don't pin this piece of shit to the wall, and soon, he's going to come after me. I'm scared, Fel. The crazy, son of a bitch scares me to death, but I'm the only one who can positively identify him."

"I know, and I can't say I blame you. He scares me too…for you. Just keep me apprised of the situation, will you?"

"I will, I promise." I started to say goodbye when suddenly I changed my mind. "Fel, I'll call you when I find out when I'll be home…will you come by?"

His voice softened. "You call me, Suga, and I'll do more than just come by."

Dave approached me as I popped the "end" button, folded the tiny Motorola onto itself and stuck it in my pocket. I peeled my jeans—and me—off the bench, checking the boards to see if I had left any denim behind. I was in luck. However, my butt was numb from contact with the cold wooden slats.

"Dare, I've talked to my captain and his advice is that we step back, and he will make some discrete inquiries as to trustee policy at Dickson County. I know you're aware that I have no official authority to do anything outside of Metro. He's also going to see if he can talk to the sheriff and can find out who was out on the road today. If the sheriff won't cooperate willingly, then the captain will go for a warrant to check his records. There's no reason to think the guy won't cooperate, unless he's using these trustees as his own private mules. I've seen stranger shit, believe me." Dave was out of breath, too many cigarettes, cold weather, and the spare-tire around his belt line.

I was disappointed and relieved in that order. I hugged Dave goodbye. He promised to keep me up-to-date on the patient's condition and all other activities concerning the case, just as soon as he knew them. The three of us walked inside to the bank of elevators, where Dave pushed the "up" button. I motioned to Lee, and we walked up the one flight of stairs to the lobby. I waved to the lady behind the semi-circular desk, before realizing that a much younger woman had taken her place. Shift change, I supposed.

The cold was brutal as we walked across the street to the parking garage. Inside the bleak structure wasn't much better. Lt. Calhoun's former parking spot was now filled by a white Ford Explorer, with orange pin striping, and bearing an "I Bleed Tennessee Orange" bumper sticker. That was a brave soul to be parking anywhere on the Vandy campus…even in the depths of the parking garage.

* *

The traffic was abhorrent, as it always is in downtown Nashville. I decided Broadway to Hermitage Avenue would probably be my best bet at this time of day. I was wrong. My mood waxed from bad to good then back again. I tried to think about seeing Fel later, but then the weather would snatch my attention. The ponderous clouds looked more like they were cranking up for a tornado than a snowstorm.

"Has there ever been a tornado this early in the year when it was this cold?"

Lee looked at me as if I'd just fallen off a turnip truck.

"What?"

"I was just wondering if those clouds could possibly be the portent of some unseasonable tornadic activity?"

"I've never heard of anything like that at this time of year. There has to be some sort of over-riding collision between cold air and warm air for such things to take place. Now, dear heart, if you can show me a warm front anywhere around here then we'll talk about it. Actually I don't think that's one of our more dicey problems right now."

"Yeah, but we mustn't forget *El Niño* and *La Niña*, smart ass."

"And don't forget to remember The Alamo and The Maine while we're at it. You going to give me back my cell phone, or are you planning on keeping it 'til you come across yours?"

I grinned at her and dug her phone out of my jeans pocket, which was no easy feat, since I was cinched up in my seat restraint. "Here, do me a favor, will you?"

"Sure. You want me to call Fel and tell him you're fine as frog hair split four ways and you're just dying to see him."

"Basically."

She talked with Fel while I drove, relaying messages from him to me and vice versa.

He would be by my house at eight if that met with my approval.

It did. I would rescue some of my revered potato and cheddar soup from the freezer, and we would dine like royalty—or like hoboes—if one cared to investigate the humble origins of the delectable tuber-stew.

He could hardly wait.

Lee relayed our good-byes before pushing the "end" button, and then made faux gagging noises for my benefit.

"Hey, you volunteered to call," I chided.

She patted my weather-chapped cheek and said, "I know, and you have no idea how glad it makes me to see you get on with your life. I would say happy, but under the circumstances I guess that's sort of pushing it. Anyhow, what I'm trying to say is Joe and I love you, and we're both so glad that you and Fel found each other." Then she added, "There's nothing like a good lay to make you forget your work-a-day worries."

"You got that, Sister." We both chuckled.

The day continued to slip away, as we neared my neighborhood. At the foot of my driveway sat a gray Buick LeSabre. Dave had wasted no time in getting my human watch dog stationed—and in a confiscated car. I motioned him to follow us up the driveway. I would offer him something hot to drink, which he would refuse, with a "Thank you anyway, ma'am." He must have been all of 21 years old, not yet dry behind the ears. I sure as hell hoped he could shoot straight if the need arose, God forbid. He drove back down to his post, where I assumed he would remain beside my driveway in perpetuity, or until we caught the asshole that was after me, which ever came first. Dave must have managed to call in some favors from his private investigating buddies because I knew Metro couldn't and wouldn't cross the Wilson County Line, not if the brass got wind of it.

"He's kinda cute." Lee was grinning.

"Yeah, in a baby sort of way," I countered.

I grabbed the remote from over the sun visor and aimed it at the garage door. We had plenty of time to say goodbye (could have held a séance) while the pitiful old door complained its way up the tracks. I got out of the car and walked Lee to her RX-7. Her doors were frozen shut, but after a few choice words and a slap or two with her hip, the driver's door reluctantly gave in, and she pulled it open. I hugged her and sent her on her way. I walked back to my car, drove through the open door, and turned off the ignition. I waited...silence. Then the door started its return trip to the floor. *As soon as it starts to get warmer, I simply must have that poor old thing put to sleep.*

* *

I dropped my boots and jacket beside the washing machine. I had my key in the lock and was about to turn it when I remembered the security alarm. *Damn, I hope they fixed the alarm system, 'cause if that sucker goes off when I open this door, I'll have a colossal sinking spell.* I glanced at my watch. Why? Katie's car was gone so it had to be after 5:00 o'clock. I turned the key and knob simultaneously, while I bit my tongue and held my breath. Nothing. Quiet. I pulled the key out of the lock and heaved a sigh of relief. I re-locked the door from the inside and punched my code into the keypad. I dropped my purse on the countertop and dug in my pocket for my cigarettes and lighter.

I lit up and looked at my empty cell phone charger and suddenly felt queasy. I knew where my phone was, or rather, I *thought* I did.

I read the note that Katie had left on the refrigerator—she knows me so well. Yes, the alarm people had come, and they pronounced the security system in topnotch working order. No, they had no specific explanation why it had malfunctioned, except that perhaps the battery backup had spiked when that truck plowed into the power station last night. Yes, they were sure it was all right now. Not to worry, they stood behind their product one hundred percent.

I wondered if that included hospitalization and burial insurance. *Not tonight, Murphy, don't think hard thoughts, you might hurt yourself.*

I lit the gas logs, put on an Elton John CD, poured myself a double Jack Daniels on the rocks and headed for the bathroom. I ran water in the tub, while I pulled a lightweight running suit out of the closet. I laid underwear and socks on the bed, before heading back to the bathroom.

I poured Dead Sea Salt into the stream of steaming water. Dropping my dirty clothes into the hamper, I stepped gingerly into the tub. *Oh, my God, that's the second best thing I ever felt.* Easing my exhausted body down into the slant of the old ball and claw, I sighed with pleasure. My aching back rested against the porcelainized cast iron, if it had been custom made it wouldn't have fit any better. Sipping my drink and soaking the weariness from my bones, I began to feel as though I might make it after all.

Before the water had time to cool down too much, I decided not to ruin a good thing by carrying it to extremes. I knew I'd better get out, get dressed, hit the freezer and retrieve the potato soup before it got any later. I did. Soon the subtle fragrance of the leek-laced concoction would be wafting throughout the house.

The only makeup I put on was a little lipstick. After all, Fel's seen me when I crawl out from between the sheets, and if that hadn't scared him away, nothing would. I blew my hair into its normal soft do and called it done.

* *

Katie had left my snail mail on the countertop. I grabbed it, along with my cigarettes and lighter, before heading into the great room. I sat on a floor pillow in front of the fire, and started separating real mail from the junk that clutters my mailbox daily. *Nothing to write home about.* I grinned at my private *bon mot.* I love clever remarks, even when there's no one but me to hear them. I drained the last remaining drops of Uncle Jack's magic elixir from my glass and stared into the fire. Suddenly I was sleepy. *Surely I can afford 40 winks, it's only six thirty-five. Fel won't be here for nearly an hour and a half—the soup's not going anywhere...it's on simmer.* I sat my glass on the hearth, pulled a throw from the sofa and shuffled cushions until I made my nest. The firelight danced around the wall—fencing with candle glow in the hushed shadows. Outside, the wind had kicked up a notch, and I could see the massive arms and twisted fingers of the old oaks reaching toward my windows. The porch light cast an eerie glow on the other side of the glass. I got up and drew the drapes, before snuggling back amongst my throw pillows.

* *

The chill drove itself into my bone marrow, and I shivered uncontrollably. What had happened to the fire, the candles and the throw? Oh, sweet Jesus, I wasn't in my great room—I was lying on the damp, leaf-strewn ground in the cold miserable woods that had gobbled Marie Zhou's life force. Was I here to give up my own as well? I heard humming...or was it whimpering? I pulled myself to my hands and knees, waiting for my eyes to acclimate to the dinginess. The night had the frigid, cloying stench of a meat locker—the odor was overpowering. My fear was almost solid, touchable, palpable. The clouds of breath, churning from my nostrils and mouth, were silver against the moonless sky. That wasn't right—there should be a moon. I looked up. It was there. It was just hidden behind a wad of snarling clouds, but it was there. I managed to get to my feet, with a little help from a low-level tree branch. I turned 360. I repeated my earlier sentiments, Sweet, Jesus.

Where was that sound coming from? I slowly turned...surround sound...I couldn't pin it down. A new sound joined the first. I knew immediately what that one was. It was the soft growling from deep within the throat of an enormous canine. It could almost be the basso-prefundo tremolo of a mountain lion, but as far as I knew, there were no "wildcats" in this part of Tennessee. Could be one from a couple of miles up the road in Kentucky though. Kentucky Wildcat—even at a time like this I think of the damndest things. I heard it again, but I had exhausted my supply of black-humor pun material. Whatever it was, it was huge. I knew in my heart that it was the bull-mastiff: that great snarling beast I had seen with Marie Zhou's femur in its mouth—the proverbial leader of the pack. I grabbed for my thighs in a feeble attempt at self-protection, as if I could hang on to them if that animal decided to have my personal drumsticks for a late night snack.

Just as suddenly as the growling had begun, it fell silent. Nothing, nada, quiet-as-a-tomb-at-midnight, quiet. Then the humming/whimpering began again. It came closer—the voice of a child—or a young girl. That damned goose was jack-booting up and down my grave. Was I time-traveling or had the painting over my mantle fallen on my head and knocked me around the bend? I was not in the woods, I was dreaming, that's all there was to it. The whimpering grew louder. I listened, like a good psychic, no more sassing the universe.

Tramping noises—leaves being kicked aside—heavy breathing. Silence again. I heard the silent pleading inside my chest. I sensed, rather than heard, a prayer, from innocent lips, calling to me from beyond the pale. Too late, it's too late. What could I do? I heard the answer in my heart.

I crawled out of that hole like Alice's white rabbit. I was late, late, for a very important date. One last diabolical growl followed me and tried to hitch a ride to the surface. I was having none of that. My heart was heaving like an old hit-and-miss steam engine. I struggled to catch my breath. Sweat beaded under my nose like an albino moustache, as I thrashed to escape that hideous scene, as though my very life was at stake. I heard a crash followed by the sound of glass shards splintering against slate.

* *

I jerked awake. In my flailing I had knocked over my cut-crystal drink glass, and it had rolled noisily off the hearth. Thank God, it had been empty. Hillary Kitten jumped like she was shot. I felt her hind claws dig into my stomach muscles, as she took off for parts unknown. I could breath again, but why did I feel as though I had left part of me behind? Or had I brought part of Marie Zhou back with me? From somewhere, I heard my own voice giving mundane instructions to someone. They should wait until the tone, then tell me who they were, along with their phone number, and I would call them back just as soon as possible. I made no effort to get up, until I heard who it was and what they wanted. Few people had my private number, though in the last few days it seemed it had been passed around almost indiscriminately. Ernest Calhoun had seen to that.

"Dare, if you're there, pick up!"

I staggered to my feet and stumbled to the phone. It was Dave's voice ordering me to answer.

I jerked the portable from its cradle and said, "Hello, Dave, I'm here."

"You sound terrible...did I catch you at a bad time?"

"No, I had fallen asleep on the floor in front of the fireplace. I'm just beat. What's up—is Cobra okay?"

"Yeah, he's gonna be fine. He's not the problem. Uh, Dare, is Felix with you?"

"No, what do you want with him?"

"I don't, I just wondered if you were alone."

"Not exactly. Your watch dog is still stationed down by my driveway, or he was when I came home."

"I know Reynolds is there, but is anyone in the house with you?"

"No." The goose did an arabesque and landed on my chest. "Why?"

"The captain talked to Sheriff Houston down in Dickson County. He said the sonofabitch is a mute when it comes to his domain. He talked to a judge down there, trying to get a court order to check the trustee sign-out sheet. Last I heard the judge was trying to decide if there was due cause."

"What does that have to do with me?"

"Well, to make a long story short, due to the fact that Marie Zhou was kidnapped, which makes it a federal offense..."

"I know all that—answer my question, please."

"The captain called FBI headquarters, and they've called a in special agent Turlock whose stationed in Jackson, and he's going to make a call on the good sheriff..."

"Dave!"

"Well, it seems there were three trustees signed out today, but only two signed back in."

"What? Who?

"The sheriff claims he doesn't understand. He says the guy that's missing is up for early release, with a good chance of getting it, and in just a few days. He claims he must have broken down or had a wreck or..."

"Or decided to visit me..."

"Well, no, that was my first thought, but I don't think so. I just talked to Reynolds. Dare, he's a good man. Try not to worry. I'll be out in about thirty minutes."

"Wait a minute, Dave...what time is it?"

"Seven forty-five, why?"

"Because Fel's coming at eight. Please call Reynolds and tell him to let him by...okay?"

266

"What kind of car does he drive?"

"I don't know what year it is but it's old—it's a Jaguar XKE."

"It's not old, Dare, it's a classic. There is a difference you know. There won't be many of them driving out your way tonight. I'll let Reynolds know. Does that mean you don't need my company tonight?"

"Don't put it that way. You can come out if you want to; I'm heating up some potato soup…"

He interrupted me mid-sentence. "No, thanks, I just didn't want you to be alone. We've put out an APB on the sonofabitch. Oh, by the way, his record reads like a dime novel. He's just a petty criminal, and not a very good one at that, that is 'til last November. His damn rap sheet goes back almost to babyhood."

"Tell me, Dave, why the hell do you suppose he didn't show back up at the jail if he was due to get out in a few days. He could have come after us at his leisure next week."

"We figure that he must have been almost to Dickson by the time the APB went out over the radio. He must have had the scanner on."

"Great, now he's running loose and God only knows what he'll do next."

"Dare, unless he's dumb as a box of rocks, he won't come near you. We don't even know that he knows where you live."

"Dave, I run a business. My address is in the phonebook.

"If he crosses the Davidson County line, we'll get him. We've notified Wilson County, and Sheriff Fletcher promised to have a patrol car drive by your house every thirty minutes until he hears from the captain. Like I said, try not to worry."

"Wilson County watching me—do you have any idea how secure that makes me feel?"

"Dare, don't be petty, we're all looking after you. Listen, if Felix isn't there in the next few minutes page me."

The doorbell rang. "Wait a minute, that must be him now…"

"You go check through your peephole and let me know before you open up…okay?

"Yeah, thanks, daddy." I took the portable and walked to the front door— Fel stood on the porch, the occasional snowflake landing in his curly black hair. "It's Fel, may I hang up now."

"See? I wrote a note while I was talking to you, and dispatch notified Reynolds to let your "squeeze" past.

"You're good. Now, goodnight. Don't call me unless it's absolutely necessary—okay?"

"Gotcha. Enjoy that potato soup and...whatever." I heard the phone click on the other end of the line. I pushed the off button and opened the door.

27

"Jesus Christ Almighty damn." The radio was playing WSM country and Ricky-Dino was having a wonderful time until the scanner spit out the all points bulletin. The drone and sputter of the police dispatcher had been in the background for entire trip, but Ricky-Dino hadn't paid any attention until he heard his name and description announced to God and everybody else. He'd heard her plain as day, and he'd turned Merle Haggard off, so he could hear every word. He probably was driving a Dickson County Sheriff's vehicle, the disembodied female voice had announced. He was wearing the denim blue that all trustees wore. It wasn't expected that he was armed, but he might be dangerous, especially if approached with force. On and on the police-speak crackled as Ricky-Dino took it all in.

"Why were they after him? Had that bitch Murphy spotted him? He had learned early in the afternoon, from the same scanner, that Cobra had been shipped up to Vanderbilt after Clarksville Memorial had said they couldn't help him. He figured that Cobra was dead in a morgue somewhere by now…and who would give a flyin' fuck? Apparently that goddam Murphy woman did. Oh, shit, now what? He couldn't go back to the lock-up. He'd be rat-bait for sure. He decided to turn the old green and white around and head up a secondary road until he came across a car to steal. He'd have to run now. Shit, there weren't no justice in this world. He was supposed to get out, now just look at the mess Cobra had got him into. He hoped that sonabitch was burnin' in hell by now.

He wheeled the squad car around in the middle of the road and floor boarded it. He turned off onto the first side road he came to. Seeing a Deep Rock service station in the distance, he slowed down and took a long hard look for any sign of official vehicles. He did likewise at the Dairy Queen and Hardees' parking lots. Nobody. He drove a couple of miles down the road until he came to a place where the gravel shoulder widened into a turnaround. He would wait. Before long he saw the low beams of an oncoming vehicle coming up in the rearview mirror. As it neared, then passed him, he saw that it was a Ford Crown Victoria. *"That sonabitch'll run."* He pulled out and picked up speed. He turned on the blue lights. The driver didn't pull over immediately, so Ricky-Dino popped the siren. That did it. The driver swerved to the shoulder and braked to a stop. Ricky-Dino drove in behind his victim— zipped up his jumper, reached behind his seat and pulled out the long flashlight. He opened his door, and shining the flashlight, he walked up to the driver's side. The power window slid soundlessly into the door.

"Evenin' officer, what'd I do? I know I wasn't speedin'. I got a tail light out or somethin'?" The driver's cautious face turned up toward the glaring flashlight.

"Get out!" Ricky-Dino was in his element. Playing cop turned him on.

"Sure officer, just let me undo my seatbelt and get out my wallet."

The driver stepped out of his automobile and proceeded to remove his driver's license from behind the plastic window in the front of his wallet.

"Give it here!" Ricky-Dino ordered.

"Sure, officer, just let me get this mother-fucker out then…"

Ricky-Dino was in no mood to wait. He drew back the flashlight and struck the man across the forehead. He crumpled into a heap on the ground without ever seeing the blow coming. Ricky-Dino crammed the wallet into his jumper pocket, then dragged the limp man off the shoulder of the road and into the high weeds beyond the berm. He hit him on the head one more time for good measure, before running back to the squad car. He drove it across the road, rolled down the window, turned off the headlights and blue flashers, then got out. While steering through the open window, and pushing the car at the same time, he rolled it into a ditch. "Bye, bye," he called, as the car careened to a crashing halt. "Good, cain't even see the sonabitch out here in the dark," he muttered as he climbed into the newly acquired Crown Vic. He dropped the transmission lever into drive and boogied.

* *

"Dare, who is that man out there? He stopped me, flashed a badge and demanded to see my driver's license. What's going on—are you all right?" His piercing amber eyes were clouded with apprehension.

"Calm down, I'm quite fine as you can see, except I just woke up." I suspected that perhaps I didn't look so fine. That guy's name is Reynolds, and he's a private detective that Dave hired baby-sit me. I guess you could call him my yard dog. He was just doing his job by stopping you."

"That's all well and good, but what's he doing out there in the first place. And why the hell do you need a yard dog?"

"Well, it seems that the bastard that killed Marie Zhou tried to do the same thing to good ol' Cobra—now he's gone missing."

"What do you mean gone missing?"

"He's a trustee at the Dickson County jail. He ran some sort of errand for the sheriff today and hasn't checked back in. I spotted him outside Vanderbilt Medical Center this afternoon. I don't know if he saw me or not—odds are he did."

"My God, Suga, is your life always this hectic?"

"Why? You ready to turn tail and run? What's the matter, can't you stand a little excitement in your humdrum life?" I asked the questions playfully and with a smile on my face. I didn't feel what I hoped the happy face would portray.

"Compared to my life, you live on a roller-coaster. But if it's what you do, yeah, I guess I can learn to stand it." He took me in his arms and hugged me tightly against his chest.

I nuzzled against his ear, "You hungry?"

* *

I was restless. Not even satisfying lovemaking had completely relaxed my brain. My body was like a limp rag; however, my mind was hitting on all cylinders. I slipped out of bed, careful not to disturb Fel's measured breathing. I padded silently into the great room. Thank God I had left the gas logs burning. Even so, that goose wiped his cold, clammy feet across my grave. I pulled a cushion as close to the fire as I could get, and lighting a cigarette, I blew the smoke toward the ceiling. I watched the cigarette quiver in my trembling fingers.

I couldn't sit still, so I got up and made my way to the kitchen. I opened the refrigerator door. Nothing grabbed my fancy. I opened the pantry and each cupboard, one after the other—still nothing. Then I remembered the hot chocolate mix that I had stashed somewhere...but where was it? I hide treats from myself like some people hide their valuables. Well, to me, they *are* valuables. The proverbial light bulb came on and I dug in the back of silverware drawer where I found the last two packets of Carnation double chocolate—*well, tie me down while I drink it*—hot cocoa mix. I ripped open an envelope and carefully, so as not to spill a single granule. I emptied it into my favorite cup. On it, was the Shoebox greeting card character Maxine, complete with bunny slippers, dressed in black leather and standing beside her motorcycle. She looked like I felt. I poured water from the Brita Pitcher into a Pyrex measuring cup, stuck it into the microwave and nuked it to a boil. I secretly wished that Fel would wake up and join me in my middle-of-the-night repast. No such luck. The timer dinged and I slowly stirred the steaming water into the fragrant powder at the bottom of my cup. Ummmm, the aroma of chocolate trips a special switch in my brain. I took a tentative sip, it stung my tongue, so I blew across the top before I tried it again.

Suddenly, without warning, the fine hairs on the nape of my neck stood at attention, and gooseflesh crawled up my forearms. Sweat beaded on my upper lip, in spite of the chill in the air. I shivered as I carried my cup back to the great room and sat down in front of the fire. I placed my cup on the hearth and hugged myself for warmth. I felt as though I might hyperventilate and pass out right there on the spot. I could feel tears backing up in their ducts, as if preparing for the dam to break. My throat ached, feeling as if it might close up. My head began to throb and my mouth went dry. What was wrong with me?

The phone rang. I jerked as if I had been shot. I jumped up, glancing at my watch as I made my way to the kitchen. I grabbed the phone from its cradle and said, "Hello?" It was a question for which I already knew the answer.

Dead air on the other end of the line, then I heard shallow breathing. I waited and listened. Still no voice, but the breathing increased in speed and in volume.

"Who's there?" I knew, nevertheless, I felt the desperate need to say something...anything. *Keep talking Dare, sooner or later he'll say something"*

Nothing, just breathing.

"Who's there? I repeated...hearing the breathing reach a fevered pitch...then a series of short gasps and finally a distant shudder. *Oh, my God!* I said inside my own head. I wanted to scream and run from this wretched creature...dig a hole and pull it in after myself. But there's no place to hide from evil...no place.

"Hey, Mz. Murphy," a disembodied voice crooned. "Dare...was it as good for you as it was for me?"

"Who are you, you son of a bitch?" I felt my lips curl over my teeth like a cowering, but angry animal.

"You know who I am, Dare, you seen me just like I seen you."

"Where are you?"

"Damn, woman, you 'on't my social security number whilst you're at it?"

"You cowardly piece of shit, come out into the open where I can see you. I think you're all talk, except when you've got a helpless little girl in your clutches."

"You really 'on't a see me? Will you open your legs for me like you do for that lawyer feller?"

"What the hell are you talking about? You know nothing about me."

"Oh, but I do, Dare. You're fuckin' that lawyer ever chance you get. Ol Dino knows all about you."

"Dino? Had he said Dino?"

"You still there, Dare? You don't care if I call you Dare, do you?"

"Yeah, I'm still here...Dino."

"Well, now that we're on a first name basis...will you open your legs for me?"

"You piece of shit! You're number one on my list, but not for what you're thinking about, I'm going to get you if it's the last thing I do on this earth. How the hell did you get my private number?"

"You ought to memorize your numbers, Dare. You got a whole list a numbers stuck down in your little case here: they's Lee's, Dave's, Fel's...even your own."

"Just shut up, you little shit. How did you get my phone?"

"Now, now, Dare, don't getchur back up...you ought to watch out after your stuff better."

"Were you in my garage?"

"Ast me no questions, I'll tell you no lies."

It took everything in me to keep from screaming. Here I sat, with a murderer on the other end of the phone, and it was like talking to a board. It would do no good to wake Fel to get him to trace the number. I knew the number—it was mine, and he could be anywhere. Somehow this creature had gotten into my garage, then my car; which I never lock inside the garage, and snatched my phone. He's probably who'd set off the alarm, and then got out, while I was coming apart at the seams. Son of a bitch. My mind was a mess. I couldn't think my way out of a wet paper bag.

"Dino, where are you?"

"You serious ain't ya?"

"What do you mean?"

"You actually expect me to tell you where I'm at, don't cha?"

"Well, it never hurts to try."

"Maybe it does, and maybe it don't."

"Are you aware that the police are after you?"

"Yeah, I heard. While we're talkin' all friendly like, will you tell me somethin'?"

"Why should I tell you anything?"

"Don't be thataway. Now, tell me how good ol' Cobra is. When's the buryin' gonna be?"

"Mr. Merriweather is not dead. Dino, he's well on his way to recovery." I could have bit my tongue off at the roots for disclosing such a well-guarded secret. *Damn it, Dare, why don't you just take him by the hand and lead him to Cobra's room?*

"Huh?" The line went dead and the silence almost swallowed me whole. I pushed the off button and laid the phone on the countertop. I walked back into the great room and slumped back onto the cushion. I picked up my cup only to find a skanky film covering my lukewarm chocolate. I sat it back on the hearth and cried into my folded arms.

"Dare?" Fel slipped his arm around me and hugged me to him. "What's wrong, Suga? You're cold as ice and stiff as a board." He kissed the back of my neck. "I thought I heard the phone, but I must have been dreaming."

I looked into his amber eyes and he saw my tears. "You heard the phone all right, it was Dino something or other. The piece of shit who murdered Marie Zhou and tried his best to do in Cobra Merriweather."

"My God, what did he want? Why didn't you waken me?"

"Well, I'm not really sure what he wanted, other than to gloat a little. I think I jarred his preserves when I told him that Cobra wasn't dead. He hung up then."

Fel gathered me into his arms and brushed my hair back from my face. He kissed me. I let him. However, I didn't help much…I was somewhere else. I was deep in the dark woods watching a man torture a young girl. I shut my eyes and squeezed the scene from my mind. I took Fel's face between my open palms and kissed him passionately. I wanted him to drive the horror from between us—to take me and make me forget.

* *

Jesus H. Christ and Mama Mary, Cobra ain't dead! What the hell am I gonna do now? Wait a minute…what the fuck does it matter anyhow? That bitch knows I done it...done both'm. I reck'n I got too big from my bitches when I called her. Piss on it. I don't give a shit...let 'er know. What can the bitch do? She can lead the fuckin' fuzz to me, that's what she can do. The TV said she tracks down all kinds a shit...people, dead bodies, lost crap like wallets, diamond rings. Shit! Git a grip on yourself, Dino. He laughed at the picture that conjured up in his head, then sobered to the seriousness of his situation. Nevertheless, he couldn't completely put the picture out of his mind. He pulled the Crown Vic out of its hiding place and nosed it northward. He wanted a woman, jerkin' off just wouldn't do it now. He craved a scared victim—the scareder the better—one who would make him feel good about himself again.

He headed toward Clarksville. *That's the last place on earth they'll be lookin' for me. If, in fact, they're even lookin' for me...a course they're lookin' for me. I heard that on the goddam radio. What's the matter with me? But that Murphy bitch might a been pullin' my leg about Cobra. He's probably deader'n a doornail...but I told her my name...dumb cocker. No, I ain't dumb...I ain't got by this long from bein' dumb. It's them fuckin' cops that's dumb. They're probably running around with their thumbs up their butts, not knowin' whether to shit or go blind. Damn, I miss Curly. I wisht I'd a found out about ol' golden tongue a long time ago. Think, Dino, think. Keep your mind between the ditches. Speakin' a ditches, I reck'n it's time to trade cars again. No, that ol' squad car's not goin' be found 'fore daylight, but I gotta think ahead...think...think. Shit, I don't have my squad car...how'm I going pull anybody over? I told you to think, cocker. Think!*

He perused the sides of the road, and carefully checked the all-night markets and service stations. Nobody out looking for him so far as he could tell. He pulled off onto a dark side road.

"I gotta piss somethin' fierce", He muttered to himself as his headlights captured a parked car in their frame. *Well, well, what we got here?* All bold as brass, he reached into the passenger seat and found the flashlight he had rescued from the doomed squad car before he'd pushed it into the ditch. He opened the door and stepped out into the darkness. He flashed the intense beam directly at the parked car—two heads bobbed into view. *Well, well, what have we here? Looks like somebody's done primin' the pump for ol' Dino.* He stepped up to the driver's door and tapped on the glass with the business end of the flashlight, careful to keep the beam focused at the scared faces. The window slowly lowered as the boy inside cranked it down by hand...no fancy, new car was this one.

"Yes sir? We was just getting ready to leave. My girlfriend here wasn't feeling too good so I just pulled off here til she…"

"Son, do I look like an idiot? I know what you're doin' way out here on the other side a nowplace. You was fuckin' your sweetie, weren't cha?"

"Well…no, sir. We were just kissin' a little…nothin' else. We don't do that…what you said."

"How old are you, boy?"

"I'm seventeen, sir."

"And you ain't been satisfyin' that pretty young thing?" He passed the flashlight beam at the terrified face of the young girl. "What's the matter with you, boy? Don't you know if you don't do it, somebody else will?"

"Sir?"

"I said…"

"I heard what you said, sir, I just don't understand why you said it. Don't police officers care what…?"

"Get out of the car, punk!" The change in tone frightened the young man, and he grabbed for the girl's pale hand. "Leave her be. Just you…get out…now!"

The boy got out, his fly was open, but he had managed to tuck himself inside before Dino made the discovery.

"Just kissin', huh. What's the matter…your pecker gotta breathe whilst you kiss this pretty little girl? I'll just bet it does. My, my, she's a pretty'n, ain't she?" He waved the light's beam from boy's crotch to girl's face and back again. "Zip up before it freezes to a permanent hard-on." Dino laughed at his own stab at humor. The boy closed his zipper with trembling fingers.

"She just touched me a little…that's all…I…"

"I don't care what she did before…let me tell you what's she's gonna do now. Now get your pretty, young sweetie outta that heap and get on back here to my car. Get in the back seat…both of you.

"This ain't a police car." The frightened girl grabbed her date's arm and began to cry."

"I never said I was the fuzz…did I? Did I haul you outta that car under false pretenses?"

"No, I reck'n not." The boy quivered and held tightly to the girl. Dino opened the backdoor on the driver's side and ordered the couple inside.

"Get in 'fore ya both freeze your asses clean off." He slammed the door behind them, pulled open the driver's door and slid inside. "Take your clothes off."

"Why? What are you going to do," whined the girl. The boy protectively put his arms around his date.

"Don't ast me why…just fuckin' do it. Now!" He watched as the two disrobed and he cranked the heater up a notch—not that he needed it. The scene he was watching was warming his cockles nicely. He just wanted the boy to be warm enough to perform. The couple sat numbly in the backseat, having no idea what was expected of them.

"Now, girlie, you lay down first and spread out for my friend here."

She looked at the boy with a stricken expression and he nodded for her to follow the instruction. Ricky-Dino saw that the boy was too scared to cause even a twitch in his penis.

"Wait a minute…change of plan. Girlie, you get up and let my boy here lay down." They did as they were told.

Now, there…you lay your head down in his lap. No, no, face down. Where you been all your life…in a church-house somewheres? I bet you can't even count past sixty-eight can you? In the mornin' you can tell all your little friends that, 'Yes, Virginia, there really *is* a sixty-nine.'" She cried, but did as she was told…again. The boy stirred.

Ricky-Dino watched with fascination as the two got into position. He massaged his erection and came at the same time the boy did. The girl cried, coughed and gagged; Ricky-Dino thought she might upchuck, but she didn't. He swiped half-heartedly at the wet spot on the leather seat where he sat. "My turn," he grinned.

28

The sun stayed in bed, why shouldn't I? I was worn to a frazzle—too sleepy to take a shower with Fel when asked. When I finally came to for good, he was gone. A note was pinned to the spot where his head was lying when I had finally fallen asleep sometime after midnight. I read his words and smiled, feeling a well-directed twitch in my innards. Then I remembered I had clients, I had to get up. Katie would be here soon. I glanced at the clock on my bedside table and groaned. It was nearly eight-thirty. I hauled myself out of bed, wondering why no one had called before now. Had I turned off the phones last night? I didn't think so. Maybe Lee was out or just allowing me my much-needed rest. I would call her after I got out of the shower.

I gathered my terrycloth robe around me and made my way to the bathroom. I turned the shower on full blast and waited for the steam to signal readiness. I dropped my robe to the floor and opened the fogged-up door. The steamy hot water immediately revived me. I heard the distant ring of the telephone. I could tell instinctively that it was my private line. I opened the shower door and leaned my head out. I heard my voice go through the "wait until the tone" litany. Then I heard a man's voice, though the words were indistinguishable due to the pounding water—was it Fel? Maybe it was Dave. I knew it wasn't that piece of shit Dino—the voice was too masculine. Well, whoever it was could wait a few more minutes. My shower waits for no one…well, almost no one. I rinsed the shampoo from my hair and smiled in spite of myself.

* *

"Dare, this is Dave, call me just as soon as you can; there have been some further developments. Oh, by the way, the detective outside your house this morning is Tom Jefferson. Think you can remember that one?"

I listened to Dave's recorded message while I dressed. I stepped into jeans

278

and pulled on a burgundy turtleneck sweater. Sitting on the chaise lounge, I pulled on socks then stepped into penny loafers. All I had to do now was dab on a little make-up, apply a tad of lipstick, blow my locks, and I would be ready to meet the world head on. First I would call Dave.

I dialed his pager and waited. Exactly two minutes later my phone rang, and I snatched it up before it had time to finish.

"You must have been sitting on top of the phone..."

"What is it, Dave?" I didn't give him time to tell me on his own, I was too impatient to hear about the new developments to lollygag through any preliminaries—even with Dave.

"Well, it seems that a Dickson County Sheriff's car was found at first light this morning. Looks like it had been rolled into a ditch about twenty miles this side of the Dickson County jailhouse."

"Well?" I couldn't wait for him to spit it out.

"Hold your horses, I'm trying to tell you fast as I can."

I could hear him sigh at the other end of the line.

"It was the one that had been checked out earlier in the day by..."

"By Dino somebody or other." I beat Dave to the punch.

"Well, for the record, his full name is Ricky Dean Harris but his fellow convicts call him Dino." How did you know that, lady?

"I'm psychic, remember?"

"Bullshit, you've been psychic ever since I've known you, but you don't very often come up with names."

"Didn't I tell you that he goes by a nickname?"

"I think so, but I can't remember for sure, I guess you want me to check my notes. Now tell me how you knew his name."

"He called me last night."

"You're kiddin'."

"Believe me when I tell you that I'm most certainly not. That's not the kicker though, the little shit called me on my own cell phone that he snitched from my car the night the lights went out in Georgia."

"You're kiddin'..."

"Damn it, Dave, will you quit saying that? I am not kidding. Even with my perverse sense of the macabre, I wouldn't come up with that."

"Well, I'll be damned..."

I couldn't tell if he was speaking to me or just mulling the situation around in his own mind. It didn't really matter at this point. "Dave...Dave, are you listening to me?"

"Of course I am, I'm just taken aback by the boldness of that little prick...calling you like that...on your personal cell phone. I'm amazed."

"Come on, David, you've been a cop for too long to let anything amaze you anymore."

"Well, almost, but not quite. This is an exception."

"Well, it seems I'm not too smart..."

He seemed incensed on the other end of the line. "What do you mean by a remark like that?"

"Well, Mr. Dino pointed out the fact that I have my own and several other numbers, stuck down in the little carrying case where I keep my cell phone. Yours is in there too, I'm afraid."

"Well, I reck'n we'll all have to get our numbers changed. My home number wasn't in there was it?"

"Well..."

"Not to worry, kiddo, I just wish he'd called me instead of you. Hang on for just a minute, will you? It seems like every county in middle Tennessee is getting cooperative this morning."

I could hear the rattling of paper as he unfolded something...an important communiqué perhaps. I heard him make a low whistle through his teeth before he picked up the phone again.

"Dare, you're not going to believe this."

"What?" Impatience re-reared its ugly head.

"If you'll just hold it in the road for a minute, I'll tell you."

"Okay, fire when ready, but please hurry up."

"A sheriff's deputy up in Montgomery County was makin' his regular rounds this morning when he came up on 1999 Crown Victoria parked back off a country road. There were two young kids, a boy and a girl, stuffed in the trunk."

"Are they alive?" The goose was dancing the fandango.

"No, but it says here that it was obvious that the girl had had intercourse, as had the boy. I hope they haven't jumped the gun on that assumption, and that they transported them very carefully. Now get this...there were what appeared to be semen stains on the front seat *and* the back seat. I'll betcha our boy sat there and forced them to take turns, or he just beat his own batter while he watched. We'll know more after the ME gets done with them, and forensics finishes with the car. You know what I think?"

"I can't fathom?" I hoped the sarcasm didn't slip through the telephone lines.

"I think his big *bang* comes when he kills. I also believe shootin' his wad is his primary objective in life. Some guys can only have an orgasm during an act of violence. Wouldn't you love to take a trip back in time and watch some of those perverts growing up? You can betcha this Dino character's folks weren't June and Ward Cleaver, for Christ's sake."

"That I'll buy," I answered. Are you going to Clarksville?"

"As a matter of fact, that's one reason I called. Do you want to go along? Your good buddy Ernest called the chief this morning. He knows our history and my interest in the case so he asked for me specifically. I guess they expect me to piece their work together and hand it back to them on a silver platter."

"Dave, sarcasm doesn't become you. I'm just glad Metro released you to go up there."

"They didn't—just the captain. It's all on the QT."

"I can't go, Dave. I've got clients all morning, and if I don't start showing up for regular office hours they're all going to think I've closed my doors. I'm sorry. I would give anything to go with you"

"Did you say you've got clients just this morning?"

"Yeah, I should be finished by one o'clock."

"I'll wait. In the mean time, I'll go check on your other friend, good old Cobra. How's that?"

"Smart ass." I laughed into the phone. "Where shall I meet you?"

"I'll drop by your place about twelve-thirty. You gonna call Lee?"

"Of course, she would never forgive me if we went off on this one and didn't ask her to come along."

"Well, perish that thought." It was his turn to chuckle.

* *

Katie said goodbye to my last client, shut and locked the office door. She flipped the sign on the door to "closed" and went back to her computer. I walked out of my office, down the hall and stood behind her chair. Finally she acknowledged my presence with a grin and a turn of her head.

"What?" She asked.

"Nothing," answered I. "I was just watching you work."

She pushed back her chair, almost running me over in the process. "Oops, sorry, I didn't realize you were still there."

"I hope you don't drive like you ride that chair," I chided, knowing full well that she did.

"What time will you be back from Clarksville?"

"I don't have a clue, why?"

"I knew you wouldn't remember you had a meeting late this afternoon, so I canceled it after I heard you talking to Sergeant Marshall. You had a board meeting at Windows on the Cumberland."

"Shit, I forgot. Oh, well, thanks for taking care of it for me." I hugged her and headed toward the upstairs.

"We aims to please, ma'am. We aims to please."

"I know." I said, thanking the universe for a friend and secretary like Katie. I passed my office and reached in and turned off the overhead light. "Hey, Katie, after Lee gets here, I don't want to talk to anyone else besides Dave or Fel. I left a message for Fel that I would call him after I get in, so I don't expect to hear from him before then. I..."

"Don't worry, I know what to do. Hey, I wish you the best of hunting...I hope ya'll catch that son of a bitch soon."

"Katie, I don't want you staying here alone this afternoon. Put the phones on voice mail and be ready to leave when we do."

"You're really concerned about this guy prowling around here, aren't you?"

"You're damned straight, Sweetie, you're damned straight."

"Hey, there's Lee now. She's pulling around back. Yell when you're ready, I'll shut this computer down and be ready to go at anytime you say."

I headed upstairs to meet Lee at the door. "You can leave at anytime," I called over my shoulder, "I just don't want you here alone after we're gone."

"That's a 10-4 good buddy," she replied, a smile in her voice. "I'll come upstairs and go out that way because I've already locked up down here."

"Good," I yelled down the stairs, pulling the door open just as Lee was about to stick her key in the lock.

"I was beginning to think there was nobody home," she grinned, pulling her jacket off and hanging it on the back of the chair.

"Oh, we're home alright," I kissed her frigid cheek. "Still cold as a well digger's knee, huh?"

"Colder," she shuddered. "Where's Dave? I thought he was supposed to be here by now."

I looked at my watch, "About fifteen minutes, five minutes one way or the other." Just then the phone rang.

"Hey, Dare, this is Dave, I haven't left headquarters yet. I'll be another 45 minutes at least."

"Why don't we meet you in the parking lot. You can drive my car, no point in you driving all the way out here just to backtrack to I-24," I offered.

"Sound good to me. I'll see you in a few minutes."

Lee poured us each a cup of coffee, stirred in my usual four sugars and dab of Coffee Mate. She opened the refrigerator and pulled out a carton of milk, dribbling a small amount into her coffee. "Should I have poured this into your traveling mug?"

"No, Not even Dave would begrudge me one cup of coffee."

I had already found my place at the kitchen table. Lighting a cigarette, I inhaled, enjoying the acidic bite of the smoke in my lungs. She sat my "Maxine" cup in front of me, and I sipped the fragrant brew, allowing it to temporarily melt the anxiety from my bones. *Not for long though—not for long.*

* *

I sat in the backseat listening to Lee and Dave talk about whatever popped into their minds. Dave had been to visit Cobra Merriweather earlier in the day. The snake charmer had suddenly developed an acute case of selective memory. He was frightened. The more his health improved, the more frightened he became. He had a TV in his room, so he knew about the murders in Clarksville, and that an APB had been issued for a missing inmate (trustee) at the Dickson County Jail. He was no fool.

Gradually my friends' conversation melted into the *squishing* sound the tires made against the rain-soaked asphalt highway. The Ford's heater didn't quite reach that part of me that was heavy with cold *and* dread. The starkness of the landscape swept past my window, and the grayness of the day settled over me like a shroud. I felt my head loll against the back of the seat. Feeling myself beginning to doze, I relaxed and went with the flow.

* *

"Dare, Daaarrrreeee."

I heard someone calling my name from what seemed to be a long way off. I tried to gather my wits around me when suddenly I realized I was no longer in Dave's official white, unmarked Ford. I sat up, alertness dodging my grasp. My mouth tasted like Sherman's soldiers had marched through it after they burned Atlanta. I knew I wasn't where I wanted to be, but I wasn't sure where that was.

"Daaarrrreeee." The cry came again. The elongated syllables rolled across the distance like waves beating monotonously upon a phantom beach. "Daaarrrreeee."

"Who's there?" I queried, afraid to hear the answer. Afraid not to.

"Daaaarrrreeee?" A young girl's barely discernible British accent melted into my mind like butter on hot toast.

"Marie, is that you?" I could feel the sweat beading along my hairline and under my nose. Why, I couldn't figure, it was cold as the foyer to hell...whatever that meant. Suddenly a chill crawled amongst my innards, and I began to shake all over. I waited.

The black scum of night enveloped me. I was back in those infernal woods, where night sounds danced in the gloom. A blood-chilling keening wound its way around my quaking body. Deeper...whining...whimpering. I could feel the gorge crawling up the backside of my throat. Sweat dampened my skin, in spite of the intense cold. Then it happened. The growling began in earnest. The mastiff was somewhere out there in the dark, I could feel his cold, piercing eyes glowering at me. The great beast was patrolling with his troops, looking for victims already dead. He wasn't interested in me except to frighten the soul from my earthly body, and he was well on his way to accomplishing that one.

"Dare!"

I looked around, jerking my neck and almost losing my footing. In my clumsiness I caught the toe of my boot under a branch, twisted my knee and truly almost fell on my face. "Marie?" I waited...nothing. "Marie, is that you?" I knew it was—just as I knew I was dreaming. "Don't wake up, for chrissakes, don't wake up. Find her, talk to her." I listened. I strained my auditory nerves—where was she? Had I lost her? Please, dear God, don't let her be lost to me...please bring her back.

"Dare, I'm here—please look at me—I'm right here." And sure enough she was. Not the hank of hair and disjointed bones I had seen in these very woods, but a vibrant young woman, a beautiful, blossoming oriental flower.

"Marie, is that really you?" I knew it was, but the rational side of my brain made me ask anyway.

"Yes, it is I." She spoke quietly and distinctly, but with a purpose.

"What is it you want to tell me?" I reached out to touch her, but only a frigid draft returned my offer. She was a specter, a phantom, a figment of my overactive imagination. "No stop it, Dare," I chided myself. She was really with me. I knew it in my bones. Her presence had returned to guide me to her *murderer...to help put him where he would never hurt anyone else, as long as he lived. That was her purpose in being here. That was her only purpose in being here.*

"I can't find Uncle's house. I can't get out of these woods, and no one has been here since that awful man left me. I'm so scared, Dare, I want to see my family. Where is my family?

I couldn't believe my eyes and ears. She didn't know...she didn't know she had passed over...that she was dead. That often times happens when death comes in a particularly violent manner, such as in battle or unexpectedly brutal murder. Trying to be articulate in a dream was an entirely new experience for me. "Marie, come closer."

"No, I'm frightened. I had no feeling when I tried to touch you...what is wrong with me, Dare, why couldn't I feel you? Why can't I get out of here, so I can find Uncle's house? My parents must be so worried. My father has patients in Hong Kong. He's been here a long time and I know he must get back soon. I must get back so I can tell him I'm all right, and he must take Mother and go back home. Oh, Dare, what is wrong with me?"

She wailed my name into the electric night. Such pain and helplessness I had not heard in a long, long time. Her agony became a part of me. I was willing to share if it would lessen her grief. I wanted to take her in my arms and soothe her, as I had done my boys when they suffered their own personal slings and arrows, but that could not be. I reckoned that the next best thing would be to talk softly to her, to try to ease her anguish. I realized she was dead, caught between this world and the next, but she didn't...and therein lay the rub.

"Marie, try to calm down; let's talk about this. I know it must be painful, but if I'm to help you and your family you must try to help me. Please, if you can, tell me what happened to you...can you do that? I knew it would be pointless to give her a date. Obviously, she had no concept of time where she was. I could see the pain well behind her eyes as she brought the images back to the surface.

"I was only a few blocks from Uncle's house, when a police car behind me started flashing its lights. At first I didn't pay too much attention because I knew I wasn't speeding nor breaking any other law. But then he turned his siren on for just a second or two...you know, like a signal to me. I pulled over into the school parking lot and rolled down my window. It was then he shined his flashlight inside the car. He held the bright beam in my face while he talked to me. It was very painful to my eyes...very distracting. He told me his

name was Officer Dino and that he had been sent from a hospital where my father had been taken. He said father had suffered a heart attack. He was driving a police car and I, like a fool, got into the car with him, and he brought me here. He did terrible things to me and made me do things to him...nasty, terrible things. I tried to get away, but he tied me up, threw me down on the ground, and raped me. He tied me, hand and foot, to those two trees over there." She broke down and sobbed uncontrollably, pointing in the direction where the two saplings had stood before the forensics team had sawed them down. Icy tears flowed down her spectral face, my heart ached for her, knowing I was in a dream did not help. Her reality had become mine.

"They cut them down," I intoned, "they're to be entered as evidence in court, if we ever catch the beast that did this to you."

"Oh you'll catch him. Just what every you do, don't give up, he's very close by. I must go now. Don't forget—he's very close by. I must go and find my family now." Suddenly the heart-rending entreaty returned to her voice. "Dare, if I don't find my family, please tell them that I miss them, and I love them very much...helppppppp meeeeeeee."

I watched as she melted into the haze. The moon erupted from the clouds and spread its glow, like a quilt, over all. I cocked my head—listening for the growl of the mastiff—nothing. Well, not exactly. I heard panting, nothing ominous, just the panting of the weary animal. I stood motionless and tried to gather my wits about me. Thank you, God.

The tenseness lifted and I was rested and was ready to do battle with whatever was thrown in my direction—at least in my dreams. He was nearby...probably in these very woods—hiding like the wild beast he is. He may be lurking anywhere.

"Dare? That you? You mess with me bitch, and you gonna be next. You'd like ol' Dino, I bet. Dino'd spread you out like Monday's warsh. He'd stick it to you and ride you like the Ol' Lone Ranger. Ain't no lawyer'd ever do again after ol' Dino fucked you. You'd be like all the rest of 'em— you'd be beggin' for more. Ain't no fuckin' like a Dino fuckin', so's I been told."

I stiffened with hatred-laced fear. **"You bastard, enjoy yourself while you can—jerk off 'til the world looks level. I don't give a shit. Just watch your back, asshole."** Dream or no dream (like this was just any dream), I was behaving pretty rashly, and knew it. Discretion being the better part of valor, I scratched my way back to the surface.

* *

"Dare, Dare, wake up…you all right?" Lee was leaning over the back seat patting (beating) my arm with a vengeance. "Wake up! Are you okay? Answer me!"

"Damn it, Lee, are you trying to kill me? I'll be black and blue in the morning. I'm all right; just let me get myself together before you beat me apart. My upper body had slumped onto the backseat, and I had drawn my legs up until I was lying in the fetal position. My left knee was cramping and throbbing. I remembered the dream.

"Damn, Dare," I raised up to meet Dave's eyes in the rearview mirror, "we thought you were awake back there 'til you started yellin' and cussin' at Dino. Lee turned around to check on you, and damned if you weren't thrashin' around back there like a blind dog in a meat house. You musta had a doozy of a dream."

"I did. Dave, Lee, the son of a bitch is somewhere in those woods where he murdered Marie Zhou—she told me."

"*She what?*" Dave believes in what I do, but he always likes to keep at least one foot firmly planted in reality.

"She told you what?" Lee was about to come over the back seat and into my lap with eagerness.

"She told me that he was nearby."

"Nearby what?" Dave's knee-jerk reaction was completely predictable.

"Look, if the two of you will take it easy, I'll try to explain." I did, I told them all about the dream—both parts.

"You really think he's out there in those woods somewhere?" Dave was sounding more and more convinced, but still a cop all the way.

"Yes, I do."

Lee jumped in with both feet. "Let's go straight out there, don't pass Go, collect $200, or anything. Let's just go on out there."

Dave reacted, "Jesus Christ, Lee, we can't do that, I'm working in somebody else's jurisdiction. That's all I need. The Captain would never get one gram of help from Clarksville-Montgomery County again, not to mention what he'd do to me. Probably bust my ass down to walkin' a beat."

"Yeah, right, out on Herman Street." Lee chided him with visions of a not too pleasant prospect.

Getting back to the original conversation, I offered my opinion. "Lee, you know better than to even think such a thought. Ernest Calhoun would be all over us like a posse on the James Boys. And if it's all the same to you, I'd just as soon not have him that close to me."

"I'm sorry, guys, I just got excited. So just shoot me."

I cuffed her shoulder. "I'd love to go after that piece of shit Dino all by myself, and if thinking the deed is as bad as doing the deed, then I'm doomed."

"Me too," said Lee.

"All of us," said Dave.

* *

Ricky-Dino was sure he was gonna freeze to death. All he had between him and eternity was a county-issued denim jumper and jeans. He didn't even have gloves. Unaware that he would be running for his life, he hadn't played Boy Scout before leaving the lockup the day before. Now he sat quivering in the front seat of an old Chevy pickup he'd hot-wired after he'd had his fun with those kids last night. The memory warmed him momentarily. He felt his jeans tighten across his lap. Boy, he'd sure like to try that again someday. A three-way was even better than ol' Curly's educated jaws. *Them kids liked it: I know they did. Hell, kids is horny all the time; everbody knows that. He went after her like a hog after slop. My dick's learning all kinds of new tricks.* He rubbed his crotch but decided to smoke instead.

The cowboy who'd owned the pickup had stashed a brand-new, unopened carton of Lucky Strikes in the glove compartment. Now if that wasn't a sign Dino didn't know what was. He opened the second pack of the day, throwing the cellophane strip on the floorboard. He punched in the dash lighter. When it popped out, he cupped his hands around it and held the glowing eye to the tip of his unfiltered cigarette. The warmth felt good. He just wished the old rattletrap had more gasoline in its tank, so he could crank 'er up and run the heater. He drew deeply and the smoke mixed with his visible breath, as he exhaled it into the chilly cab.

He wiped the side window with the back of his chapped red hand, looking out into the dreary afternoon. He had pulled the pickup farther up into the woods than he'd ever been before. He didn't want anyone to spy him before nightfall, when he planned to go out foraging for another, better vehicle, one with a full gas tank and a *workin'* heater. He needed to pick up a good jacket and gloves, and maybe a cap somewhere too.

He thought about Cobra layin' up there in the hospital all nice and warm.

Dammit, what a major fuck up. I shoulda made certain that bastard was dead for sure. I cain't believe he lived through that cuttin' up I give 'em. Fucker shoulda been better'n dead, he shoulda been half way to hell by now.

Violence, or even the thought of it, gave Ricky-Dino a hard-on. This was no exception. His zipper was biting through his raggedy drawers and into the tender flesh between his legs. *"Cain't fight the feelin,'"* he chuckled, as he gently tugged the zipper over the lump in his lap. He had to move from under the gigantic steering wheel in the antiquated pickup, and make himself some maneuvering space. He still couldn't get a good handle on the situation, so he had to pop the snap at his waistband. Suddenly his family jewels were exposed to the cold and dampness of the interior of the truck. *Wait just a minute there, Hoss.* The touch of his frigid palm coupled with dankness of his surroundings had caused a momentary wilting of the flower. He reached over and cranked the engine 'til it wheezed like an old asthmatic, coughed twice and caught. A cold blast of air hit his exposed balls, sending a bone-shattering chill throughout his body. He grabbed himself and held on for dear life until a semblance of warmth began to sneeze in fits and starts through the vents. He slowly began to relax and enjoy himself. His hands had warmed between his legs, and he was once again in full bloom, nothing else mattered. He couldn't think past his immediate need for self-gratification. The world beyond the frosted, cracked windshield of the rusty old Chevy disappeared. Ricky-Dino was lost in a world of his own making.

29

Look, Ernest, I know he's somewhere out there in those woods." The Lieutenant didn't want to go out in the cold rain—he didn't fool me.

"You sure that's not just wishful thinking?" He was stirring saccharine into a muddy looking cup of coffee. He shuddered with the first swig, before walking around the desk, where he sank into his swivel chair. His expression was disdainful and condescending.

"Dare had a dream." Lee spoke up from the fringe of the conversation."

Ernest Calhoun coughed smoke from his lungs and ground out his cigarette. "A *dream*? We're sealing fates by dreams nowadays?"

"Look, Ernest," Dave put his own cigarette out and sat on the edge of the Lieutenant's broad desk, "you know perfectly well how Dare works. Sometimes she dreams solutions to crimes that would have taken hundreds of man-hours to glean the same information. But if you have honest doubts about calling in Will Bealer, then I'll be happy to do it on my own. Without so much as glancing at Calhoun, Dave asked if he could use the telephone. Before the answer came, he was well into dialing Bealer's number. "Yeah, this is Sgt. David Marshall, Metro-Nashville PD. Is Chief Deputy Bealer there?...No?...Well, ask him to call me at Lieutenant Ernest Calhoun's office, just as soon as he gets in. Tell him it's imperative that I speak to him ASAP." He dropped the receiver onto its cradle, eased off the desk, pulled a ragged package of Marlboro Reds out of his rumpled jacket pocket and lit up. Only then did he look at me. "I hope that deputy gets that message to Will soon. I don't want to wait around here all day, but someone with direct jurisdictional authority sure will make things a lot simpler when we get this case to court. We don't need any technical fuckups tossin' this case in the crapper before it even gets to trial. We can't afford to lose this shithead. The former was an indirect dig at Calhoun.

"All right...let's go." Apparently forfeiting the role of prima donna, Ernest Calhoun was up and headed for his coat-rack. He zipped himself into a Mackinaw, wrapped a wool scarf around his neck, donned earmuffs and a baseball cap. He reached into his pockets and pulled out silk glove liners over which he pulled fur-lined leather gloves. "Ya'll comin'? I'm ready. I thought ya'll were in such an all-fired big hurry. Get your shit on and let's go…" The phone rang—it was Bealer. After an abbreviated conversation of explanation, Lieutenant Calhoun announced that we would all meet at Sharkey's, and go as a unit.

We finally caught up, pulling on our winter gear. "I'm ready," we each called in turn, like first graders lined up at the restroom.

"Good," muttered the Lieutenant, "let's get outta here. I rolled my eyes at Lee and headed for the door.

* *

If possible, the weather had deteriorated even further since we had driven up earlier. Thunder rolled in the distance. I expected to see flashing pitchforks from heaven at any moment. Clouds hung like heavy theatre curtains awaiting the onset of a drama. The atmosphere was electric with anticipation.

Dave, Lee and I were riding with Will and his wife/sidekick Rolanda. His old Blazer sloshed its way over wet macadam before turning off toward the woods. As soon as we left the relative security of pavement, he stopped the vehicle and got out to convert its freewheeling front end to four-wheel action. He got back inside the vehicle and pulled onto the old logging road. The stark, bare deciduous trees looked like ebony skeletons reaching for us with bony fingers. *There goes that damned goose again.* As we neared the woods, the rutted road grew thick with gumbo-like mud. The Blazer slued sideways briefly, before the heavy-duty tires chewed deep into the mire, and the old SUV chugged its way toward the forest from hell.

* *

Ricky-Dino's ears perked up. *What the hell was that?* He thought he had heard a car door slam somewhere. He sucked on his cigarette, rolled down the window and tossed the butt onto the sodden ground. He listened for further sounds. He heard voices, muffled by distance. He couldn't distinguish if they were men or women, but he had heard something, nevertheless.

Shit, what the hell 'm I supposed to do now? His head was churning. He couldn't decide if it was time to panic or not. *Maybe some young'ns cuttin' school. Prob'ly come out here to fuck in the daylight. Shit, yeah, I'll bet that's all it is—wantin' to see, not just feel.* He rolled the glass almost to the top, but he left a crack open just in case. He hunkered down in the seat and wrapped his arms around himself to retain what little heat was left in his quivering body. He felt himself dozing in the gloomy afternoon. He shook his head, trying to stay alert. *I heard tell when you're getting' ready to freeze to death you get sleepy,* he said inside his head. *Gotta stay awake. Damn, it'd be a pisser if somebody come up on me while I was takin' a beauty nap, now wouldn't it?* He chuckled, and resituated his body on the seat of that ol' clunker of a pickup, he had so unwisely hotwired and made off with the night before. *God, I wish I'd a stole me a Caddie or Lincoln. This here pickup's for the fuckin' birds. Hell, that's about all it's good for, damned ol' heap.* His head was beginning to nod when he heard the voices again. He could hear a woman's voice. *Shush,* he cautioned himself, *I know that voice.* He cocked his head toward the window and listened intently. There it was again. *Jesus Christ Awmighty and his sweet mama Mary, that's that Murphy woman and her gang. Now what, asshole? You gonna sit here 'til they walk right up here and handcuff you to this piece a shit truck, or are you gonna get the hell outta here while you still can?* He swung open the driver's door as quietly as the aged hinges would allow. He dropped to the ground, and the mucky forest floor almost sucked the sneakers from his frigid feet. "*Shit!*" he muttered aloud as he steadied himself and picked his way from the truck, through raggedy briars, and into the ominous dimness of a clump of conifers. Straining his ears so hard that the rest of his body followed suit. He realized he had to pee. *Holy shit, my dick's gonna freeze and fall off out here.* With half frozen fingers, he wrestled his cold-shrunken penis from inside his jeans, and held it tenderly. "*Damn it, Hoss, we ain't gonna be froze forever.*" When he had finished, he crammed it back inside his britches and patted his crotch. "*No siree, we ain't.*" He clung to an ancient hemlock and listened to the silence.

* *

"He's here. The little worm is somewhere in these woods, even as we speak, so everyone be especially quiet. I'm going to stroll a little ways into the woods, sans Lee or any of the rest of you."

Lee started to protest when I put my index finger to her lips.

Dave did protest, but quietly.

"Forget it," whispered Will and Rolanda, while Ernest fumed silently on the sidelines. He had no jurisdiction over these woods. We were now in the county and, therefore, in Will Bealer's bailiwick.

"Please, I must go in alone...I must feel his presence. Otherwise, we may lose him. I'm sort of like a bloodhound, I guess. I will get his scent and then, if we play our cards right, we'll have him. Please, don't fight me on this. I promise I'll be careful—I'm no fool. *Yeah, right.* I don't care if you draw your weapons and hold me in your sights, but I need to go in alone. All of you stay here and twiddle your thumbs, if you must, but don't move until I give you a signal. Okay?" Grim but silent faces were my only answer.

I dug deep inside my purse and pulled out a jacketed container of pepper-spray. "Here." I handed my purse to Lee who slung the strap over her shoulder, opposite her own pocketbook. I'll arm this little squirt and be ready to fire as soon as I get close enough."

"Dare, that's not always effective...especially on nut cases." Dave's eyes pleaded with me, but he knew from personal experience that when my mind was made up, nothing short of bodily restraint would stop me. "Oh, well, shit...please be careful. If you're gone more than five minutes, Will, Ernest and I will be right on your tail, so if you're gonna find him, do it quick." With that he hugged me. Lee was right behind him.

* *

Little did I know that they had no intention of allowing me to go in alone. The lawmen were fanning out, preparing to circle around whatever or *whoever* might be lurking about.

* *

I picked my way past slimy weeds left over from last summer. Briars bit through my jeans and snagged my long silk underwear. My boots protested the muddy trail. Stopping quickly, I thought I heard what sounded like a rusty hinge groan in the distance. Could have been a possum hanging high in a tree. They make a sound exactly like an old car door squeaking to and fro. I proceeded with careful steps.

A crack appeared in the clouds, and for the briefest moment, the sun broke through. Then just as quickly the portal closed. I got the message—"*though I walk through the valley of the shadow of death, I will fear no evil; for thou are with me...*"

* *

The brief, but glaring, appearance of the unfamiliar sun caught Ricky-Dino by surprise. *What the hell is going on here?* Careful to speak only to himself. He hugged the hemlock even closer. He was scared of spooks and portents. Nothing earthly frightened him in the least, but the unknown caused his balls to shrivel and made him want to run. He heard a voice in his head. That Murphy woman was stalkin' him. He could feel it in his bones. "Where are you bitch?" He spoke before he thought. *Shit, fool, why don't you just walk out with your hands over your fuckin' head and surrender?* He clamped his tongue between his teeth and stood still as a post in the woods—waiting. It didn't take long. From his spot behind the hulking hemlock, he saw her draw near the truck. He also saw that she had something in her hand.

That don't look like no gun I ever seen. Hey, wait, that's just goddam mace, pepper spray or the like. He watched as she peered through the window, then into the backend of the rusted hulk. He saw her shoulders relax a little, but her feeble weapon appeared at the ready. He watched as she turned slowly around, as if preparing to hone in on her prey. She stopped and looked directly into the dimness where he stood. His balls tried to crawl inside his body. She walked tentatively in his direction. She wavered, then began again with purpose. He waited. He was going to get his chance at her after all. He couldn't remember the last breath he had taken. It was as if time had stopped since he had spied her there near the truck. She was almost within his reach. One more step…two at the most.

"Darrreeee?" He reached out just as she pressed the valve on the pepper spray. He twisted her hand, and they both got a fleeting dose of the burning mixture. Coughing ensued.

"Dino," I croaked through the dissipating fumes. He had both my wrists in one of his hands. The tiny aerosol container dropped to the ground. It was just as well since I had dosed myself as well as him. My eyes burned. I could barely see. He pulled my face to his, and that was infinitely worse than the pepper spray. His breath reeked with tooth decay and rotting gums. Yellow teeth grinned from his rancid mouth. His purple lips stretched tightly in a demonic snarl. In spite of his evil appearance, I could tell he was much younger than I had anticipated…early twenties at most, but his red-rimmed eyes were vacant, old and rheumy, way past their years. While I was attempting to gather my wits, he grabbed me and threw me down like a ragdoll. How could anyone so scrawny be so agile and strong? *Psychopaths are often powerful beyond their physical appearances,* I remembered, as I hit the ground. Feeling the spray container under my hip, I felt encouraged. He stood over me, straddling me like the Colossus at Rhodes. He tore open the button at his waist and ripped his zipper open—his engorged penis jumped out like a trained seal. He pushed his pants down to his knobby knees, and he dropped to the ground to likewise relieve me of my clothing. I reached down and pulled the pepper spray from under me and hit the valve without aiming—luck was with me.

His fingers clawed at his eyes, and he screamed between gasps for clean air. "You motherfuckin' bitch, I told you I'd get you if it was the last thing I ever did. Now I gottcha."

Yeah, right. I pushed him backward and crawled from beneath his writhing form. When I regained a modicum of equilibrium, I gave him a good swift kick to the chest. His hands grabbed blindly. He gasped and vomited into his bare lap. I rolled aside, and for a second, I felt something akin to pity, as I saw his miserable, barf-covered reason-for-living, dangling between his skinny legs. *Big Man,* I thought. I heard running footsteps rushing in from all around me. I turned to see Dave, Will and Ernest—pistols drawn—crashing through the brush toward me. They didn't slow until they were staring at the temporarily blinded, pathetic lump of humanity at my feet.

It seems that they had fanned out too wide, in their desire to protect me, so their timing was off. The battle was won before the cavalry arrived.

"By God, she did it!" Ernest Calhoun was astounded at the sight before him.

Dave jumped in with both feet, "I told you if anybody could do, she could. Didn't I say that?"

"Yeah, but I figured you were pissin' into the wind, as usual."

Will Bealer just stood looking aghast. Suddenly he regained his composure, turning around. He yelled at his wife and Lee, telling them to come on up. "Pull up the son of a bitches pants," he said to any one of us that might be willing. He bent over and grabbed Ricky-Dino's filthy hands away from his burning eyes and clamped them behind his back. The punk jerked and whined as he felt the cold bite of the steel handcuffs around his scrawny wrists. Will had the distinct honor of being the arresting officer, while Dave smiled and Ernest coveted. When they frisked the punk, they found my cell phone, along with my personal phone list crammed down in his denim jumper pocket.

It was over. The realization of what had just taken place hit me. It was my turn to vomit. I ran behind the tree that had previously hidden Dino and hurled everything I had eaten for a week. Lee was immediately beside me. How she could stand it, I'll never know, the same way she stands a lot of other things about me, I guess.

They hoisted the prisoner into Will's Blazer. Dave got in the backseat beside him, glaring him into submission. The rest of us climbed into the confiscated Taurus that Ernest used on the job. I sat in the backseat with Lee, while Rolanda rode up front with Ernest. Lee patted my knee and whispered, "Good job," in my ear. I laid my head back and shut my eyes. I knew if I said anything I would cry, and if I did, I figured Lt. Ernest Calhoun might enjoy it too much. He thinks I'm a fearless bitch, and I'd like to keep it that way.

Ernest turned in his seat and looked at me for what seemed like minutes. "Dare, I'm going on record as saying, you're good at what you do. But damned if you're not a canker sore on the mouth of humanity." He grinned then gunned the motor.

All of a sudden I liked him better. "I love you too, Ernest."

* *

All the lights were out except in the kitchen. Lee turned down a cup of coffee, saying it was late. She needed to get home and tell Joe all about the day's events before he saw all the gory details on TV. I hugged her, and watching her get into her car. I waited until the Mazda's exhaust plumed into the frigid evening air. I turned my attention to my garage door as it creaked and groaned its way overhead. Pulling underneath, I hit the remote once more. The crotchety old door halted midway down and heaved a mournful sigh. It was finished. Its heart had finally given out. Sears could bury it when they replaced it with a new, sleek, hopefully as faithful, electronic portal. The end of a day—the end of an era.

The answering machine was blinking a welcome as I tossed my purse on the countertop. I pulled my long-lost cell phone, my cigarettes and lighter from my pocket. After plugging the phone into the charger, I lit a cigarette and settled down to check my messages. The only one of interest was from Fel. He would be by after work. Maybe we could go out to dinner or *something*. I grinned through my weariness at his tone. I checked my watch. He would be leaving his office soon. I dropped two ice cubes into a glass and poured in a very healthy measure of Black Jack.

I sat on a chair and unlaced my boots, then peeled off my jeans, sweatshirt, long underwear and socks. I threw them beside the back door, picked up my drink and made my way to the bathroom. I ran *very* warm water into the tub, dumping aromatic bath salts under the tap. I went to the closet and pulled out a sexy, mid-thigh length silk nightshirt from Victoria's Secret—a gift from another lifetime.

The bath did what it was designed to do. I lay in the steaming water, allowing the stress and tiredness to wash from my body and soul. I took the occasional sip of Uncle Jack and thought about later. Quiet jazz eased its way over me. God was in his heaven, and all was right with the world.

* *

When the doorbell rang I had just finished doing my hair. I had dabbed on pale lipstick and pinched my cheeks before peeking through the spy-hole. It was Fel, in all his glory. I unlocked the door and fell into his arms.

"Hey, let's at least close the door. I know your neighbors can't see, but it's cold as hell out there," he laughed. I stepped back and he shut the door while I reset the alarm system. He pulled off his topcoat and suit coat and hung them in the foyer closet. He loosened his tie and unbuttoned his collar button. "Wow! Why haven't I seen that before?"

I did an exaggerated model's twirl so he could view my attire from all sides and underneath. "This old thing?" I teased, "I've had it for years…"

EPILOGUE

No food, no drink, no conversation—just passionate, cathartic sex. Lovemaking would come later, along with the sweetness of words and actions, but not until I had rid my mind and body of mental rents and tears, that nothing else could fix quite so expeditiously. Fel filled all the hollowness that had, over time, become such a large part of my life.

He seemed surprised, but not at all disappointed, at the fierceness our coupling had taken. He kissed me deeply then with genteel sweetness. He told me he loved me. It was my turn to be surprised, but I did love him and told him so. We lay in front of the fire, wrapped in a warm, easy embrace.

We didn't sleep much that night, and only after my empty stomach made itself loudly known, did we eat. He scrambled eggs and toasted bread while I fried a half-pound of turkey sausage. He made faces at the latter's prospects. We washed our midnight meal down with cups of delicious Macadamia coffee, before making our way to my bedroom. We lay comfortably silent in each other's arms.

With total peace of mind and heart, I said goodbye to Marie Zhou. "Sleep peacefully, Marie." I felt her assuring presence for a fleeting moment before I fell asleep.